BITE
OF SIN

SHADOWS OF WAR BOOK 1
KAY RILEY

Cover Design by: Dark Ink Designs

Edited by: Editing by Gray

Proofread by: VB Proofreads

Formatting: Dark Ink Designs

Note to Readers

Bite of Sin is a dark vampire romance set in a dystopian world. This is book one of a series and does end on a cliffhanger. For more information on the content, please refer to the author's website:

https://www.kayrileyauthor.com/books

To Amanda,
My friend who first heard about this story and
gave me the confidence to step outside my
comfort zone of contemporary dark romance.
Thank you for helping this story come to life!

♡ Kay Riley

Prologue
Zan

Seven years old

"We should leave." Pax gave me a push forward. "Dad is going to be so mad if he finds out we're here."

Viggo grabbed my arm to keep me from stumbling into the wall before shooting his twin a glare. "Don't be so scared, Pax. We come down here all the time."

Pax's frown was a mirror of his twin's as they stared at each other. Since I'd known them my whole life, I was one of the few who could tell them apart even though they were identical in almost every way. On the outside, anyway. Their personalities were the exact opposite. Where Pax was quiet and a rule follower, Viggo was reckless and outspoken. They were my best friends by choice, and my brothers by blood. Only on our father's side, since Pax and Viggo had a different mother.

All three of us froze when a door slammed somewhere in the maze of halls. We were underground, and it was as large as the mansion above us. Whenever we were bored,

5

we'd sneak down here, even though our father forbade it. But we never were allowed to leave the property grounds because of the war happening. A war that had been going on since before I was born. I could count on one hand how many times I'd been past the high walls.

"Let's go back upstairs," Pax urged, worry in his voice.

"Don't you want to know what's happening?" I asked as I began walking again. "Everyone was running around this morning. No one ever tells us anything. If we want to know, we can just listen to their meetings, like we always do."

"Because we're kids," Pax muttered.

Viggo shook his head. "There are kids fighting outside the walls. We should be out there too."

Pax and Viggo were three years older than me, and we'd heard rumors that ten-year-olds were helping however they could, to make sure our side won. Viggo wanted to join them, but our father made it clear that the three of us wouldn't see the bloodshed until we were ready.

"We'll just see where Dad is, and then we'll go back upstairs," I soothed Pax, nodding to the office door.

Pax sighed in defeat and slowly followed me to the vent that we'd used before. Viggo crouched down and quickly undid the screws that we'd left loose last time. I kept watch, making sure we were alone until he slid the grate to the side and crawled inside. Pax grumbled under his breath before getting to his knees and following his twin. Peering down the hall one last time, I awkwardly scooted into the vent tunnel, grabbed the grate, and set it against the opening. The hallway was dark, and with whatever was going on, no one would notice. At least I hoped they wouldn't.

We moved on our hands and knees, going slow to keep quiet. This was the third time we'd traveled through the vents, and we'd already memorized the way to the office where our dad held important meetings. Soon the narrow space opened wider, and my heart began pounding when muffled screams filled the air. We were close enough to know it was coming from the office. Viggo scooted to the side, nearly lying on his side to make room for me and Pax.

My shoulders were squished against Pax's as we all crammed into the space so we could peer through the vent slats. My stomach dropped when I finally looked into the office. The lights were on, giving us a clear view of the large desk. Music was playing, helping conceal us even more. Pax sucked in a breath as all of us lay there frozen.

Our father was standing on the side of the desk with no shirt on and his jeans unbuttoned. A woman was sprawled on the desk, her legs wrapped around his waist. This wasn't the first time we'd seen sex happening. Even if our father wanted to protect us from the war, the things we'd seen in this house were sometimes just as bad.

"Amaros," the woman pleaded my dad's name. "It hurts."

He stopped moving, watching the tears fall down her face with a blank expression. He moved so fast it took me a moment to realize that he'd wrapped his hand around her throat. My blood turned to ice in my veins as my heart beat faster. Pax shifted, his wide eyes going to me. He wanted to leave, but none of us moved.

"We're celebrating," my dad stated in a deadly voice, bringing my attention back to the desk. "Today is a special day. Don't you want to keep me happy?"

"Yes, of course," the woman choked out.

"Then be good while I eat."

Pity for the woman filled me as I watched my dad's face carefully. He opened his mouth, and when his fangs appeared, a piercing scream filled the air as the woman tried escaping his hold. He lowered himself onto her and moved his hand from her throat before he sank his fangs into her. She writhed while screaming and crying, her feeble attempts to get away growing weaker as he sucked, and soon, her head slumped onto the desk. He didn't stop feeding, and memories flooded through me as I watched the woman take her last breaths.

It was on my fifth birthday when my father first fed on a human in front of me. He wanted me to see what I would become. The vampire who would rule, with Pax and Viggo by my side, once he stepped down.

"When you become a man, you'll turn," my father said with blood dripping down his chin. "You will carry on everything I've worked for, Zan. Failing is not an option."

Once he was satisfied, he pushed the woman's body away from him and pulled his jeans back up. He wiped the blood off his lips as he strode out of the office, none of us moving a muscle until the door slammed shut behind him.

"Come on," Pax whispered, wiggling to move backward.

Since there wasn't a meeting happening, I moved to follow. We wanted to hear what was happening with the war, not witness this. We crawled through the vent, and once we got to a fork, I paused, hearing a faint noise. Instead of going toward the exit, I turned my head the other direction as the noise got louder. It almost sounded like a woman crying. But not from pain. The cries sounded heartbreaking.

Without thinking about it, I turned, going in the opposite direction. Pax and Viggo were whisper-yelling at me to stop, but I ignored them as I kept going, squeezing my shoulders tighter as the opening narrowed more. Quiet thumps from behind me proved that my brothers were following me as I went toward the noise.

After a few minutes, we were deep in the vent system,

and I hesitated, hoping I wasn't getting us lost. Dad would not take it well if he found us down here. The cries were now echoing around us, and I stopped in front of a vent where the cries were the loudest. The space was tight, and Pax and Viggo stayed behind me as I peered through the slats.

A large bed was in the middle of the room, and it was the only piece of furniture that I could see. A woman was lying there, tears streaming down her face as she sobbed. Her long hair was deep brown with red highlights and was wrapped in a loose bun. Her nose was red, and her eyes were squeezed shut as she rocked back and forth. Until she suddenly went still.

My heart stuttered when her eyes snapped open, and a moment later, her gaze locked on me. I wasn't sure if she could see me through the vent, but her stare didn't waver as I swallowed thickly. Before I could motion for Pax and Viggo to move back, she began speaking.

"I know you're there," she said softly, her voice motherly and sweet. "Come out. Help me. Please."

I didn't move, and I heard Pax's quiet arguments. I'd never seen her before, and I knew everyone on the grounds. But she didn't look dangerous. If anything, she looked nicer than any adult I'd met. My chest constricted as I thought about my mother. The mother I'd never known or met. More than anything, I wanted a mother to tuck me in at night. To sing to me and keep me safe. Like Pax and Viggo, I'd never gotten that. Other than our strict nanny, our father was the only parent figure we knew.

More tears welled in the lady's eyes, and that was all it took for me to push against the metal vent. It shook a little, and I knew the screws holding it were short and not sturdy, just like the screws in the grate we always snuck through. I slid back, giving myself more room for my arms.

"Zan," Pax hissed. "Let's just go back. Don't."

Instead of doing what he wanted, I slammed my palms against the metal two more times, ignoring the pain jolting through my hands. The grate loosened, and after hitting it a couple more times, it finally gave and clattered to the floor. Panic slid through me, worrying the noise would attract attention.

"It's okay," the woman coaxed, giving me a warm smile. "Come here, dear boy."

"Hurry up," Viggo grumbled from behind me. "I need to get out of here."

Pax sighed. "This is a mistake."

Taking a deep breath, I pushed myself forward until I was going headfirst into the room. My chest hit the floor, and I groaned as Pax fell on top of me. I pushed him off and rolled to the side before Viggo landed on me too.

"Who are you?" Viggo asked bluntly once he climbed to his feet.

The lady smiled, and small wrinkles covered her forehead. "I know who you are, Viggo. Along with your brothers, Pax and Zan. Your father wouldn't be very happy to find you here, would he?"

"We're leaving," Pax mumbled, glaring at me.

"It's okay. I'm not going to tell him," she whispered. "Can you boys do something for me?"

Curiosity filled me as I stepped closer to the bed, my body tensing when I saw what was connected to the bedpost near the foot of the bed. It was a thick chain, and it traveled under the blanket, making me believe it was connected to her. Viggo nudged me in the shoulder, noticing the same thing.

"Are you a prisoner?" Viggo asked, his voice sharp. "Are you against us?"

The woman shook her head gently. "No. But I'm sure your father wouldn't agree."

"We don't talk to traitors," Viggo spat out.

I stared at her, not agreeing with Viggo. Her eyes were warm and sweet. She didn't look dangerous at all.

"I'm not leaving this place alive." Her voice caught, and she cleared her throat. "But I don't want my daughter to share the same fate."

All three of us went silent with shock as she shifted and raised her arms to show a baby bundled in a blanket. My gut churned as I looked at the tiny baby. When traitors were brought here, they were killed—along with any of their family that were caught too. I'd never seen them kill kids or babies, but we all heard rumors.

"Take her. Please," the woman pleaded, pain lacing her voice. "You boys know a way off the grounds, don't you?"

Viggo exchanged a glance with Pax. There was a tunnel we'd discovered a few months ago. We'd only used it once so far to leave the mansion. But to sneak a baby away? No way we could get away with that.

"She needs to live," the woman implored, her voice rising. "She is vital to everything. The war—"

"What?" Pax questioned, looking doubtful.

"Where there is death, there needs to be new life." She stared above us as she spoke. "The balance cannot be disturbed. One cannot survive without the other."

"I think it's time to go," I muttered, not understanding the lady's ramblings.

"Zan." She spoke my name with a love I'd never experienced before, making me halt. "You're going to do great things. One day, your father will fear you."

My fingers curled into fists. "You don't know who I am."

"You're young," she said, her gaze staying on me. "Soon, you'll learn of what's happening in the world. And when you do, it's all going to change."

"He would never do anything to our dad," Pax said stiffly.

Her smile held nothing but sadness. "You'll all see. But you're not ready yet."

"How old is she?" Viggo asked, his eyes dropping to the baby in her arms.

The lady hugged the baby tighter. "She was born last night. She hasn't even seen how beautiful a sunset is. You three can help her live."

"We can't do this," Pax said quietly, looking at Viggo, then me. "If Dad finds out—"

"We could be back before he even knows," Viggo cut in, shifting on his feet. "A baby is an innocent, Pax. Are you really okay with her death, knowing we could have stopped it?"

Fear slid down my spine at the thought of Dad finding out what we were doing. Because Viggo was right. If the woman was a traitor, then her death was warranted. But the baby's? It wasn't fair.

"We'll take her," Viggo answered for all of us as he stepped up to the side of the bed. "I can't promise anything else. She can't stay here. Once we get her off the grounds, there's nothing else we can do."

"You won't need to do anything else," she murmured before pressing a long kiss to the baby's head. "It will work itself out in time."

"We're going to get in so much trouble," Pax muttered, running a hand down his face.

"We need to go if we're doing this," Viggo told the lady, holding his arms out.

She looked at me. "Zan, can you carry her?"

Nerves swarmed me. "Viggo's older. He should do it."

I'd never held a baby before and didn't want to drop her. But the woman wasn't taking no for an answer. She shooed Viggo away and beckoned me closer. I wiped my hands on my jeans as I crept toward her, my pulse thudding.

"You'll protect her," she whispered, tears falling as she hugged the baby one more time. "Don't follow the same path your father did, Zan. You're not meant for that."

I didn't argue with her. Once the baby was off the grounds, I'd never see her again. And I *would* follow my father. It was the reason I was born. But seeing as her life was coming to an end, I didn't feel it was important to tell her that.

She held out the baby to me, and I carefully took her in my arms as she showed me how to keep the baby's head supported.

"There's a note in the blanket," she told me, her voice thick. "Don't lose it."

I nodded, worried my hold was too tight, but I didn't want to risk dropping her. I looked down at her as she slept peacefully. Her head was covered in a pink hat, and she didn't stir as I backed away from the bed.

"The balance will stay intact," the woman said, sagging against the pillows. Her gaze didn't leave the baby, and an ache carved its way into my chest at the raw pain on her face. Was my mother just as sad when I was taken away?

Pax was staring at her as if she was out of her mind, but he stayed quiet. Viggo jogged to the door, cracking it open to see if the coast was clear.

"I'm sorry," I told her as I slowly backed away. Sorry for

what, I wasn't sure. For knowing we were leaving her to die? Or taking her baby away from her, even if it was what she wanted? There was no doubt that this day would plague my mind constantly. The woman's eyes were kind yet haunting, like she'd seen terrors I couldn't fathom.

"Let's go, Zan," Viggo said under his breath, his hand keeping the door open. "There's no one out here right now."

The woman was sobbing, waving her hand for us to leave, and I was aware of every step I made as I slipped out of the room. I didn't know much about babies, but I did know they were fragile. Luckily, the tunnel was close to here, and it wouldn't take us long to reach it. About a mile behind the property was a train station where we could take her. That would be the risky part. No one could know we'd left the property.

"We're so screwed if someone catches us." Pax shoved Viggo as they ran ahead of me. "Listening to meetings is one thing, but this? He'll beat us for days if he finds out."

"He won't," Viggo said, his lack of confidence making me more on edge. "It's a baby, Pax."

I stared down at the baby as Pax and Viggo pushed open the false wall to reveal the tunnel entrance. She was sleeping so peacefully. She had no idea of the darkness in this world.

I hoped she found happiness in this life.

Chapter 1
Kali

Twenty-Four Years Later

The entire crowd held its breath as the man lifted the knife, making the blade glint in the sunlight. My heart was in my throat as my gaze swept over everyone who stood on the raised platform in front of me. In a few months, that would be me. The thought had bile burning my throat. Fingers closed around mine, squeezing in a comforting way. I glanced out of the corner of my eye, giving my best friend a small smile. Warner pulled me closer while checking that his sister, Helena, was still on the other side of him before we all turned our attention back to the platform.

The man holding the knife was an elected official in our city, and he did this every month. Norman Wallace was a large man in his forties, and his long brown hair was slowly going gray. His skin was leathery from his lifelong smoking habit, and he wore a permanent scowl on his face. He fucking terrified me. His job seemed to get him off in a sick way, and I detested that soon I'd be the one he'd be touching.

"Give me your hand," Norman ordered, stopping in front of the first guy in the line.

This happened during the first week of every month, and this time, there were only four people up there. Sometimes it was more, and other times there were zero. Ever since the war had ended, not a single month was skipped.

The guy was shaking slightly as he held his hand out. Norman snatched it, raising it high for everyone to see. Bringing his other hand up, he slowly sliced the guy's forearm. Once the cut was a couple of inches long, Norman lowered the knife, but he kept a tight hold on the guy's arm, keeping it raised. When the bright red blood trickled out of the cut, everyone let out a sigh of relief. The guy let out a small cry as he pulled his arm to his chest, cradling it as Norman strolled over to the girl who was next in line.

"Warner," Helena breathed out, her face scrunched in worry as she glanced at her brother. "She can't be—"

"She'll be fine," Warner cut in gently, wrapping an arm around her.

"We don't know that." Helena stared at her best friend, who Norman was standing in front of.

I shared Helena's fear. Our friend Lisa was an orphan, just like me. And like Warner and Helena. We had all lived in the same foster home until we turned eighteen. Not knowing who our parents were was dangerous in this life. Everyone had to go through this ritual on the month of their twenty-fifth birthday, but it was us who were parentless that had the most to lose.

We hadn't seen Lisa in over a month, but she looked healthy. At least they'd fed her while waiting for this blood check.

My mouth went dry as Norman raised Lisa's arm and sliced her skin just like he'd done with the previous guy. Gasps filled the air, and Warner tightened his hold around Helena when she tried lunging forward. My heart sank into my stomach as I watched the blood drip from Lisa's arm.

Because it wasn't red.

It was as black as a starless night.

Meaning only one thing. That we'd never see Lisa again.

Helena was openly sobbing, Warner's arms around her the only reason she was still standing. My palms were clammy as my fingers closed into fists in an attempt to stifle the trembles rolling through me. Lisa was crying as she scanned the crowd until her gaze stopped on us. We were the only family she had, which meant we would be able to say goodbye. My reddish-brown hair was sticking to my neck, and I brushed it away as I gave Lisa a look that I hoped conveyed reassurance. Norman muttered something to Lisa that we couldn't hear, and she held her bleeding arm, her eyes going to the black blood while Norman went to the next person.

Helena ran her hands through her hair as she fell to her knees, while others around us stepped back to give her space. I wasn't even paying attention to the last two people on the platform as I knelt to console Helena. I was close to Lisa, but not like Helena was. They were joined at the hip most of the time.

"Don't," Helena choked out before I said a word. "It's not going to be okay, Kali. Nothing you say can change that."

I only hugged her, knowing she was right. Hot tears trailed down my cheeks as I stayed kneeling next to Helena, softly stroking her blond hair while sobs racked her body.

Warner was shifting on his feet beside me, his face scrunched in pain for both Lisa and his sister.

"That concludes the blood check for this month," Norman said in a loud voice, addressing the crowd. "The family of Lisa Howard can go to town hall."

Helena scrambled to her feet, rushing forward while Lisa and the other three people left the platform. Norman had a tight hold on Lisa's arm, his body tense. There had been times in the past where people refused to go with him. More city workers surrounded them as Norman and Lisa left the town square.

"Helena, wait," Warner yelled, racing to catch up with his sister. "You need to calm down or they won't let you see her."

We weaved through the crowd, following Lisa as they marched her to the town hall building. Nausea swirled in my stomach, my lunch threatening to come back up as I ran. Fear was also flooding through me. Fear for myself, and for Helena and Warner. What if this was us in the coming months?

The town hall came into view as they ushered Lisa inside, and Helena reached the door before it closed. Warner held it open for me, and I stepped inside, tension sliding through my limbs. Nothing good ever happened in this place. Lisa was sitting in a metal chair on the other side of the empty room, and Norman stood behind her.

"Lisa," Helena cried out as she crossed the room. "I'm so sorry. Maybe there's something—"

"There is nothing you can do." Norman cut her off sharply. "She's going to get the help she needs. Say goodbye and leave."

"Show some sympathy," Warner snapped, squaring up to Norman. "At least pretend you have a fucking heart."

"Warner," I murmured, tugging on his arm, trying to remind him that we didn't hold the power here. Norman and the other city officials did. They could ship Lisa off right now without letting us say goodbye.

"Watch yourself, boy," Norman warned, crossing his arms. "Unless you want to spend time in the cells."

"He's sorry," I rushed out, stepping between them. "We just want to talk to our friend."

Norman frowned. "Friend? Only family is allowed to say goodbye."

"We are family," Helena shot back. "She grew up with us."

"Oh. You're all orphans," Norman spat out, his voice filled with distaste. "You kids should be more grateful. This city took you in. If not for us, you'd be dead."

I glared at him, not saying a word. It wasn't like we had a choice where we were sent. During the war, kids who lost their parents had been sent to safe cities wherever there was space. I had no idea who my parents were or where I was from. Helena and Warner had lost their parents when they were six, so at least they had some memories. Although I wasn't sure that was any better than not knowing at all.

"You have ten minutes," Norman stated, backing away. "She needs to start treatment as soon as possible."

A cry escaped Lisa at his words, and she tried wiping away the dried blood as if she could fix it. Her arm was stained with the black blood, and I shrugged out of my zip-up hoodie and put it on her so she didn't have to look at it anymore.

"You'll be okay," I told her, barely able to keep my voice from cracking. "They'll help you."

"And then what?" Lisa asked, her lip trembling. "No

one has ever come back after they go to treatment. So what happens to me?"

"I'll find you," Helena promised. "You won't just disappear like the others."

My heart sank as they kept talking. I wasn't sure Helena would be able to keep her promise. We never saw the others again. Whether the treatment worked or not was a mystery. Ever since the war, society had turned into a dictatorship. The Peace Alliance Response Administration controlled our life now.

Everyone called them PARA, and when the war started, they were the government agency that created these safe cities. But now, it was more than about safe havens. Civilians had no say. No power. We followed PARA or suffered the consequences. From what I'd learned in school, our country used to be fair. Citizens used to be able to vote. I wondered how life had been before the war.

The war between humans and vampires. So many lives were lost in the decades-long fight. Humans wanted the vampires extinct, while the vampires fought to take over everything. When I was a child, the war finally ceased. There was no winner—only a tense compromise that was still holding this world together today.

Vampires weren't allowed in our cities, but the humans who wandered outside the walls were free game. People could make extra money by selling blood, and it helped to keep the vampires peaceful. The rules in our cities were strict to keep people safe. Women especially were under a scrutinizing eye. During the war, a truth had come out that only made things worse.

Certain male vampires could impregnate human women. It wasn't clear why only specific vampires could, but from what I learned in school, not all male vampires were able to. And people with black blood were the result of that.

They were called Shadows. The name had been around since before I was born, and it was the worst thing that could happen to someone.

The children who were half-vampire were no different from humans in the first part of their life. They bled red, and there was no test that could prove if they were human or half vampire. Until they turned twenty-five. That was when the changes began happening. The first thing was the blood turning black within a couple of days of their birthday. Then, within six months, the sickness would start.

We never saw what the symptoms were because they were taken right after the blood check, just like what was going to happen with Lisa. There were rumors about what happened to the people after they were taken away, but no one knew the truth. The city officials assured us that they were doing everything they could to take care of the sick people and were working to find a cure.

Every city had strict rules about blood checks. We hadn't seen Lisa in weeks because, like everyone else, she had been taken a week before her birth month. There was a building that was only used to house people during their birth month. They weren't allowed to leave and were watched every second. PARA didn't want a chance for people to try to escape if they found out they were Shadows. In the past, some had tried running and hiding, but in a city that was so locked down, there was no place where PARA couldn't find them.

People would stay in that building for their entire birth month, and then the first week of the next month was when the blood checks were.

"Time's up," Norman grunted as he shoved past me and took hold of Lisa's arm.

Helena lunged forward, screaming when Warner grabbed her around the waist to hold her back.

"That wasn't even five minutes," I said, trying to keep the panic out of my voice. "You said we could have ten minutes—"

"The convoy leaves soon." Norman cut me off sharply. "She needs to be on it. To get the help she needs before it's too late."

His words had ice sliding down my spine, and I couldn't help but feel he wasn't sincere. Maybe it was because I knew he was a cold-hearted bastard. He seemed to thrive on other people's pain, and it was killing me that Lisa was about to be left alone with him.

"Please don't take me," Lisa sobbed as Norman dragged her away. "I don't want to go."

Helena was screaming as Warner held her, and I stood next to him as three men, all wearing military-type clothes with guns on their hips, stood in front of us, making sure we stayed where we were as Norman pushed Lisa through the back door. My heart was in my throat, my nails digging into my palms as I forced myself to stay where I was. Trying to go after Lisa was a death sentence. The city officials didn't take kindly to disobedience, and I'd learned that the hard way in the past.

Once Norman and Lisa were gone, the three men ushered us out of the building, and I swallowed my words when one of them grabbed my ass as he pushed me onto the sidewalk. I whipped my head over my shoulder to look at him, nausea building in my stomach as he gave me a leering smirk.

"Come on," Warner gritted out, taking my hand and glaring at the man who'd touched me. "Let's go home."

We were halfway down the block when Helena halted in her tracks, turning until she was in front of us. Her eyes were red and puffy from crying, but they were bright with a burning rage as she leaned closer.

"We're going to find the convoy," she hissed under her breath, "and follow. I want to know where Lisa is going."

My pulse quickened as I hurriedly glanced around to make sure we weren't overheard. Helena couldn't just blurt things out like that. We'd get thrown into the cells in an instant.

"No," Warner replied in a hushed voice. "It won't change anything other than you getting in trouble."

"Fine, I'll do it myself."

Her palm flew up, crashing against her brother's nose, and he let out a curse as she raced away. Warner wiped the trickle of blood away, not wasting a moment before chasing after her, and I was hot on his heels. We had to catch up to her before she got to Lisa, or there would be hell to pay.

Chapter 2
Kali

"Helena, wait," Warner demanded in a low voice as he raced to catch up with her. "You're gonna get yourself killed."

Helena ignored him as she darted around a corner, and my heart pounded when we lost sight of her. Warner pulled farther ahead of me, and I scanned the street, hoping none of the city officials were watching. The narrow roads were lined with attached homes and apartments that were falling apart. The sidewalks were overgrown with weeds, and the roads were cracked and full of deep potholes. Not that it mattered, since almost no one who lived here had cars. Vehicles were a luxury that only government workers had.

Luxury. The only reason I knew that word was from school. I'd only ever known survival. Working for the scraps of food to curb the hunger pangs I used to think were normal. As an orphan, I'd always felt unwanted. Because we were extra mouths the city had to feed. Everyone had their own problems here and couldn't afford to worry about children who weren't theirs.

But I wasn't a scared child anymore. I'd found friends

who became family, and we leaned on each other for everything. Swallowing my fear, I ran around the corner, my stomach twisting painfully when Helena slipped out of sight again. But I knew exactly where she was going, and from how Warner swore under his breath, so did he.

The tall walls that surrounded the city came into view, and like always, dread filled every inch of me. We were taught from an early age that the gray bricks were the protection between us and the vampires. For our own safety, no one was ever allowed out. But the older I got, the more one question plagued me. Were the twenty-foot walls that were layered with barbed wire really here to keep us safe? Or to keep us where the government wanted us?

Warner stumbled to a halt when we saw the grate lying on the ground next to the tunnel.

"Stay here, Kali," he ordered as he crouched down.

"Like hell I will," I hissed. "I'm not just waiting here for you."

"It's too dangerous—"

"I don't care," I cut him off sharply. "You and Helena are my family. I'd have nothing left if something happened to you."

He shot me a glare but didn't argue with me any more. There wasn't time to sit here if we wanted to catch up to Helena. He pushed his blond hair out of his eyes before lowering himself into the tunnel. I sat down, letting my legs dangle in the darkness as apprehension churned in my stomach. Once we went through the tunnel, we'd be in vampire territory. This wasn't the first time, but we'd always gone there prepared with weapons, which we weren't now. Anything could go wrong.

I scooted forward, falling into the tunnel, and even if it was only about a six-foot drop, it seemed a lot longer when I couldn't see. There was a rope, but I only needed it when we came back into the city. The soles of my leather boots slammed to the concrete ground, and Warner's arm wrapped around my waist, steadying me. The musty air hit my nostrils, the dampness settling on my skin. It was much cooler down here, and a shiver ran down my spine.

"I hope someone doesn't see the open grate," he muttered, letting me go. "We don't have time to reposition it."

"I'm sure it'll be fine."

At least I hoped so. If anyone caught us leaving the city, we'd be punished. I forced that thought out of my mind, reaching my arm up and slowly moving until I felt the rough wall. Usually we brought flashlights, but this time we were going blind. As long as we stayed near the wall, we'd be able to find our way.

Warner was in front of me, and we quickly moved through the darkness, my ears straining for any sound of Helena. Footsteps from far ahead echoed around the tunnel, and Warner called out her name softly. But if anything, that only made her go faster.

After what felt like forever, a small light protruded from the darkness ahead of us, and I let go of the wall, racing ahead. Helena had left the cover off, and we climbed through the narrow hole. I sucked in a lungful of fresh air as I scanned the forest around us while Warner heaved the heavy cover back over the hole. Usually we put weeds and dirt over it, but there was no time for that now.

"Come on." Warner grabbed my hand, pulling me with him as we started running. The sun was going down, and my nerves crept through me, making my pulse thud. Night was when the vampires came out, and we'd be sitting ducks without stakes or our other weapons. We delved deeper into the forest, the shadows growing larger as the sun dipped behind clouds.

"There she is," I breathed out, catching sight of Helena before she ducked behind a tree.

Warner let go of my hand, rushing to catch up to his sister. He disappeared for a second before I heard Helena shriek. I caught up to them as Warner pulled Helena into the small trail clearing.

"Let me go," she demanded, struggling against him.

"We're going back." Warner slapped his hand over her mouth when she started screaming. "Are you trying to get us killed?"

Helena tore away from him, batting his hand away. "I'm following Lisa, and you can't stop me, Warner."

"The fuck I can't," he hissed.

"Helena." I tried soothing her, catching her arm before she could back away from me. "Even if we follow her, what could we do?"

"We can bring her back with us," she cried. "Or at least know where she's going."

"No." Warner's one-word answer left no room for argument, but Helena didn't back down.

"I won't go with you," she promised fiercely. "I'll fight and scream."

"And lead any vampires in the area right to us?" I snapped, losing my patience. She wasn't thinking clearly, and none of us would make it home if she didn't calm down.

"Then let me follow them," she screeched, shoving me away. My heart hammered in my chest, hoping no one had heard her. "They won't even know we're there. I just need to know where they're taking her. Please."

Warner glared at her, his jaw clenched as he weighed the options. Helena was stubborn, and I had a feeling she'd fight us every step of the way if we tried taking her back to the tunnel. With night falling, we couldn't afford for any vampires to hear us. Or the guards patrolling the grounds near the city.

"We can take the bikes and stay far enough that they won't know we're following," Helena continued quickly, sensing she was winning the argument. "Don't you want to know, Warner? Especially with Kali doing this in a couple months? What if they take her too?"

"I wouldn't let that happen," Warner hissed. "Fuck. Fine. But we do this my way."

Helena nodded, relief sweeping over her face. My own emotions were a tangled mess. I wanted to know where Lisa was going, but this was a death sentence if we got caught. I'd spent my entire life surviving, and my instincts were screaming at me to turn around and go back to the tunnel. My life wasn't exactly great, but at least I was safe behind the city's high walls. Ignoring the fear sliding through my limbs, I followed Warner and Helena deeper into the forest.

We got to a small clearing, and Warner muttered under his breath about this being a bad idea as he crouched down beside some bushes and stuck his arm through the thick leaves. It took him a while, but he finally leaned forward, using both hands to drag out a small motorbike. Stepping next to him, I grabbed the handlebars, rolling the bike away as he got the second one out.

"The group is not going to be happy," I muttered as I swung my leg over the bike. "We're supposed to log it every time we use these."

"I'll handle it once we get back," Warner replied tightly, walking the second bike next to mine.

Our group. The Clovers. Faith, hope, love, and luck. Faith that humans would overthrow the vampires. Hope that humans could someday live in a world where we weren't controlled under a dictatorship. Clovers brought others in and proved there was still love in this world. And we needed all the luck that someday our numbers would grow enough to displace PARA.

The Clovers wanted a world where humans weren't trapped in a small city for their entire lives. Where we didn't work to the bone to survive. Where we weren't terrified to step a toe out of line because we'd be thrown in the cells or worse, killed. PARA controlled everything, and that was how they wanted to keep it. But it was also the vampires that needed to be taken down. We couldn't live in peace with them running free.

The Clovers had taken me in when I was a child and taught me everything I knew. Clover members spanned everywhere in this world, and there were other freedom groups we worked with.

PARA saw us as threats because the Clovers challenged their authority. We'd trained on how to protect ourselves from both the vampires and the government. I'd been with the group for years, just like Warner, Helena, and Lisa. And it was a secret we'd take to our grave. It was a trusted circle, and if someone broke it, they'd pay with their life. If the city officials ever found out, we'd be executed.

The larger our numbers grew, the more we expanded. Growing up, I did small jobs, and now I'd leave Project Hope to find food and train. Older members did the larger jobs, like finding out the secrets PARA wanted to keep from us. For now, we stayed quiet in Project Hope, but other cities were having larger fights. Members would tag buildings with our symbol, the four-leaf clover, letting PARA know rebellion was happening. It gave civilians hope. It also put a larger target on the group, making our secrecy even more important.

"Do you hear that?" Helena asked, looking over her shoulder. "We need to go before we lose them."

We stayed silent, and the hum of engines filled the air. The convoy that Lisa was with must have left the city. There was only one road that was maybe three hundred feet from where we were in the forest. My stomach flipped, nerves skating down my spine. The Clovers had tried following the convey in the past, but PARA found them and killed them. Ever since then, we were told to stay in the city when the convoy left. They were more on guard and had more security on the nights they took the Shadows out of the city. And our group couldn't afford to lose more people right now.

"We stay far back," Warner ordered, catching my eye. "Keep your lights off. The moon is full, so it shouldn't be too hard to see the road."

I nodded as Warner got on the bike and then helped Helena get on behind him. I kickstarted my bike, putting it into gear, and let Warner go first on the narrow trail that led to the road. Even with the moon, it was still nearly impossible to see more than a foot in front of me. Branches scratched my bare legs as I rode, making me regret wearing shorts today. It wasn't long before we made it to the dirt road.

We veered left, following the taillights of the last vehicle in the convoy. They always traveled with at least three, in case they were attacked. My pulse was going haywire as we rode slowly, keeping our distance but making sure we didn't lose them. I wasn't sure who terrified me more right now—the city officials if they found us or vampires roaming the woods. Either way, I'd end up dead.

I frowned in confusion when, only a little way up the road, the convoy stopped. Warner pulled to the side of the road, and I followed. We watched as men jumped out of the truck and headed into the woods.

Helena hopped off the bike, already running toward them, and Warner didn't risk yelling for her to stop as he went after her. She was creeping near the tree line, and my annoyance grew. I understood she was upset, but the way she was acting went against everything we'd been taught our entire childhood. We didn't take unnecessary risks. Ever.

Warner and I caught up to her, and she threw him a look of warning. She wasn't about to leave quietly if her brother tried forcing her hand. He let out a long breath, falling into step with her, and I was right next to him.

"They're heading to the river," Helena whispered as we got closer. "What are they doing?"

"Maybe they figured out someone was following," Warner shot back under his breath. "This is such a bad fucking idea."

But we still didn't turn back. We pushed through the leaves, following their flashlights as they moved closer to the river. I could hear the roaring of the fast-moving water, and we found a berry bush to hide behind that gave us a clear view of them. My heart dipped when I saw Lisa among the men. They were standing in a half-circle, surrounding her, with the river behind her. Helena grabbed my hand, her fingers tightening around mine as we stayed crouched down.

"What are you doing?" Lisa sobbed, wrapping her arms around herself. "I thought I was going to treatment."

"You are," Norman soothed her as he stepped closer. "We need to cross the river to get there."

"Cross here?" Lisa asked doubtfully.

"Right over there." Norman pointed into the darkness. "There's a bridge."

When Lisa turned toward the river, Norman pulled a gun out from under his shirt and quickly put it to the back of her head.

"No!" The scream tore from my throat right when he pulled the trigger.

Helena's yell was cut off when Warner raised his arm, putting his hand over her mouth before dragging her back. Lisa's lifeless body crumpled to the ground, but the men weren't focused on her. They were shining their flashlights our way. I stumbled back as tears streamed down my face.

"Someone's out there," one man said.

"Vampires," another voice rang out.

"No," Norman snapped, his eyes scanning the trees. "They wouldn't be hiding. We have civilians out here. Find them."

Raw panic sliced through my grief as I turned toward the road. Warner was dragging Helena with him, and he turned to look at me, his eyes wild with fear as he whispered to me.

"Run."

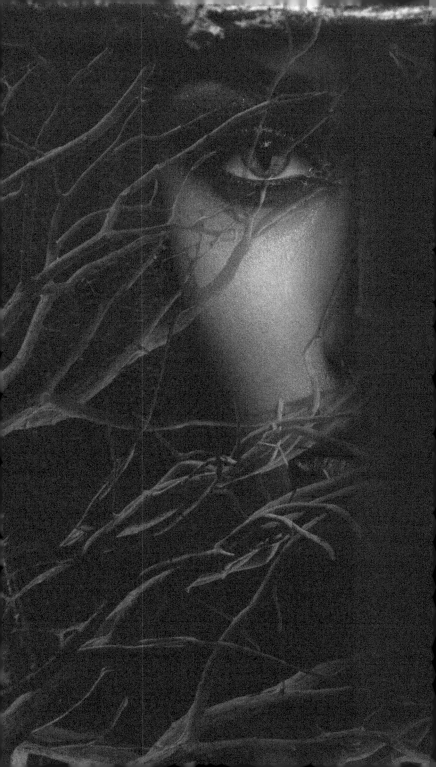

Chapter 3
Kali

We were halfway back to the bikes when new flashlights sliced through the darkness. A lump grew in my throat as Warner grabbed my wrist, hauling me the opposite way. There must have been more men in the trucks, and they were too close to our bikes. We couldn't take the chance of going that way.

"We're going to have to split up," Warner said tightly.

I shook my head. "No—"

"There're too many of them," he cut me off. "Get back to the tunnel. Don't wait. They didn't see our faces, so we're safe as long as they find us back inside the walls."

"I'm so sorry." Helena's voice shook as we pushed through the branches. "It's my fault. We never should have come."

"Don't worry about that right now," I breathed out, my panic swallowing me when the footsteps behind us drew closer. "Focus on getting home."

"And don't let them see you," Warner reminded us. "Or we can never go home."

"Be careful," I muttered, squeezing Warner's hand before I let go.

"Get to the tunnel," he whispered before veering to the left. Helena raced straight ahead, and I turned toward the right to keep the river in sight. I'd been in this forest so many times in the last three years that I could easily find my way back on foot.

As long as I didn't get turned around in the dark.

There were at least a few men chasing me, and one was yelling at me to stop. Clouds were blowing in, hiding part of the moon and making it easier for me to disappear into the darkness. It also meant I needed to be extra careful not to run into anything. I weaved between the trees, hissing out a breath when I stepped on a rock, nearly twisting my ankle. A jolt of pain shot up my leg, and I darted to the left, not running in a straight line.

"Stop. Now," someone bellowed from behind me.

The voice was much too close for comfort, and I sucked in quick breaths, trying to keep my fear controlled. If I let the terror in, it would strangle me, and then I'd never survive. I could let it take over if they caught me. It was nearly pitch black as more clouds covered the sky, and I risked slowing a bit so I didn't run face-first into a tree.

"I have a shot."

"Take it."

My mouth went dry, hearing the shouts behind me. They really didn't want any witnesses to what they'd done. I pushed myself faster, my eyes straining to see in the darkness. A silenced gunshot went off, and bark flew off the tree near the left side of my head. I bit back my cry, lunging away, zigzagging as much as I could between the thick tree trunks. One second, my feet were on the ground, and the next, I hit nothing but air.

I couldn't stop my yell of shock as I dropped. My momentum made it impossible to get my limbs back under control as I rolled and flipped down a steep hill. Branches and rocks cut and tore into my skin. Pain ricocheted through my skull when I hit something solid as I kept bouncing down the dirt. Protecting my head as much as I could, I attempted to stay in a tuck and roll position.

It felt like forever before I finally came to a halt. Every part of my body was aching, and I could feel warm blood sliding down my arm. I sucked in breaths, my head still swimming when I noticed lights sweeping the ground near me. Scrambling to my hands and knees, I groaned in pain as I scurried away from the bottom of the cliff. I spotted a wide tree trunk and threw myself behind it, letting my back rest against the bark as I caught my breath.

The lights continued to search the area, but as I peeked around the tree, I didn't see anyone coming down after me. The moon peeked through the clouds, revealing how massive the hill I'd just rolled down was. I was lucky I didn't break anything. I counted in my head, and when I was just passing one thousand, the lights disappeared. A slice of relief cut through me, and I rested my head on the tree trunk.

I couldn't afford to stay here much longer. We'd be prime suspects, and we needed to be safely home before they came and searched for us. I shakily climbed to my feet, patting myself down for any injuries that might be serious. Other than some nasty cuts and a throbbing headache, I seemed to be okay.

"North of the river," I mumbled, trying to remember the way back. As long as I stayed on this side of the river, I only had to go north to find the city again. Glancing up, I frowned in disappointment. The clouds were hiding the stars. It would be easier if I could track my way back that way. Swiping my hands down my face, I attempted to wipe away the caked-on dirt as I jogged. I just needed to find the river again.

Soon, I could hear the flowing water, and I rushed forward when the river came into view. Dropping to my knees, I cupped my hands. I began washing off my face before throwing water on my arm and rubbing off the drying blood from my scrapes. I shook my hands dry before climbing back to my feet, more confident now that I could follow the river back to the city walls.

I turned around and froze in my tracks when I saw a figure in the shadows. It moved toward me, and I spun to the side, racing away. If it was Warner or Helena, they would have called out to me so I wouldn't be startled. Whoever—or whatever—was chasing me was not a friend. Heavy steps followed me as I lost sight of the river again to try and get away.

My chest was tight as I kept running, my tired body begging for a break. I sucked in breaths with each step, willing myself to keep going. The moon was bright again, making it easier to move faster.

"No," I screamed when I was pushed from behind.

My chest slammed into a tree, and I grunted in pain when a hand landed between my shoulder blades to keep me in place.

"Quiet," a voice demanded under their breath. "Don't make a sound, and I won't hurt you."

I complied. Not to follow his orders, but because I wasn't sure if it was Norman's man who had me or something much worse. But either way, I didn't want to attract any more attention. If it was only one person, I could fight my way out.

I went rigid when fingers wrapped tightly around my upper arm, turning me around. He let me go once I was facing him, and my heart bounced in my chest, terror seeping into my bones. This wasn't one of the city's men. I doubted he was a man at all. He was wearing a T-shirt and jeans, looking out of place deep in the forest. Only one creature would be wandering these woods at night with no weapons.

Because they didn't need any. Their strength and teeth were more than enough.

The vampire cocked his head to the side, studying me curiously. His eyes swept down my body, and I grew more uneasy by the second. My cuts were still openly bleeding, making me feel so much more vulnerable.

I didn't dare take my eyes off him as I kept my back pressed against the tree. He looked like a normal human. All vampires did until their fangs came out. The moonlight made it possible to see some of his features as we stared at each other. If I didn't know what he was, I'd consider him cute.

Tattoos covered his mahogany skin on one arm where his shirt wasn't covering, and he was maybe half a foot taller than me. His black hair was cut short, and he had stubble running along his jawline. His ears were pierced, the diamonds glinting in the dim light.

Our tense stand-off was broken when another voice rang through the trees.

"Pax. Where'd you go?"

In a second, the vampire, Pax, was pressing me against the tree, his hand covering my mouth, his glare a silent warning to stay quiet.

"Smell that?" another voice asked. "He found dinner."

"I'm eating alone tonight," the vampire holding me yelled back. "Both of you fuck off. I'll find you later."

My eyes widened, pure fear invading every cell in my body as I began fighting. He quickly pulled me away from the tree, moving behind me and keeping his hand over my mouth as he forced me to walk farther away from the river. His free arm wrapped around my waist and arms, keeping them trapped at my sides.

"Don't fight," he murmured in my ear as we walked. "You'll have a much worse night if my brothers find you."

This time I ignored his command, writhing and wiggling to slip out of his hold. When that didn't work, I lifted my feet, attempting to use my dead weight to throw him off balance. He only chuckled, effortlessly carrying me through the trees. Sinking my teeth into his fingers that were still covering my mouth, I bit down as hard as I could. He jerked his hand for a moment but didn't release me.

"Feisty little thing," he muttered, sounding more amused than anything else. "Now, I'm going to let you go so we can talk. But if you try to run, it won't end well for you."

Before I could process his words, I was free of his grasp, and I stumbled to my knees, trying to scramble away from him. My hand touched a large rock, and I wrapped my fingers around it, holding it tightly as I jumped back to my feet.

"I saw you running—and then falling down that hill," he stated as I turned to face him. "Why were you running?"

Confusion swarmed me as I stared at him. Why the hell was he stopping to question me? Every other vampire I'd come across tried killing me the second they found out I was human. Or they tried capturing me. The Clovers had trained me from a young age to take care of myself. They needed capable people who could handle themselves when leaving the city. Orphans were usually recruited since no one ever paid attention to us. We were the kids no one wanted.

I learned how to fight. How to kill. When I had my weapons on me, I was never scared of walking these woods. Right now was different, since I had nothing. But I refused to let him see that fear.

He took a step toward me, and I warily moved back, my eyes darting around while I tried to get my bearings. I had no idea where I was now that I couldn't see the river.

"Put the rock down," he murmured, arching an eyebrow. "You really think that would hurt me?"

"I don't know, *Pax*," I shot back, spitting out the name the other vampire had called him. "Have you ever been hit in the face with one?"

A hint of surprise flickered across his features before he grinned. "All I want is an answer, and I'll let you go."

"I don't believe you."

He shrugged. "Have I hurt you yet? Actually, I saved you. Because if my brothers had found you first, then you'd already be dead."

My heart thudded, and his gaze dropped to my chest, as if he could hear the change. I swallowed thickly, taking another few steps back.

"Don't run," he repeated, his smile fading.

"Why?" I sneered. "Not a fan of fast food?"

He gaped at me before he let out a loud laugh. "Do you taunt all the vampires you meet?"

"No," I answered casually. "I usually don't have much time to chat before I kill them."

"Mm," he hummed out. "I'm not the first vampire you've met."

"Not even close."

He stalked closer, but instead of coming after me, he circled me. I turned with him, not letting him out of my sight. The knots in my stomach tightened with each passing second. I needed to get back home, and I wasn't sure how I was going to escape him without any weapons.

"Humans were chasing you," he stated, still prowling around me. "You were running from your own kind. Why?"

"Does it matter?" I snapped.

"Were they taking you to the river?"

The blood drained from my face when Lisa's murder flashed through my mind. Agony crushed my chest, and I couldn't stop the tears from welling in my eyes.

"How do you know about that?" I angrily wiped my face, refusing to show him weakness.

"What if I told you we were out here to save the Shadows they killed every month?"

My eyes cut to his in disbelief. "Why?"

He grinned. "Can't tell a human all our secrets."

"If that's the truth, then you failed. Because they killed her."

"We don't always get there in time. They change the time and place to evade us."

"Do you know of a cure?" I asked, the hope in my voice impossible to mask.

He stared at me for a few moments before completely changing the subject. "We're not all that different, you know."

I scoffed. "Please."

He lunged at me, catching my wrist when I tried ducking away. I swung my other arm, and he caught it before I could smash the rock against his jaw. He squeezed a pressure point, and I hissed out a breath as he forced me to drop the rock.

"Let me go," I snarled, covering my fear.

He ignored me, holding both my wrists in an ironclad hold as I tried twisting away from him. My spine slammed against a tree, my already battered body protesting. He pulled my hand up, pressing it against his chest.

"My heart beats just as yours does," he murmured, keeping my palm on his chest. "Blood runs through my veins just like yours."

I could feel his calm heart beating against my hand, not understanding where he was going with this. I tried tugging away, but he held me in place, his stare boring through me.

"You're dead," I hissed. "And your kind is trying to kill or capture mine."

"You've already admitted to killing my kind. I'll say it again—we really aren't that different."

"I do it to survive."

"You live in Project Hope. That's the only reason you're this close to the city with nothing on you." He named the city I lived in. "I hear civilians aren't allowed to go past the walls. You're going to get in trouble."

"You have no idea what you're talking about." Suspicion burned through me, wondering how much he knew about the way our city operated.

"So you're not planning on sneaking back in unnoticed?"

"Get off me," I bit out.

He laughed. "How do you plan on doing that when you're all cut up? I could smell your wounds before I even saw you. But even with human eyes, it would be impossible to miss."

"What's with all the questions?" I burst out, losing patience. "Stop playing. If you're going to try to kill me, then just fucking do it."

"I find you entertaining. Come with me."

My lips parted in shock. "What?"

"Did you know that there are humans living with us? By choice?"

My heart pounded. "You're lying."

"They say it's better than being trapped in the city. They have freedom with us," he whispered, his eyes locked on mine.

"Freedom to do what? Be a food bank?" I asked in disgust. "I'll never choose that life."

"Or I could turn you."

His words had me freezing in fear. He watched me intently as I glared at him. That was one secret humans didn't know. The whole process of how vampires turned humans was a mystery. The vampires kept that quiet. We knew that they could bite us without us turning, but that was it.

"Why don't you tell me how you'd turn me, and I'll think about it," I said snidely, trying to calm my nerves.

He chuckled. "Humans have been trying to figure that out for decades. You think I'd tell you?"

"I think you're playing with me, and I'm getting bored."

"You won't come back with me?"

"No," I snapped.

"Fine. Then go." He released me and took a couple of steps back.

I didn't move a muscle, not sure if he was playing some kind of twisted game. He could easily overpower me. Vampires had brute strength that humans couldn't touch. They were also faster. Not super-speed fast, but more than enough to overtake anyone trying to outrun them. Without weapons, I didn't stand a chance.

"You're letting me leave?" I asked skeptically.

"Yes."

"Why?"

"Because not all vampires are as bad as you think." He paused. "Most are. But we're all different too. And I don't particularly care to feed on girls who have that much pain in their eyes. Whoever they killed at the river must have been close to you."

"She was," I muttered, still not believing his words. "But I don't understand why you care."

"I'm considering it my good deed of the week." He gave me a boyish grin, making me almost forget what he was for a moment. "Better run along before I change my mind."

I hesitantly took a step back. Then another one when he made no move to follow. I slowly crept around him, my hands clenched into fists, waiting for him to attack. But he stayed completely still. I didn't stop walking, and once darkness made it impossible to see him, I turned and bolted.

I couldn't hear him coming after me, but that didn't put me at ease. He wouldn't just let me go. What if he followed me back to the city? Letting a vampire find the tunnel would put everyone at risk. But I didn't have anywhere else to go. I had no food or anything else I needed to survive out here.

He was right about my wounds. When they came to question me, they'd realize in an instant where I'd been. I'd have to leave before they found out. But I needed to pack first, so I'd have a chance at surviving outside the walls.

I searched for the river as dread filled me. Life was about to change, and not for the better.

Chapter 4
Zan

"**M**aybe we should have waited for him," Viggo muttered, glancing over his shoulder.

"Pax is fine," I replied as we strode through the woods. "And we even left him the fucking truck."

Viggo sighed. "You know how he is. He's always getting himself into trouble."

"Really? That sounds more like you."

"He cares too much," he mumbled as he scrubbed a hand down his face. "I thought it would change after we turned. But it's been seven years, and the sympathy he shows them is going to bite him in the ass."

"He had one girl." I dismissed his concerns. "He can handle her."

I didn't get a look at her but heard her muffled cries when we were searching for Pax.

"Something was different tonight," he murmured, giving me a long look. "Usually they leave right after they're done at the river. But they were searching the forest. Probably looking for the girl Pax took."

"We saw them getting in their trucks," I reminded him, pushing a branch to the side as we walked. "We wouldn't have left Pax if they were still there."

"We shouldn't have let them leave at all."

I scowled. "Don't. You know they always come prepared. We came to watch tonight. That's it. They only killed one person. Next month, we'll be ready."

Viggo didn't respond, but his lips were pressed together as if he was keeping his thoughts to himself. We'd been at this for months, trying to catch PARA before they could go through with their killings. But they took precautions, and we'd been too late every single fucking time. Tonight, we got there to find the woman's body on the ground with the men combing the woods. Viggo was right about it being different this month. They usually did the killings quickly and left as soon as they could before we caught them.

"Dad was expecting this done." Viggo's words made my stomach tighten. "We were supposed to move on to another city already—not be here for over a year."

"I know," I snapped. "Next month it'll happen."

"Not if we keep getting to the river late. Soon they'll start going somewhere else if they have a hint that we're watching."

I ignored him, pushing through the last of the bushes, glad to be out of the damn woods. I needed a fucking drink. Two drinks, actually. The first would be straight whiskey. And then I'd indulge in something warmer. I upped my speed, hearing Viggo grumble behind me as he raced to keep up. We crossed the abandoned highway, getting to the edge of a crumbling city. Before the war, I was sure this sprawling skyline was stunning. But now, it was overgrown with weeds and trees, while the buildings deteriorated more every day.

The night was quiet, and to anyone looking in, this city would seem like all the others that had fallen during the war. Desolate with no sign of life. But that wasn't the case. We'd been here for over a year, and I'd been building up our numbers the entire time. No one stepped foot in our area without us knowing about it, although the humans had tried. Their city, Project Hope, was on the other side of the forest, and we had eyes on their gate at all times so they couldn't catch us by surprise.

We entered the city, striding down a street that was lined with buildings that used to be high-end stores. Most of the windows were broken, and everything had been taken long ago. A head popped up out of the darkness, and I jerked a nod toward him as we passed. We had watchers prowling the outskirts of the city around the clock to keep an eye out.

"We need to get everyone ready for next month," Viggo stated as we kept walking. "Our numbers have to be larger than theirs."

"We will."

The closer we got to the city center, the louder it got. Lights shone from inside the buildings, and there was laughing and yelling. When the other vampires saw Viggo and me, they greeted us with respect, giving us space as we moved forward. Night was when everyone came out to play. They were bound to the dark since the sun would kill them, and the second sundown happened, the streets were full.

Music got louder, and I raised my gaze to see our main place. We called it Impulse, and vampires from all around came to party here. Even though we were here on a mission, we made sure to keep life fun. Which was all part of the overall plan. Vampires wouldn't want to follow if we led with a cutthroat hand. It was in our nature to crave chaos.

So we supplied all the blood, booze, and drugs they could handle. Human vices were still just as addictive after death. And after the war, they were a hot commodity.

"If he's not back soon, I'm going looking for him," Viggo muttered under his breath as I pulled open the front door of Impulse.

I arched an eyebrow, glancing at him before going inside. Viggo had a lethal reputation. Other vampires feared him, just like they did me. But his one soft spot was his twin. He worried about Pax much more than he'd ever admit out loud. Viggo might only be two minutes older, but he took the big brother role seriously.

"Zan. Want your usual?"

Lifting my head, my gaze fell on Gia. We owned everything in this city, but she ran Impulse to make sure everything went smoothly. Her fiery red hair was a couple of shades lighter than the bright cherry lipstick she loved to wear. She had hazel eyes that were always bright, and she was the cheeriest vampire I'd ever fucking met. But she wasn't one to mess with. She had trained under my father and was deadlier than nearly all the other vampires in this city.

"How's the night going, Gia?" Viggo asked as we made our way to our usual spot. "Anything to report?"

Gia shook her head. "It's actually been a quiet night."

I chuckled, taking a seat in a plush black chair before scanning the room. The space was loud and busy. Music pulsed as dancers took up the middle of the room. Fights were a nightly occurrence. There were couches and chairs scattered everywhere, with tables crammed wherever they could fit. Pool tables and dart boards were in the back, next to the private rooms. A long bar ran along the entire left wall with two workers behind it, busy making drinks.

I never knew what life had been like before the war, but from what I'd learned, this was how humans spent their free nights. Partying in places like this. Some vampires remembered those days, and they loved telling stories about it.

Although I was sure the cages around the room were something the human clubs didn't have.

My eyes drifted to the closest one, where a man was sitting in the middle. His arms were wrapped around his legs, and he was keeping himself as small as possible. The cages were tall enough to stand in, but I was sure this particular human was exhausted. He'd been in there for at least a week. Fear flickered across his face when a vampire sauntered up to him and stuck her arm into the cage. He scrambled back, his spine hitting the bars as he tried to evade her.

She laughed when he was grabbed by another vampire who snuck up behind him. The man screamed when his arm was pulled through the bars, and the vampire sank his teeth into the man's forearm.

My gaze cut back to Viggo, uninterested in watching someone else's meal. The people trapped here were our enemies. The cages were reserved for the humans who tried getting into our city or attempted to attack us. I hadn't felt empathy in seven years, but even if I did, I wouldn't feel anything for those assholes. They wanted us dead.

Viggo made himself comfortable in his chair as Gia came back with our drinks. Our little corner of Impulse made it easy to watch the entire room. We lived upstairs, and I had to admit, I considered it home after being here for so long. The freedom here beat the hell out of living on my father's property.

"Damn. He wasn't gone long." Viggo was staring at the entrance, and I followed his gaze to see Pax stalking toward us, a pissed-off scowl on his face. We'd left him the vehicle, so it would have only taken him a few minutes to get back here compared to our twenty-something-minute walk. Pax dropped into the last chair in our half circle, nodding at Gia to get him a drink.

"How'd she taste?" Viggo asked, cocking his head as if already knowing the answer.

"I didn't go after her to eat," Pax replied tightly.

Viggo scoffed, shaking his head, but didn't say a word. Pax fed on humans just like us, but he was much more particular in his tastes. Because he had sympathy that Viggo couldn't stand. If he stumbled on a human he felt bad for, he wouldn't feed. My father fucking detested it, and it wasn't a secret that he looked at Pax as the weakest of his sons.

"She was running from them," Pax explained in a low voice, leaning forward. "She's from Project Hope."

"So?" Viggo asked, sounding bored.

"So she couldn't just walk past the gate. I wanted to follow her to see how she got back into the city."

That got my attention, and I peered around, checking to see if anyone was listening. I really didn't care if vampires overheard. But there were humans in here too, and this was not for their ears.

"And?" I asked, getting impatient. "Did you follow her?"

If we had a secret way into the city, that would help speed up our plans. When Pax shook his head, I leaned back in disappointment.

"I let her out of sight because she was already suspicious as fuck. Then she jumped in the damn river, making it harder to catch her scent again," Pax gritted out.

Viggo let out a howl of laughter. "One human girl got away from you?"

Pax shot him a scathing glare. "Before I could catch up, I ran into a few of the guards they have patrolling the woods over there."

"You took care of them?" I asked, noticing the small splatter of blood on his shirt.

He nodded. "Yeah. But they called backup, so I decided to leave."

"PARA was chasing her?" I murmured, curiosity getting the better of me. "Why?"

"She wasn't exactly chatty with me," Pax replied, taking his drink from Gia.

"If there's another way into their city, we need to find it," Viggo said. "We could finish this in a heartbeat if we had that information."

"We'll send scouts out to look." I downed the rest of my drink.

The humans thought the war was over. They had no idea we'd never stopped plotting. And they wouldn't know until it was too late.

Chapter 5
Kali

Something was wrong.

I had the tunnel entrance in my sights, but it was the chaos inside the walls that had my blood running cold. There was a curfew, and everyone had to be in their homes when the sun went down. Nights were deathly quiet in my city. But right now, I could see the glow of lights, and I could hear a voice over a loudspeaker. I rushed forward, my heart pounding painfully when I noticed the cover of the tunnel was moved. Which meant Helena or Warner had already gotten back.

Or people were leaving the city.

Either way, I needed to sneak back in. I wouldn't survive long out here if I didn't have my supplies. And I couldn't leave without finding Warner and Helena. I was almost positive I'd lost the vampire once I swam in the river, but if he was trailing behind, I didn't want him spotting the tunnel.

Once I was in the tunnel, I tried hauling the heavy cover over the hole, but couldn't place it perfectly by myself. But it would have to do, and I wouldn't be in the city too long anyway. Keeping my hand on the rough wall, I ran as fast as I dared through the darkness. My heart fell into my stomach when I stumbled to a stop under the exit. It was uncovered, just like we'd left it.

Dread clung to me as I grabbed the dangling rope and hauled myself up. My muscles burned as I held myself up while I slowly poked my head out, scanning the street. The second I made sure there was no one around, I climbed out and put the metal grate back in place. The voice over the loudspeaker was echoing, but it sounded like it was coming from the city center, where the monthly blood checks were held.

I stood still for a moment, considering my next move. Going to my place and grabbing my bag should be the first priority. But as the voice grew louder, I found myself heading the opposite way instead. What if it was about Warner and Helena? If they got caught outside the walls, the government would make an example out of them.

I began flat out running, cutting through the small yards, my shoes crunching on the dead grass, and soon, I wasn't alone anymore as others were making their way to the city center. Forcing myself to slow down, I ran my hands through my tangled hair, hoping it didn't look too messy. It was still damp from jumping in the river, but at least I wasn't covered in specks of blood anymore.

"Kali."

I spun around, seeing a man who was a Clover. He was older than me and was one of the people who trained me. Even if he couldn't help me out of this situation, there was still a slice of relief to know I wasn't by myself. I fell into step with him as we kept walking.

"What's going on, Tim?" I asked in a hushed voice.

"Mandatory attendance." He glanced over at me. "They think people are missing."

Shit. One look at me, and I was fucked. Tim's steps slowed as he studied me, a scowl forming on his face. My cheeks flushed, knowing he was not going to be happy. Going through the tunnel without informing the group would be a breach of trust.

"What happened to you?" he hissed, grabbing my arm. "Did you go into the woods? We had nothing planned."

"Something happened—"

I snapped my mouth shut when a bunch of soldiers came around the corner. Long guns were strapped over their shoulders, and they marched behind us, trying to corral everyone toward the city center. Tim cursed under his breath, shrugging out of his zip-up hoodie before throwing it over my shoulders. I gave him a grateful smile as I zipped it up. It didn't go much longer than the hem of my shorts, but it was better than seeing the tears in my shirt.

"Did they see you outside the walls?" he asked, leaning close to me.

"I don't think so."

"Who else was with you?"

I pressed my lips into a thin line. Even though I doubted it would stay a secret, I wasn't about to voice Helena's and Warner's names. Maybe they could get out of this somehow. The people in the crowd were murmuring with curiosity as we entered the large space in the middle of the city. Everyone was here, and I felt suffocated as I was pushed forward into more bodies. We had over a thousand people here, and it was impossible to fit in this long rectangular space without being squished together.

Tim kept a hold on my arm to keep us from being separated as we moved with everyone else. I searched the crowd, trying to catch sight of Warner or Helena. Panic tightened the knots in my stomach when Norman stepped onto the platform. He was wearing the same black uniform that he'd had on in the forest, and he lifted a microphone to his mouth.

"Everybody, please be patient," he bellowed. "There was a breach of security, and we need to account for everyone to make sure you're all safe."

Bile rose in my throat. This wasn't about safety. It was about finding the people who'd witnessed them killing Lisa. They were trying to cover their tracks.

"How did you get caught?" Tim whispered furiously in my ear. "We taught you better than that."

"I didn't get caught," I shot back. "I'm here. They have no idea who it was, which is why they're doing this."

"They'll realize it the minute they see your face." He brushed his knuckles over my cheek. "Your jaw is already bruising."

"I could say I got into a fight."

He scoffed. "You know that won't work."

I knew that. Norman would be looking for anyone who stood out, and since his men saw someone tumble down a cliff, they were expecting someone to be hurt. I glanced over my shoulder, my fear growing larger when I realized all the exits of the city center were being guarded.

I had no way out. I should have gotten my bag first. I might have a chance if I had my weapons.

"We have a traitor among us." Norman's voice echoed as he spoke into the microphone. "Helena Mackley was caught outside the walls. Running to vampires to sell out our secrets."

Shocked gasps exploded throughout the crowd as Tim's fingers tightened on my arm. I barely acknowledged him as

I watched in horror as a man dragged Helena onto the platform. Her wrists were tied in front of her, and her mouth was gagged with a thick cloth. She was walking with the man on her own, not fighting or trying to escape. I lunged forward, only for Tim to haul me back to his side.

"There's nothing you can do for her now," he said softly. "I know you're close but—"

"Helena was beside herself that we needed to take her friend, Lisa, to treatment." Norman spoke again, drowning out the rest of Tim's sentence. "Instead of coming to us, she decided she didn't want to be with us anymore. Her actions could have put us in jeopardy."

His lies brought a surge of action from the crowd, and a few began yelling, their anger focused on Helena. Just like they wanted. Helena was staring over everyone, as if she wasn't listening, her body sagging in defeat. I raised on my tiptoes, seeing blond hair weaving and pushing through the bodies.

"Kali, don't," Tim ordered when I slipped out of his hold.

I ignored him, shoving through the crowd, keeping my eyes trained on Warner. He was attempting to get to the platform without raising too much attention, and I slowly gained on him as Norman spoke up again.

"We can't have people like this in our community. They are a threat. We must always choose the human race before ourselves, or we won't survive." The crowd cheered at his words. "She can't be trusted anymore."

A chill ripped through me. My worst fear—her being made an example of—was coming true.

"Traitor," someone screamed from the crowd.

"Punish her."

"Lock her away."

The yells had my heart sinking. The people here put so much trust in PARA—they wouldn't believe anything else. They were the reason we'd survived the war. They were respected. Feared. No one ever went against them.

"Warner," I called his name as I got close.

He whipped around, his frantic gaze softening a fraction when he saw me. He hesitated, giving me a chance to catch up to him. He had two backpacks on, and he shrugged one off and pushed it into my arms.

"I stopped at home first," he said in a rush, his eyes going back to the platform. "I thought Helena was safe. I didn't know they had her."

I put the backpack on, ignoring the few curious glances we were getting. Most were too focused on Norman to notice us, but now suspicions were high.

"I put extra supplies in there," he said. "You should be good for a while. You remember there's a faction of the group that lives free. Find them, Kali."

"We don't know where they are," I said, my voice shaking. "And I'm not leaving you here, so stop talking like I am."

"Yes, you are," he growled. "I'm getting my sister. And you're leaving right now. Before they get a hold of you too."

"No—"

"Run," he cut me off. "Leave and find someplace safe. You know that abandoned city on the other side of the forest? Stay in one of those buildings. I'll find you once I get Helena."

He was talking as if it were simple. There was no way to get Helena away from Norman. The crowd would get involved to stop him now that they saw Helena as a traitor.

"The cells aren't enough for her," Norman said, his voice cruel. "We can't let her try it again."

The people screamed in agreement, and I froze when Helena suddenly attacked the man who was holding on to her. Like me, she was trained to fight, and it only took her a couple of simple moves to free herself. She raised her tied hands, pulling the gag out of her mouth.

"They killed her," Helena screamed. "Your precious government is murdering innocent people in cold blood."

She was yelling as loud as she could, but I could barely hear her, and I was near the front of the crowd. Norman lunged at her, and she ducked out of the way, looking determined.

"Lisa never went to treatment." Her voice caught. "They shot her in the head near the river."

"Spewing lies," Norman snarled into the microphone.

"I didn't go to the vampires," she shouted, running to stay out of Norman's reach. "They killed her. I saw it. They're murderers."

Warner was shoving forward toward the platform, and I followed behind him. My hands clenched into fists when I spotted two more men hurrying onto the platform. They quickly caught Helena's arms, shoving her to her knees before she could do anything. Norman stalked behind her, and I cried out when he raised a knife.

"Let this be a lesson to anyone who dares go against us." Norman put the blade to her throat.

"No!" Warner roared, not caring who he was pushing out of his way as he tried getting to his sister.

The noise of the crowd swallowed his cry as Norman slid the knife across Helena's throat. Blood gushed from the large wound, and my heart cracked when I watched her eyes widen and her tied hands go to her neck. Someone stepped in front of me, blocking the platform, and I swallowed a sob, darting around him.

Tears blurred my vision as Helena slumped to the floor of the platform when the two men released her. Warner had gone still, and I made it to his side and grabbed his arm.

"Warner," I choked out. "I'm sorry."

"I'm going to kill him—"

"She wasn't alone," Norman spoke up. "She has a brother who is always with her. And we got word that three people were involved. They need to be found."

Cold fear slithered through me and squeezed as eyes were already finding us. Warner wasn't hiding the fact that he was upset, and he looked just like Helena. A circle was already forming around us, and I tensed.

"Go, Kali," Warner gritted out, tears wetting his cheeks. "Get out while you can."

"I'm not leaving you here," I hissed under my breath, watching warily as more people surrounded us.

Fingers curled around my wrist, jerking me away from Warner. I moved to defend myself until I realized it was Tim.

"You need to get out of here," he bit out, trying to tug me away.

"Not without Warner—"

"Take her," Warner cut me off.

I glanced back at him, my heart crumbling. He and Helena were my only family. There were others in the Clovers, like Tim, but it wasn't the same. I had grown up with Warner and Helena. I'd lived with them and shared everything with them. I didn't want to survive by myself.

"We'll help get him out too," Tim promised, dragging me away.

"That's the brother," someone shouted on the other side of Warner. "Look at how upset he is."

"Don't touch me," Warner snapped when another guy tried grabbing him.

"Let me go," I begged, fighting against Tim. "I can't leave him."

"Kali, think logically," he breathed in my ear as he pulled me farther from Warner. "You need to leave the city to survive. You can be our outside ear. You can still be part of the Clovers."

"I don't care," I cried, my body trembling. "I don't want to leave."

"Go through the tunnel. Hide. I'll leave a note for you at our tree. Check for it in two weeks."

He kept talking about plans, and I tried comprehending it as I lost sight of Warner. There were still some stares on me, but most were now focused on Warner. I could hear him fighting, and I protested when a second pair of hands grabbed me. I turned my head to see Jill. She was another member of our group, and even if she didn't know what was going on, she was following Tim's lead to get me out of here.

"Who is she?" a woman screeched, glaring at me. "Another traitor?"

"No," Tim answered. "She can't stand the sight of blood. She fainted."

"Stop fighting or you'll get us all killed," Jill whispered desperately.

Her words shook me out of my growing hysteria. She was right. If I looked guilty, she and Tim would suffer right along with me now. For trying to save me.

"I think I might get sick," I mumbled loudly, not needing to pretend much. Pain was invading every cell in my body.

"We need to get her to a doctor," Jill said, her voice full of nerves.

When I began gagging and heaving, people parted to the side to let us pass. It didn't take long for us to make it to the edge of the city center, and two guards stepped in our way. Warner's yells cut through the muttering crowd, and it took everything in me not to go back to him. How could I leave while he was stuck here? I was a terrible fucking person.

"You're needed on the platform."

Another guard came out of the shadows, and Jill let out a sigh of relief. This particular guard was with us. His name was Collin, and he was saving our asses. The two men glanced at each other before nodding at Collin and walking away.

"Hurry," Collin urged, moving to the side. "What the hell happened?"

"We'll talk about it later," Tim replied tightly, pulling me onto the side street. "Thanks."

Collin nodded before turning his attention back to the city center. Tim and Jill stayed on either side of me, holding my arms to force me to run with them.

"We need to go back for him," I cried, glancing behind me. But we were far from the area now.

"We will," Tim said. "You need to go. Remember what I said. Two weeks and go to the tree. I'll bring you more supplies."

"Why?" I asked hoarsely. "Why are you saving me?"

"We take care of our own, Kali," he said gently as we stopped at the entrance of the tunnel.

"Stay safe," Jill whispered, giving me a tight hug.

I hugged her back, my body on autopilot. For the first time in my life, I was leaving Project Hope with a plan to never return. And I was going to be alone. I'd never been by myself. I'd always had Helena and Warner.

"Get in." Tim lifted the grate. "Hurry, before someone sees us."

I couldn't stop the tears as I jumped into the tunnel. I barely felt the pain when I landed hard on my feet. Looking up, I watched Tim place the grate over the hole before they ran off. Slowly, I wandered through the dark, not sure what to do after this. I'd had enough training to survive on my own. But right now, I wasn't sure I wanted to.

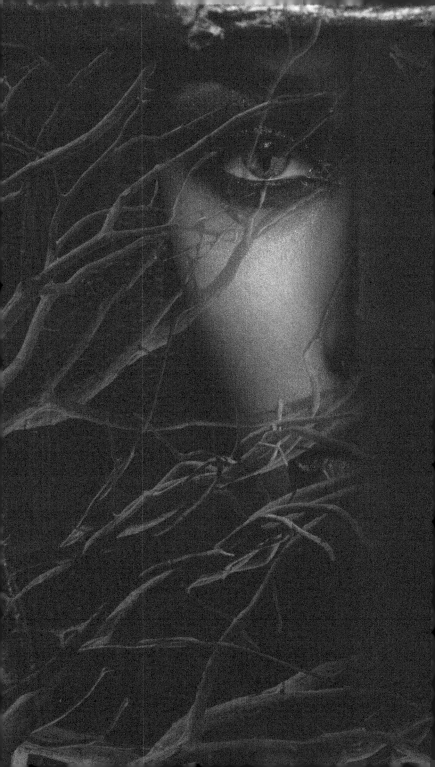

Chapter 6
Kali

The chirping of birds woke me from my troubled sleep, and I blinked a couple of times, my eyes adjusting to the late afternoon sunlight. The old boards creaked under me when I turned on my side, and I slowly stretched, my body stiff from the uncomfortable position. I'd been using the backpack as a pillow, and luckily, it was nearly summer, making it warm enough that I hadn't frozen without a blanket.

My mind was hazy, and I silently counted how many sunrises there had been since I'd left Project Hope. Three. I'd been gone three days, and I hadn't moved from this spot. Which was stupid of me.

My stomach panged with hunger, and I realized I really hadn't eaten much. I'd been numb, not feeling anything. Uncaring. Helena's last moments had been replaying over and over. I had no idea if Warner was alive or not. The thought of him possibly still being alive was the only thing I was clinging to so I didn't fully give up.

I hadn't even taken any precautions to ward off vampires since being here. It was fortunate one hadn't stumbled into my hiding spot. It wasn't much, and I knew I couldn't stay here much longer. PARA would be searching the woods for me, and it was only a matter of time before they came here. Yet I was not motivated to move on.

I was high up in a tree in an old hunting spot. Some of the wood was rotting, and there was no ceiling. Just four walls that were a couple of feet high. Warner and I had found it about a year ago when we were searching for food. Pain slashed my heart as memories of our adventures popped into my head.

When we left the city, we were always on edge, but at the same time, they were the only times I'd felt free. There were no high walls cutting off the outside world. No guards strolling the streets. No rules. The first time I ever went through the tunnel, I decided I would not live the rest of my life in Project Hope. I just never foresaw being forced out by myself.

"Shit," I breathed out, rolling out the kink in my neck. My body was protesting from not moving for so long.

But I still didn't get up. I lay there, peering at the clouds as they slowly moved across the sky. I wasn't sure how much time passed, but for the first time since everything had happened, feelings began stirring within me. And the longer I focused, the more it all spiraled into one thing.

Rage.

Norman was number one on my hit list, but he would be difficult to get to. He left the city regularly, but never without a convoy. Getting to him would take a lot of careful planning. But I'd kill him. I didn't care how important he was to the city or the government. I didn't give a fuck if I died doing it. As long as I buried him first.

Norman was the long game. Until I could plan that, I could sate my need for revenge with the creatures that had started this whole mess. The *vampires* were the reason we lived like this. Before they'd tried taking over, the world had been different. Not that I'd ever witnessed it. But the older people would tell stories, and I'd listen for hours.

I wasn't sure how many vampires were in this area, but since I had nothing else to do, I was going to find out. I'd killed more than a few in the three years I'd been exploring outside the city. A couple times by myself, but usually I had Warner or Helena with me. I had enough supplies to be okay on my own if it was only one vampire. They usually hunted alone anyway.

With renewed energy, I finally sat up and grabbed my bag. After unzipping it, I slowly took out each thing, one at a time. Warner had thought of everything. I had a couple of wooden stakes. A small handgun with an entire extra case of wooden bullets. There was a bag of dried-up hawthorn flowers, along with some berries. A knife small enough to keep in my boot.

After taking the hair tie off my wrist, I pulled my hair up, realizing how greasy it was from not washing it for three days. I'd have to go to the river soon. I stared at the weapons, recalling my training.

There were three ways to kill a vampire.

Wooden stake through the heart.

Cut off their head.

Tear out their heart.

I'd only ever used the stake for my kills. Even if I was larger than my five-foot-six frame, it was still the best way to go since vampires were stronger than humans. We had to get the element of surprise. The hawthorn plant helped with that. They were toxic to vampires. Not deadly, though.

Hawthorn plants also helped against the mind control vampires could use on humans to do their bidding. We called it entrancement, although there were a few other words to describe it. Whenever a vampire would look a human in the eyes, it only took seconds for a human to fall under the vampire's control.

Hawthorn made that impossible. I had to either have it on my body or ingest it for it to work. It had come in handy twice when fighting against a vampire. If I drank it, it would stay in my system for a few days, but I always had it on my body too.

While planning on what to do next, the conversation with that vampire bubbled to the surface. Pax was his name. I hadn't forgotten what he'd said about vampires saving the humans who bled black. Whether it was a lie or the truth, I had to admit, the question wouldn't stop plaguing me. If I ran into any vampires, I might be able to question them if I was able to gain the upper hand.

I pulled out the last two items. A large container of lotion and a small bottle of spray. My eyes widened in surprise that Warner had these on hand. They were only for the PARA officials who left the city. It allowed us to be near vampires without them smelling our blood. The lotion masked the scent, and the spray was an extra layer of protection.

PARA had spent years perfecting the recipe, and after many errors, they seemed to have gotten it right. It let humans walk outside the cities without having targets on their backs. By sight, it was impossible to tell the difference between a human and a vampire. They relied on the smell of our blood. The lotion stopped that, allowing humans to roam on foot if they could keep up the pretense of being another vampire.

I nearly jumped when thunder cracked through the air. I'd been so focused on my growing plans that I hadn't even noticed how dark the sky had gotten. I hurriedly shoved everything into the waterproof backpack, not wanting anything to get wet.

"Check over there."

I froze, my heart falling to my stomach. Creeping over the wooden boards, I peeked over the edge, seeing two soldiers striding through the trees. Both were wearing black clothes, and they had guns in their hands. They were moving fast, most likely trying to search before night fell.

Rain began falling as I slipped my bag over my shoulders before quickly climbing down the ladder that was luckily on the opposite side of the tree from where the men were scouting. My mind raced over options for what to do next, and Warner's words about the abandoned city repeated in my head. PARA might check there too, but there were a lot more places to hide in buildings than out here in a forest.

I snuck a glance around the tree, and when the men were focused in a different direction, I ran the other way, staying as low as I could. My racing heart slowed as I got farther, hearing no sign that they were following. I could have used my weapons on them, but I'd rather save those wooden bullets for the vampires.

The rain came down harder as I ran, and I didn't slow my pace. I didn't have to worry so much about vampires during the day, but there were rumors that they could come out when the sky was cloudy, so I kept a lookout for anything moving. Plus, sundown was coming at any time, and I had no idea when, since the sun wasn't out. The abandoned city was a good three miles from here, and I focused on my breathing, not wanting to stop unless I had to.

My lungs were begging for relief, my body covered in sweat despite the rain, when I finally got out of the trees. I halted, sucking in breaths as I peered at the city that was just on the other side of an old road. There were buildings spanning as far as I could see, and I felt calm for the first time in days. It wasn't perfect, but I could easily find a place to hide out for weeks here.

After adjusting my backpack, I walked toward the buildings, fully set on planning my revenge.

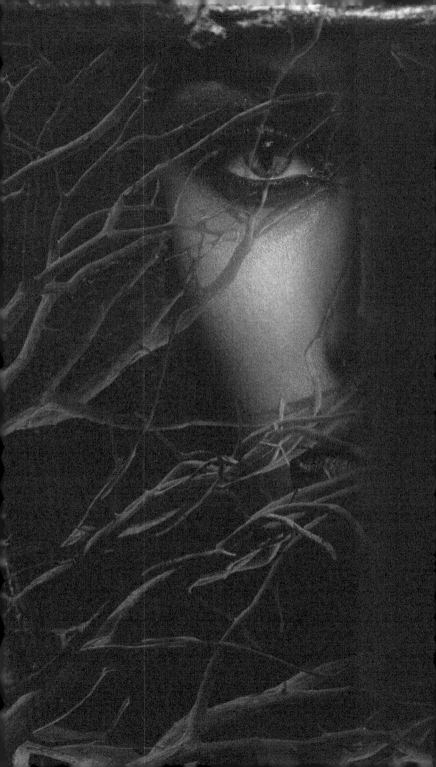

Chapter 7
Kali

I'd barely made it across the wide road before voices cut through the wind. The rain had slowed a little, and I wiped water from my face as I swung my gaze to the side, looking for a place to hide. Before I'd made it even two steps, a deep voice cut through the air. Fear washed through me. I didn't think the sun had set quite yet, but maybe vampires were out because the storm was blocking out the sun. I figured I'd have more time to find a hiding spot.

"What do we have here?" he asked, the excitement in his voice making a chill run down my spine.

I wasn't in the city yet, and there was nothing around me at all except for flat roads. I could possibly make a break for the buildings, but if it was a vampire behind me, I wouldn't be able to outrun him. Adrenaline coursed through my veins, and I closed my eyes for a second, remembering my training. This wasn't the first time I'd faced a vampire, and unlike when that one named Pax had cornered me, I had my weapons this time.

I spun around, my heart pattering when I realized there

wasn't one vampire, but two. They were both staring at me with hunger in their eyes, making it obvious they'd already smelled my blood.

"One of Impulse's girls?" the one with blond hair asked. His question was clearly for the other vampire, and I shuffled back a couple of steps when they glanced at each other. I had a stake in my boot but didn't want to pull that out until one of them got close enough for me to use it. The gun in my bag would be the most beneficial since there were two of them, but they'd get to me before I'd be able to dig through my bag for it.

"Maybe," the other vampire drawled, his leering gaze going back to me. "Let me see your neck, sweetheart."

Forcing a smirk on my lips, I tilted my head slightly. "No thanks. But you're more than welcome to try and look yourself."

A flash of surprise hit both their eyes for a moment before the blond one straightened his shoulders in challenge. The other vampire was the one who made me more nervous. He wasn't cocky like his friend, and he was watching me intently. But I kept my confidence, knowing if I played this right, I could kill both of them. There was still a healthy dose of fear flowing through me, but it only spurred me on more. Going up against vampires was always scary, but it was about survival. And I'd been training for moments like this for years.

The blond sauntered forward while his bald friend hung back, his scrutinizing stare staying on me. My mind raced with the best approach, but I didn't get a chance to say anything else before the blond vampire was inches from me.

"I just need to see something." He slowly reached for my neck, and I forced myself to stay still. It didn't seem like he wanted to attack right away, and I could use that to my advantage. When his cold fingers brushed my neck as he pushed my wet hair back, my stomach churned, seeing his change.

"Well?" the other vampire asked gruffly.

"No mark," the blond exclaimed, the dark excitement in his voice making me tense as he tightened his grip around the back of my neck. "Where'd you come from?"

"Let me go," I demanded coldly.

The blond barked out a laugh, glancing behind him. "You hear her? The little human thinks she can give me orders."

I suddenly let my body drop before he could get a firmer hold on me, and he yelled in surprise when I fell to the ground. I went for my stake first and stabbed him in the leg, giving myself the distraction I needed to get into my bag to reach the gun. The blond howled from the wood stuck in his calf, and I swept my legs under him, knocking him down. I was already scrambling to my feet, fumbling with my backpack.

I didn't make it a step before fingers wrapped around my ankle, taking me back to the wet grass. I let out a shriek when he tried climbing on top of me, but too bad for him, I already had the gun in my hand. I was jerked around roughly until I was on my back, and I didn't waste a second before clicking off the safety and shooting my first wooden bullet into my attacker. It was the blond vampire, and his eyes went wide with shock when I shot him in the stomach. This gun held twelve bullets, and I needed to use each one carefully.

"Bitch," he choked out, pain thick in his voice. His warm blood seeped through my clothes as I struggled to raise my arm high enough to shoot him in the head. My heart was racing, knowing I only had so much time before the other vampire intervened. My finger tightened on the trigger, and the echo of the shot vibrated through my skull when the bullet hit him in the forehead. It was enough to knock him out, but I'd dropped the stake to reach for the gun, meaning I had no way to kill him right away. But at least the bullet in his head would keep him knocked out for a while.

"What the fuck?" the other vampire bellowed. His footsteps were coming fast, and I scowled, unable to see him with the blond one's dead weight smothering me. Keeping the gun tight in my grip, I finally was able to roll him off me, and I raised my weapon, making the bald vampire skid to a halt a couple of feet from me.

"Wooden bullets," I informed him coldly. "I'll fucking drop you if you come any closer."

His eyes narrowed into slits as he glared at me. "You're going to regret that."

The rain was still coming down, and it was hard to see through the water and falling darkness, but he was close enough that my shot wouldn't miss. I pushed myself up, slowly climbing to my feet while holding the gun aimed at the vampire. His entire body was rigid, waiting for the moment to rush me.

"How many more of you are around here?" I asked him. Getting information was the only reason I hadn't shot him yet.

The vampire sneered at me. "Doesn't matter when I'm going to kill you."

A cruel smile tipped up my lips as I lowered the gun and shot him in the leg. He let out a string of curses, falling to the ground while grabbing his knee. He'd heal, but since the bullet was wooden, it would take longer. Not that it mattered because I wasn't letting him get to his feet again.

"Fucking bitch," he swore, glaring at me. "All we were going to do was feed. But now you're dead."

I breathed out a laugh. "Me? You're the one bleeding out."

"Want some?" he shot back, making my stomach churn. "How about I feed you some of my blood and see how long that fucking smile stays on your face."

Fear surged through me at his threat, and I tightened my hold on the gun. Vampire blood *killed* humans. One sip from their vein, and death would happen soon after. For years, there were rumors that vampire blood could heal. Until the harsh truth came out when our city, along with others, decided to test it.

They'd taken a prisoner to the platform and made him drink vampire blood. Within minutes of ingesting it, the man had died. And it wasn't a fast, painless death. I'd witnessed it years ago, but that man's death was still a horrible memory that was burned in my brain. The government wanted the civilians to see that vampire blood was not something to chase after.

"I'm guessing you know what my blood does to you," the vampire said, pulling me back to the present. "If you don't drop that gun, I'll make sure to drag your death out."

I raised an eyebrow. "You're not as scary as you think."

His eyes darkened at my taunting, and he quickly moved to get back on his feet. But I was ready. He let out a roar of pain when I shot him in the other knee, and he went down again. Out of the corner of my eye, I noticed his blond friend begin to stir and realized I needed to get to my stake quickly. I thought that bullet would have kept him knocked out longer.

I scanned the ground, searching for the stake I'd dropped when I went for my gun. My eyes locked with the vampire's when he realized what I was looking for. His bleeding leg was forgotten as he whipped his head around to find my weapon. He had the advantage since he could see much better in the dark than I could, and a wave of panic hit me. He was moving too much for me to shoot in the head, so I aimed and put two wooden bullets in his chest. He choked out labored breaths as he fell onto his back.

I ran to where the blond vampire was and fell to my knees running one hand over the wet grass while keeping the gun in the other. My heart hammered when I finally found the stake, but before I had a chance to stand, the blond vampire rolled over, grabbing my arm.

"Get off," I snarled, trying to wrench free.

"That fucking hurt," the blond vampire gritted out, anger lacing his voice. "But not as much as you'll be hurting when we're done with you."

I pressed the gun to his chest, but he swiped it away with his free hand while keeping a hold of me with the other. My fingers tightened around the stake, and I twisted my body until I had access to his chest. Without any hesitation, I slammed the stake into his body, right where his heart was. He made a noise of surprise as I shoved the stake deeper. His body sagged as his life left him, and I didn't have a moment to move before I was suddenly yanked backward by my hair.

I screamed as I was dragged back, my instincts the only reason I held on to the gun and stake. The other vampire threw me down, and I let myself relax, rolling over the grass to create space between us. The second I stopped, I lifted the gun, aiming it in his direction. He was already charging at me, and I shot at him, hitting him in the shoulder and the stomach. He slowed, a grunt of pain leaving him. My heart was racing out of control, and I shot again, aiming at his legs. He let out a bellow when I hit his knee again.

"Fuck," he hissed, nearly face-planting in the grass.

I blew out his other knee to make sure he stayed down before cautiously creeping closer so I could make sure my next shot wouldn't miss.

"You'll never leave these woods alive," he threatened, pain thick in his voice. "One fucking human little girl won't get far. You're nothing."

I pressed the barrel of the gun to his skull, making him freeze.

"I'm enough to kill two of you," I said in a deadly voice. "I guess that's what happens when you underestimate humans. Especially one *little girl*."

I didn't give him a chance to respond, shooting him in the head. He slumped to the ground, and I hurriedly crouched down and rolled him onto his back. I dropped the gun and wrapped both hands around the stake. Without another thought, I drove the stake into his chest. His body jerked before he went completely still. Blood seeped from the wound, and I stared at him.

My heart was still racing as I leaned closer to the vampire, wanting to make sure he was actually dead. The gun was tight in my grip, and I squinted, waiting for the clouds to break. After a couple of minutes, the moon shone through the clouds, and I searched for the telltale sign. My pulse calmed down while I watched his skin slowly turn gray. He wasn't getting back up.

I fell back, sucking in large breaths. Fuck, that had been close. I peered around me, not able to see much through the darkness. It wasn't raining anymore, and I wondered when it had stopped. The wind was still strong, and I slowly stood up and made my way to my discarded backpack. I went still, hearing the familiar sound of moving water.

After slipping the bag back over my shoulders, I followed the noise to find a ditch near the road that was full of fast-moving water. I glanced down, knowing I needed to wash the vampires' blood off. With a sigh, I tossed my bag back to the ground before stripping off Tim's hoodie and climbing into the ditch.

"Shit," I breathed out, my body adjusting to the cold water. The water must empty out somewhere because it was moving too fast for it not to have an outlet. I scrubbed my body with my hands, trying to get all the blood off. Once I was satisfied, I dipped my head under the water in case there was some in my hair.

Goosebumps covered my body as I climbed out of the ditch. I fell to the ground, my muscles exhausted from the fight. I glanced at Tim's hoodie before grabbing it and throwing it in the water. There was too much blood and too many tears on it to salvage. After squeezing the excess water out of my hair, I closed my eyes for a moment.

I leaned back on my palms, staring at the dark sky as I let my body dry. Before I went any farther, I had to use the lotion to cover my scent. If I ran into any more vampires, I had a better chance if they couldn't smell me. I could easily act as one of them as long as they didn't catch the scent of my blood.

I wasn't sure how long I lay there as my mind wandered over everything that had happened. My heart squeezed when I thought of Warner. I hoped he'd gotten out of the city. My gaze went toward the tall buildings, and I decided I'd stay there for a while to see if Warner found me.

I stood up after a while, giving my shorts some time to

dry, and once they were only damp, I grabbed my bag. Taking the lotion out, I carefully unscrewed the cap and set it on the ground. I slathered the lotion everywhere. My arms, legs, and under my clothes. I put an extra layer on my neck. I needed to use it sparingly, but at the same time, I had to be sure I put enough on to completely cover my scent. My hair was still damp and tangled, but I didn't have a brush, so there wasn't much I could do about that. I grabbed the spray and squeezed, letting the mist cover my head and hair, hoping it worked as well as the lotion.

Far away voices caught my attention, and I immediately dropped to the ground, panic taking hold. I only had so many wooden bullets before I ran out.

"What the fuck?" The voice came out of the darkness, and I narrowed my eyes, straining to see.

"They're both dead," another voice rang out. "PARA?"

"No," the other answered. "They wouldn't have left the bodies."

"We let them go out in the storm." He sounded nervous. "We weren't supposed to, and look what happened."

I was barely breathing. Thank fuck I'd already put the lotion on. I just needed to keep my heart calm and hope like hell they didn't hear it. Luckily, the rushing water in the ditch would help hide my heartbeat from them. I didn't move a muscle, only seeing their shadowy forms in the darkness.

"We can fix it before anyone finds out. We'll drop the bodies in the woods."

It sounded like there were only two of them, and I frowned in confusion as I listened. They almost sounded... scared. But what did they fear?

"This is on us. It's our watch. If they find out two were killed because we let them go out—"

"No one will know," the other snapped harshly. "Come on. Grab the other one. We'll be back before anyone realizes we're gone."

I watched as they picked up the bodies of the vampires I'd killed and kept arguing, but soon their voices faded out as they crossed the road, heading toward the woods. I quickly grabbed my bag and bolted in the opposite direction, toward the city. I planned to be far from here when they came back. Their words had confusion rocking me, but I didn't have time to think about it now.

I followed a street that led into the city, and once I was between the tall buildings, I slowed down and studied my surroundings. There was an eerie silence that had my neck prickling, and I kept walking until I was a few blocks away from where I'd entered the city. I put my stake back in my boot before opening the door to the closest building. The area was small, with broken furniture scattered around.

I spotted an empty duffel bag on the floor, and I moved toward it. There was a chance I could find supplies here. With a deep breath, I slipped my own backpack off and unzipped it. A lump grew in my throat when I pulled out the hoodie. It was Warner's. I slipped it on before grabbing the spray bottle and covering my clothes again. The hoodie was nearly as long as Tim's, the hem going down to my mid-thighs and covering my shorts. Probably a good thing, because I wasn't sure the blood had washed out of the denim.

I closed up my backpack and hid it under one of the broken desks. It would be safe here while I scrounged around. I hefted the empty duffel bag over my shoulder, scanning the rest of the room.

There was nothing useful in here, but there were a bunch of other buildings I could search. I'd have to be fast since I didn't want to stay in this city too long. Not when I knew there were at least two other vampires hanging around. I'd just check out the street before coming back for my bag.

With a deep breath, I stepped back outside before heading toward the next building.

Chapter 8
Kali

Coming to this city was a horrible fucking idea.

But by the time I realized it, I'd gotten turned around and it was taking forever to find the building where my bag was. The deeper I went into the city, the more alive it became. The place was filled with vampires. Trying to avoid them was the reason I'd gotten lost. I'd already abandoned the empty duffel bag, not wanting anything in my way if I needed to go for my stake. The vampires were *everywhere*. Running in the streets. Going in and out of buildings. Some places seemed livable. I even saw someone making food and serving it like an outside restaurant.

It went against everything I'd learned as a child. We were told that vampires were solitary creatures, and if they did travel together, it was only in small groups. That was the reason the war had ended. Because vampires couldn't form an army without fighting among each other, but there were still too many to overtake them.

My eyes darted to two vampires making out against the side of the building. I kept my pace casual, passing them while holding my breath. The lotion seemed to be working, and I hoped it stayed that way. I wished I hadn't left my backpack in the first building I'd stopped at. But I never expected to walk into something like this. I had the wooden stake in my boot, and it was against all my instincts not to have it in my hand.

Fear was running rampant, causing the hair on the back of my neck to stand up. My gut was knotted to the point that I thought I was going to get sick. I was surrounded by vampires who would kill me in a second if they knew I was human. I just needed to get back to my bag, and I'd be long gone. Taking my chances in the forest would be better than this.

I was backtracking, and if I remembered correctly, the building was only a block away. I upped my pace, a shiver running through me when I heard footsteps behind me. I listened carefully as I kept walking, only to come to a halt when someone stepped in front of me. Keeping my eyes on the ground, I shuffled to the right, my heart dipping when they moved with me. My hands curled into fists, and I took a long breath as I tried again to go around.

"I've never seen you here before."

The voice was deep. Panic smothered me when I finally raised my gaze. The vampire was only a couple of feet in front of me, standing right under a dying streetlight that was blinking. My breath caught in my chest when we locked eyes. He was breathtakingly fucking gorgeous.

How was it possible for a creature who lurked in the night to look like *that*? His black hair was longer, the messy waves nearly covering his left eye as he studied me. His eyes were lighter, maybe green or blue, but it was impossible to tell in the dim lighting. His facial features were sharp and rigid, but they fit him perfectly. He was wearing a black T-shirt and jeans, with a pair of black boots. He was leaner, but as he crossed his arms, it was impossible to miss his flexing muscles. I took an involuntary step back, and he cocked his head to the side, curiosity flaring in his eyes.

"You went out in the storm?" he asked, glancing at my slightly damp hair. "Risky. The sun could have come out."

I didn't say a thing, unsure what to do or say. One wrong word, and I'd be dead. The stake pressed against my ankle, and when suspicion flashed across his face from my silence, I nearly grabbed it. Unlike the two vampires I'd killed hours ago, this one screamed violence. I had a feeling I wouldn't get as lucky if I went up against him.

"You hear that, Viggo?" he asked, looking past me. "She's scared. Her heart is racing. The question is why."

My face paled when footsteps came up from behind me. Vampires had heartbeats just like humans, but I didn't know if they went through emotions like we did. Could they feel the same type of fear that had me paralyzed? I didn't dare take my eyes off the vampire in front of me even as another one came up beside me. He paused for a moment before striding forward until they were both in front of me. Shock tore through me when I stared at the second vampire. He was the one who had cornered me in the woods the night Lisa was killed.

His stare didn't reveal a speck of recognition as he looked at me, and questions raced through my head. The other one called him Viggo. I could have sworn they'd called him Pax that night. My fear rose as I stared between the two of them. I doubted my one little stake was enough now. I needed to talk my way out of it.

"She's cold, Zan," the vampire called Viggo murmured, his eyes going to my arms. I was regretting pushing up the sleeves of the hoodie I was wearing. "Look at her goosebumps."

"She's still susceptible to the weather. She's new," Zan replied. He stepped closer, and it took all my will to stay where I was. "When were you turned?"

A lump grew in my throat as I fumbled over an answer. Why did they think I was a new vampire? Right now, I decided to play into what they already believed.

"Around two weeks, I think," I said quietly, trying to keep my voice steady.

That was clearly the wrong answer because the vampire named Zan scowled as he stepped into my personal space. This time I couldn't stop myself and stumbled back until my spine hit the crumbling brick wall of a building.

"Two weeks?" he bit out. "Why the hell aren't you at the center?"

The *what*? Fuck. There was so much I still didn't know about them. I thought with all my training that I was prepared to survive outside Project Hope. Maybe I was wrong.

"I—I didn't want to be there. So I left."

His cold laugh had terror jolting through me, and my heart pounded against my ribs. His eyes dropped to my chest, as if noticing the change. I knew vampires had good hearing, but now I wondered how good. I'd learned breathing techniques to calm myself, but that wouldn't help now when he already knew I was panicked.

"You left?" he sneered, raising his arm and resting his palm on the bricks next to my head. "You can't just leave there. No one is allowed out until they hit the year mark."

"I was never there, okay?" I nearly screamed. "A vampire turned me, and I woke up in the woods by myself. I have no idea what you're talking about."

My lie would either bury me or save me. I bit my tongue before quickly stopping myself. He was so close that he'd be able to smell the blood if I accidentally bit down too hard. The lotion seemed to be working, and I couldn't mess this up.

"You don't know who turned you?" he asked, his voice dangerously soft.

I shook my head. "No."

"Irresponsible fucker," Viggo cursed from behind Zan. "Word is supposed to be everywhere by now. If this is happening, we have a problem."

Zan turned to face him, and I barely listened to them, sagging against the bricks, relieved that they believed me. They exchanged a few more words, and I subtly crept along the wall, ready to get the hell out of there. Until a hand caught my arm, tugging me back.

"Where do you think you're going?" Zan asked, his hold going tight as he kept me against the wall.

"I'm leaving," I said firmly. My confidence was much higher now that they believed I was one of them.

"Can't let you do that." Zan's gaze swept over me. "You're too new. You know nothing. That's why you should be at the center."

"I'll have someone take her there—" Viggo began to say until Zan cut him off with a shake of his head.

"Not yet." Zan raised his hand, brushing hair out of my eyes. "Consider me curious. We never see them this young."

"Don't touch me," I snarled, shoving his hand away. Fear had invaded every part of me, but I didn't want to show them that. I wasn't sure how new vampires were supposed to act, but I didn't want any of them getting this close to me.

Zan chuckled. "You should watch your attitude until

93

you can back up your words."

"I can back them up just fine," I retorted.

"Really?"

His hand was suddenly around my throat, and he squeezed tight enough to cut off my air. I grabbed his wrists, my nails digging into his flesh, pure terror swallowing me whole. Reaching my stake was impossible as my lungs burned from lack of air, and I writhed and struggled uselessly until stars danced in my vision. A moment later, he loosened his hold just enough that I could suck in a shallow breath.

He leaned closer until his lips were an inch from mine. "You know nothing of your new race. The humans don't teach the truth. That's why you're supposed to learn at the center."

"Learn what?" I choked out.

"Your changes come slowly. It takes an entire year for you to grow into your true self. You've been a vampire for two weeks?" He pried one of my hands off his wrist and slammed it against the wall. "You're practically still human. You can survive without blood for at least another month."

"I don't understand." My head was spinning. New vampires were weak? Why didn't we know about this?

"The cravings. The strength. It's not instant, even though the humans think it is." Zan's words had my mouth parting in shock. "We let them think that's how it is."

I wanted to run back to the forest and leave a note at the tree for Tim right now. This little piece of information could help us in so many ways. The new vampires were the weakest, which was why they kept it such a secret. If we could stop their population from growing, we could get the upper hand.

I stayed silent before asking a question. He believed I

was clueless, which I clearly was. I needed to learn everything I could. "So new vampires aren't crazed for blood like everyone thinks?"

"Oh, that does happen," Viggo spoke up. "But not until around the six-month mark."

"I'm sure you've noticed the small changes," Zan murmured. "Your taste buds changing. Your hearing becoming a bit sharper."

"Yeah," I muttered, my lies coming easier now that I had a handle on the conversation.

"Your feelings have changed toward humans," he continued, watching me closely. "You don't have the same commitment to them."

"I only want to survive," I bit out.

My answer came from what I'd learned, and I hoped it was the right thing to say. Tim had always taught me that once someone is turned, they lose empathy. They don't care about the war anymore. They only want to look out for themselves.

"Come on." He pulled me off the wall, keeping his hold on my wrist.

I planted my feet. There was no way in hell I was going anywhere with them. I needed to get out of here as soon as I could.

"No. Let me go," I demanded fiercely, pulling away from him.

He fell still, his grasp going even tighter while he peered at me as if my reply was something he'd never heard. "No?"

"I don't know you. I don't know where you're taking me. Get off," I growled. "I can find the center on my own since that's clearly where I belong."

His eyes lit up in challenge, and I swallowed thickly.

"You're not going to the center," he informed me,

amusement in his voice. "We have vampires here who can teach you what you need. You'll stay here for now."

"The fuck I will." Panic engulfed me as I fought against him.

"Maybe she should go to the center," Viggo said, sounding bored. "She's no use to us this young."

"No. She stays here."

"You can't do this," I screamed, not caring if I was drawing attention. I was a second away from pulling my stake out and taking my chances against both of them. I had no idea what he wanted with me, but I really didn't want to find out.

My struggles had him scowling, and he grabbed my other wrist, bringing them both behind my back and pressing them against the bottom of my spine. His chest was crushed against mine as he held me in place, and I had to crane my neck to look up at him.

"Who knew vampires could be assholes too?" I spat out. "You're as bad as any man who takes what he wants."

He lowered his head, brushing his lips over my cheek. A shiver rolled through me, and I attempted to tear my face from him, but he was holding me too tightly.

"I'm much fucking worse than any man," he whispered harshly. "And if you don't stop fighting me, then the chains I'll put you in will be much shorter than the leash I'm graciously giving you right now."

I stared up at him, my body trembling from his words. I was scared. There was no denying that. But I was also pissed. Vampires had taken enough from me. If he thought he could keep me here, he'd soon find out how wrong he was.

The second I had a chance, I was driving my stake through his heart.

Chapter 9
Zan

Viggo was staring over the girl's head at me as if I'd lost my mind. *Maybe I had.* I didn't know what fucking had possessed me to bring her back with us. We should have handed her over so she could go to the center like she was supposed to. My father had a strict order about all newbies. They needed the training. It was the first step in trying to teach vampires to follow. It was the only way to keep going with the plan.

We walked toward Impulse with the girl between Viggo and me. I wasn't touching her but stayed close in case she decided to bolt. Not that she could outrun us. But it would be easy to lose sight of her if she managed to slip into one of the buildings. I studied her out of the corner of my eye as she glared straight ahead.

It looked like she'd been through hell. After inspecting her closer, I could see scabbed over cuts marring her skin. There was a bruise on her cheek. A few more months, and those kinds of injuries would heal in minutes. But she was fragile with how new she was. I was curious about where she'd been for the last two weeks.

Her dark hair was tangled and knotted, and her oversized hoodie was a couple sizes too large. It nearly went to her knees, covering most of her body. But none of that hid the fact that she was fucking beautiful.

She hadn't said a word after I threatened her, and I wondered if she was really backing down that easily. I highly doubted it. The fire in her eyes was still bright and dangerous. She was furious, even in her silence. And for some reason, it made excitement burn through me.

I was Zan fucking Kane. Son of Amaros, leader of the vampires. I got what I wanted when I demanded it. Vampires fell to their knees to do whatever they could to please me. I owned this city and had power over every vampire except my father.

No one ever denied me anything. They never told me no.

But she had.

She spat that one little word at me like being in my presence was the last thing she ever wanted. She didn't know who I was, and I was sure it wouldn't take long for her to find out if she was staying near me. Would she bow down like all the others when she did? Her disobedience and fiery attitude would get her into trouble here if she didn't rein it in. Although I wasn't sure I wanted her to.

I'd met other vampires who challenged my authority.

None of them caused the reaction she did.

It had anger bubbling in my veins, but in the same breath, her fight had my dick getting hard. My reaction to her had my head fucking spinning. The number of women who would fall into my bed was endless. I never had to go looking or even say a word. They all wanted a chance to be with a Kane brother. Viggo loved it, while Pax tended to be more selective with the women he slept with.

"Where are you taking me?" the girl clipped out, still refusing to look at either of us.

"Impulse," I answered, putting my hand on her lower back and leading her around the corner. She went rigid at my touch, and I half expected her to pull away.

Her eyes cut to me for a brief moment. "What's that?"

"The best spot in this city," I told her.

"Doubtful," she muttered.

"I'm sure it's more fun than what you've been up to since you turned," Viggo replied, giving her a once-over.

Her glare shot to him as her jaw clenched. She didn't respond, and I reached past her and opened the door, giving her a little push when she didn't move. Impulse was busy tonight, and the crowd was thick as I guided her to our usual corner. She jerked when a fight broke out near the pool tables. Her head was on a swivel, and I could tell she was growing more uneasy when stares fell on her.

Pax was sitting in his chair with a drink in his hand and a girl on his lap. He seemed less than impressed with her and whispered something in her ear that had her slipping off his lap with a frown on her face. We got closer, and when Viggo fell into the chair next to his twin, Pax glanced over at me as he took a sip of his drink.

His eyes wandered toward the girl, and suddenly, he was spitting out the whiskey, choking and coughing. Viggo leaned over, slapping him on the back while laughing.

"What's wrong, little brother?" Viggo asked in amusement. "Got a thing for newbies?"

I snagged a chair, dragging it closer and putting it next to mine. I motioned for her to sit, and she stiffly lowered herself in the chair, her demeanor tense as she looked between Pax and Viggo with questions in her gaze. They were identical in every way, and I was sure her seeing double was throwing her through a loop. Only my dad and I could tell them apart.

"Newbie?" Pax asked hoarsely, wiping the alcohol off his chin. "When did she turn?"

"Two weeks ago."

My answer had him looking back at the girl, and his intense stare had me bristling. He was never fucking interested in any woman I was with. But something about her was making him sit up straighter and take notice.

"Two weeks?" Pax repeated. "Why is she here?"

"Because I said so," I snapped. "Is that a fucking problem?"

Both Viggo and Pax looked at me in shock while the girl shifted uncomfortably in the chair. I caught Gia's eye and nodded my head for her to come over here. She quickly poured my favorite drink behind the bar before sauntering over to us.

"Hey, Zan," she greeted me cheerfully, handing me the drink.

"Gia, I found you a new helper. This is—" I turned toward the girl. "What's your name?"

She didn't answer, glaring daggers at me. With the noise in this place, I couldn't hear her heart like I could when I first saw her on the street, but I was positive she was still scared. Although, there wasn't a hint of fear on her face now. After downing my drink, I turned toward her and caught her jaw in my grasp. Her eyes widened, and I tightened my hold when she tried pulling away from me.

"Tell me your name," I ordered in a threatening voice. "Or I'll give you one of my own."

After a few seconds, she finally gritted out, "Kali."

I leaned back, focusing back on Gia. "This is Kali. She

can help you out around here for now. I know you're always looking for help."

"Zan," Pax piped up, sounding worried. "What are you doing? We don't need someone like her around here. She knows nothing."

"She'll learn," I shot back. "And she won't leave the city without one of us. I'll make sure she can't wander away."

Viggo groaned, already knowing where I was going with this. He jumped up and headed toward the stairs that led to our living quarters. Pax's attention was still on the girl, but he looked at me once his brother was out of sight.

"What are you doing?" he murmured. "We can't trust her."

His words held truth. New vampires were wild cards. They had no loyalty to anyone except themselves, especially in the first year. Which was why they were trained from the moment they turned. We were sure PARA had theories about how weak new vampires were, but we tried to keep it a secret. Mature vampires knew to turn humans only when they were alone and to bring them to the center. Clearly, whoever had turned Kali failed to follow those orders.

We'd been doing it this way for decades, which was how we'd built up our numbers. We made sure that vampires didn't just roam around, trying to turn every human they could. For one, that would cut our food source. We needed human blood to survive.

"She can't work here looking like that," Gia said, studying Kali. "But once she's cleaned up, she'll fit in perfectly."

"No, I won't," Kali snapped. "I don't have any other clothes."

Gia raised an eyebrow at her tone before her gaze slid to

me. No one talked to us like that, and Gia was waiting for me to correct Kali's behavior. But I was biding my time. I was curious to see how far she'd go before she learned who I was.

As for Pax's question about what I was doing with her—I had no fucking idea. All I knew was she elicited emotions in me that I hadn't felt in seven years. And in the short time she'd been in my presence, it was becoming addictive.

I wanted to keep her near me, and until I grew bored, that's what I was going to do.

Chapter 10
Kali

The redheaded vampire was still shooting me curious glances as she and Zan spoke in whispers low enough that I couldn't hear. I was on edge, my foot bouncing as I scanned the room again. Zan had called this place Impulse, and it was so different from anything I'd ever experienced. We had music in our city, but people played it in private. Only on holidays was music played throughout the city's loudspeaker to celebrate.

The atmosphere here was electric, full of fun and chaos. The vampires were all laughing and having a good time. It was a stark contrast to the somber mood of Project Hope. Although the cages around the room were a cruel reminder that humans didn't belong here. There were men and women locked inside the cages, and terror twisted my gut. I'd be in one of them if they realized I was human.

I found myself looking at Pax again. He was still staring at me, his eyes dark with suspicion and anger as he slowly sipped his drink. I wasn't sure why he hadn't blurted out the truth. He knew I wasn't one of them, but he hadn't outed me yet. Maybe he was waiting for the right moment.

Viggo was still gone, and I hoped it stayed that way. I couldn't tell them apart at all. And while I was sure they were both deadly, Pax didn't seem as bad as his twin. Danger lurked in Viggo's eyes, where Pax seemed less intense. Although right now, he looked anything but happy that I was here.

With every second that passed, I became more panicked about being stuck here. I didn't have my bag, and even though the lotion was supposed to last twelve hours, I was worried about it fading. With so many vampires surrounding me, I was fucked if they caught the scent of my blood. I'd never felt so vulnerable in my life.

But I was also confused.

I thought I knew everything about vampires, but it was obvious I knew absolutely nothing. How many more secrets did they have? I wondered if I could learn from them and bring it all back to Tim. I lifted my gaze to see Zan watching me, and my heart stuttered. No way could I stay here. It was too risky. I'd already learned new things that could be helpful. The second I had the chance, I was leaving. But I really hoped I had a chance to use my stake on Zan before I ran.

He was an arrogant asshole, and his smug grin had me seeing red. He was used to his orders being followed; that much was clear. Others here respected him. No one came to this little corner where we were sitting. Glances were coming our way, but no one except the vampire named Gia spoke to us.

"Here."

I startled when Viggo stepped up beside Zan and dropped something in his hand. Before I could get a look at it, Zan slipped it into his pocket and focused back on me. Viggo retook his seat while waving someone over.

"You're going to work here," Zan announced as Gia

strode away. "Every night. After the sun goes down, you come straight here."

I bit back my refusal, crossing my arms and staying silent instead. From the way it sounded, he was going to let me leave. If that was the case, I wasn't going out of my way to piss him off.

"Hi, Viggo," a girl purred, coming up and jumping into Viggo's lap. "I missed you."

"Mm, my favorite girl." Viggo wrapped an arm around her while grabbing her wrist with his free hand. "I'm starving tonight, Dee."

I watched with rapt attention when the girl he called Dee giggled before kissing him on the neck. Viggo brought her wrist to his lips, and a weight fell on my chest when his fangs came out. He bit into her wrist, and she didn't even flinch. I sat there in disbelief as he fed on her, not believing what I was seeing. She was human. And was willingly letting him feed. She had to be entranced.

"You look surprised," Zan murmured.

I tore my eyes from Viggo to see Zan leaning close to me. I jerked back, my spine hitting the back of the chair.

"You have humans here," I muttered, curious to see what else I could learn before I made my escape.

Zan cocked his head. "How do you think we eat?"

I stayed silent, my eyes going back to Viggo. There was a place in all human cities where we could go to donate blood to give to the vampires. And there were also people who refused to live in the safe havens, deciding to risk living near the vampires. But I'd never expected to see this.

"She's not entranced," Zan said, as if reading my mind. My chest tightened for a moment. Could vampires read minds? We'd learned they could only use mind control, but after tonight, I wasn't sure what else there was that I didn't know. "She's here because she wants to be."

Before I could stop myself, I looked at Pax. He'd told me the same that night in the woods, and I hadn't believed him. Pax didn't say a word. His jaw clenched as he stayed sitting at the edge of his chair.

"And the people in the cages?" It took everything to keep my voice neutral. A new vampire wouldn't care about the lives of humans. I needed to keep playing the part.

Viggo chuckled, pulling his mouth away from the girl's wrist. Blood dripped from his lips as he took a cloth from his pocket and put it over Dee's bleeding arm.

"Some humans stay here because they want to. Like Dee," Viggo explained. "Others are here to be punished. They either stay in the cages or are entranced."

"I love it here," Dee sang out, giving me a wide smile. "I give a little blood and get taken care of."

"Taken care of," I repeated, still in shock.

"Show her, Dee," Zan commanded. He didn't even finish talking before Dee lifted her dark blond hair, revealing the side of her neck. There was a large *K* tattooed in black ink. "That shows others that she's not to be hurt. She's under our protection."

"Did you come from a city?" Dee asked me, her eyes hardening. "Isn't this way of life so much better? The freedom? The fun? Who wouldn't want this?"

Ice chilled my veins as I forced myself not to react. Was this on purpose? Were the vampires turning humans against their own race? How many other humans were here?

"I found clothes for you. I'll have them ready for you tomorrow." Gia stepped in front of me. "You have a place to shower?"

"Yes," I lied. None of it mattered. I was leaving this city

as soon as I could. I'd never see them again. Gia nodded and walked away, going back behind the bar.

"She should stay with us," Pax mumbled.

"No need," Zan replied, his voice confident. "She'll be here tomorrow exactly as I told her. Won't you, Kali?"

I nearly grinned but managed to keep my cold stare on him. I could taste my freedom. "Yes. I'll be here tomorrow night."

He slipped his hand into his pocket, pulling out a necklace with a thick chain. "I want you to put this on. It'll show others that you work here, and they won't bother you."

I should have been snatching the necklace out of his hand to keep him happy, but his smug fucking tone had rage engulfing me. I would almost rather let them kill me than take orders from a vampire. The one thing stopping me was the small hope that Warner was still alive. I only hesitated for a few seconds, but it was enough for Zan's patience to snap. I cried out when he grabbed me, hauling me onto his lap.

"Don't fucking touch me," I snarled, trying to get back to my feet. His arm snaked around my waist, crushing my back to his chest while keeping my arms trapped at my sides.

"I asked you to put it on," he said, his lips brushing against my hair. "I don't ask things twice. You should learn that sooner rather than later."

"If we're being technical, you didn't ask—you demanded," I snapped, my chest heaving from being so close to him. I should feel disgusted that a vampire was all over me. But I didn't. The hate was deep in my bones, but his touch wasn't doing what I expected it to. And I really didn't like it.

"That *is* me asking nicely," he shot back. "You have a lot to learn if you're going to stay here."

Viggo lifted Dee off him and got to his feet. He grabbed the necklace from Zan, ignoring my protests as he pushed my hair to the side and wrapped the chain around my throat. It wasn't tight, but rage still shot through me as he took forever getting the clasp clipped. He finally got it and stepped back. Zan released me, and I flew to my feet, my fingers going to the small charm on the necklace.

The chain was just long enough for me to glance down at it, and I stared at the round shaped charm in suspicion. It looked old and had an intricate design on the outer part of it with an oval in the center. It was heavy enough that it seemed like something was in the hollow center.

"This is a temporary mark," Zan said, making me shift my attention to him. "Unless you'd rather have a tattoo like Dee's."

"No," I bit out.

"Good. Then I'll see you tomorrow night."

His words had me freezing. It couldn't be this easy. Viggo was watching, his lips lifting in an amused grin.

"Good luck trying to get it off," Viggo said, as if he couldn't hold it back. "There's a lock on the clasp."

I brought my hand to the back of my neck, my stomach sinking when I felt around and realized there was a tiny padlock-type thing on the chain. How the hell would I be able to get this off without help? I didn't care. I could leave and hide it under my clothes. Either way, I'd be gone before the sun came up.

"I think she's going to run, Zan," Viggo taunted, talking as if I wasn't there.

"No, she won't," Zan responded, his eyes staying on me. "She'll behave."

"Can I go now?" I ground out.

Zan stepped to the side, but when I walked past him, he grabbed me above the elbow, tugging me close.

"That necklace claims you as mine," he breathed out. "I'm protecting you from everyone else in this city. Do not make me regret it."

"I didn't ask for this," I hissed, my face flushing in anger.

"Doesn't matter."

He released me, and I rushed away, not daring to look back. If they were following me, they'd make their presence known anyway. I stealthily weaved through the crowd, not touching any vampires. Relief filled me when I burst through the doors, the night air hitting my face. My ears rang from the sudden silence after being in such a loud atmosphere. I stumbled down the street, my mind racing from what had happened. I stopped in my tracks, turning in a full circle, trying to get my bearings. I didn't know this city at all.

I turned down a side street, searching for anything I recognized as I tried to find the building I'd left my bag in. Until I was suddenly grabbed from behind, a hand covering my mouth. I was lifted off the ground, and I fought uselessly as I was carried into the closest building.

The hand left my mouth, and my back slammed into a wall. My eyes fell on the vampire who'd grabbed me, and I sucked in a breath. It was Pax. Or Viggo. Either way, he was pissed.

"What the hell are you doing here?" he asked sharply. "Pretending to be one of us?"

It had to be Pax. My racing heart calmed slightly at that.

"I saw you days ago, and you were human," he accused. "You masked your scent. I don't smell your blood like I did that night."

"Let me leave—"

He grabbed my wrists when I tried pushing him away. "Answer my fucking question. Why are you here?"

"Because I can't go home," I snarled. "You saw me running that night. They want me dead. I'm hiding."

"From the humans?"

"Yes."

"Why?"

"Because I saw them kill my friend." My voice cracked when I thought of Lisa. "They don't want witnesses."

"You can't stay here."

"Why didn't you tell them about me?" I asked, curiosity getting the best of me.

"I don't know," he gritted out. "I felt bad for you. And if I told them, they'd kill you."

"I just want to leave," I told him quietly. "I have no intention of hurting you or your friends."

"Not sure I believe that either."

"Then why did you keep my secret?" I snapped.

"Fuck," he muttered. "This is going to end badly."

"Just let me walk away," I pleaded. "I'll leave and never come back—"

He laughed humorlessly, grabbing the necklace they'd locked on me. "This makes that impossible."

I scoffed. "Please."

He backed away, not giving me any other answers. "You're not a threat right now. But if you become one, I'll kill you myself."

With that, he spun around and left the building. I stared at him for a moment before moving to leave. I needed to get my bag and get the hell out of this city.

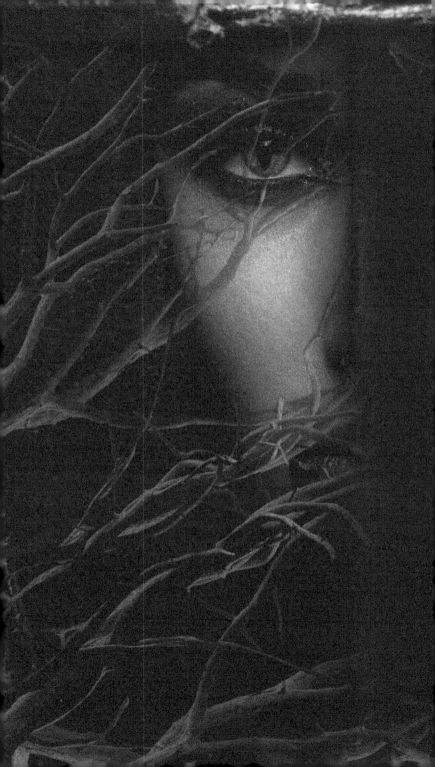

Chapter 11
Zan

"I can't believe you finally used the necklace that Dad gave you," Viggo mused before downing his drink. "And on a newbie?"

I didn't answer, leaning back in the chair as I thought about Kali. The way she'd run out of Impulse had me believing that she'd try to leave the city as soon as she could. Pax left after her to follow so we could find out where she was staying. It would be interesting to see if she succeeded. Not that it mattered. She wouldn't get far with that necklace on. I'd be able to track her anywhere she went.

"Call it a test," I muttered. "If she gets out, then it means the watchers aren't doing their job."

"And if they fail, that means we're going to be chasing her ass all over the damn woods," he complained. "You should have just sent her to the center."

"No."

"Never thought I'd see the day where Zan Kane had a crush."

"Fuck off," I snarled. "I don't have a crush."

"But you want to fuck her," Viggo taunted, his eyes

lighting in amusement at getting under my skin. "I don't blame you. She's fucking hot."

"She's *mine*," I snapped before I could think about it.

His eyes widened in surprise before he chuckled. "You have it bad."

"I don't," I retorted through clenched teeth. "She's a way to keep me busy while we sit here and wait for Dad's orders."

"Whatever you say."

Pax interrupted our conversation when he stalked past me and dropped into his chair. Viggo raised an eyebrow at his twin as I stared at him, waiting to hear why he was back so soon.

"I lost her," Pax admitted with a scowl. "She slipped into one of the buildings."

Viggo let out a loud laugh. "She's going to be trouble."

He wasn't wrong. The thing was—I wanted her kind of trouble.

Pax focused on me. "You don't need distractions. Dad is counting on us. You should just let her be."

"We can't do much until next month anyway," I said, trying to keep the annoyance to myself. The twins were older than me. We made all decisions together, and they never left me out because I was the youngest, but sometimes they acted like they knew better.

"Want to make a bet on if she shows up tomorrow night?" Viggo asked, crossing his arms. "I bet she doesn't."

It all depended on whether she got out of the city tonight. With how new she was, she could still handle the sun too. But leaving here was much more difficult than it looked from the outside. In the time we'd been here, we'd built this place up into a fortress.

From the outside, it still looked like a crumbling city.

That wasn't the case. There were only a few ways to enter or exit, and two of those were secret tunnels. We left two roads unblocked but always had vampires watching. The rest of the roads were covered with debris and crushed cars. The buildings that were on the outskirts of the city were boarded up, and the first levels of them were stacked floor to ceiling with anything we could use to make them impassable.

Which made me wonder how the hell she'd gotten into the city. Vampires could leave as they pleased, but most didn't venture out. Not with Project Hope only ten miles away. There were always soldiers in the forest, and they killed vampires on sight. Plus, we had the watchers do a head count for everyone that left and came back to make sure we didn't lose anyone. Everyone who had left in the last three weeks had come back before the sun rose. There was no odd number. Which meant no one counted her when she came in.

Either she'd found a crack somewhere or my workers weren't doing their jobs on the perimeters of the city. And both of those were a problem that would need to be fixed. We couldn't let our guard down so close to a human city.

I would have asked her how she got here, but I doubted she would tell me. Her eyes had screamed hate ever since I approached her in the street. I'd ask her at some point when she'd calmed down from being forced to stay here. I could be patient when I needed to be. Although I wasn't sure it would last long in her presence. I had a feeling she was going to try and push me to my limits.

"One of our scouts told me that there were more men in the woods than usual," Viggo said, growing serious as he brought up business. "Looks like they're searching for something."

"Or someone," I added. "They were doing that the night we saw them at the river."

"Maybe one of them got away before they could kill them," Pax murmured, looking troubled as he stared past us.

"We should be looking too, if that's the case." Viggo snatched Pax's drink. "I'll give the order to have more eyes in the forest this week."

I nodded in agreement, subtly studying Pax. He seemed more upset than usual. Though he was like this every month when the humans killed at the river. I couldn't blame him. When we were still human, he had fallen in love with a girl who was with a group that lived free. They'd set up their own camp not far from our dad's property, and Pax used to sneak out all the time to see her.

Until PARA found them. And Pax's girl had just turned twenty-five. They'd cut her, and she bled black. They killed her right there. I didn't know if Pax would ever get over it. Ever since, his sympathy for civilian humans had grown and his absolute hate for PARA had increased to a point that he couldn't think logically without emotions getting in the way.

We wanted to save the Shadows, but it was for an entirely different reason than Pax. His need to save was purely emotional, while ours was calculated.

My mind should be focused on the job Dad had given us, especially with him coming to visit next month.

But instead, all I could think about was her.

BITE OF SIN

KAY RILEY

Chapter 12
Kali

I grabbed my bag, relief filling me now that I had my supplies again. Unzipping it, I double checked that everything was there, even though it was still in the hiding spot I'd stashed it in earlier. It had taken me much longer to find my way back than I thought it would. When Zan dragged me to Impulse, it had gotten me all turned around. But none of that mattered now. I was leaving.

The city was full of vampires wandering around, but I planned to walk right past them all and go out using the street where I entered. If the lotion covered my scent with Zan being so close, then I didn't need to worry about passing some in the street. I tightened the straps of the bag over my shoulders and hurriedly made my way out of the building.

As I walked through the streets, I ran a hand over my chest until my fingers brushed against the necklace they'd locked on me. Pax seemed positive that I couldn't run away with this on, but even as unease filled me, I wasn't staying here. The chain was too thick and the lock too strong for me to break, so I'd have to wear it until I came across a tool I could use to cut it off.

A chill ripped through me. Usually I would go to Warner or Helena for help. Helena was dead, and Warner might be too. Even people from the Clovers like Tim and Jill couldn't do much, since it was too big of a liability for me to try and go back to Project Hope. I needed to find the Clovers who lived free. But they were always on the move, and I wasn't good at tracking. I might never find them.

A bit of my fight left me, exhaustion curbing the anger that had been pushing me forward. What was I going to do to avenge Helena by myself? Against PARA. And to stay alive when surrounded by vampires. The lotion that Warner had given me would only last so long. I'd learned so much, but never had I imagined having to navigate this cruel life by myself.

I turned the corner, relief sweeping through me when I recognized the street. This was how I'd entered the city. Straightening up, I quickened my pace, only to pause when I noticed two vampires milling around about fifty feet in front of me. Lifting my chin, I surged forward. If I could sit in a place they called Impulse, with dozens of vampires surrounding me, I could walk right past these two. Both of their heads snapped up when I got closer, their conversation ceasing.

One of them threw up their hand, stopping me in my tracks. "No one is allowed out tonight. Turn back around."

My jaw fell. "What?"

The vampire ran a hand through his long brown hair to push it out of his face. "You know how it works. Whenever the humans are hunting, we stay in the city. They've been out nonstop the last couple of nights. No wandering until they stop."

The other vampire scoffed. "You're the tenth one to try and leave tonight. Everyone is getting antsy. But orders are orders."

Orders? There was a hierarchy here? I knew vampires had leaders. Every human knew who Amaros Kane was. He was the vampire who had led the war when it first began. Rumors were that he was still in charge, even if he hadn't been seen in years. He kept himself hidden because PARA was out to execute him. Along with his sons. Though, from what Warner had told me, they were even harder to find. No one knew what they even looked like. But ever since the war had ended, the search for them had slowed.

The one with long hair suddenly stiffened, his nostrils flaring. I took a step back when he looked back at me, his glare scrutinizing. He sucked in another large breath through his nose before advancing toward me.

"You're Zan's," he hissed. "You aren't allowed to leave."

My mouth grew dry, dread climbing down my limbs. "No, I'm not—"

"We were already told about you," the other vampire spoke up. "Everyone who watches the streets has already been ordered not to let you through. I wouldn't try to leave again."

I swallowed thickly at his threat as I backed away from them. Neither tried to follow me, but I could feel their stares as I turned and jogged down the street, darting around the first corner. I slumped against the closest building, letting my pulse slow down. What kind of power did Zan have around here? Their communication was still shocking. Those vampires were taking orders. It contradicted so much of what I'd learned.

And how the hell did they know about me? He smelled something. I dipped my head down, grabbing the necklace from under my hoodie and raising it to inspect it. I had no idea how, but this had to be the reason. I narrowed my eyes, lifting the necklace as high as I could and sniffing it. I couldn't smell anything, but vampires had an excellent sense of smell. What was inside it?

I rolled the hollow necklace through my fingers, realizing there was an even greater urgency to get this the fuck off me. Letting the necklace fall back to my chest, I rubbed my eyes, wishing I could just erase the last few days. But there was no going back. There was only surviving. I wasn't about to give up now.

I pushed off the wall, heading to the next street, my heart dipping when I saw the entire road was blocked. Cars and other large items were stacked at least twenty feet high, and it looked anything but stable. One wrong move and the entire thing would come crashing down, making enough noise to alert all the vampires within earshot. With my heart in my throat, I moved to the next street, trying to maintain a casual pace so I didn't look suspicious.

"What the hell?" I breathed out, seeing the same home-made wall as the previous road. Were they all blocked? Panic crept across my chest, making my heart pound faster. Maybe this was why Zan seemed so confident that I wouldn't leave the city.

I spent the next hour going to every street that led out, only for them all to be blocked just like the first two. Vampires were still out, and I looked at every one of them, just waiting to see Zan or the twins. But they never appeared. Not that they needed to. My hope of leaving was fading more every second.

The doors were open at the next building, and I glanced inside. I clenched my teeth, seeing the entire place was impassable. I couldn't even walk five feet inside because it was full of random items that looked like they had been shoved inside. Was every building on the outskirts of the city like this? I wasn't sure I'd have the time to check. The sun would be rising, and I needed a sure way out before then. I couldn't get caught in the sunlight while still trapped here. They'd find out I was human. Or maybe new vampires could walk in the sun. But I couldn't take that chance unless I was positive I could leave.

"Fuck," I muttered, running my hand through my hair, only to wince when my fingers got caught in the tangled mess.

I would wait. The vampires couldn't patrol the only open street in daylight. It was my best chance to leave. Once the sun was up, I could walk out with none of them able to chase me. At least for that day. I could find a good hiding spot in the forest by then. With a deep breath, I spun around and headed for a building closer to the city center. I estimated I had a couple of hours of darkness left. I wanted to find out as much as I could about this place while I was here.

After walking around for a while, I stopped in front of a huge building. From the old rusting sign, this used to be a hotel. The books I used to read in the library were the only reason I knew what a hotel was. There were so many things I didn't know about life before the war, and if I wasn't surrounded by vampires, I'd be fascinated with this city. I'd only ever seen Project Hope and the forest. What else was in the world that I didn't know about?

My steps were hesitant as I made my way across the worn tile floor. There was a cardboard sign reading *Community Showers. Second Floor.*

A sudden burst of laughter had me whirling around. Two women vampires were staring at me, their eyes dancing with mischief. One had blond hair that was wrapped in a bun on top of her head. Her pale blue eyes darted past me to the sign I'd been looking at. The other one had black hair that went nearly to her waist, and she twirled a strand around her finger.

"I'm sure the showers are free since everyone waits until sunrise to come inside," the blond one drawled, her gaze darting to my tangled hair. "But you don't live here. We've been staying here for months and we've never seen you."

"I think she needs more than a shower." The other one snickered. "She's a fucking mess."

"You're giving vampires a bad name by walking around looking like that," the blonde sneered.

I bristled, biting down on my tongue to stay quiet. Both were leering at me, their smirks cruel. Until their expressions changed and they took a step back.

"Zan," the black-haired vampire breathed out, fear flashing in her eyes.

"Use the showers. No one will bother you," the other one rushed out.

What. The. Fuck?

I watched in shock as they spun around and strode back outside, leaving me alone again. What the hell did this necklace do? I had a feeling I wouldn't get very far out of this city if I kept it on. I glanced back at the sign, wishfully thinking about how good a shower would feel right now.

Ignoring the nagging little voice in my head that told me to keep looking for an escape route, I found the stairs and quickly bounded up the steps, keeping an eye out for any other vampires. But the blond one was right about no one being inside at night; there wasn't anyone around. I wandered around for a while until I found the showers. The room was huge, with curtains separating the shower stalls.

Soaps and shampoo were on the benches, along with a couple of brushes. I didn't miss that the shower supplies were the same we used in Project Hope. Were the vampires stealing our items?

I crept inside, pulling the door shut behind me and flicking the lock. I wasn't sure if that would keep vampires out, but it made me feel better. Fuck it. I could take a quick shower before leaving. After this, who knew when I'd see a shower again? Plus, I couldn't leave the city until the sun came up anyway. I had time to burn. I just needed to make sure no one walked in before I could apply more lotion.

Taking a deep breath, I pulled the hoodie off. Moving into one of the enclosed shower stalls, I turned the hot water on before going to grab some soap and putting it in the shower. Luckily, I had a couple of changes of clothes in my bag. I quickly slipped out of the rest of my clothes, my panic rising from being so exposed.

But when the hot water hit my skin, a spark of pleasure filtered through the dread that had been clinging to me for days. I nearly moaned when I put my hair under the water, giving myself a moment to enjoy it. The weight of the necklace on my chest reminded me that I couldn't spare any more time. This city would be a death sentence if I didn't leave.

I scrubbed shampoo into my hair, massaging my scalp and rinsing before using a ton of conditioner to help with the knots. The soap had a lavender scent, reminding me of home. Helena loved flowers and had a tiny garden on our balcony in Project Hope. She'd find seeds any time we went into the forest and would always bring some back. Tears pricked my eyelids. I squeezed my eyes shut, pushing it all away again. If I thought of Helena and Warner, I'd wallow in sadness and I wouldn't be able to concentrate. For now, all I needed to focus on was getting out of here.

I shut off the water, staying in the stall as I squeezed as much water out of my hair as I could. There wasn't a towel in sight, and I needed to be completely dried off before I could apply the lotion. After making sure the door was still closed, I stepped out and grabbed a brush, not caring that it wasn't mine. Well, it was now since I planned on taking it. There wasn't one in my bag, and I'd need to cut my hair if I couldn't brush it.

"Shit," I gritted out, working through the knots as I waited for my body to dry. It took longer than I wanted, but finally, my hair was tangle free. Grabbing the lotion, I applied a layer before digging through my backpack and pulling out a pair of baggy pants and a long-sleeve shirt. Then I put more lotion on, hating how the container was slowly emptying. With the two containers I had, there was maybe enough for a couple of weeks.

Time to go. Making sure I had everything in my bag, I left the showers and made my way back outside. The sky was beginning to lighten, and I rushed back to the street, ready to bolt as soon as the sun came up.

I peeked around the corner, watching the same two vampires who were standing watch earlier. They seemed impatient, and one of them grinned when two others came out of a small door from the side of the building.

"Finally," the long-haired vampire said, speaking just loud enough for me to hear.

The two newcomers didn't respond as they took their place in the middle of the street. My breath caught in my throat when one of them turned, and I saw the tattoo on the side of his neck. The same *K* tattoo that the girl, Dee, had. Were they human? My great escape plan was nonexistent now. If they had humans watching the street in the daylight, I couldn't exactly stroll past them. If they caught me, they'd take me to Zan, who would realize I was human.

I watched a little longer, my heart sinking when it became apparent that they weren't going to leave before the sun came up. Making a quick decision, I spun around and raced through the streets, going back to the hotel building.

I'd have to stay longer before I figured a way out of here. Fuck me.

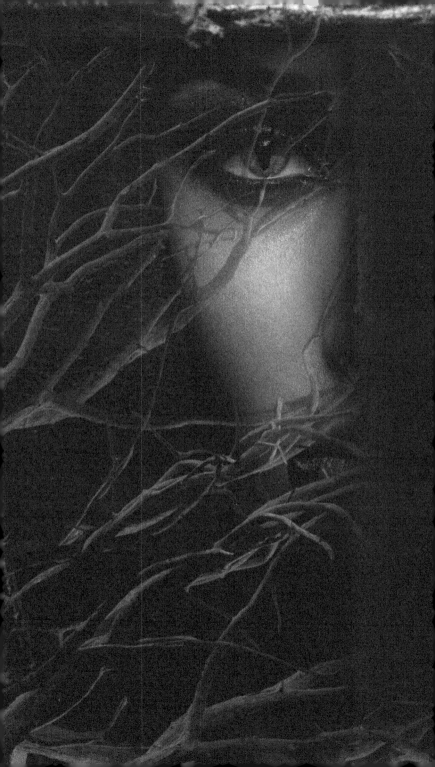

Chapter 13
Kali

I stared through the cracked window, watching the sun slowly disappear. I'd stayed in this room all day, with a dresser in front of the door. This hotel had hundreds of rooms, all with beds and bathrooms in them, even though the water pressure was abysmal. Paint was peeling off the walls, and the mattress was ripped and dirty. But the room I'd found seemed vacant, and I'd been left alone.

I was on edge and antsy, trying to come up with an idea on how to leave. My best bet was to use the gun with wooden bullets that Warner had given me. I could shoot the vampires on watch tonight and run. The bullets wouldn't kill them, but they would slow them down enough for me to get a head start. And I could also stake them if I needed to. There was no way I was staying here another night. The second I didn't show up at Impulse, I had a feeling Zan would come looking, and I needed to be far away.

I finished eating the granola bar before taking a couple small sips of water. I needed to conserve my water until I could get to the river to replenish it. I sighed, pulling off my pants before slipping on a tighter pair that had a pocket for my gun at the waistband on my back. I tucked in the small gun, feeling it press against my spine. After putting on my boots, I put the stake inside my right boot. The leggings also had side pockets, and I froze when I brushed my fingers against one of them, feeling something in it.

The second I pulled out the piece of paper, a sob escaped me. Warner had thought of everything. I thought this was lost forever when I fled from Project Hope. Falling onto the bed, I carefully unfolded the old paper, reading the words I'd memorized years ago.

Kali,

My sweet daughter. You can choose to be the light or the dark, and one cannot survive without the other. You are so special, Kali. When you become a young woman, you choose the path you desire, because even destiny cannot decide that for you. Just like I wasn't able to choose your life when you were born. I love you so much and wish I could be there to see you grow. Please remember that you were wanted. Life just needed you for a larger reason.

Love,
Your mother

I always tried imagining what my mother looked like. This note was all I had from her, and half the time, I wondered if it was ramblings. It didn't make any sense. I was nothing but an orphan. But I always kept it because this was the only thing she'd given me. I was only days old when I was found abandoned at a train station, wrapped up in a blanket. I didn't even know the real day I was born. The date on my birth certificate was a guess. But since I was less than a month old when I was found, I knew my birthday was in June.

Footsteps from the hall caught my attention, and I shot to my feet, quickly putting the letter in a small pocket of my backpack before wiping the tears from my cheeks. This wasn't the first time I'd heard vampires in the hall. There had been a couple of them that walked past the room, but this time was different.

The footsteps were slow, and when they stopped outside my room, I silently lifted my bag and tiptoed forward, setting it right on the wall near the door. It was big and bulky, and if I had to fight my way out, I had a better chance without it on. There were no other sounds until a few seconds later when the footsteps moved away.

My heart raced, and I took small, quiet breaths as I counted to sixty. It was still silent, and I kept my bag where it was as I pushed the dresser away from the door. Keeping one hand behind my back in case I needed the gun, I used my other to grasp the doorknob. I twisted it, cracking the door an inch. My breath hitched when my eyes locked on a pair of bright green ones. Before I could do anything else, the door was shoved open hard enough to make me stumble back.

I righted myself, glaring at the vampire filling my doorway. Zan didn't make a move to come into the room as he crossed his arms and leaned against the doorframe. A wicked smirk tipped up his lips as his eyes trailed down my body.

Terror held me hostage, and I forced myself to keep

looking at him instead of my bag that was just out of his sight. If he rummaged through that, I was so fucked. My fingers twitched, my instincts screaming to go for my gun. One shot to his head, and then I could stake him in the heart. If there were no other vampires in the hall, I'd be able to get away with it since the gun had a silencer on it.

Until another head popped into the doorway when one of the twins glanced inside. I couldn't be sure if it was Pax or Viggo, but I had a feeling if one of them was here, so was the other one.

"Damn," the twin exclaimed with a shake of his head. "I was betting you'd be gone."

"You were supposed to be on your way to Impulse already," Zan murmured, ignoring the twin. "I told you to go right when the sun went down."

"I couldn't remember the way there," I lied.

Zan cocked his head to the side. "Really? You mean you weren't going to try to leave? My watchers informed me that you were on their street last night."

"Watchers?" I repeated.

"The vampires who wouldn't let you leave the city."

I scowled. "How'd they know who I was?"

His eyes fell to my chest, where the necklace was hidden beneath my shirt, his growing grin making anger tear through me.

"They smelled something," I snapped. "What is it?"

He moved to step into the room, and I shot forward, my palms slamming into his chest before I thought better of it. His fingers instantly wrapped around my wrists while his eyes flared in surprise. But instead of pushing me away, he just kept me in place with my hands on him. His touch was cold, his hold staying firm when I tried tugging away.

"I thought you wanted me at Impulse," I said tightly. "So lead the way."

He arched an eyebrow, and I caught a flash of amusement before he stepped back into the hall, taking me with him. The twin reached behind me, slamming the door shut before taking out a black marker and drawing a *K* on the door. Zan finally released me, and I took a large step away, making sure to keep facing him as the weight of my gun felt even heavier. The long-sleeve shirt I had on was loose and flowy, making it easier to keep the weapon hidden, but if he grabbed me like he did last night, he'd find it immediately. At least he hadn't seen my bag.

The twin turned around, staying behind Zan. He caught me watching him as he put the marker back in his pocket. His lopsided grin had me believing it was Viggo, since Pax was less than happy about me being here. "No one will go into your room now. Not with the mark on your door."

"Great," I ground out.

My attention cut back to Zan when he advanced closer, forcing me to back up until I was pressed against the wall. I went still when he raised his hand, letting his fingers brush against my neck.

"You hiding something in your room?" he questioned, his voice soft but still full of danger at the same time.

"No. But it's mine. And you weren't invited in."

He scoffed. "I'm sure you know by now that vampires don't need to be invited to get inside someone's place. That rumor did go around a decade ago, though."

"I know that." I kept my voice steady, trying to act like his fingers still grazing my neck weren't affecting me. Because his touch shouldn't—but I couldn't stop the goosebumps from skating across my skin. "I'd rather the assholes who kidnapped me didn't go in my personal space."

Zan kept his eyes on mine as he spoke again. "Kidnap? We aren't holding you hostage. You have your own place, according to you. What do you think, Viggo?"

Well, at least I knew which twin it was now.

Viggo glanced over Zan's shoulder at me. "We gave her a job and a home that's a hell of a lot better than the center. I'd say we did her a favor."

"A favor?" Their audacity had rage heating my veins. "Does that mean I can decline the job you so fucking *graciously* offered me? And I can leave?"

Zan chuckled. "You're my responsibility now since you're not going to the center."

"Because you decided it," I gritted out.

Instead of answering, he grabbed the chain of the necklace and pulled it out from under my shirt. He slid his fingers down the chain until he was grasping the round pendant, his eyes not leaving mine.

"Do you remember what I said this necklace does?" he asked in a low voice.

I scowled. "Your exact words? That it claims me as yours. But let me make myself perfectly clear—I will *never* accept that."

He tugged on the chain, and I arched my back to keep from falling against him. My hand lashed up, grabbing his wrist to keep him from pulling me forward more. Not that my strength was anything compared to his. But he stilled, his gaze going to my hand before going to my face again.

"It also means that you can't go anywhere without me finding you." His words had my heart skipping a beat. "How do you think I found you here? Even if you did get out of the city last night, it wouldn't have changed anything.

I thought I'd let you know so you don't waste your time trying to escape again."

"What's in the necklace?" I hissed.

"In a few months, once your senses are honed, you'll be able to smell it yourself." He let go of the necklace before taking a step back and motioning for me to start walking. "You're late. I'm sure Gia is waiting. Let's go."

The walk to Impulse was silent, and I made sure to keep up with Zan and Viggo so they had no reason to touch me. How the hell was I going to keep this gun hidden? I remembered what Gia had said about finding me clothes. I wouldn't be able to keep it concealed if the clothes were tight. Panic clung to me as Zan opened the front door, ushering me inside, just like he had last night. Only this time, the place was still empty. The red strobe lights that had shadowed the room last night were off and the overhead white lights were dim, but the space was still visible.

Gia and the girl who Viggo had fed on last night, Dee, were clearing the tables. Gia swiped an armful of empty bottles into a garbage can before straightening up and glancing at me.

"We open in an hour," she told me with a cheery smile.

"It looks like the party just ended," I mumbled.

Dee didn't stop sweeping the floor as she responded. "We don't clean up when we close. We do it before we open. Days are for relaxing and sleeping."

The humans here must follow the same schedule as vampires. Dee was wearing sweats, and her dirty blond hair was thrown in a messy bun, looking like she just rolled out of bed. I stared at the tattoo on her neck, wondering what was so special about the *K* symbol. Depending on how long I was stuck here, I might find out before I leave. Zan's words clouded my mind, and I stiffened. Was he telling the truth about being able to find me with this necklace? I guessed I'd find out. Because his threat wasn't going to stop me from leaving.

"Your clothes are in there." Gia pointed to a door behind her. "Go change to make sure it fits."

"I can just wear this—"

"No," Gia interrupted me. "This club has a reputation, and what you're wearing won't do."

I opened my mouth to protest, needing to find a way to stay in my own clothes so I could keep my gun. Before a word left my mouth, Zan grabbed my arm, stepping in front of me.

"I wouldn't argue with her," he murmured under his breath, leaning closer to me. "She might always be smiling, but she'll be the first to rip your throat out if she gets annoyed. She has a short temper."

"It's not polite to gossip, Zan," Gia chastised with a wink as I glanced at her over Zan's shoulder. "And my temper is much better than yours."

It wasn't lost on me that she'd heard his words even though she was across the room. Anything I said here wouldn't be private, and I'd have to remember that.

"You told me this necklace protects me from other vampires," I said, tilting my head. "Or were your words lies?"

Shock lined his features for a moment before he masked it. With a grin, he leaned even closer until his lips were inches from mine. "I haven't lied to you. But it's still not a good idea to rile up vampires until you reach your full strength. Especially when you have no idea how this city works. Now go change like Gia wants."

I gritted my teeth, his orders pissing me right the fuck off. But seeing as I was hiding a gun and a stake, I backed away a few feet before turning around and striding to the door Gia had pointed to. I quickly slipped inside, shutting the door behind me, grateful there was a lock. The room was small, with just enough space for two short couches pushed against the wall and a small glass table in the middle, where a pile of folded clothes and a pair of heels were sitting. I slumped against the door, sucking in deep breaths.

The lotion I'd put on should last the night, and if I didn't fuck up, I should be able to walk out of here alive. I lifted my head, scanning the tiny room again. My stomach twisted painfully, not wanting to part with my gun. But one glance at the clothes Gia had laid out proved I wouldn't be able to hide it on me. With a sigh, I stepped forward, grabbing a back cushion off one of the couches. It had a zipper, and I slowly unzipped it, hoping it wasn't loud enough for any of them to hear through the door.

Once it was open a few inches, I took out my gun and stashed it inside. I closed the cloth back up, repositioning the cushion. I hoped to everything that whoever sat here wouldn't be able to feel the gun through the cushion. I sat down, checking for myself, feeling a little better when I didn't notice it.

Then I grabbed the clothes, my lips parting as I looked at them. I'd never worn clothes like this in my life. I lived in things that were practical and easy to move in. These were the exact opposite. The top was black leather and strapless. There was a corset-type tie that ran along the front, which I was grateful for. At least I could make it tight enough to keep from slipping down if I needed to run.

I swallowed thickly, realizing it was going to show off part of my tattoo. The ink covered my entire back, from my shoulder blades all the way to the top of my ass.

Tattoos weren't allowed in Project Hope, but this one was important. It was needed. If the vampires found out the reason I had it, I'd be just as screwed as if they found my weapons.

I slipped off my shirt and then took my boots off with every intent of wearing them after I changed. I couldn't bring myself to part with my stake. Plus, the heels that were left out for me were at least four inches high, and I'd break my damn neck if I wore those. The pants Gia had left for me were black leather just like the corset top. It took me forever to pull them up. I sucked in my stomach, buttoning them before reaching for the shirt.

"These clothes are fucking ridiculous," I grumbled, annoyance filtering through me. It took me another couple of minutes to tighten and tie the strings of the corset, and I froze when I realized how much it pushed up my breasts. I'd never shown cleavage like this in any of my regular clothes.

There was a knock on the door. "Gia still needs to show you what you'll be doing. Hurry up."

Since it was a feminine voice, I was guessing it was Dee outside the door. I bent over and slipped on my boots, glad the stake could stay hidden. There was no mirror in here, so I ran my fingers through my hair, wishing I'd pulled it up before Zan showed up at the hotel. My hair had natural loose curls, and I usually slept with my hair braided to help keep it from frizzing. Most of the time, I kept my hair in a ponytail, but unfortunately, my hair ties were in my backpack.

Wearing my hair down like this was just another vulnerability. It was easier for people to overpower me if they got a hold of my hair. These clothes made it even worse. I couldn't move as freely as I liked. Not that any of it really mattered when I was surrounded by vampires here. I couldn't fight my way out, even if I wanted.

Taking a deep breath, I shut out everything. My worry. My fear. I relaxed the muscles in my face until I knew I wasn't portraying any emotion before I reached forward and opened the door. Gia was behind the bar, and she beckoned me over when she saw me. The place was still empty, and Dee was nowhere to be seen. It was quiet, but I knew that wouldn't last much longer when they opened the doors to this place.

I was halfway to the bar when I heard a sharp intake of breath and then a muttered curse. A glance over my shoulder revealed Zan and the twins sitting in the same corner they'd brought me to last night. The only reason I could tell which twin was Viggo was because of the white shirt I'd already seen him in. Pax was wearing a hoodie. All three of them were staring at me until Viggo whispered something in Zan's ear and then let out a laugh. Zan's face darkened with a scowl, and he shoved Viggo away.

"Why aren't you wearing the heels?" Gia asked sharply, making me look back at her.

"They didn't fit. And I've never worn them," I explained stiffly. "I wouldn't get two steps without tripping."

She nodded, seeming to accept my reasoning. "Fine. The boots match the outfit perfectly anyway. Even though they're a bit worn."

"I didn't spend my days drinking and partying like everyone here," I mumbled, letting my tongue run loose before I could stop myself.

Gia's usual grin was gone in an instant, and she studied me. "It might look like fun here, but this was not how we spent our lives before this. Don't judge. It's rude."

"Sorry," I forced out, not wanting to test her patience after what Zan had said.

"I'm guessing you've never made drinks before?" she questioned as she continued washing the glasses.

I shook my head.

"Then you'll serve the drinks." She eyed me. "You can carry a tray, right?"

"Sure."

"Don't look so glum." Her smile was back. "This place is great. You'll learn what you need to without knowing the shit life at the center. Consider yourself lucky."

Lucky. I was lucky to escape Project Hope with my life. But being here and lying to stay alive was hell. And I had a feeling it was only going to get worse.

My gaze fell on one of the cages and the woman inside who was curled up, sleeping. There were eight cages throughout the room and five had humans in them. Guilt crept in before I could stop it. Maybe I could find a way to get them out.

"You don't need to worry about them," Gia said, coming up beside me. "I have someone who deals with them only."

"These humans are different from the ones last night," I observed, glancing at the other cage.

"Yes." She waved her hand toward a door in the back. "We have a whole room back there where they stay. We switch them out. Where they get showers and bathrooms."

I turned to her in surprise. "Why?"

"Because the smell would be unbearable if they stayed in here."

I nodded because that made more sense. For a moment, I'd considered that they cared about the humans, but that clearly wasn't the case.

"Go finish wiping down the tables," she ordered. "We'll

be opening the doors soon, and it'll only take minutes for this place to fill."

She tossed me a rag, and I moved to do what she said. The back of my neck prickled, keeping me fully aware that there were eyes on me. I subtly looked out of the corner of my eye, noticing Zan was still staring while the twins were talking to each other. Biting my tongue, I turned away from him, cleaning off a table before moving to the next one.

Gia kept me busy for the next half hour, and I'd finally stopped fidgeting with my top, feeling confident that it wasn't going to fall. Zan's necklace was on full display, and I caught Dee and Gia glancing at it more than once.

The overhead lights suddenly went out, and the red strobe lights lit up the place. Dee pushed open the front doors, and vampires immediately began piling in. Three of them began throwing punches, trying to reach the pool table first. Gia tugged me behind the bar as the music started.

"I know it's all overwhelming, especially when your body is changing." She was yelling in my ear to be heard over the music. "But don't worry about anything. That necklace will make sure they all keep their hands to themselves. Go take some orders."

She gave me a little push, and I stumbled forward, hesitantly moving for the closest table, where four vampires had just sat down.

"What can I get you?" I asked, keeping my voice strong. I didn't say it very loud, but all four heads swung my way. Nerves bubbled in my stomach, catching the gaze of the vampire to my left. His brown eyes flashed with desire, and a leering smirk appeared on his lips.

"Who are you?" He stood up quickly, and it took everything in me to stay still. "You look downright fuckable. One of Gia's new girls?"

"Kellen." The other vampire grabbed the arm of the one who had stood up. "She's his."

Fear was thick in his voice, and Kellen glanced at him before looking back at me, his gaze trailing to my chest, stopping where the pendant sat. His eyes bulged, and he scrambled back, nearly tipping the table over. Once he was standing far from me, he looked over toward the corner, and I couldn't help but do the same.

"Sorry," Kellen sputtered out, staring at Zan. "I didn't know."

The raw panic he was displaying shocked the hell out of me. Why were they scared of Zan? What power did he hold to have these vampires terrified of crossing him?

But when I glanced at Zan, a jolt shot down my spine. He looked downright fucking terrifying. His eyes were narrowed, his face murderous as he glared at Kellen. He was sitting down, but that didn't diminish the confidence radiating from him. He owned this place. Owned everything.

All the vampires and the tattooed humans around me were watching the interaction with interest, and none of them would look me in the eye once Zan went back to talking to Viggo and Pax. I had a feeling Gia was right about no one messing with me here.

"Coke," Kellen stammered out, turning back to me. "Coke is what we want for the table. Please."

I licked my lips, nodding stiffly. "Sure."

I spun around and relayed the order to Gia at the bar. She reached under the counter and tossed me a small baggie of white powder. I caught it out of instinct, staring at her in confusion.

"Four glasses of coke," I said slowly, wondering if she'd

missed what I'd told her. Soda was a luxury in Project Hope, but I'd tried it once during a holiday.

Gia giggled, shaking her head. "We only serve three things here. Alcohol. Blood. And drugs. There's only one kind of coke here."

"Oh. *Oh.*" It took me a second to understand. I'd learned about drugs in school but was told they didn't exist anymore after the war. Just another thing to add to the list of information I had no damn idea about.

"It affects vampires almost the same as humans," she explained. "But it leaves our system faster. Personally, I don't enjoy it. Seeing as they'd allow you to try it at the center, you're more than welcome to do it—"

"I'm good," I cut her off quickly. I wasn't sure what it would do to me, but there was no way I was trying anything like that while I was here.

"Smart girl," she praised while pouring a beer. "Don't ever let your guard down here. Even with that necklace. Vampires can smell the weak, and they prey on them. The center teaches why we need to work together, but it's impossible to break the sheer instinct of being predators—even of our own kind. The feeling will grow as you get older. You'll need to learn how to control it. We don't condone killing each other unless it's warranted."

Her words stayed in my head as I went to a new table and took their order of glasses of whiskey. No wonder the war had lasted as long as it did. Vampires were much more organized than I ever knew. The next table's orders had bile rising in my throat. O negative blood. They served it like a drink here, and I wouldn't ever get used to it. Was this where the donated blood went to? Or did they get the blood in a more sinister way?

I didn't stop moving for the next couple of hours. Running back and forth from the bar to deliver orders. No vampires ever paid for anything, creating more questions. Did they barter or trade? Or maybe it was all given freely. But I kept my chin up and stayed quiet. There was already enough attention on me from the damn necklace, and I just wanted to get this night done with so I could leave for good. Gia glanced behind me, but before I could move, someone spoke.

"Kali is taking her break."

Chapter 14
Kali

Z an's voice cut through the music, and Gia nodded before I turned to see him standing a couple of feet behind me.

"I don't need a break," I said, reaching for the glass I was about to take to a table.

He caught my wrist, tugging me from the bar and dragging me away, ignoring how I was attempting to pry his fingers off my arm.

"Get off me," I ground out, knowing he could hear me even over the music.

He didn't respond, and I realized he was bringing me to the area where all the vampires were dancing. The second he stepped onto the open floor, the crowd parted, leaving the entire center open for him. My stomach flipped when he abruptly stopped, yanking me against him until my back was crushed to his chest.

Thank fuck I stashed my gun.

His hand landed on my waist, keeping a bruising grip on it to keep me from going anywhere. He rested his chin on my shoulder, his lips right near my ear.

"Dance with me." It wasn't an offer or a question, but a command. One he clearly intended for me to follow. This time, I couldn't have done it even if I wanted to.

"I don't know how," I muttered.

He stilled, keeping his fingers digging into my hip. "You've never danced?"

"No."

It was the only truth I'd given him. Because I doubted he was going to let me off this floor, and from the way the other vampires were moving around us, there was no way I could hide it. Women were rolling their hips, grinding on the male vampires, some bent over with their hands touching the floor. Other couples were facing each other, their hips moving in rhythm with each other's. There were larger groups, their hands moving everywhere they could touch. It was like they were all having sex with their clothes on.

Did vampires enjoy sex like humans? Not that I had much experience. I'd had sex a total of five times. I didn't understand what was so good. It only stressed me out. And the two guys I'd slept with were only chasing their own pleasure. I had a lot of practice getting myself off over the years.

Before the war, there had been something called birth control, but it wasn't available anymore. PARA needed women to have babies so our race could survive. Which was funny, considering orphans were treated like burdens. They needed babies, but there weren't enough resources to take care of them all properly.

I had absolutely no desire to bring a baby into this world. Not when I had grown up without parents. Or with how easy it was to die. Life wasn't fun. Or happy. It was a chore. One I would never bestow on a child. Which was why I barely ever indulged in sex. Many people did it because it was fun. But I'd seen the accidental pregnancies, and I'd promised myself years ago that it would never be me.

"Have you heard this kind of music before?" he asked, pulling me from my thoughts.

"No."

He made a noise that made me believe he was annoyed with my one-word answers. His other hand went to my free hip, and he held me firmly as he began moving back and forth to the beat of the music. I tried jerking away, but he didn't give me an inch, keeping me pressed against his hard body. He moved me with him, the dancing causing new sensations to skitter through me.

"So you'd never been to a vampire city before you were turned," he murmured, keeping his mouth near my ear so I could hear his quiet words.

I stiffened, realizing he was trying to learn about me.

"Are you from Project Hope?"

I stared straight ahead, acting like his continued moves weren't affecting me at all.

"Or did you live with one of those free groups?"

I watched two female vampires kiss as they danced a few feet in front of me. Which was not helping the heat that was spreading slowly through my veins. The sexual tension surrounding me made my own body react as Zan's moves grew faster.

"Where are you from, Kali?"

When I didn't answer, his hands left my hips, and he suddenly spun me around. I managed to swallow my gasp when my chest slammed against his while he wrapped an arm around my waist. He raised his other hand, grasping my jaw to tilt my face up.

Fuck. I'd rather he kept me turned away from him. His unrelenting stare seemed to burn through me as I glared at him. He didn't stop moving his hips, still dancing with the music.

"Where are you from?" He repeated his question, his eyes boring into mine.

"You can't entrance me. I'm a new vampire," I forced out breathlessly.

It was only a half lie since I wasn't a vampire. But he couldn't entrance me. The hawthorn plant had made sure of that. I hadn't been without it since I started sneaking out of Project Hope.

He scoffed, dropping his hand from my face. "I'm aware. I'm only asking you a question."

"Fuck. Off."

He raised an eyebrow, his apparent amusement beginning to grate on me. "You see how all these vampires fear me, and you still talk to me like that?"

My stomach tightened. "I talked to you like this the first time we met, and you didn't do anything to me."

"I haven't done anything to you *yet*. You shouldn't push me."

I grinned, wondering just how far I could go. He had some kind of point to make with me, and from the growing bulge in his jeans, he wasn't finished with me. Not that I'd have sex with him—ever. But the fact that he was attracted to me could play in my favor.

"Or what?" I purred, enjoying his moment of surprise. "What happens if I push you?"

"Kali." He said my name as a warning, coming out gruff and low. His eyes snapped to mine when I rolled my hips without any help from his hands.

"Did you do all this because you're attracted to me?" I tilted my head, happy that I flipped the conversation.

"I'm keeping you here because you're new," he gritted out. His teeth clenched tight as I continued to find my own dance moves.

It was impossible to miss his hard-on now, proving he was affected by what I was doing.

"You want to kill me," Zan murmured. "Don't you?"

That was a question I didn't mind answering. "Yes. You're forcing me to be somewhere I don't want to be."

"The urge will only grow as you gain strength." He chuckled, putting his other arm around me, making sure there wasn't an inch of space between us. "You'll learn to live with it. And not give in to that desire. Because let me tell you—you can't kill me. No matter how hard you try. Vampires have tried before."

"If I was at the center, would I learn to fear you like they all do?" I asked in a whisper.

"Yes. They were taught well, weren't they?"

"Why? Who are you?"

"Who are you?" he countered. "Where did you come from?"

I pressed my lips together, not saying a word. A wicked gleam hit his eye, and he suddenly wedged his knee between my legs, forcing them apart. My heart leaped in my throat, his arms not letting me move away. He pressed his thigh against me, and I held my breath, keeping his stare. The leather pants were the only barrier between his leg and my clit.

"Keep dancing." His hands went back to my hips, making my body grind against his.

"What are you doing?" I snapped. But it was clear that

he was playing into my game, and I was now regretting it because I had no idea what he was going to do.

"I'm teaching. Since I'm keeping you from the center, that's my job." He smirked, leaning forward so he could whisper in my ear. "You need to learn the rules. But the way we keep new vampires in line is by showing them all the good we can give too. The alcohol. The drugs. This club. How even the simplest things can feel fucking amazing once the changes start happening after you turn. I bet your body is buzzing just from my touch, isn't it?"

My lower stomach twinged in a way I'd only felt a few times in the past, and I hated to admit he was right. The instant reminder that I wasn't really a damn vampire sobered me right up. He was giving me pleasure. *And I was enjoying it.*

"No," I breathed out, refusing to give into it. He was a vampire. And a smug asshole who was keeping me here against my will. I wouldn't give him anything.

"Answer my questions," he demanded in a low voice. "Or I'll keep you on this dance floor all fucking night."

I couldn't deny the jolts of pleasure, and I allowed myself to indulge because, fuck, I hadn't had nearly enough experiences in life like this. Experiences that made me crave more. Made me forget the hardships of this life.

"I don't think my new boss would be happy about that," I rasped.

"She answers to me. Just like everyone else here except Pax and Viggo. I can do whatever I want to you, and no one would stop me."

That threat really should have made me panic. Instead, all I could focus on were the waves of pleasure that were growing with each passing second. He knew exactly what he was doing to me if his heated gaze was anything to go by.

Before I could try to push him away, there was a sudden commotion, and the music grew quieter. The vampires around us turned their attention toward the front.

Zan's head whipped in that direction, and he moved his thigh from between my legs, spinning me around with him. He turned me until he was at my back again, but his arms never strayed from my waist.

Two vampires were dragging someone between them, and once they got away from the front door, they threw the person to the floor. I wasn't sure if it was a human or vampire, and it was impossible to see their face because they were covered in blood and dirt. But as they struggled to climb to their feet, my blood ran cold.

Even though his back was turned to me, I would recognize him anywhere. It was easy when I'd known him my entire life. He swiped his hand over his face, trying to see through the smeared blood, and I silently screamed.

Warner whirled around, his hands clenching into fists as he swung at the closest vampire. Every muscle was frozen as I stared at my best friend. Anguish ripped through my chest. This wasn't fucking happening. He couldn't be here.

"Look what we found," one of the vampires sneered, shoving Warner back to the floor.

"He was caught trying to get into the city. Took out two of us before we could disarm him."

No, no, no. My heart squeezed painfully, my mind screaming to do something. But what could I do? They'd kill both of us. Zan was still holding on to me, and I was sure he noticed how tense I was. But I couldn't force myself to relax. Not when Warner was right here.

Viggo jumped up from his chair, sauntering toward Warner with a cruel grin playing on his lips. The crowd moved out of his way, and it didn't take long until he was standing a few feet in front of Warner.

"Is that true?" Viggo asked. "You killed two of our kind?"

"I'll fucking kill you all," Warner snarled, lunging at Viggo, who easily dodged the move before punching Warner in the head hard enough that he crumpled to the floor. I didn't breathe until I witnessed his chest rising to prove he was only unconscious.

"You know what to do." Viggo nodded at the two vampires who had brought Warner inside, and they hauled my best friend up and dragged him to an empty cage. Gia strode up and locked it with a key after they slammed the cage door shut.

"This city is ours," Zan breathed in my ear. "No one leaves or gets in without us knowing about it."

I swallowed back a sob, glad Zan was behind me when I barely blinked away a lone tear as I stared at Warner.

There was no way I could leave now.

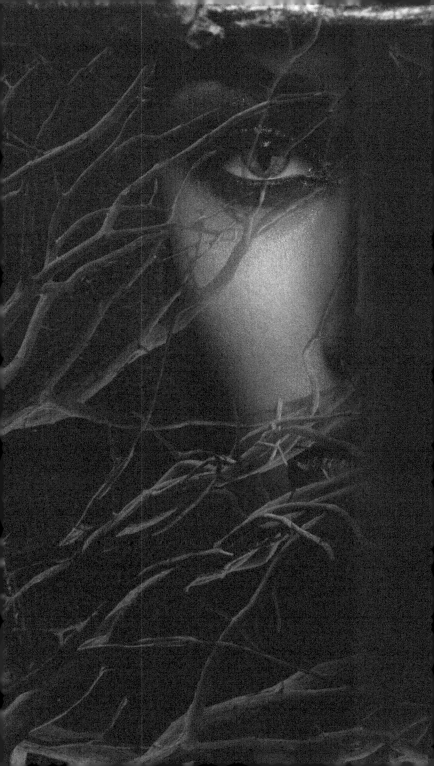

Chapter 15
Zan

"This should last us at least three months," Viggo muttered as he pushed the last box into the back seat of the truck.

We were about two hours from our city, picking up supplies to stock our club. The drugs were easy enough to keep in stock because we had them being made in the south. Alcohol was a bit more difficult. There was barely any left from before the war, and making it was time consuming. But it was worth it to keep the vampires happy and in line like we needed.

"Amaros is expecting an update next month."

I gave a curt nod to Brett. "We'll be at the meeting."

Brett hesitated, fear lining his face as he stared at the ground. Viggo exchanged a glance with me, raising an eyebrow.

"Spit it out, Brett," I drawled. "What's going on?"

"We were raided a few days ago. Amaros was already made aware. He wasn't pleased."

I stared at him, my skin prickling. The humans were getting more aggressive, and I didn't fucking like it. They weren't happy about the fact that vampires were taking over uninhabited cities. We had been keeping it quiet, but PARA was catching on that we were setting up near their cities.

"How bad?" Viggo asked tightly.

"The city is gone. Half of us got out," Brett mumbled.

"Shit," I breathed out. "Not fucking good."

"We were quiet like we were supposed to be," Brett rushed out. "But...we had a couple of rogue vamps who decided feeding was more important. They drew attention."

"Were they dealt with?" I asked sharply.

"Your father handled them."

"Good. We'll take back what we lost," Viggo replied, forcing a smile to his face. "We'll see you next month."

Viggo and I got in the truck, and I started driving back home. The news that Brett shared was troubling, and I needed to make sure our city stayed intact. We'd have to add more watchers and scouts to keep a closer eye on PARA.

"Dad is going to put more pressure on us after this," Viggo muttered.

"I know."

"We need to find a way to get into Project Hope."

I sighed. "We will."

"Your new obsession might get in the way." He turned his head, giving me a shit-eating grin. "I can't blame you, though. If you hadn't claimed her first, I'd be doing the same."

I gritted my teeth, knowing he was fucking with me. "I'm not obsessed."

"Really? Then why did you have Pax stay behind when he always comes to drops with us?"

"Fuck off," I grumbled, keeping my eyes on the road.

It had been three nights since Kali had come to the city. She showed up at Impulse the second night without me having to drag her there. I had been expecting her to try and run again, but something had changed. Her attitude was still very much intact, but she didn't seem to have the motivation to escape. Maybe she realized life in the city was far better than being on her own. I'd had Pax hang back so he could keep an eye on her, on top of the vampire I kept posted outside the hotel where she was sleeping.

"If Dad finds out you gave that necklace to a newbie, he's going to be furious," Viggo said, as if I didn't already know that. "You know what he wanted you to use that for."

"Once she's older and knows her place, I'll take it off. He doesn't need to find out."

He chuckled. "Sure."

Fuck me. I should have just taken her to the center like Viggo wanted the first night we found her. It was too late now. I didn't want her to leave. She got under my skin every time she spoke, but that didn't stop me from wanting to push her even more to see how she reacted. She was unpredictable. Something in this life that wasn't tolerated at all.

We demanded obedience from every vampire. But I wasn't forcing it on her like I should be. Even Gia was surprised. But she was just as bad. Already taking Kali under her wing and teaching her our ways without the cruel hand that the center lived by.

I pushed the pedal down more, pushing the truck faster. The headlights were off so we didn't attract any attention, and with the moon hidden behind the clouds, it was pitch black out tonight. Not that it bothered me. My sight was perfect, even in the dark, just like every vampire.

"In a hurry?" Viggo taunted with a laugh. "You realize she hates you, right? Every time she looks at you, I can see her planning your death. But I can see the appeal. The fun of the unknown."

I could feel his stare on me, but I kept my eyes on the back road, avoiding the potholes. "She'd never get close to killing me."

Her strength was nothing compared to mine. Even as she got older, her skills would never come close.

"I'm surprised no one has tried anything with her."

I bristled. "She's claimed as mine. No one would fucking dare."

"You know that's not true," he shot back. "There are always vamps who try to challenge us when the urge gets too strong. And she's an easy target, being so new."

He was right. As much as we did to keep them all in line, it was a precarious balance to keep them compliant when a vampire's instinct was to control and dominate. The majority did fall in line, but there were always a few who refused to follow.

"Pax is there. She'll be fine," I finally answered. Yet I still sped up even more, tearing through an open field to cut time off the trip.

This was the first night I hadn't set eyes on her since she came to my city, and the unease strumming through me put me on edge. Which was another problem in its fucking self. She was filling my mind more than I'd ever admit out loud. My priority was Project Hope, but I'd been practically living at Impulse since she showed up, just to keep an eye on her.

I should send her away.

I should. But I wouldn't.

Chapter 16
Kali

"You seem to be getting along well in here."

Gia's words had me stiffening, but I smiled at her anyway as I leaned on the bar. It had been a few hours since the doors opened, and like the last two nights, it was nonstop busy. But tonight was different. Because Zan and Viggo were missing. Pax was here, in his usual spot, and I'd caught him keeping an eye on me more than once while I took orders. Tonight was also the first time I was able to see Warner again.

Apparently, having an unconscious and beaten human in the cages was no fun, so they'd taken him to the back room. A room I had absolutely no access to. But I'd been watching. Gia had a copy of the keys for the cages, along with another vampire who had a mohawk. I was guessing his job was to deal with the humans, since I'd only seen him in and out of that back room.

He had brought Warner out earlier and thrown him in a cage in the back of the club near the wall. I didn't want Warner seeing me—not yet anyway. Not until I could explain what I was doing. If he alerted anyone here about knowing me, it was going to be a problem. But Warner hadn't looked this way once. He was sitting up with his arms around his knees and his face toward the wall, not paying attention to any curious vampires who came around him.

My heart panged as I stared at his back. He looked so weak, making me wonder when he'd eaten last. He hadn't had his backpack on him when they'd dragged him in here two nights ago. His head sagged down, and it was taking all my willpower not to reveal myself to him. But first I needed to talk to him without any vampires overhearing, and I wasn't sure when that would happen.

"Has anyone bothered you?"

Gia's question had my eyes snapping away from Warner and back to her. "No. They see the necklace and nearly trip over themselves to get away from me."

"Just be careful. There will always be one who'll try to challenge Zan. And since you're wearing that, you'll be the first target."

"Where is Zan?" I asked.

She grinned. "Missing him?"

My face flushed, and I scowled. "No. It's just the first time he hasn't been here."

"He's busy. Like always. The only reason he's spent so much time here lately, I'm guessing, is because of you."

"Right," I muttered, ready to change the subject. "Do you own this place?"

"I just run it. I have a feeling you know who owns it."

"Zan."

"Along with Viggo and Pax." She leaned over the bar, as if wanting to keep the next words between us. "Everything in this city is theirs."

I frowned, glancing at Dee as she handed out drinks to a table. "What do the *K* tattoos stand for?"

Gia paused, looking at me thoughtfully. "Kane."

My lips parted, fear racing down my spine. "As in Amaros Kane?"

"Did you know about him when you were human?" She raised an eyebrow. "Or did someone mention him after you turned?"

I shook my head. "We grew up learning about him. And his sons. He's the reason for the war. For all the death."

She clicked her tongue, her eyes darkening. "I'd say the humans played a large role in the deaths too."

"Is he in this city?" I whispered. "Amaros?"

"No. His sons are."

My stomach twisted painfully as I stared at her in shock. The Kane sons were this close to Project Hope? This was the kind of news I needed to bring back to Tim. If I ever found a way out of this city. Realization hit me, and I straightened up, pushing off the bar. The blood drained from my face, panic filling every inch of me.

"Ahh, looks like you figured it out." Gia laughed, going back to washing the glasses.

"Zan," I choked out. "He's a Kane?"

"Along with Viggo and Pax. Half brothers," she answered cheerily.

Holy shit. Not only had I been pissing off a vampire who could kill me in a second, I'd been defying one who was part of the most notorious vampire family. The one who'd spearheaded the war. Why the fuck hadn't he killed me yet? I should have figured it out sooner with how the other vampires acted around them. But I just thought they had control here in the city—not all over the fucking country.

"Gia, you know you're not supposed to blurt that out."

I whirled around to see Pax striding toward me, his lips set in an annoyed frown.

"She was going to find out," Gia said from behind me, not sounding worried in the least. Unlike others in here, she didn't seem to fear them. I wondered how important she was. "And with that necklace, she's not going to run off and tell anyone. She would have learned it at the center."

Pax swiped a hand down his face. "They don't learn until they've been trained enough to *trust*. She has not."

"Oops."

Gia walked off, leaving Pax glaring at her before he turned his attention to me. "We need to talk. Now."

Before I could say anything, he grabbed my arm and practically dragged me through the club until he stopped in front of the room I'd changed clothes in on my first night here. He pushed me inside before stepping in behind me and shutting the door. Grumbling something I couldn't hear under his breath, he fell onto the couch where my gun was hidden, making my heart skip a beat.

"Sit down," he ordered, nodding to the couch across from him.

Crossing my arms, I moved slowly, sitting down where he'd motioned. He leaned back, and I bit my tongue, knowing my gun was literally on the other side of the cushion. I was rigid, wondering what he wanted. This was the first time he'd directly talked to me since the night I got here.

"This is becoming a problem," he said gruffly. "I'm keeping your secret and lying to my brothers."

My eyes widened, and I glanced at the door.

"It's a soundproof room. No one can hear us."

His words had me looking back at him, and I didn't like

what I was seeing. He didn't want to keep my secret anymore.

"If you help me get this necklace off, then I can just leave—"

"That's not an option anymore," he cut me off sharply. "You've learned too much. How this place operates. The weakness of new vampires. And after what Gia just told you...there's no way I can let you walk away now."

He sounded almost sorry, but the resolve on his face proved he was telling the truth. Panic smothered my chest, and I scrambled to think of a way to get out of this.

"How much longer until you run out of that lotion?" he asked, his pointed stare staying on me.

"How do you know what that is?" I asked hoarsely.

He scoffed like I'd insulted him. "Humans are easy to interrogate. We know more than you'd think. How much longer until you can't mask your smell anymore?"

"Not long," I muttered. I had enough for maybe two weeks if I used it sparingly.

"I'm going to turn you."

I leaped off the couch, terror shooting through my veins. "No the fuck you're not."

He stood up, only the glass table separating us. "It's the only way. Unless you want to be killed. Because that's what is going to happen when they find out you're human. I can turn you, and you can go on acting how you've been. And I'll know our secrets are safe since you'll be one of us."

He sidestepped the table, making his way closer to me, and I stumbled back until I hit the wall, holding up my hands. "Wait. There has to be another way. Please."

I just needed to keep him talking until I could get closer to my gun. It was a soundproof room. I could shoot and stake him without anyone hearing. I could try to leave. But what about Warner? I couldn't just leave him. Fuck, my mind was racing, and Pax lost patience as he stalked toward me.

"You can entrance me," I nearly screamed just as he stopped in front of me. "Make me forget about it all."

He froze, studying me closely. "You have access to that lotion. And I doubt you've been surrounded by vampires for nearly a week without precautions. I bet you have hawthorn coursing through your system right now."

"I do," I admitted. "But I'll give it all to you. And I'll stop taking it. You can even search my room. How long does it take to get out of my system? A couple days?"

"Five days," he replied quietly, looking deep in thought.

I sucked in a breath, calming myself since it didn't look like he was going to attack at any moment. It didn't matter if he took the hawthorn from my bag. I had another way to keep from being entranced, but that was something he didn't need to know.

"Please," I begged, letting my voice crack. "I've lost everything. Don't take my humanity too."

"Fuck," he mumbled. "Fine. We'll try it your way first. But I'm warning you—if you do anything to try to leave before then, there's going to be a problem."

"I won't," I promised.

"I only turn people who want it," he said quietly. "I wouldn't enjoy if I had to do it to you. But I'd do it without hesitation to protect my family."

I stared at him in confusion. "I thought vampires didn't care about anyone but themselves?"

"Partly true. But if you had a special bond with someone as a human, then that stays with you even as a vampire. It doesn't usually happen unless you're around that human after you turn." He sat back down on the couch, and I relaxed a fraction. "I will do anything for my brothers. They mean as much to me as they did when we were human."

"But you care about my choices, and I mean nothing to you," I pointed out.

He raised an eyebrow. "I saw the pain in your eyes the first night I met you. You have burdens. Just like me. Well, just like everyone. But for some reason, I felt bad. Consider yourself lucky."

"Thank you for keeping my secret," I mumbled, my stomach knotting from feeling thankful for a damn vampire.

"Go back to work," he said, ending the conversation abruptly. "No more ingesting hawthorn. If I can't entrance you, I'll turn you."

"Got it," I clipped out, moving toward the door.

"Don't make me regret this," he warned as I opened the door.

I glanced over my shoulder, managing to give him a small smile. "I won't."

My stomach bubbled with my lie. He wouldn't be able to entrance me. Now I just needed a plan to get both Warner and myself out of here before he figured it out. I allowed myself to look at Warner, and he was nearly shaking as he sat in the cage. When was the last time he'd had food or water? He couldn't die before I was able to get him out of here. Pax had stayed in the room, and I found Gia arguing with some vampires near the pool tables.

I walked casually behind the bar, grabbing an apple from the basket of fruit. I could just set this in his cage without him even seeing me. And since he was situated in a corner, it would be easy to get away with it. Vampires barely acknowledged me because of Zan's necklace. I crossed my arms, keeping the apple hidden as I slowly crossed the room, making sure no one was watching me.

My pulse thudded as I stepped up to the side of the cage. Warner was still staring at the wall, and he couldn't see me from this angle. It took everything in me not to call out his name. But it was too dangerous with so many ears around. I spotted Gia still on the other side of the dance floor, and I uncrossed my arms, reaching out to set the apple between the bars.

Until someone came up beside me, and a hand dropped on my arm, fingers curling tightly around my wrist.

Chapter 17
Kali

My heart fell to my stomach when I snapped my head up, panic invading every cell in my body. The apple fell from my grip, hitting my foot before it rolled to the floor.

"What is this?" Zan murmured. His hold on my wrist was tight as his eyes stayed locked on mine.

I opened my mouth, but not a sound came out. I didn't know what the hell I could say to explain this. I hadn't even seen him come inside the club. Something moved out of the corner of my eye, and Viggo stepped into my sight, staying behind Zan.

"What are you doing, Kali?" Zan's dangerously soft question pulled my attention back to him.

"Kali?" Warner's voice was full of shock, and I turned my head to see him staring at me. Relief filled his eyes, and he scrambled to his feet, moving until his hands gripped the bars in front of me. His face was a mess, with a black eye and a swollen cheek. But he still shot me the comforting smile that had always grounded me when we were kids. Until his gaze fell on my clothes and then darted to Zan.

His shoulders tensed, murder filling his eyes when he realized Zan was touching me.

"You know him?" Zan hissed, his voice full of suspicion.

"Everyone out. Now," Viggo shouted. It only took a few seconds for the music to shut off before everyone raced to the door, leaving their drinks and drugs scattered on the tables. Only Gia remained, watching us curiously as she stayed behind the bar.

"What the hell is going on?" Pax asked, coming out of the small room and walking closer to us.

"Kali was just going to explain that. Weren't you?" Zan released my arm, only to step fully in front of me.

But Warner spoke before I could. "Kali, look at me. Please."

He barely choked out the words, and his heartbreak was too much to ignore. I sucked in shallow breaths, turning away from Zan to look at him. His face fell, his eyes searching mine for anything.

"How do you know him?" Zan gritted out.

When I didn't answer, fingers caught my chin before Zan forced me to tear my gaze from Warner. He kept his hold on my jaw, refusing to let me look away from him.

"This is not a question you can ignore like all the others I've asked you," he warned. "Who the fuck is he?"

I swallowed thickly, fear lighting through me, and I sagged in relief when he let me go. But his eyes gleamed dangerously, and he turned toward the cage. His arm flew out, his fingers wrapping around Warner's throat before yanking him forward, making his nose slam into one of the bars. Then he started squeezing until Warner was choking out breaths.

"Stop," I screamed. I lunged forward, only for someone to grab me around the waist, yanking me back. I didn't take the time to check if it was Pax or Viggo as I was dragged backward.

"Who is he?" Zan asked again, his voice perfectly calm, yet steeped in violence. He stared at Warner, looking bored as he tightened his grip.

"He can't breathe," I shrieked, my mind clouding with panic when Warner's face turned a shade darker. "You're killing him."

"No. You're killing him," Zan shot back. "Answer my question. And I swear, if you lie to me, neither of you will leave here alive."

"I've known him my whole life," I choked out, unable to stop the tears from flowing.

Zan's face didn't reveal anything, and I screamed when he didn't stop. The arms tightened around me, keeping me back as I struggled.

"His name," Zan spat out. "What is it?"

"Warner," I cried. "His name is Warner."

Zan relaxed his hold, and a sob escaped me when Warner sucked in choppy breaths as Zan kept his hand around Warner's neck. Viggo moved beside me, making me realize it was Pax who was holding onto me.

"A bond strong enough for her to hold on to after transition," Viggo muttered, giving Zan a long look.

I frowned in confusion until I remembered what Pax had told me. Human bonds survived even after people were turned into vampires. They still believed I was a vampire. I wasn't sure if that helped right now. My heart was racing out of control, and I was sure all three of them could hear it with how quiet it was now that no one else was here.

"Do you love her?" Zan cocked his head, his stare on Warner.

Warner glared daggers at him, keeping his mouth

closed. Disgust and loathing covered his face until Zan squeezed, and Warner flailed when his air was cut off again.

"Zan," I pleaded, my voice raw with emotion. "We grew up together. He's like my brother."

"He's not looking at you like a sibling." Zan glanced at me, his eyes cold. "Have you been with him?"

I hesitated for only a second, but it was enough for Zan to think I was lying. With a snarl, he shoved Warner back hard enough that he fell to the floor of the cage. I'd never been with Warner, not sexually—not even a kiss. But we'd talked about it. Promised each other that if we lived past twenty-five, we were going to try it. Build a life in this hell together and have each other to lean on.

I loved him because he was *always* there for me. He was my comfort. My safe place. He'd never let me down. It wasn't sparks of love or lust, but I never expected to find that in this life. Warner was reliable. He was as close to a home as I'd ever had.

Warner climbed back to his feet, his devastated expression cracking my heart. Pax slowly let me go, and I looked over my shoulder to see him glowering at me. He was definitely regretting keeping my secret now.

"Did he turn you?" Warner growled hoarsely, hitting his hands on the bar. "I'll fucking kill them—"

"He doesn't know?" Viggo cut him off with a callous laugh. "What a shit way to find out."

I threw him a scathing look, and he gave me a shrug. Zan's eyes darted between me and Warner before he reached forward and grabbed me, pulling me in front of him. He situated me just like he had on the dance floor a couple of nights ago, with my back pressed to his chest. I was facing the cage, and Warner watched, his jaw muscle flexing when Zan wrapped one arm around my waist.

"She's with us now," Zan said, the possessiveness in his tone making the back of my neck prickle. "Where were you when a vampire turned her?"

Warner let out a shout of fury, horror crossing his face when he looked at me again. "Fuck, Kali. I'm so sorry I wasn't there."

Anguish sliced my heart as we stared at each other. He was already mourning me. He thought I was gone. And I couldn't blurt out that I was still human. No matter how hard it was. I knew how devastated I'd be if I were in his position. If we had any chance of getting out of this, he had to believe I was a vampire.

I jerked when Zan's fingers softly touched my skin. He slowly traced my collarbone, and I stilled, not understanding what the hell he was doing. Warner watched him, rage quickly replacing the sadness when Zan's fingers dipped lower, grazing my skin around the necklace.

"You left her alone and look what happened." Zan's voice was mocking. Cruel. And it had the effect he wanted, because Warner recoiled like he'd been hit.

"It wasn't his fault," I snapped.

"Mmm," Zan hummed out. "Protecting him? Now I understand why you've been so compliant the last two nights. And here I thought you were warming up to me. But no—it's because he's here."

I didn't dignify that with a response. Viggo took out a pack of rolled cigarettes and took one out before putting it to his mouth. He lit it, his stare staying on Warner as his brows furrowed.

"Should I turn him?" Zan whispered in my ear. "Give the two of you eternal life together?"

My blood turned to ice, and I stayed silent because any

answer was dangerous. He was playing a game that I didn't know the rules to.

"Bad idea," Viggo retorted, blowing out a lungful of smoke. "Her bond with him is strong, and his will be the same. He'll never follow our orders. Not when it comes to her."

"True," Zan mused. "Kill him then?"

"Don't," I breathed out, unable to hold it back.

"Fine. Then he stays in the cage," Zan said simply. I was suddenly free, and I spun around to see him backing away.

My eyes cut to Pax and then to Viggo before going back to Zan. "What are you doing?"

"Letting him live." Zan strolled to the bar where Gia already had his favorite drink waiting. "Go home, Kali. You have the rest of the night off."

"What?" I sputtered, planting my feet. "I'm not going anywhere."

"Go," Gia ordered. "We'll see you tomorrow."

I snuck a glance at Warner. "I've seen two humans die in these cages. Vampires feed on them all night."

"Warner will be fine. Right, Gia?" Zan drawled before sipping his drink.

"If that's what you want," Gia replied in her bubbly voice. "It's your club."

"Wait, wait," another voice called out. "I know her too."

I turned to see a man in a cage on the other side of the room, gripping the bars desperately. His graying hair was everywhere, and his unshaven beard was halfway down his neck. He was still wearing a tactical uniform that was ripped and filthy.

Zan raised an eyebrow. "You know her?"

The man nodded frantically. "Yes. And she wants me to stay alive."

Pax grabbed my arm, warning me to stay quiet with a shake of his head. I wasn't going to say anything anyway. I didn't know this man, but I wasn't going to make life harder on him either. Zan advanced toward the guy's cage, stopping right in front.

"Okay, then what's her favorite fruit?" Zan asked, sounding curious.

"It's, uh, strawberries," the man stammered out, looking at me like I could help him.

"Wrong." Zan's arm shot through the bar, his hand going around the guy's throat just like he did with Warner. "It's apples. You know what happens when humans lie in here."

"Fuck you," the guy spat out with fury. "Fucking bloodsucker. You're all devils. You and all the others walking around like real men. The female vampires walking around like sluts. Just like her. When the humans invade this city, they'll give her what she deserves and make all of you watch."

"Too bad you won't get the chance to watch anything else."

With those words, Zan tightened his grip, squeezing until blood trailed down the guy's neck from where he dug in his nails. The man writhed, his mouth open in a silent scream. My chest heaved as I watched, knowing anything I said wouldn't help. Pax didn't let me go until the man's eyes rolled and the only thing holding him up was Zan's hold.

After a few more moments, Zan released him, and his body hit the floor of the cage with a thud. I didn't have to check to know the guy wasn't breathing. He was already dead. Zan turned back toward me.

"Warner will live. For now." He locked his stare on me.

"Go home. Actually, go for a walk. I'll even tell the watchers you're free to leave the city tonight. Enjoy your time off."

I clenched my teeth when I finally figured it out. He was using Warner against me. He knew I wouldn't leave now because the person I cared for was here locked in a cage. There was no need for threats or chains. Not when he could hang Warner's life over my head.

He grinned, his eyes still screaming danger as he waited for me to argue. Instead, I raised my chin and gave Warner one more look before walking stiffly toward the front door. Warner was screaming threats at Zan, but I didn't look back. It wouldn't change anything. I wasn't even sure Pax would go through with his plan to entrance me after this. I needed to come up with a new idea. Before Zan lost his patience and killed Warner. Or me.

Chapter 18
Zan

"I'm getting bored," Viggo complained, sagging in his chair. "Please tell me we aren't spending another night here."

"Then go," I snapped. "I'm not keeping you here."

Pax shook his head. "You've been in a fucking mood since last night. Go feed and cool off."

"I ate earlier."

Viggo scoffed. "A blood bag is not enough. You need it straight from the vein to calm you down."

"I'm calm," I forced out through clenched teeth.

Impulse was still empty. Gia and Dee were rushing around cleaning up, and I expected Kali to show up the second she could leave the hotel once the sun went down. Although with how new she was, she could still stand the sun. I wondered if she was aware of that. Probably not since she knew nothing of being a vampire.

I turned my attention toward the cage in the back, my anger rising even more. *Warner*. He was standing and leaning against the bars, his glare focused right on me like it had been since I entered the room. I shot him a cold smirk, and his fingers tightened around the bars. I should have fucking killed him.

"You know, we can entrance him to find out about her," Viggo spoke up, making me look back at him.

"I don't need him for anything," I replied, not admitting I'd already thought about that. I wasn't above doing that if needed, but I wanted to learn it from her.

Viggo snickered. "She wasn't forthcoming before last night. I doubt she's going to say a word to you now. You saw her face, Zan. Her emotions have been locked down since you dragged her here, but she couldn't hide anything when you nearly killed him."

"But I didn't. He's still alive."

Pax frowned. "And why didn't you kill him?"

"Isn't it obvious?" Viggo snorted. "He wants her, and killing the one human she has a bond with would wreck that completely. Although I don't think you had much of a chance with her anyway. I don't know why you have a hard-on for the only one who wants nothing to do with you."

"Fuck off," I snapped.

"Apples?" Pax shook his head. Unlike Viggo, he wasn't giving me shit. He was honestly confused about why I was so focused on her. "You know her favorite fruit. Learning about her is more than just sex."

"She eats at least two every night," I muttered. "It's kind of hard to miss."

"I never noticed," Viggo replied. "But I'm also not obsessed."

I stared at him, silently warning him that he was pushing me past my limit.

Viggo raised his arms, giving me a taunting smirk. "Hey, maybe I'm wrong. She might be so thankful you didn't kill him that she'll fall right into bed with you."

The front door slammed, and I raised my head to see Kali striding inside. Her gaze went to Warner first before glancing at me. Her eyes lit up with loathing, and I could practically feel the burn of her glare. Her lips tipped in a scowl before she turned and moved toward the bar.

"Nope," Viggo drawled, clearly still intent on pissing me the hell off. "She's definitely not going to fall to her knees to thank you. Might as well kill him since it won't make a difference."

"I think you should remember that she's a fucking newbie," Pax said stiffly. "Getting close to her is a mistake. And since she's not at the center, she's not going to fall in line and obey when you're giving her special attention. She's going to be a liability."

"Then I'll deal with her if that happens."

I didn't wait for either of them to reply as I jumped to my feet and made my way to the bar. Gia saw me coming, and she poured me a whiskey, setting it on the counter before returning to setting up for the night. Kali stiffened as if sensing me coming, and she peeked over her shoulder, quickly ducking around the bar to stand beside Gia. Grabbing a rag, she began drying glasses, purposely ignoring me.

The red strobe lights came on, and there was a commotion behind me when vampires started coming inside. The second the tables started filling, Kali rushed off to take orders. I continued to stand at the bar, watching her. She wasn't going to keep giving me the silent treatment, but I impatiently waited until I decided what to do.

I raised an eyebrow when she faltered slightly. The fullest table was right next to Warner's cage. She straightened up, looking at the vampires instead of the cage, and I focused on her, drowning everything else out. With the music and chatter, it was harder to pick up the quieter noises, but if I fixated, then I could do it. Just like I thought he would, Warner attempted to get her attention.

"Kali," he said in a loud whisper. "Fuck. Just look at me."

Her shoulders tensing was the only proof that she heard him. She didn't look at him, and he frowned, looking unsure before he called out to her again. I swallowed, my fists clenching. Some humans would completely turn their backs once their loved ones were turned. Others would still try to save the vampire's humanity because they couldn't let go. It was easy to see that even if she wasn't human anymore, he wasn't ready to give her up. Would that change once she fully transitioned?

"I couldn't get out for another day," Warner said quietly, his voice full of pain. "I'm sorry I couldn't protect you."

Kali finally looked at him, but her back was to me, making it impossible to see her face. Until she glanced over her shoulder, catching my eye immediately. Her expression fell flat, and she turned back around, focusing on the vampires. I chuckled before finishing my drink. She was smart enough to know I was listening.

Warner whipped his head up, the possessiveness in his gaze making me snap. She wasn't his anymore. She was a vampire, and he needed to fucking learn that she would never be with him again. The only reason I hadn't killed him was because I remembered how the bonds felt after transitioning. I'd always been close to Pax and Viggo, but it grew even stronger after. If she felt the same way about him, then her actions wouldn't even be her own anymore. She'd only want revenge.

So I was letting him live. But it didn't mean I needed to sit here and do nothing while he pined for her.

Pushing off the bar, I stalked toward her as Warner watched me with murder in his eyes. I kept his stare while stopping behind her and wrapping an arm around her waist. All the vampires at the table went silent, nodding at me in respect. Kali fell still, letting out a cry when I tightened my hold and swung her around. She raised her head to look at me, her lips pressed in a line, keeping her words to herself.

"We need to talk," I informed her before leading her away from the table. Warner wasn't being quiet now when he yelled Kali's name. The asshole was going to get himself killed if he kept attracting attention when the bar was full. Although Gia wouldn't let that happen when I told her that I wanted him kept alive.

"Kali will be back later," I muttered to Gia as we passed the bar.

When she realized I was taking her out of Impulse, she began struggling, but I kept my arm banded around her waist as I brought her outside. Once we were on the street, I let her go only to grasp her hand, interlocking my fingers with hers.

"What are you doing?" she hissed, failing to pull away from me.

"Giving you a chance to do what you've been wanting ever since I met you."

"What does that mean?"

I didn't answer, not slowing down as we walked through the streets. I glanced at her when we turned a corner, and panic was in her eyes as I took her farther away from the city center. After cutting through a building and passing two more streets, we made it to the park. The grass was dead and brown, and there was debris scattered on the ground, but it was the largest spot in the city with no buildings. There were picnic tables with rotting wood and trees surrounding the grassy area. A few vampires were messing around, and they all froze when they spotted me.

"Leave." My command was followed instantly, and they raced out of the park.

I pulled Kali into the center of the park before finally releasing her hand. She scrambled back, putting at least ten feet between us. She stared at me warily, her body staying rigid.

"You admitted you want to kill me," I murmured. "Here's your chance to try."

Her eyes widened. "Excuse me?"

"Go ahead," I pressed, taking a step toward her. "Try it."

Her eyes darted around, as if checking that we were actually alone. She didn't make a move to come at me, but she wasn't backing away either. Her heart was beating faster than normal, proving I had her on edge, which was exactly what I wanted. She refused to answer my questions any other time, so I was going about this a different way. I was also curious to see what she'd do when we were alone.

"I'm no match for you," she spat out. "We both know it."

"Scared?" I taunted, slowly retaking the space between us.

"No. I'm just not stupid."

I tsked. "Lying to me is stupid. You should have told me you knew that human the second he came into the club."

Her eyes flared with anger, her hands curling into fists. "It was none of your business."

"I'm making you my business," I stated, closing in on her. She was watching every step I took, but she still didn't try to run. "And I'm tired of you not answering my questions."

She raised her chin to keep her glare on me as I stopped right in front of her. "Well, we can't always get what we want. I'm tired of a certain asshole vampire trying to control me, but here we are."

I arched an eyebrow, a spark of excitement jolting through my veins at the fiery glare she was giving me. "I'm giving you a chance to stop me. Why are you stalling?"

"Because you're fucking with me," she snapped.

"You're going to fight me—"

"I don't know how to fight," she cut me off irritably. "You want to hurt me, then just do it."

"If I wanted to hurt you, I would have kept you at Impulse and made you watch while I tortured that human you're soft for."

Her jaw clenched. "Then why are we out here?"

"I'm giving you free rein to try to kill me." I grinned. "But when you fail, and I pin you, then you owe me a truth. Then we'll go again."

She frowned, staring at me with open suspicion. "Why'd you bring me all the way out here to do that?"

"Because I didn't want an audience."

"How do you know I won't lie to you?"

"Believe me, Kali, I'll know if you lie to me," I murmured. "And you won't like what happens. I want truths only."

"*If* you can pin me," she tossed back. "Maybe I'll kill you before that."

I couldn't hold back my laugh. She had no chance, but apparently, she was up for the challenge. I reached forward and lightly grabbed the necklace on her chest. She didn't move, her eyes not leaving mine.

"Do your worst," I ordered in a low voice, letting the pendant drop back to her skin and waiting for her to make the first move.

She fidgeted with the shirt Gia had gifted her. It was a

black tank top, and lucky for her, it wasn't strapless like the corset she'd been wearing the last two nights. The jeans she was wearing were tight, but probably not as restrictive as the leather pants. She still had the boots on that she'd come into the city with. Her hair was pulled in a high ponytail that she seemed to favor over wearing it down.

"How am I supposed to kill you when I don't have a stake?" she ground out.

"Get creative."

My mocking tone had her bristling, and I got impatient when she didn't make a move to come after me. I lunged forward, and she twisted away, ducking just out of reach. She stayed light on her feet, moving in a small circle, scrutinizing everything I did. When I angled my feet to go left, she immediately shuffled to the right. She could read my moves. Interesting. I had a feeling she wasn't being completely honest about not being able to fight.

There was only one way to find out.

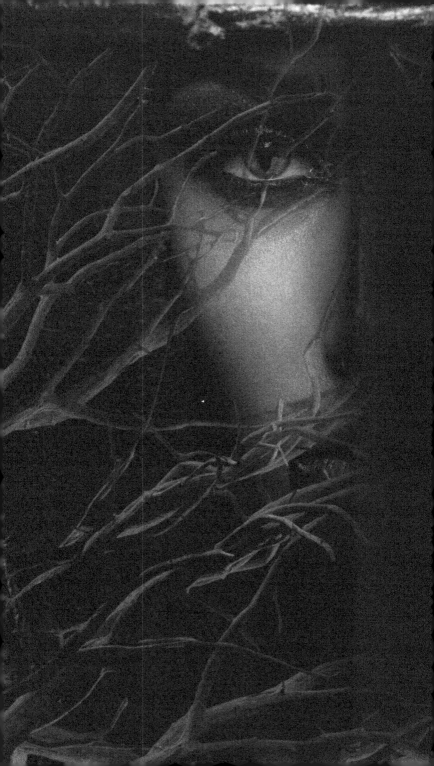

Chapter 19
Zan

This time I came after her with more speed, making it impossible for her to guess my next move. I snatched her wrist while kicking her feet out from under her. She let out a cry when she went down, and I jumped on top of her. I still had a hold of one of her arms, and her other fist slammed into my ribs. It was a sloppy hit and felt like nothing. Before she could swing again, I grabbed her wrist, forcing both of her arms over her head as I leaned over her.

"Give me a truth," I said, giving her a smug grin. "Or I don't let you back up."

She twisted in my hold, a frustrated shriek escaping her lips. She bucked her hips, attempting to throw me off, but I didn't budge. Her chest heaved as she glared up at me.

"What truth?" she hissed.

"How old are you?"

"Sixteen. What a big bad vampire you are to scare a little girl."

I didn't respond to her lie right away, listening to her heartbeat. I frowned, realizing how slow it was. It was still slightly elevated, but not as erratic as I was expecting it to be. She tilted her head, watching me curiously as I tightened my hold on her wrists even though she wasn't struggling anymore.

"How old are you?" I asked again. "And please, an answer that's fucking believable."

"Twenty-one."

There was no jump or skip to her heartbeat when she answered, and I paused, annoyance flaring through me. It could be her real age, but there wasn't any part of me that believed she'd tell the truth about anything. Plus, she looked older than that.

I let it go and climbed off her. She jumped to her feet, and I was on her in seconds, taking her to the ground again. This time she landed on her stomach, and I straddled her back. I fisted her ponytail, arching her neck back as she hissed curses at me.

I aimed to make my next question more emotional. "Do you love him? Warner?"

Her heart didn't miss a beat when she answered. "No."

With a snarl, I moved to stand, letting go of her hair. She hauled herself off the ground, taking the time to brush dead grass off her jeans. To my shock, she grinned at me, her gaze taunting.

"Are you lying?" I gritted out.

Her eyes widened with bullshit innocence. "Am I? You told me that you'd know if I was, so why are you questioning it?"

Her voice was overly sweet, a tone I'd never heard from her. She danced away from me when I went for her again.

"Oh, wait," she exclaimed, darting behind a picnic table to separate me from her. "I know why you brought me out here."

I studied her, annoyance coursing through my veins. "And why's that?"

"Is the silence helping, Zan?" She cocked her head. "Can you hear if I'm lying?"

I prowled closer to her, and she kept moving, keeping the picnic table between us. She knew what I was trying to do. Listening to heartbeats was the best way to catch lies if I couldn't entrance. I'd perfected it in the last seven years.

"Lie to me again, and I'll kill him," I threatened, needing to shake her enough to hear how her heart reacted to it.

Her heart didn't patter or skip from my words. It stayed even as she stared at me. *Fuck me.* She'd had practice. Which meant she'd had training to protect herself against vampires. I wanted to know what else she'd learned.

"You've been holding out on me," I said in a low voice. "Controlling your heartbeat like that takes skill."

"I didn't hold out. You never asked."

I scoffed. "Because you would have told me."

"Sure, I would have." She paused for a long second. "Or not. I don't know. Can you tell if I'm lying?"

"You've made your point," I gritted out. "Were you PARA as a human?"

"Still asking questions when you know I won't tell you the truth. Not very smart, are you?"

I gaped at her, anger rushing through me. This was not how I was expecting it to go when I brought her out here.

"No, not PARA," I answered my own question, determined to get back on top of this game. "Tattoos are illegal, and I've seen the one on your back. Where'd you get it?"

The flowers that covered the top of her back made me want to see the rest of the tattoo. I'd been curious about it since I saw it the first night she wore the new clothes. Tattoo ink was hard to come by, especially to humans.

She didn't say a word, so I asked another question. "Why did you let me find out? Why not play it off like you were telling the truth?"

She narrowed her eyes. "Would you have believed me if I answered every single question truthfully?"

"No."

"Then you would have realized it anyway. I just saved time."

"What kind of secrets are you keeping?" I suddenly jumped on top of the picnic table and leaped down, landing right in front of her. Surprise filtered across her face, but she didn't move.

"How long have you been a vampire?" she asked.

"I'm the one asking things tonight," I snapped.

"You won't get the truth out of me. Not this way."

"Shall we go back, then?" I grabbed her arm, tugging her closer. "Because I know of a way to get you to talk."

The threat of hurting Warner had her anger rising again. "You told me I had a chance to kill you. I haven't gotten to try yet."

"We both know that's not possible." I'd brought her here to learn about her, but now that it was off the table since I couldn't tell her lies from her truths, I was done with this game.

"How about if you give me your word that you won't hurt Warner for a week, I'll tell the truth to your questions?"

I went rigid when she wrapped an arm around me, willingly pulling me closer to her for the first time since we'd met. She had to keep her head tilted back to look at me, and I searched for any signs of deception.

"A week?" I queried. "That's too long."

"Seven days of his safety for my truths."

"And how do I know you won't lie?"

"When I make a deal, I keep my word."

"Hmm," I mused as she shifted against me. "Fine. Deal. But a word of warning, Kali. If I find out you lied, then I won't just threaten his life. I'll fucking take it. And I don't break my promises. Do you understand?"

She nodded curtly. I didn't move, not hating how she felt pressed up against me.

"I wasn't with PARA," she stated. "I'm not twenty-one. And yes, I love Warner. Because he's the only person I have left in this world."

I stared down at her, processing her words until a sharp pain seared through my lower back. I hissed out a breath, shoving her away before swiping my hand over where the pain was radiating from. I clenched my jaw, yanking out the thing buried in my skin. Bringing my hand back in front of me, I stared at the wooden stick in disbelief.

"Did that hurt?" Kali asked in the same sickly sweet voice.

I whipped my head up to see her already on the other side of the picnic table again with her eyes gleaming with danger. My gaze fell to the ground, seeing branches and twigs littered around. I hadn't even seen her pick it up.

I forced out a chuckle, acting like she hadn't just gotten the drop on me. "You missed my heart."

"That stick isn't big enough to touch your black heart," she shot back. "But this is."

She kicked at the seat of the table, breaking off a piece of wood that wasn't rotting. It was thick, and when it snapped off, it made a pointed end, close enough to resemble a stake. She twirled it in her hand, watching me expectantly.

This was a far cry from the girl who shuffled around the bar, keeping her head down. She'd been hiding a lot from me. Too much. And I wanted to find it all out.

"You're going to try that even though you know you won't be able to stake me?" I asked, noticing how firmly she was holding the piece of wood. And expertly. This wasn't the first time she'd held a stake.

"Are you scared?" she mocked.

"There's little in this world that I fear." I rounded the table. "One new little vampire will never make that list."

She backed away, moving into the open area again where there were no trees or tables. That was a mistake on her part. Being able to separate herself from me would be an advantage.

"Have you killed a vampire before?" I asked my first question, wondering if she'd be honest.

"Yes."

No change to her heartbeat. Although, I couldn't rely on that when it came to her. But she did care for Warner, which meant she'd do what she could to keep him safe. If the truth kept him alive for seven more days, then I had a feeling her answers would be true. And it really pissed me off that I cared that she was doing all this to protect a man.

"What's your last name?"

"Smith."

"Smith," I repeated in surprise. "That name is reserved for—"

"Orphans," she cut me off. "That's what I am. A lonely orphan."

"What you *were*." I kept an eye on her makeshift stake

202

as I got within arm's distance of her. "You won't be alone again. Not as a vampire."

Uncertainty swept over her face. "I'll never be happy here."

"You better try," I murmured. "I have no interest in letting you go anytime soon."

My words made her snap, and she lunged at me in a practiced move. The stake was going straight for my heart while she jabbed her other hand into my throat. I let her nearly crush my windpipe to go for her wrist that was holding the weapon. I could survive without breathing, even if her hit did hurt like a bitch.

The stake was inches from my chest when I stopped her attack, and her eyes blazed with determination, trying to push against my strength. I shot her an amused smirk, slowly moving the stake farther from me.

"How'd you get into my city without anyone knowing about it?" I asked another question as she stumbled away once I let her go.

"I walked right in from the street," she pushed out between heavy breaths. "Your watchers aren't doing their job very well. I had no idea it was a vampire city when I came."

Well, shit. That was going to need rectifying. "When did you get here?"

"The same night you found me."

I'd have Pax look at who was on duty that night. At least I'd gotten one piece of useful information out of this. She hesitated for a moment before reaching behind her and tucking the stake into the waistband at her back.

"I'm done," she said with a roll of her eyes. "It's a waste of time when I can't kill you. And I don't feel like sharing anything else."

"Too bad. I'm not finished with you. I want more." I strode forward, catching her arm before she could scramble out of reach again. "Tell me something. Something you've never told anyone else. Not even him."

Her eyes widened before she scowled. "That's not fair."

"The truth," I reminded her. "Unless you want me to leave here and have fun with Warner."

She swallowed thickly, not fighting me when I pulled her closer until her chest smashed against mine.

"I..." She stopped and cleared her throat. "Do you read books?"

"What?" Her question threw me off.

"Fiction. Made up stories."

I shook my head. "No."

"That's all I did growing up. There was a library in my city, and I would spend hours curled up in the corner reading. It's how I learned so much about how life was before the war." She was almost whispering, and for once, her heart rate changed, pumping faster. "And I read so many stories about people falling in love. I remember wishing that I'd feel it. The amazing feeling of true love. Finding my person. But I never did. And I realized why it's just in books. That will never happen in this world."

I went still as a statue when her hand slipped under my shirt, her fingers trailing softly over my abs. Fear was blatant in her gaze as she looked at me, but there was something else there too that I couldn't decipher.

"But when *you* touch me, I feel something," she breathed out. "And I don't understand it."

Now it was my heart that was pounding against my ribs as she kept touching me. She raised on her tiptoes until her lips were hovering so close to mine that I could feel her shallow breaths. She hesitated, as if waiting for me to refuse her, but my head was still spinning. I'd never talked to a woman like this. It was always just about sex.

"And now I'm wondering what else you can make me feel," she whispered.

Her lips crashed to mine, and I brought my hand behind her neck, bringing her closer. I pushed my tongue into her mouth, letting out a groan. She tasted better than I fucking imagined. She eagerly kissed me back, her small moan making my dick grow hard. The things I wanted to do to her—

There was a stinging pain on my chest, and terror lit through me when I realized it was right over my heart. I ripped my mouth away, my eyes cutting to hers. Only wicked determination was filling her gaze, and my rage exploded. I glanced down to see the stake pressed against my chest, hard enough to break skin.

"Strength isn't the only way I can beat you," she purred, her voice full of dangerous promises. "I could have killed you right here."

"Then why didn't you?" I hissed, tearing the stake from her hand. Fury was radiating from me, and I stepped away to get back in control.

"Because you're a Kane." She crossed her arms. "I'd be dead the second I walked into Impulse without you. Like I said before—I'm not stupid."

It wasn't a surprise that she knew who I was. Pax had told me that Gia ran her mouth. The shock was that I'd fallen for her act. She drew out a weakness that I didn't even know I had. Fuck. She was becoming my weakness. There was no way I'd let that happen again.

"I need to get back to work," she sang out, turning away from me. "And the whole thing about me reading is a truth, by the way. So don't touch Warner."

I watched her walk away. She would make a great vampire. My father would love her. Once she came to full strength, she'd be a perfect soldier. Strong and cunning.

Half of me wanted to strangle her. But the other half wanted to fucking kiss her again. She was growing more abrasive, like she knew I wouldn't kill her. The problem was, I wouldn't. Even after what just happened.

Chapter 20
Kali

I trudged through the streets, my stomach churning
with nerves. Another night at Impulse. I wasn't sure
how long I could do this. After I went back to the club
last night when Zan took me to the park, Warner had tried
to talk to me, and I couldn't even look at him. I wanted to
say so much to him, but not when Zan and the twins were
listening. What if I said something that screwed everything
up? I couldn't chance it.

I was even more apprehensive about facing Zan. I had
no idea how he was going to act after what happened last
night. He was probably going to be even more on edge
around me now. But it didn't matter. He was a Kane. I
couldn't kill him, or I'd be hunted by vampires for the rest of
my life, even if I did escape. The Kanes were vampire
royalty. Killing them was my last resort now. But if I could
do it without getting caught...it was a possibility. Especially
if it gave Warner and me a chance at freedom.

I'd also stabbed him because I needed to see how far I
could push him. He'd had chance after chance to hurt or kill
me, but here I was. He didn't want me dead. When I shoved

the stake into his chest, I half expected him to end me right there. But he didn't.

I pushed open the front door, unable to swallow my grin at the memory of Zan's face. When he realized I had the stake to his heart, the disbelief was worth it all. Even though I was sure he wouldn't fall for that twice.

"What's got you so happy?"

Gia stopped sweeping the floor to look at me, and I shrugged. "I slept well."

My gaze went to the cage Warner had been in, and my heart skipped, seeing it was empty. I turned my head, scanning the cages, finally stopping at the one near the corner. The corner where Zan and the twins always sat. Warner was inside, lying down, his chest moving up and down slowly as he slept.

"He's still alive," Gia said, following my gaze. "And no need to try to sneak more food to him. He's eating better than any other human in here."

"Why was he moved?" I asked, guilt eating me alive. Here I was, walking and living free—well, free-ish—while he was trapped in a cage.

"Zan wants to keep an eye on him. But I'm sure you already know that."

"He can watch him fine from any cage in here," I grumbled.

"Don't," she warned, her smile fading as I looked at her. "You push him too far and he'll snap."

My curiosity regarding how far I could push him was growing even more. After last night, he knew I was much more capable than I'd been letting on. Was he going to act differently now? He'd made a deal not to hurt Warner for a week, which was what I wanted. Because I needed to plan a way out before those seven days were up. Pax wasn't going to keep my secret much longer. He would either turn me or reveal I was human. I needed to be far away before he lost patience.

"Where'd he take you last night?" Gia asked, hooking my arm with hers and leading me to the bar. "I've never seen Zan Kane have such an interest in anyone, and I'm curious."

"How long have you known him?" I asked. It was rare to talk to Gia without anyone else around. Usually Dee was here, or Zan. The humans still filled the cages, but they weren't paying us any attention.

"Years," she answered.

She went behind the bar, and I sat down on one of the stools in front of her. "How old are you?"

"I'm thirty-five," she said with a wink, her usual cheery demeanor in place. Zan had warned me that she was dangerous, but I hadn't seen that side of her. She reminded me of a motherly figure. Or at least what I imagined a loving mother would be. She treated Dee and the other girls here like they were one of them. She gave me anything I needed with a smile on her face.

"How long have you been thirty-five?" I pressed.

"Seventy years."

"Is that how long you've known Zan?"

"No." She laughed as she pulled bottles of alcohol out of a cupboard. "Zan isn't nearly as old as me."

"How old is he?"

"Gia."

I tensed when his voice filled the room, slowly peeking over my shoulder to see Zan and the twins coming through the back door. I learned a couple of days ago that they lived upstairs, and no one ever went up there except the three of them.

"Hey, Zan." Gia greeted him, not sounding flustered at all, even though I'd heard the warning in his voice when he spoke her name. "Care to tell your girl how old you are?"

"I'm not his," I gritted out in a low voice, fully aware that he would still be able to hear me.

"Until she tells me her age, then she doesn't need to know mine," Zan clipped out.

Gia raised an eyebrow, looking between Zan and me before breathing out a laugh. "Hmm, something happened last night. I can feel the tension. Want to share?"

I bit my tongue, looking behind me to Zan again. Instead of the frown I was expecting, a smirk was playing on his lips, his calculating gaze swinging to the side before landing back on me. I straightened, realizing Warner was awake. He was sitting up, his entire body rigid as he glared at Zan. His face was still black and blue, but he looked a lot better than the first night he was here.

"Kali and I spent time alone," Zan drawled smugly. His arrogance had me bristling, and I stood from the stool to face him. The way he spoke made it clear his words were for Warner. Pax and Viggo were already sitting in their usual spots, and I took a moment to study them. I was sure it was Pax who was staring at me intently while Viggo smoked. I'd been able to start telling them apart by their mannerisms, which was the only way, because when it came to looks, they were identical unless their tattoos were visible.

"Alone?" Gia questioned, her humor flowing freely. "And what did you two do?"

I focused on my breathing, watching Zan cross the room with his usual confidence. He was listening to my heartbeat, wanting to get my reaction as he fucked with Warner's head since he couldn't physically touch him after the deal we'd made last night.

"Mmm," Zan hummed out, stopping right in front of me, keeping his words loud. "What did we do, Kali?"

I tipped my chin up defiantly, searching for the best way to play this. He was going to blurt out that I kissed him to hurt Warner. I could see it in his eyes. He was pissed that I'd gotten the upper hand last night, and here he was trying to claim control again.

Forcing a smile, I looked at Gia. "Zan asked me to try and kill him."

Gia didn't even blink, her amused smile growing even bigger. "Really?"

One of the twins—Viggo, I was guessing because of the cigarette between his fingers—had stood up and was strolling closer to us, sharing Gia's amusement as he caught my eye.

"How did that go?" Viggo asked, cocking his head.

My eyes cut back to Zan, and he was watching me expectantly, letting me answer first. Behind him, Warner was watching us with a scowl on his face.

"I had a stake digging into his chest before he knew what was happening," I stated.

Viggo howled with laughter. "Bullshit."

"She did. Even broke skin."

Zan's words had the entire atmosphere shifting. Gia nearly dropped the bottle she was holding, and her eyes swept over the empty room, as if making sure no others were here for this conversation. Viggo's grin dropped in an instant, his accusing glare shooting to Zan. Pax was still sitting with his mouth hanging open. His uncertainty about me was crystal clear when he caught my eye, making me swallow thickly. If he saw me as a threat, he wouldn't keep my secret.

"You let her get that close?" Viggo hissed, coming to stand next to Zan.

"Believe me, it was worth it." Zan erased the space between us, coming close enough that his chest brushed mine, backing me into the bar counter. "That kiss? I'd bleed for you again just for another taste."

"Zan," Gia scolded from behind me. "You can't let anyone get that close to you—even a pretty girl promising sex."

"I didn't promise anything," I forced out, keeping my voice steady. "In fact, the only reason I kissed him was to distract him."

"Maybe it started off that way." The dark grin tipping the corners of his lips had emotions warring inside me. "But after learning that you can control your heartbeat—"

"She can do *what*?" Pax cut in sharply from across the room.

"Yes," Zan mused, his eyes not leaving mine. "It seems the young little vampire has human secrets she's been holding onto."

I gritted my teeth, not saying a word. I couldn't control my heart rate perfectly. I had still been learning when I had to flee Project Hope. I had to concentrate and focus ridiculously hard. The only reason I was able to do it at the park last night was because I was expecting it once Zan asked me for truths. If it was in the heat of the moment, I couldn't do it. Not right away anyway.

"But when we kissed, she let her guard down," Zan continued, dropping his head until his lips were a breath from mine. "Her heart gave her away. She might have done it for ulterior motives, but she loved it."

"Or maybe that's what I wanted you to believe," I quipped, feeling my neck flushing and hoping to everything my cheeks weren't heating. Discussing what happened last night in front of everyone was not what I expected to happen when I walked into Impulse.

"Shall we test that theory?" Zan's hands were suddenly on my hips, crushing me to him. "I want to hear what your heart sounds like when you're not scheming. I bet it'll sound the same as when you were moaning into my mouth."

Fuck. He was calling my bluff. There was an angry snarl from somewhere in the back of the room, reminding me that Warner was listening to everything. Zan had made sure to speak loud enough for all the caged humans in the room to hear. It was the whole reason he was doing this. To prove that even though he would keep his word about not touching Warner, he was still very much in control, contrary to what I had done to him last night.

Warner's voice filled the air for a split second before Pax overrode it with a threat to shut up. My heart pattered despite myself, and I could feel all their stares on me. Warner was still worried for me. He still *cared*. Even though he thought I was a vampire. And from how I just reacted to his voice, every vampire in here knew that he affected me.

"Let me go," I demanded, my voice stone cold.

Zan didn't move, keeping me trapped between the counter and his hard body. But before he could respond, there was a loud banging coming from the front. Viggo cursed under his breath, striding to the door, and flicked the lock. He swung the door open, revealing a vampire who looked ready to piss himself.

"When these doors are closed, it means no one comes in." Viggo's words were steeped in danger, and I now understood why the vampire looked so terrified. "You better have a damn good reason to interrupt us."

"I'm sorry," the vampire squeaked out. "But the watchers—they told me I needed to announce his arrival."

Zan instantly shot away like I'd burned him, his eyes looking behind me. Viggo was furiously whispering something to the vampire outside the door, and I couldn't see Pax from here, but I didn't have a chance to gather my thoughts before I was suddenly yanked away from the bar.

"Don't come back here tonight," Gia ordered, her voice sharper than I'd ever heard. She nearly dragged me toward the back, where there was a hallway with an exit door at the end.

"What's going on—"

"If you don't want to die, then no more questions." Her voice held firm as she pushed me toward the hall. "Go back to your room and stay there."

Right before she stepped into the hall behind me, there was a new voice that rang out, and Gia shoved me farther down the shadowed hall.

"Gia, there you are," a deep voice said. "You running off on me?"

Gia gave me one last look of warning before her cheery smile was back in place and she turned around to answer the newcomer.

"Running off on you?" She let out a laugh. "Never. It's good to see you, Amaros."

Chapter 21
Kali

Every one of my muscles locked up when Gia said his name. Did she purposely say it to scare me enough to leave? Amaros Kane was here. In the same building as me. The most wanted vampire. The one PARA had been searching for since the war first broke out. There were so many rumors about him that it was impossible to know which were true. But all stories held the same bottom line—Amaros Kane was cutthroat and ruthless. And he detested humans unless they were his meal.

Gia was out of sight by now, and I could hear a couple of the humans yelling insults and curses at Amaros until there was one blood-curdling scream and then a loud thud. I refused to believe that it was Warner because I wasn't sure I'd be able to handle that. Not after losing my other closest friends just under a week ago. Had it really only been a week since I'd gotten here? My pulse pounded in my ears from the silence until Zan spoke up.

"We can go upstairs," he said in a respectful tone I'd never heard from him before.

"No," Amaros answered, his cruel voice making a shiver

run through me. "These humans know where they stand here. They make another sound, and I'll kill them all."

I squeezed my eyes shut, slowly counting down from twenty, trying to calm my heart rate. Luckily, with the other humans here, it would be easy to hide myself unless Zan or the others were specifically listening for me. Did heartbeats sound different from each other? I guessed I was about to find out, because there was no way I was leaving. Not when I could learn about Amaros.

I spun around, purposefully dragging my feet a bit as I quietly walked to the exit door. Gia would be listening for me to leave, and most likely Zan too. So I pushed open the door, and left it open for a few seconds before pulling it shut again, hearing a small click. I didn't move, sucking in the tiniest breaths as I listened to their conversation.

"We weren't expecting you until next week," Viggo said, sharing the same tone of respect that Zan had. "Everything okay, Dad?"

Their voices drifted farther, and fear trickled through my veins as I tiptoed silently back down the hall so I could get closer to them without being seen.

"Project Hope is still standing," Amaros stated, danger lurking in his powerful voice. "It's been months. What's the holdup?"

"The security is tighter than any other city we've dealt with," Pax spoke up. "We're working on it."

"I know it's tighter. That's why we need to get inside. Whatever they're hiding, I fucking want it," Amaros snarled. "That's why all three of my sons are here. Because this is important. You've never failed me before."

"We won't fail." Zan's voice matched the fierceness of his father's. "We all knew Project Hope would be more difficult than all the others."

"PARA isn't completely stupid," Amaros murmured. "They're getting antsy. They can tell we're up to something."

"All the more reason to be cautious with Project Hope," Gia interjected. "They can't know we're coming until we're already inside or it won't work."

"Fine," Amaros bit out, sounding anything but happy. "Four more months. If you don't get in by then, we're changing the plan. Understood?"

"It'll be done," Viggo promised.

"You three never come to visit home anymore. I haven't seen you in four months," Amaros said. I frowned. His voice almost sounded...fatherly. Like he truly cared for his sons. Even if I'd never laid eyes on him, Amaros Kane was a monster in my head. Someone incapable of any type of emotion. Did Zan and the twins love him? Did they have the kind of bond with their father that Pax had told me about?

My stomach roiled, reminding me of what I'd done. I'd kissed Zan to play him. But I'd fucking liked it. Not only liked it—it sparked something in me I'd never felt before. It made my body burn in a way that made me crave more. Enthralled me enough that I almost didn't push the stake to his chest. Because I didn't want it to end. But I had to remember who he was—what he was. A Kane. A cold-blooded vampire who had probably murdered more humans than I could count. Who would no doubt kill me if he found out I was human.

Dread climbed down my limbs when another thought occurred. Maybe he wouldn't kill me. He'd use me. They wanted to get into Project Hope, and Pax had guessed that was where I'd come from and that I had another way inside. They knew my connection to Warner, meaning they'd use him too. I forced myself to keep breathing evenly, attempting to keep my heart steady as the thoughts raced. They couldn't find out.

"We've been busy," Viggo replied. "Your property isn't close to here."

That piqued my curiosity. That could be a weakness.

"Not that far. It would only take you a—"

"Want a drink, Dad?" Zan cut in, his voice sounding farther away as footsteps slapped the floor. I clenched my teeth, hoping he hadn't interrupted Amaros because he thought I was here.

"My usual." Amaros must have been walking too because there were suddenly more steps. Panic had my chest tight, and I pressed myself against the wall to hide in the shadows more. Though I didn't think that would help when vampires could see perfectly in the dark. "How many humans do you have here?"

"Enough to keep us entertained," Pax answered. Unlike his two brothers, he was curt with Amaros.

"The ones in cages can be replaced?"

Amaros's question had terror flooding through me, my nails digging into my palms to keep myself still. I slowly flexed my fingers, not wanting to draw blood. Now was not the time to reveal that I was human.

"They're all replaceable," Zan said coldly. "That's why they're here."

"Good. That conversation wasn't for their ears. We'll catch up after I eat."

The next sound was screaming. Pain-filled yells that turned into groans. Until other humans began shrieking and begging for their life. The sounds made my ears bleed, guilt smothering me that I couldn't do a damn thing. Warner's face flashed in my head, and I took a single step closer before realizing what I was doing. Movement caught my eye.

I went absolutely still, not even breathing when Zan's gaze fell on me, not looking the least bit surprised that I was here. He had a bottle of whiskey in one hand and a glass in the other. Hot fury brightened his eyes when he pierced me with a glare, his anger nearly palpable. I pushed off the wall, straightening up and returning his rage. Warner was out there, and Zan knew how much he meant to me. But here he was, fetching drinks while his father slaughtered the people out there.

He barely moved his head, but it was a clear order for me to leave. Anguish squeezed my heart, hearing the screams continuing. I couldn't leave Warner. I physically couldn't. Not after watching Helena die. And Lisa. If Warner was gone, I'd have nothing. A second later, Zan tore his eyes off me, stalking out of sight. I stared at the spot where he'd been standing, unsure that he was really gone.

More painful shrieks rang out and I moved closer, wanting to reach for the stake in my boot. I knew I couldn't kill them all. But Amaros was right there. He was the brain behind all of this, and if I could kill him, then maybe all the vampires' plans would crumble. Even if I didn't make it out alive.

"I had a meeting planned with the watchers," Zan said, making me freeze. "We've had issues with security lately. I need to go deal with it; I'll be back later."

"I'll be here, son," Amaros said, sounding distracted. "Don't be long."

Oh shit. I scrambled back, but it was already too late. Zan appeared, striding into the hall and catching me before I made it two steps. His hand went over my mouth, and he spun me around, wrapping his arm across my waist and lifting my feet off the floor before he quickly moved down the hall. My muffled arguments were swallowed by the screams of the humans getting killed, and Zan didn't stop, pushing the door open, letting it slam shut behind him.

My struggles did nothing as he carried me down the street. He kept his hand covering my mouth for another block before finally releasing me. My feet hit the cement, and I swung my fist at him. He saw it coming, catching my wrist and then pulling me farther from Impulse.

"He could be dying," I shrieked, fighting against him.

Zan stayed in front of me, not turning to look, keeping a tight hold on my wrist. "Even if he was, there was nothing you could do. My father would have killed you for interfering."

"We had a deal," I hissed, tears clouding my vision. "That—"

"That I wouldn't hurt him," Zan cut me off, his voice nearly vibrating with anger. "I didn't touch him."

"I hate you," I breathed out, fury settling into my bones. "You're a fucking monster, just like your father."

I cried out when he suddenly spun me around, my back hitting the front of the building we'd been passing. His hand wrapped around my throat just like he did the first time I met him, but this time he didn't squeeze, only applying enough pressure to keep me in place.

"The human you would get yourself killed for is perfectly fine." There wasn't a speck of emotion other than anger on his face, but his voice was eerily soft. "Pax got him out of the cage and into the back room before my father even saw him."

"He's alive?" I choked out. The weight lifted from my chest, and I sucked in a full breath.

"Yes." He studied me for a moment before continuing. "You should not have heard that conversation."

A new wave of panic hit me. "I didn't hear anything."

"I don't even need to listen to your heart to know that's a lie."

"Then why did you get me out instead of serving me to Amaros?" I snapped. I wasn't tiptoeing around him anymore. If he wanted me dead, he'd do it. I had a feeling nothing I said would change his mind once it was made up about something.

"Because that necklace around your neck makes you mine. And I'm not ready for that to end yet." He leaned closer, brushing his lips against my cheek. "But always remember—I am my father's son. He trained me to be an even better monster than he is. Do not think you can cross me and get away with it."

His threat of making sure I stayed quiet about what I heard wasn't lost on me. Not that I had anyone to tell. Not while I was trapped in this city. I'd caught a vampire following me back and forth to Impulse a couple of times. Zan had eyes on me even when I wasn't working at his club. Which was why he felt perfectly confident that I wouldn't breathe a word of this to anyone. If I did, he'd hear about it.

He withdrew his hand from my neck but didn't make a move to step away. "If I catch you eavesdropping again, I'll move you in with me so I can watch you at all times."

My eyes snapped to his, defiance burning through me. "Even the worst monsters can be killed. They all have weaknesses."

He chuckled. "Good luck finding mine. Go home, Kali."

He turned and walked away, leaving me in the street. Even if I couldn't see anyone, I was sure there was someone lurking close to follow me back to the hotel. Which was exactly where I started heading to, because I had nowhere else to fucking go.

I was so tired. Of the lying. The constant worry. Having to sneak showers and put on the lotion. I'd been slowly coming up with a plan to get out of the city just to get a note to Tim, and I was going to need supplies if I couldn't get Warner free before I ran out. And I needed to tell them everything about Amaros and new vampires.

I shook my head, forcing out the thousands of things that could go wrong if I made a mistake. What was the worst that could happen? I got caught and killed? Or tortured for information? They'd do that when they found out I was human anyway. No, I needed to get a note to Tim right away.

Chapter 22
Kali

I crouched in my hiding spot, my heart thudding much too loudly. Most of the vampires were already heading inside since sunrise was minutes away. The place I'd chosen didn't have any windows pointing this way that I could see when I scouted it out. I stared at the end of the street that was blocked off like all the other routes that led out of the city. But this one didn't seem as inaccessible as the others. I'd been studying it for the last three nights after leaving Impulse, and I was sure I could get over the high wall of debris without it tumbling down. At least I hoped I could.

I reached into my leggings' pocket, making sure the folded napkin was in there. I'd found a pen in the hotel, and I'd written down everything I'd learned. I just needed to get it to the tree so Tim could find it. Maybe he could help me and Warner get the hell out of here if I wasn't able to. I had a knife in one boot, a stake in the other, and a hammer I'd found in my hand. I was wearing a hoodie with the hood up. If a vampire did spot me, I hoped I could conceal who I was.

The sky continued to lighten, and I sucked in a large

breath. Zan's face popped into my head, making nerves skate down my spine. If he found out about this, I was so fucked. But I was running out of options. My lotion was running out, and I had no idea how I could get Warner out. I knew where Gia kept the keys to the cages, but I was never alone at Impulse. Even with my gun still hidden there, I didn't have a chance.

I scanned the area again, adrenaline pumping through my veins. Staying low to the ground, I kept myself pressed against the wall as I made my way down the street. I stopped in front of the makeshift wall, instantly finding what I was looking for. There was a crushed-up car at the bottom of the pile, and the inside was filled with smaller things. The front window was already cracked, and I tapped the hammer against it, testing its strength. It splintered a bit more, and I cringed when I hit it again. The sound wasn't even that loud, but to me it was deafening.

From the information I pulled out of Dee, most humans here kept to the vampires' schedule. Which meant they should all be inside by now except for the ones who were guarding the open street. But that was at least half a mile from here, and they wouldn't be able to hear it. Both buildings surrounding me had nothing inside them, and from what I could tell, no vampires resided in them. But even if they heard it, there wasn't much they could do to investigate now that the sun was up.

I hit the window for a third time, and it finally shattered. Using the hammer, I knocked out the rest of the glass before grabbing the first thing I could reach. The car was full of random shit, and it took me much longer than I wanted before I even made a dent. The entire time, my heart was racing out of control, and I knew there was no way I could have gotten away with this at night. Not when vampires roamed the city.

I climbed inside, throwing more stuff behind me so I could make my way through the car to the other side. Sweat began trickling down my back, a reminder that I hadn't been keeping up with my workouts. In Project Hope, I trained every day to stay in shape. There wasn't much I could do here while cooped up in a hotel room all day.

The other window came into view, and I let out a cry, seeing trees beyond the glass. I hurried up, shoving the last two things out of my way before grabbing the hammer again. The window was still intact, and I swung hard, listening to the glass crack. I hit it again and again until it finally busted. Swiping the glass shards again, I awkwardly climbed out headfirst, landing on my hands. I crawled out the rest of the way, and the second I was back on my feet, I bolted across the wide road toward the trees.

With my chest heaving, I darted behind a huge tree trunk and sagged against it, letting myself calm down for a moment. Then I peeked around the tree, looking back at the city. I didn't see anyone in the windows or any humans moving around outside. I stared, the taste of freedom surging through me. This could be it. I could walk away and leave for good. I'd find a way to cut off the necklace and run far away.

But I couldn't. Not when Warner was still trapped.

With a sigh, I pushed off the tree and began walking. I had at least a two-hour walk there and back, meaning I needed to make sure I hurried. Even though I had much longer than that until the sun went down, I needed to make sure I got back by nightfall to get to Impulse.

I kept my head on a swivel, watching my surroundings warily as I trudged on. I didn't need to worry about vampires right now, but I was still wanted by PARA, and I knew they scouted these woods during the day. Which was why I'd brought the knife along with the stake. Although one little blade wouldn't do much if I came across a group of men.

After a while, I finally heard the river, and my emotions slammed into me like a wall. I raced forward until I stopped at the edge of the river. I watched the rushing water while letting myself get lost in memories. This place was my first happy place when it was my turn to finally leave Project Hope for a day run. Tim had wanted us to get familiar with the area, so Warner and Helena and I spent hours walking around. Then we just lay at the edge of the river, listening to the water. It was the first time I'd ever felt truly free. It was when I'd made the decision that I wouldn't spend the rest of my life in Project Hope.

"Fuck," I breathed out.

Tears filled my eyes, and for once, I let them fall on my cheeks. I didn't have to hide out here. There were no vampires watching my every move. It was just me. Alone. I swallowed a sob, thinking of Helena and Lisa. They were gone. Warner was knocking on death's door being trapped inside Impulse. I was toeing that same line until I could find a way to get out.

I wasn't sure how much time passed, but I finally stepped away, heading back into the trees. The sun filtered through the leaves, and I welcomed the warmth. The window in my hotel room didn't open, and I couldn't chance wandering out in the daylight in that city.

I rotated between jogging and walking, trying to get to the spot faster. It felt good to move—to run—after being cooped up at Impulse every damn night. I stopped a few times to drink some water, and after a couple of hours, I finally spotted the tree. Excitement hummed in my veins when I stepped up to it and reached into the small hole that was in the trunk. Until I swept the leaves out of the way and realized there was nothing in there. I bit my lip, my body feeling heavy with disappointment. Tim had said he'd leave something in two weeks, but I was hoping he'd be able to do it earlier.

I carefully pulled the napkin out of my pocket and read it again. I listed everything. That the Kane sons were here. That humans lived with vampires. I explained everything I could about how the city operated. That Amaros had property somewhere. That the vampires were trying to get into Project Hope. I'd written small and still filled the entire front and back of the napkin.

I hesitated for just a second before I put it deep in the hole and then covered it with leaves again. Kissing Zan flashed through my head, and I grumbled under my breath. I was going to have to forget about that, and fast. He was a vampire, and he was clearly planning something against humans. I shouldn't feel a shred of anything when it came to him. This was about survival, and there was no way I'd sit back and let them try to take over human cities.

I slowed my pace while walking back, knowing I had plenty of time before nightfall. The sun was high in the sky, and I slipped out of my hoodie, only walking in my bra and soaking up as many rays as I could. For once, I wasn't tense. I was still keeping an eye out for soldiers, but it was a million times better than being at Impulse or the hotel. Guilt filled me for having a moment of peace while Warner was stuck in a cage. But leaving that note was essential, and I'd gotten it done.

The sun was lower in the sky by the time the highway came into view, but there were still a couple of hours of daylight left. After pausing and pulling my hoodie back on, I sprinted across the cement, hating that I was in plain view. I skidded to a stop in front of the car, grabbing the hammer I'd left behind before crawling back through. My pulse thudded as I hurried and shoved some of the debris back inside to cover the hole I'd made.

Creeping through the two streets was giving me the most anxiety because I wasn't out of view from buildings here, but there was no other way to get back to the hotel. I breathed a sigh of relief, seeing the side door still cracked open like I'd left it. I peeked through the narrow opening, making sure the hallway was empty before kicking the rock out of the doorway and stepping inside. A smile tipped up my lips as I made my way back to my room. Until I opened my door and saw someone sitting on the small desk.

My heart dipped when Pax's head snapped up, his glare focusing on me.

I hesitantly stepped into the room, shutting the door behind me. "What are you doing here?"

My eyes widened when I saw my closed curtains. How the hell had he gotten here when the sun was still up?

"Sewer tunnels are a great way to get around during the day." Pax answered my silent question as he pushed off the desk. "Where were you?"

"Exploring the hotel," I said with a shrug. "Staying in here was making me stir crazy."

He frowned, crossing the room in a few steps. "I've been waiting for you all damn day. You're lying."

"I'm not," I hissed. "This place is huge—"

He reached forward, grabbing the back of my neck, pulling me close until his lips were right near my ear. "I can smell it. You were in the woods. This room isn't soundproof, so be careful what you say to me unless you want your secret out."

His words had barely been over a whisper, and once he was done, he moved back half a step. Fury was brewing in his eyes, and I crossed my arms.

"I needed a break," I said in a whisper. "I didn't leave."

"You can't leave," he shot back. "Zan would have found you."

"So I keep hearing," I muttered. "Why are you here?"

"I want your hawthorn."

I almost had to read his lips to catch the last words, and fear jolted through me. His patience was gone. He was either going to turn me or entrance me. Seeing as he wanted my hawthorn, I was guessing the latter.

"I can't just leave Warner," I said stiffly. "You entrance me, and then what? He dies?"

He mumbled a curse, running a hand over his short hair. "I'll figure it out."

"Not good enough—"

"You have no say here," he cut me off, a threat in every word. "I'm done. You're learning too fucking much. Fight me on this, and I'll just turn you."

We were still talking in whispers, but my panic was rising, and I had to remember to stay quiet. My hands curled into fists, and I cried out in protest when he whirled around and went for my backpack that he'd already found under the bed.

"Don't," I demanded in a strangled voice, lunging toward him. "I'll give it to you."

He was already digging through my bag, turning around to keep me from reaching it. A second later, he just dumped it all over my bed. He unzipped the small pockets, and my heart seized when he pulled out my mother's note. With a snarl, I snatched it from his hand, and he whipped around.

"What is that?" he asked, suspicion written all over his face.

"It's personal," I said, my voice trembling. "A letter from my dead mother. Want to take that from me too?"

That deflated him a bit, and he eyed my hand one last time before turning back around and digging through my things. Since the gun was at the club and my stake was on me, all that was in there was clothes, food, the lotion, and the hawthorn. I'd hidden the bullets for the gun in another abandoned room, and after this, I was definitely putting my backpack in there every day too.

"Five days," he said, pocketing the bag of hawthorn. "Once I know it's out of your system, we're ending this."

"I need to change," I forced out. "Get out."

"You should be more grateful that I'm not just killing you."

"Thank you so much for sparing my life," I drawled sarcastically. "Now, can you leave?"

"Don't wear any of those clothes to the club," he warned as he headed to the door. "You smell like pine needles."

With those words, he disappeared down the hall. I slammed the door before falling onto the bed with all my things. Fuck. I didn't exactly need the hawthorn, but that didn't matter much. I only had five days to figure a way out for both Warner and me.

Chapter 23
Zan

"Consider this my brotherly advice of the month."
Viggo dropped his hands on my shoulders,
giving me a push forward as we went down the
stairs from our place to Impulse.

I shot him a glare. "What the hell are you talking
about?"

"You need to do things differently," Viggo said.

"What things?"

Pax pushed open the door, walking into Impulse with
me right behind him. Gia gave us a smile from the bar
before continuing her talk with Dee. Warner was back in
the cage next to our spot, though he was still far enough
away not to hear us if we spoke quietly. He was pacing the
four steps he could take around the cage, his eyes wild when
he caught sight of me.

"Why am I still alive? What do you want?" he hissed,
his voice lacking its usual vigor. Staying locked up was
getting to him.

I arched an eyebrow, assessing him with a cold gaze.
"Nothing I don't already have."

He scoffed, finally coming to a stop and grabbing the bars. "You don't have her. If you did, I'd be dead."

His words pissed me off more than they should have, but I didn't let him see that. Viggo came up and threw an arm around my shoulder, leading me to our chairs. Once we were seated, Viggo waved Dee over. Pax didn't say a word. His brows were furrowed like something was bothering him. He'd been like that for the last week but refused to admit what was wrong.

"He's right, you know," Viggo said in a low voice. "You don't have her."

My jaw muscle flexed. "Thanks, asshole. I do have her. She's mine. Everyone here knows it."

Viggo rolled his eyes. "But you don't *have* her."

"Stop talking in riddles," Pax muttered. "It's annoying."

"Hey, Viggo," Dee purred, jumping into his lap. "Hungry?"

"Not yet." He wrapped his arm around her, running his other hand down her arm, massaging her skin as he stared at me. "Dee, do you think Kali likes Zan?"

Dee let out a nervous giggle, her stare begging Viggo not to include her in this conversation. I eyed my brother warily, wondering why he was bringing her into this. He laughed before nuzzling his nose into her neck and groaning when he got a whiff of her blood.

"Don't be scared," he coaxed her, shooting me a smirk. "You're safe from my little brother. Tell us what Kali thinks of him."

"She hates him," Dee said quickly, playing with the tips of her hair. "The only reason she listens is because of the human and the necklace."

Viggo brushed his lips along her throat, giving her soft kisses. "You think she'd leave if she had a chance?"

"Yes," she panted, her focus solely on Viggo's touch. "She's tense all the time. Don't you notice when she smiles?"

"It's not real," I grated out. "I already know all of this, Viggo. What's your point?"

"My point, little brother, is that you want her. I don't care if you want her in bed or more than that. Either way, you aren't doing it right. You've been insufferable since she got here, and now it's even worse after you kissed her." Viggo brushed Dee's hair to the side, exposing the other side of her neck. "Try a new tactic."

My patience was about to snap. "And what did you have in mind?"

"Be nice to her."

Pax leaned forward, glaring daggers at his twin. "Bad idea. There's no reason for him to get closer to a newbie. She's a fucking liability."

"Yeah, yeah. I know you don't like her," Viggo said. "Doesn't really matter. Zan has no plans on letting her go, do you?"

"No." The answer was out of my mouth before I could think about it. But it was the truth. As if on cue, the front door opened, and just like every night, Kali stepped through, her gaze going for Warner first before her eyes met mine. She stared at me with indifference, acting like I wasn't even worth her time. My annoyance flared, and I had every intention of following her to the bar until Viggo spoke up again.

"See? You're going to go over there and pull her away, pissing her off all over again." Viggo shook his head. "She isn't a typical vampire who learned who you were at the center. She doesn't respect you, fear you, or want to fuck you. You've never dealt with someone like her. You literally locked a necklace on her and forced her here. She knows you're a Kane and is still acting that defiant? She's not going to change unless you do something different."

"I don't need to change," I growled. "This is my fucking city."

Viggo shrugged. "Fine. Enjoy having blue balls, then. Because I haven't seen you look at anyone else since she got here."

He lost interest in the conversation, turning his attention to Dee as his fangs slid down. Fisting her hair, he tilted her head back before sinking his teeth into her neck. She let out a small cry when he broke skin, but she ground against his lap, silently telling him she was enjoying it.

My gaze darted to the bar where Kali was talking to Gia with a hint of a smile on her lips. She seemed to tolerate Gia better than the three of us. Although Gia was always friendly. I replayed Viggo's words in my head, wondering if maybe they held some truth. I focused back on Kali, wanting to hear what they were talking about.

"You've been everywhere," Kali said to Gia, sounding wistful.

Gia laughed. "I've been around a long time. You'll see everything too."

"Doubtful," Kali muttered, her voice dropping so low I almost didn't catch the next words. "I'll probably never even see the ocean before I die."

Her head snapped up as if realizing she'd revealed something she hadn't meant to. Her back straightened, a telltale sign I'd learned she did when she thought I was listening.

"You've never been to the ocean?" Gia asked in surprise.

Kali hesitated before shaking her head. "No."

Viggo pulled away from Dee, licking the blood off his lips. "She's never seen the ocean, Zan."

I blew out a breath, giving him a glare. He was acting like he was God's gift to women when he'd never had to deal with one as infuriating as Kali. They were all like Dee. Human or vampire, it didn't matter; they fell into his lap without him having to say a word.

Viggo snickered. "You're more stubborn than both Pax and me."

"Or maybe he's being smart and not giving into a new vampire who literally had a stake to his heart," Pax grumbled.

"Where's your friend, Dee?" Viggo asked.

"In the back."

Viggo gently pushed her off his lap. "Go get her."

Dee rushed to comply with his order, and I frowned at his smirk, knowing he was playing at something.

"We should be talking about Project Hope after Dad's visit the other day," Pax said in a quiet voice. "What we're doing isn't working."

"Not tonight," Viggo replied with a wave of his hand. "All work and no play is not the way we live."

Pax scowled. "It seems that's all Zan has been doing. Playing with Kali."

"Fuck off," I snapped. "I kept her from the center, which means I have to make sure she learns what she needs to."

Viggo leaned back in his chair. "And what have you taught her? How much of an asshole a vampire can be? I don't see you teaching her anything. She's almost a month old now. Her senses have to be changing. You remember how that feels. No wonder she's always in a bad mood."

"I doubt that's the reason she's acting like that," Pax muttered, swiping a hand down his face. "I need some air."

Viggo watched his twin exit the club, a flicker of concern passing over his face. "He's hiding something."

"He always gets like this after Dad visits," I replied, even though I agreed. Pax had been acting differently even before Dad came.

"Here she is, Viggo."

Dee and her brown-haired friend walked up to us, and Viggo jumped to his feet. He shot me a grin before grabbing the girl's hand and pulling her closer.

"Zan, you remember Jessica?" Viggo asked.

I gave a curt nod. I knew all the girls in here, just like the twins did. We'd been bringing humans to our cities for years, showing them that our way of life could be good too. The humans here of their own free will were always treated well. There were men too, but not nearly as many. Having humans here that we could feed on freely was an advantage we didn't want to turn away.

"Jess, I think Zan is bored. Can you help with that?" Viggo phrased it like a question, but I saw it for what it was. A challenge. He thought I was so obsessed with Kali that I didn't want anyone else. And when Jess gave me a shy smile and then touched her palm to my chest, I realized he was right. Because Jess's touch did absolutely nothing for me. I wasn't even in the mood to feed right now because I was so focused on Kali.

Fuck it. I could try his way one time. Only because I was curious to see if it would work. I wanted to learn about her, and for some damn reason, I wanted her to give it up willingly. I could easily threaten Warner, or even entrance him. But I wouldn't—not yet.

Bite of Sin

"Not tonight," I said, brushing her hand away. "I'm sure Viggo would love some company, though."

"I would," Viggo agreed, sweeping up Jess and sitting down with her on his lap. "Zan is no fun anyway."

Jess giggled, but I was already heading toward the bar. Gia's glance at me alerted Kali that I was coming up behind her. She spun around, already on the defensive before I even stopped in front of her.

"Come with me." I realized those words sounded like every other command I'd given her. Clenching my jaw, I forced out the last word. "*Please.*"

I could very clearly hear Viggo's snicker from across the room while Kali openly gaped at me. Gia had a similar reaction as she stayed behind the bar. Kali quickly schooled her expression, her eyes narrowing into slits.

"Why?" she snapped. "So you can try to interrogate me again? That didn't end well for you last time, did it?"

My patience was already wearing thin, and she was ridiculously close to sending me over the edge, but I didn't move as I took a long breath. Gia was still watching, her eyes dancing with amusement as she listened.

"I want to show you something," I grated out.

"Show me what?"

Gia gave me an encouraging smile, and I nearly scowled. I didn't fucking need to do this. But I could feel Viggo's eyes on me, and he was just waiting for me to do exactly what I wanted—which was to just grab her and haul her out the door.

"It's outside the city."

My words had Kali going still, and I could tell she was already plotting. She wanted out, and finding a way out of the city could be beneficial for her. This wouldn't help, but she didn't know that.

245

"You're asking me to go?" she asked slowly.

A muscle ticked in my jaw. "I think it's something you'd like to see."

Her eyes flicked behind me before she met my gaze again. "I'll go. If you add another seven days."

This fucking girl.

Even though annoyance was flaring through me, there was a slice of amusement. The one time I asked her to do something, she wanted to set her own conditions. She'd go willingly if I left Warner alone for longer. Smart. Although her connection to him angered me more than her defiance. I leaned toward her, and she glared, standing her ground.

"No," I answered simply. "Come or don't. I just thought you'd want a night out after being stuck here for over a week. But I guess you must love it here if you'd rather work another night."

She stared at me for a few long moments, a small flash of uncertainty crossing her features. My actions were putting her on edge because they were in stark contrast to what I'd been doing.

"Fine. I'll go."

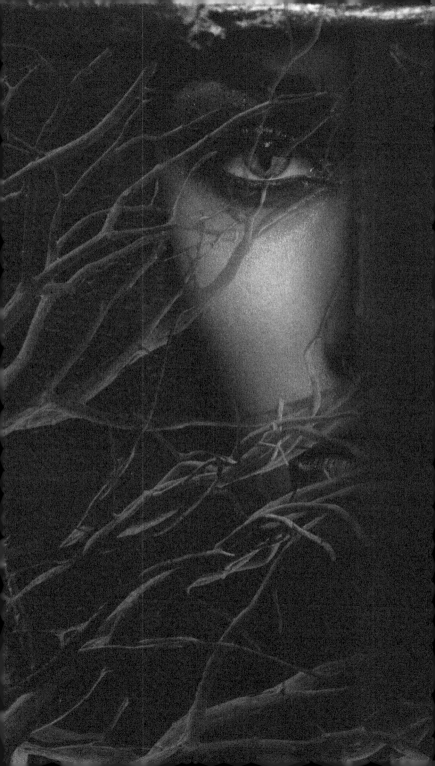

Chapter 24
Zan

I motioned for her to go first, and she glanced at Warner one last time before spinning around and heading toward the door. I followed behind her, nodding at the line of vampires waiting for the doors to open. I fell into step beside her, noticing how tense she was.

"Why didn't you just drag me out like you did the night you took me to the park?" was her first question as we turned down another street.

"I was curious to see if you'd choose to come."

"I'm surprised." There was a smug edge to her tone. "The last time we were alone, I almost made you bleed."

"Feel free to try it again," I murmured, catching her eye as we kept walking. "The only reason you were able to do that was because you kissed me. And I told you I wanted another taste."

The flush creeping up her cheeks had me swallowing a grin. She wanted to act like it didn't affect her when it clearly did.

"And why don't you just take what you want?" she

snapped. "You obviously have no issue trying to control me."

She brushed her fingers along the necklace, shooting me an irritable glare. I stepped ahead of her, getting in her way, making her stop in her tracks. She scowled when I caught her chin, tipping her face up.

"I might be horrible in your eyes. But forcing myself on someone? Whether human or vampire—it doesn't appeal to me. Sex is supposed to be fun. If both parties aren't screaming only in pleasure, then what's the appeal?"

She studied me, her brows furrowed. "I don't believe you."

I arched an eyebrow. "Why? I haven't touched you. Actually, you're the one who kissed me."

"And you've had no issue saying you want to do it again," she snapped.

"Oh, I don't have any issue with it," I murmured. "I have no problem admitting that you tasted like delicious trouble. And now I want to rip those clothes off and taste every fucking inch of you."

Her eyes widened, her throat moving as she swallowed thickly. I watched in amusement while it took her a few seconds to get her next words out. Talking about sex with her seemed to jumble her thoughts a bit, making it easier to see her true emotions.

"That won't be happening," she finally said, her voice a notch higher than normal. "Because I say no. Unless you're lying about your only redeeming quality."

I chuckled. "Believe me, Kali. I have no redeeming qualities."

I began walking again, hearing her footsteps as she moved to catch up with me.

"Where are we going?" she asked.

I didn't answer, knowing her curiosity was enough for her to keep following. We walked toward the back of the city, looking beside me to see Kali scanning the area.

"Never been this way?" I questioned.

"I came in through the other side," she muttered. "Didn't have much time to explore before some asshole dragged me to his club."

I scoffed. "Have you talked to any other vampires about the center?"

"No."

"Even if you hate being here, it's much better than there."

"If you're waiting for me to say thank you, you'll be waiting a long time."

"The center shows vampires how to hone their abilities," I told her, guiding her down another street. "They're also shown the fun we can have. But we teach them to follow. And what happens when they don't listen."

Kali paused, glancing at me out of the corner of her eye. "I'm guessing those methods are painful."

"Good guess," I mused. "If you spoke to anyone there like you did to me..."

I trailed off when she shot me a scathing glare. We walked in silence for a few minutes before she spoke up again.

"You made that sound like a threat," she said, staring straight ahead. "But I don't think it is. You like that I challenge you."

"You infuriate me," I ground out.

"And you *like* it. If you didn't, I wouldn't be here. You could have anyone. But you're obsessed with me."

I snapped my head to the side to look at her. "I am not obsessed."

"Sure you're not."

I swiped a hand down my face, not responding as we walked down the last street. She kept pace with me, making sure to keep a couple of feet between us. I grabbed her arm, stopping her before she passed the door.

"We're here," I muttered, pulling a key from my pocket.

She stared at the metal door, her eyes dropping to the large padlock as I stuck the key inside it. It clicked, and I pulled it off before grabbing the handle and pulling it open. Kali froze as she took in the stairs leading into darkness.

"You want me to go down there? With you?" she accused, her voice giving away her nerves. "You're crazy."

"You seem pretty confident that I have no desire to kill you," I taunted, stepping onto the first stair. "So why are you scared?"

"I'm not scared," she retorted. She was rigid as she cautiously moved forward and stepped next to me. I closed the door and slid the dead bolt. Her heart was beating faster, and I heard her suck in a few deep breaths.

"I can't see anything. It's pitch black," she said tightly.

That wasn't an issue for me. I could see her pretty damn well, and I turned slightly, sweeping her up in my arms. She yelled in surprise, squirming in my hold until I began descending the steps.

"It will take us forever if you walk," I explained. There were no other sounds except my footsteps and the pounding of her heart, which had started racing faster when I picked her up.

"Or we could have brought a flashlight."

"I don't need one. In a couple of months, neither will you." I got to the bottom of the steps and followed the narrow tunnel. "You're nearly a month old. You're going to need to drink blood soon."

"I can't believe vampires don't need blood for the first month," she muttered. "Humans don't know that. At least not civilians."

"That's the point. Can't show them our weaknesses." I glanced down, watching her awkwardly adjusting her arms. "You know you can put your arms around my neck. I won't bite."

"If I were human, you would." She crossed her arms instead. "When does the blood craving happen?"

"Between four and six months," I answered. "Vampires can't control it. Not even around humans they have a bond with."

"I would attack people I care about?"

"Yes. The craving of blood...it controls you. Doesn't matter who it is."

"You're telling me that I'd kill someone I've known my entire life?"

The tunnel came to an end, and I began climbing the stairs, feeling Kali shift in my arms.

"If you care for Warner, you should probably stay far away from him when your cravings start." *If he lived that long.*

"How long do the cravings last?"

"It's different for each vampire."

"How long did it last for you?"

"It doesn't matter," I said gruffly. "We're here."

I set her down on the top step and slid the lock before pushing open the door. Letting her go out first, I followed behind, making sure to close it and lock it. We were on the outskirts of the city, and I grabbed her hand, pulling her with me. We passed a wide road, and Kali pulled against me when she saw a cliff.

"Where the hell are you taking me?" she hissed.

"Don't worry. There're stairs."

She caught sight of the railing, and even though the metal had seen better days, it was still stable enough to use. I would know. I came here all the time. I bounded down the steps, the full moon lighting the area enough for her to see. She didn't even make it to the first step before her movements stopped. I glanced over my shoulder to see her staring down past me.

"What's that noise?" she asked.

"What do you think it is?"

She squinted as if that would help her see better while tilting her head to the sound in front of us. Shock crossed her face, and her eyes cut to me.

"Is that...is that the ocean?" she nearly whispered.

"Yes. The Atlantic Ocean."

"It was this close?" she mumbled. "I had no idea it was here."

"You never asked."

I continued down the stairs, and she quickly followed. The stairs ended right on the beach, and I stepped onto the sand. Kali appeared beside me, and she immediately crouched down, scooping up a handful of sand. She watched it fall between her fingers with a smile creeping across her face. Until she remembered I was right next to her. She tilted her face back, shooting me a quizzical look.

"Why did you bring me here?" she asked.

"You've never seen the ocean."

She frowned. "But why do you care?"

I didn't answer, walking toward the water instead. I wasn't about to tell her that seeing the smile she'd flashed when holding the sand was enough to bring her out here every damn night. Because then that would be admitting something I wasn't ready to accept myself. I kept her in my city because of my curiosity about her being a new vampire. Nothing else. *Shit.* Maybe if I fucked her, I could get her out of my head. Although I didn't see her agreeing to that.

She came near the water, watching the dark waves crashing onto the beach until she closed her eyes and sucked in a deep breath of the salty air.

"I wish I had your eyesight right now," she muttered. "I want to see it all."

"You can come back out when your transition is over." I reached for her hand again, tightening my hold when she fought against me. "There's one more place I want you to see."

She huffed out an annoyed breath but kept pace with me as we moved in the sand. A little way up, there was a pier, and we climbed the stairs carefully. Once we got to the top, I pushed her behind me.

"Walk exactly where I walk," I ordered. "The wood has spots that aren't stable."

"And how do you know which spots those are?" she asked, following behind me.

I sighed. "This is one of my favorite places to go."

"Then why have you been at Impulse every night?"

I looked over my shoulder. "You really need to ask?"

"Obsessed," she muttered under her breath.

"Not obsessed. Making sure you don't get into trouble," I corrected her. "You're my responsibility, since I kept you from the center."

We slowly made our way down the pier, and I stopped before getting to the end. Half of the railing was missing, and the wood was rotting too much to walk any farther out. Kali moved next to me, her gaze taking in the sight. Thanks to the moon, even with her vision, she could see more than when we were on the beach. Cliffs were on one side of us, and she slowly turned in a full circle, her eyes wide.

"I wish I could see this in the sun," she breathed out before snapping her mouth closed as if she hadn't meant to say it. She glanced at me. "Why do you like it out here?"

"It's peaceful. Quiet. I didn't get a lot of that growing up."

"Amaros Kane raised you," she said carefully, a glint of fear hitting her eye.

I gave her a pointed look. "He is my father."

"He's not your real father," she countered.

"Tell me, what kind of stories do the humans come up with about how Amaros had his sons?" I already knew the answer but wanted to know what she thought.

She licked her lips. "The story is that even though certain vampires can mate with humans, Amaros couldn't. So he found humans who he believed would make strong sons."

"And?"

Pity clouded her face. "And that he killed the human parents so he could raise the sons as his own. Then he turned them when they became adults."

I stared out at the ocean. "For once, humans have the right story."

"You never met your parents?" she whispered.

"Amaros is the only parent I know—or have ever known."

She stayed quiet, her gaze on the water. For some reason, it was easier to talk to her out here. Maybe it was because the atmosphere was different. Or because she was happy to be near the ocean for the first time. But even our stretched silence wasn't tense.

"I never met my real parents either," she finally said. "I don't even know their names."

"Siblings?"

She shook her head. "Not that I know of. The only person I have—"

She cut herself off, her eyes hardening as she glanced at me. I didn't say anything, even though we both knew the name she was going to blurt out. The man I had locked in a cage. In all honesty, I didn't know what I was going to do about him yet. But I didn't need to worry about that tonight.

"Do you come out here to swim?" she asked, changing the subject.

I grinned. "Sometimes. Why? Want to try?"

She went still. "No."

"Don't know how to swim?"

"Never learned."

Her voice was cold, and I studied her, wondering why she'd suddenly closed back up. "You don't have to fear water as a vampire. You can't drown."

"Really? Even a new one like me?"

I paused. "Actually, I'm not sure."

"Yeah, I'll wait until I know I won't die before swimming," she muttered.

"I wouldn't let you die. It would be a shame to not feel the water your first time at the beach."

Panic lit up her face, and she took a step back. "I'm perfectly happy not going in the water."

I snatched her hand before she got even farther from me. She struggled against me as I pulled her toward the edge.

"Zan, no," she shrieked. "That has to be a thirty-foot drop."

"Perfectly safe," I answered. "I do it all the time."

257

"You know, you haven't been half the asshole tonight that you usually are," she snapped, her voice nearly shaking. "Why don't you keep that going?"

I pretended to ponder. "No. I'd rather swim with you."

"No—"

"Don't let go." I pushed forward, quickly taking the last three steps to the edge, my hold on her wrist staying tight. She yelled and cursed at me, and when I jumped, she let out an ear-piercing scream.

The wind whipped around us, Kali's scream not ending until we hit the water. We went under, and I made sure to keep hold of her arm as I kicked, pushing us back to the surface. Kali's head popped up next to me, and she yanked out of my hold to wipe her face. She caught my eye for a split second before she turned around and began swimming back to shore. And she was moving fast.

"You're a liar," I called out, swimming to catch up. "You do know how to swim."

"Do you know how hard it is to swim in boots? And the water is cold," she shot back, not stopping.

My heart beat unevenly, hearing the raw panic in her voice. I didn't know what her issue was. She could clearly swim. It took her only a few minutes to get to shore, and I treaded water for a moment, letting her calm down before I joined her. Until she suddenly bolted. Taking off down the beach like someone was chasing her.

"What the hell?" I muttered, kicking my feet to swim faster. "Kali. Stop."

But she didn't. She was flat-out sprinting. The only things slowing her were the sand and her wet boots. My feet hit the sand, and I clamored out of the water, running after her. She was nearly to the stairs at the cliff, and I lunged forward, catching the hem of her shirt and yanking her back.

"Let me go," she snarled, trying to rip from my hold.

My stomach churned, feeling her body trembling. Was the water really that frigid? I didn't process temperature the same way she did, but the water here never got cold in the summer.

"What's wrong?" I asked.

She raised her arm to hit me, and I growled in annoyance, grabbing her wrist to stop her. She jerked back, slipping away from my grip. I rubbed my fingers, realizing they were greasy. She had some type of oil or lotion on, making it harder to keep a hold of her. She got two steps before I wrapped an arm around her waist, crushing her chest to mine.

"Calm down," I gritted out. "What the hell is wrong?"

"You're going to kill me anyway," she screamed. "Just get it over with."

I stared down at her, but she refused to look at me. "Why would I—"

A new scent caught my attention, and I stilled. Kali was still struggling, but I locked my arms around her waist, not caring if any of her hits landed. I sniffed, whipping my head around. It was blood. I was sure of that. There shouldn't be any humans in the area. But this scent...was so good. Sweet. Kali had stopped fighting me and was shifting her body. She lifted one of her legs, but I focused on the smell, not really caring when she tried stomping on my foot.

The scent of this blood was strong. So damn addicting. Everyone's blood smelled slightly different, and I'd never come across one so potent. One that I instantly craved. I closed my eyes, and when Kali shifted again, I blinked, the realization slamming into me. I wasn't sure whose heart was pounding faster, mine or hers, as I reached up and fisted her hair, tilting her head back and exposing her neck.

Her eyes finally met mine, and the truth was written all over her face. Terror flashed in her gaze before I lowered my head, running my nose up the side of her throat. The scent surrounded me. Engulfed me.

"Not fucking possible," I breathed out.

"Zan—"

"Human," I hissed, still in disbelief. "How the fuck did I not catch this? You've been here for days."

She didn't answer, her body shaking as I inhaled more of her scent. She had masked it somehow. The water had washed off whatever it was. Before I could question her further, I saw her raising her arm out of the corner of my eye, and ice filled my veins, catching sight of a fucking stake. I let go of her waist, twisting away fast enough that she couldn't hit my heart.

Instead, she stabbed me in the lung. Pain spasmed through me, and I fell to my knees, gasping. I didn't even need to breathe to survive, but the burning pain of the stake was still agony from such a deep stab. I grabbed it, yanking it out. By the time I looked back up, Kali was at the top of the steps, disappearing from view.

Chapter 25
Kali

Oh my fuck. This was bad. So fucking bad.

I kept running, crossing the road and getting farther from the beach. My eyes darted around as I tried to think of where to go. I wanted to go back into the city where Warner was. But I wouldn't get a foot inside Impulse without the vampires smelling me. The door to the tunnel was in front of me, and I slowed down, whipping my head around.

There was nothing else here. No buildings or forest. Just a long stretch of road and cliffs. I wasn't even sure which way the trees were. If I ran either way, there was no place to hide. He'd catch up with me before I could get away. The necklace hit my chest as I ran, reminding me that he had another way to find me, even if I did escape. I could go through the city and get out through the car like I had the other night. My heart stuttered. *But what about Warner?*

There were other humans here. Maybe the vampires wouldn't take much notice, especially with Zan's necklace warning them off. It was the best choice I had. I couldn't save Warner if I didn't get out myself.

I lunged forward, ripping the door open and slamming it behind me, making sure to engage the dead bolt. I reached for the wall, feeling around because I couldn't see a damn thing. My chest was heaving, and I sucked in breaths as I carefully made my way down the stairs. A few seconds later, I flinched when there was a thunderous noise that echoed through the tunnel. Zan pounded on the outside of the door again, and I hoped the door held.

The disbelief and betrayal in his eyes when he smelled my blood was seared into my brain. Anger was mixed in there too. If he caught me, I was so fucked. I knew he'd want to kill me, but yet when I'd gone to stab him, a small nagging voice had me feeling guilty. Which should absolutely not have happened. This life was kill or be killed. That was especially true in a vampire city.

Keeping my hand on one wall, I got to the bottom of the steps and started running. Water was still dripping off my clothes, and my boots were heavy and wet, but at least I hadn't lost the stake when I hit the water. My lungs begged for me to slow down, but I pushed forward until my feet hit something hard.

"Shit," I hissed.

I fell forward, my knees slamming into the rough cement steps. I caught myself with my palms, pain jolting through me. I climbed back to my feet, my knees stinging as I began racing up the steps. My left knee was much worse off, and I gritted my teeth, refusing to slow down. It was hard to tell, since I was still soaking wet, but I was pretty sure I busted skin and was bleeding. Which was fucking great.

I made it to the top and blindly searched for the dead bolt I'd heard Zan close when we came down here. I finally found it and quickly unlocked it, pushing the door open before stumbling into the street. I glanced around as I began running again, noticing a few vampires. One of them turned their attention to me until his eyes fell on my chest. He turned back around, acting like I wasn't even there. Nice to know that this necklace was good for something.

My injured knee was forcing me to limp slightly as I ran, and I pushed forward, trying to remember which way to go. This part of the city was new to me, and I hadn't learned the roads yet. I turned down one street, muttering a curse when I saw it was a dead end. Spinning back around, I crossed to the other side, heading down another street. After two more turns, I recognized where I was and turned again, heading toward my escape route.

Until a figure popped out from behind a corner. I didn't have time to stop and slammed right into him. Fear lit through me, my stomach knotting painfully when he gripped my upper arms to keep me in place. I forced myself to look up, my breath locking in my chest when I met Zan's gaze. He looked just as terrifying as the night I first met him. Fury swam in his eyes, his face hard and cold.

"You thought you could outrun me in my own city?" he murmured, his voice lethal. "And as a human? You didn't stand a chance."

He didn't wait for a response before he bent down and threw me over his shoulder. His arm banded tightly around my thighs, and he strode forward. I braced my hands on his back, the blood rushing to my head from being upside down. My struggles didn't faze him in the least as he walked briskly down the streets, and I soon realized we were heading to Impulse.

"Zan—"

"Not a fucking word," he snapped. "You don't want to push me right now."

"Why not?" I shot back. "Will begging or pleading change what you're going to do?"

He didn't answer, slamming open the front door to the club. I couldn't see anything, but the chattering quieted when he stepped inside.

"What the hell happened to you two?" Gia asked. "Why are you wet?"

"Everybody get the fuck out. Now," Zan bellowed.

He headed toward the bar, and I let out a cry when he pulled me off his shoulder and I landed on the counter. Vampires were rushing out the door, and I clamored away, feeling Zan's stare burning through me. I slid off the bar, pain jolting through my knee when I landed on my feet.

"Do not leave this room." Zan's threat was clearly for me, but when I glanced toward him, he was focused on Gia. "Where're my brothers?"

Gia frowned, shooting me a look. "Viggo is upstairs with Dee and Jess. I don't know where Pax is."

"Get Viggo," Zan snapped. "And then go spread the word that I'm looking for Pax."

I was inching away from them, my heart pounding against my ribs. Running would be useless, but if I was going to die, I wanted to be near Warner. Gia gave Zan a long look before she headed toward the back, where the stairs were. She passed me, halting in her tracks. Her nostrils flared, and she snapped her head to the side, her eyes dropping to my legs. I followed her gaze, seeing my jeans stained with blood on my left knee.

"Well...that's interesting," she murmured, studying me. She didn't seem to share the rage that Zan was simmering with. But I didn't miss the frown on her usually cheery face.

"Gia. Go get Viggo," Zan ordered sharply.

She hovered near me for another moment before going

to the stairs. Zan continued to watch me as I backed up more. He reached over the bar and grabbed a bottle of whiskey. His black shirt was stained with dark blood from where I'd stabbed him, but he didn't pay it any attention as he took a long drink from the bottle. I debated the odds of rushing into the back room and grabbing my gun, but there was no way I'd be able to get it out of the cushion before Zan caught up to me. My spine hit bars, and I jumped when a hand landed on my shoulder.

"Kali," Warner whispered from behind me.

I spun around, meeting his stare. Fear for both me and him welled inside me, and I bit my lip.

"I'm sorry," I choked out, not even trying to be quiet. "I tried getting us out."

Warner's eyebrows rose in confusion, and I opened my mouth to tell him I was still human, but Viggo rushed into the room, interrupting me. I turned away from Warner to watch Viggo skid to a halt, his gaze stopping on Zan first.

"What happened, little brother?" Viggo asked quietly.

"Ask Kali."

Zan's answer had Viggo turning toward me, suspicion crossing his face when he noticed me pressed against Warner's cage. I didn't move a muscle as his eyes trailed down me, stopping on my legs, just like Gia's had. His shoulders tensed as he advanced toward me. My instincts screamed to run. To fight. To do anything. But what the hell could I do against two vampires when I didn't have a weapon on me?

Viggo stopped a foot from me, the shock he was trying to mask still peeking through. He sniffed again, scoffing in disbelief.

"What a good little liar you are." Viggo's words were laced with anger, his eyes not leaving me. "This is what happens when we break the rules, Zan. Instead of a new vampire, we've been teaching a fucking human everything. We should have brought her to the center."

"Human?" Warner breathed out. "Kali, you're not a vampire—"

Zan heaved the bottle of whiskey at the wall, shattering the glass. My body trembled no matter how hard I tried to contain it as I watched the liquid spread across the floor. My clothes were still wet, making me cold, but that was the least of my concerns when Zan crossed the room, stopping right next to Viggo.

"Why'd you come here?" Zan asked. "To learn all our secrets?"

I shook my head. "No. I had no idea what this city was—"

"We can't believe a word that comes out of her mouth," Viggo cut me off, side-eyeing Zan. "Not unless we know it's the truth."

"She's been here for over a week," Zan ground out. "Slathered in that fucking lotion that PARA has. You really think she doesn't have hawthorn too? I doubt I can entrance her."

"He doesn't have any." Viggo's gaze darted behind me to Warner. "He's been here nearly as long."

"I snuck him some the other day," I said, my voice shrill. "He can't be entranced until it's out of his system."

Zan's eyes flared with fury at my words, but I didn't look away. It wasn't exactly the truth. I hadn't gotten the chance to give Warner any hawthorn, but he had a bracelet that he wore around his ankle with hawthorn in it. As long as he kept it on, they couldn't entrance him. This way, it gave us another couple of days to think of something if they wanted answers.

Viggo cocked his head. "I can think of other ways to

make him talk without us having to wait. You're going to think that cage is heaven compared to what I'm going to do."

"No," I screamed. "He hasn't done anything."

"Have you?" Zan shot back. "Did you tell humans what you've learned here?"

"No," I gritted out. "I haven't left the city since you found me that night."

There was no controlling my heart when I spilled out the lie, but it was beating so erratically right now I wasn't sure he'd be able to pick up on it. Before he could reply, the front door slammed open, and Pax rushed inside. His eyes widened when he took in the scene, and he froze.

"Oh shit," he muttered.

"*Oh shit*?" Viggo repeated, turning his attention to his twin. "Why does it sound like you already know what's happening here?"

Of the three of them, Pax was the most open about his emotions, and the guilt that spread across his face had both Zan and Viggo whirling around toward him.

"You *knew*," Zan accused in a low hiss. "This whole fucking time?"

"Yes," Pax admitted, his voice thick with emotion. "But it was for a good reason—"

Viggo snorted. "A good reason? What the hell are you doing? She learned things that the humans can't find out about. I knew your sympathy was going to bite us in the ass. But to lie to us? I never saw that coming."

"She's the girl," Pax gritted out. "The one I met in the forest that night we went to the river. She was running— from PARA. The one who knew a different way into Project Hope."

Silence fell across the room at his admission, and I stayed still, feeling Warner right behind me. I was scrambling, trying to come up with a way out of here, but I was coming up blank.

"You knew who she was when I brought her here that night," Zan said slowly. "Why the hell didn't you say anything?"

"Because our sweet brother was worried that we'd kill her," Viggo answered, his voice cruel. "He chose the life of a human over his family."

"The second you locked that necklace on her, I knew she wasn't going anywhere," Pax snapped. "I took her hawthorn the other day and was going to entrance her for answers. I realized I should have said something the night she came, but I didn't. And then I felt like shit and knew you were both going to be pissed. So I was going to fix it myself."

"How?" Zan asked in a low voice. "By getting answers and then turning her? That would be the only way. Unless you killed her, which you clearly don't want to do since you're the one fucking protecting her."

"Has she left the city since she's been here?" Viggo's question had lead filling my veins.

Pax glanced at me. "Yes. I caught her coming back from the woods the other day."

Viggo cursed under his breath while Zan slowly turned to focus back on me. Panic engulfed me as he stepped closer, raising his hand and gripping my chin.

"What did you do in the woods?" he asked, threat dripping from every word.

"I needed a day in the sun," I gritted out. "Away from vampires."

"Bullshit," Viggo argued.

"Leave her alone," Warner hissed.

When Warner's arm came through the bars, Zan

snatched it with his free hand and twisted until Warner grunted in pain.

"Try to touch me or her again, and I'll kill you," Zan threatened. His voice held only truth, and he let go of Warner, his glare not leaving me. "Do you have hawthorn running through your veins?"

"Yes."

He tilted his head, searching my face. "I'm calling your bluff."

"Go ahead," I snarled. "Ask me something."

He chuckled darkly. "No need. Did you know that we can tell it by your blood? All I need is one taste."

Chapter 26
Kali

C old fear held me hostage as we stared at each other. I did know they could taste hawthorn. I also knew that it hurt them enough that most vampires never bit anyone who might have it in their system.

"I'll go get someone," Viggo muttered.

"No," Zan growled. "I'll do it."

"If you ingest hawthorn, it's going to put you on your ass for the rest of the night," Viggo snapped. "Get someone else to drink it."

"I think she's lying," Zan murmured.

"I'm not," I hissed. "You can't entrance me."

He released my jaw, snagging my arm and yanking me away from the cage. A scream tore from my throat when he pushed me into Viggo, who grabbed my arms, trapping them behind my back. Warner was shouting, pleading for them to let me go. Zan stepped up to me, his arm snaking behind me until he was gripping my hair.

"Stay still," he ordered roughly, tilting my head back even more until he had complete access to my throat.

I squeezed my eyes shut, wondering if this was it. When he realized I had no hawthorn in my veins, would he drain me? Kill me? Did it hurt? I'd never been bitten before.

A shiver jolted down my spine when his warm breath hit my skin, and I sucked in short breaths, refusing to show him my fear. My pulse went haywire when his fangs grazed my throat, and a second later, I swallowed a cry when there was a small pinch of pain as he bit me.

He sucked slowly, and other than the sting from him breaking skin, it didn't hurt like I always imagined. I tried pulling away, and his hold on my hair tightened, not letting me move an inch.

"You son of a bitch," Warner snarled.

"Shut up," Viggo retorted, keeping my wrists locked behind me.

Zan didn't drink for long, and he slowly pulled away from me. I could feel the trickle of warm blood running down my neck, and I forced my eyes open, my chest tightening when I found him staring right at me.

"Fuck me," Zan muttered, wiping my blood from his lips, his face completely unreadable.

"You're still standing." Viggo released me, and I stumbled away, moving in front of the cage again with my hand on my throat. "Which means she doesn't have hawthorn in her system."

"Has anything you've said since you've gotten here been the truth?" Zan hissed.

Viggo crossed his arms. "Entrance her."

"I'm telling you, it's in her system," Pax said, sounding nervous. "I tried entrancing her the other day about going into the woods. It didn't work."

My stomach flipped. He tried entrancing me? Zan scowled, pacing in front of me.

"Then she has it on her body somewhere," Viggo replied, growing impatient.

"She was in the ocean. Anything on her body, the salt water would have ruined." Zan stopped in front of me, his eyes going to the hand I still had pressed against where he'd bitten me. "Do you have hawthorn on you?"

His voice didn't change, but he was still meeting my gaze. I wasn't sure if he was trying to entrance me, but either way, I was going to lie.

"No," I answered, trying to keep my voice steady.

He didn't say a word, his frown growing deeper. His gaze flicked to Warner before landing back on me.

"Every human can be entranced," Viggo grumbled. "She's lying."

"Unless she found a permanent solution to it."

My heart skipped at Zan's words. No matter how hard I tried to calm it, and from the small smirk on his face when his eyes dropped to my chest, he caught it.

"What's on your body that's added?" he questioned, almost to himself.

My jaw clenched, and I realized it wouldn't take him long to figure it out. This time when he reached for me, he spun me around until my chest hit the cage. Warner crouched, putting his face in front of mine. My fingers wrapped around the bars, and I squeezed them tightly, feeling Zan grip the hem of my tank top. Warner reached forward as if to cup my face, but he stilled when Zan spoke up again.

"I wouldn't," Zan warned dangerously. "I told you what would happen if you touched her."

I swallowed thickly, knowing Zan wasn't bluffing about killing him. A muscle in Warner's jaw flexed as he glowered at Zan while keeping his hand inches from my face.

"I'm fine," I whispered. I met Warner's gaze and attempted to give him a small smile. "Don't get yourself killed right now."

"When did you get this tattoo?" Zan asked, lifting my shirt to reveal my lower back.

"Two years ago," I answered honestly. Dread weighed down my limbs as he studied the artwork that had taken hours upon hours to finish. It took up my entire back, and I'd chosen to make it a landscape of the river because it was the first place I fell in love with after leaving Project Hope. Blue water wound up my spine, with trees and flowers surrounding it. It was beautiful, and the person who'd done it was a true artist. The details were immaculate and worth every hour I'd spent on a table while he tattooed me.

But it also served a greater purpose.

Because every single part of that tattoo had powdered hawthorn plant in the ink. That was the reason it took up my entire back. There needed to be enough in the tattoo ink for it to seep into my skin and stay. As long as I had this tattoo, I couldn't be entranced. The hawthorn sat in my skin at all times, just like Warner's bracelet did for him.

All the women in the group had one, and the men were slowly getting theirs. Warner was supposed to get his next year. Tattoo ink was hard to come by, and it was decided that women needed to have it first since vampires usually went for them before men.

"There's no way," Viggo mumbled. "Hawthorn in ink? I've never heard of that."

Zan dropped my shirt before grabbing my arm and spinning me back around. "Is it the tattoo?"

"No."

I could easily see that he didn't believe me, and Pax stayed behind his brothers, staring at me with pity.

"She's useless if that's the case," Viggo said pointedly. "If we get wrong information about Project Hope, it could ruin everything. We need to make sure it's the truth."

My value and chances of staying alive were declining with every word, and I searched for a weapon or anything that could get us out. Viggo was watching me intently, as if knowing what I was thinking, so I stayed pressed against the cage, not moving a muscle.

"What about you, *Warner*?" Zan spat out the name, lifting his eyes toward the cage. "You have ink too?"

"No," Warner bit out.

"Take off your shirt."

"Fuck you."

Viggo stepped up next to me and reached inside the cage, snatching Warner's arm. He yanked him close until he could reach his neck and then wrapped his hand around that, keeping Warner right in front of him.

"Take off your shirt," Viggo repeated, keeping his eyes locked on Warner's. It was clear he was trying to entrance him, and I let out a breath when Warner pretended to follow the direction and slipped off his shirt when Viggo released him. He raised his arms and spun in a slow circle, proving he didn't have a tattoo.

"I've had eyes on Kali all week," Zan murmured. "There's no way she had time to slip him any hawthorn."

"I did," I protested.

Viggo was still standing next to me, and he glanced at Zan. "Hold her."

"Wait. What are you doing—"

Zan pulled me away, wrapping his arms around mine and keeping them pressed to my sides. Viggo crouched down, and in a quick move, he snatched Warner's ankle and pulled, sending him to the floor of the cage. He went down hard, hitting his head on the bar, and he spat out curses when Viggo gripped his pant leg and pulled it up to his knee. Warner tried kicking him away, but Viggo just pulled him forward, sliding Warner's leg through the bars as far as it would go. Viggo did the same to the other leg, holding them tightly as Warner kicked and tried to crawl away.

"Get the fuck off me," Warner snarled, panic rising in his voice that I was sure none of them missed.

"What is that?" Zan asked in a low voice.

I saw it too but clenched my teeth together, not making a sound. I noticed it the second Viggo tugged up the second pant leg. The small black bracelet was wrapped around his ankle.

"Now, who wears something like that on their leg?" Viggo inspected it for a moment before easily ripping it and tossing it on the ground.

"Get the key, Pax," Zan said, his arms tightening around me.

I wanted to scream and promise them that I'd talk. But they'd believe nothing that came out of my mouth anyway. Not when they knew they couldn't entrance me. I watched helplessly as Pax tossed the key to Viggo, who went to unlock the cage. Warner was already on his feet and charged at Viggo the second the door was open. Viggo ducked away, throwing his fist into Warner's ribs hard enough to knock his breath away.

"We have some questions for you," Viggo muttered, wrapping his hand around Warner's throat again and slamming his back against the cage.

"I can't wait to see the day when you all die," Warner snarled, his eyes wild with loathing. "It's coming."

Viggo lowered his head, getting right in Warner's face. He didn't say anything, only stared into Warner's eyes. Ice slid down my spine when, after a few moments, all the emotions faded, and he looked back at Viggo with a blank expression as his entire body relaxed.

"That's better." Viggo kept his eyes locked on Warner's. "Let's start with an easy one. Where did you live before you came into our city?"

"Project Hope," Warner answered, his voice completely monotone.

I sagged in Zan's arms, knowing it was all over. Warner was going to tell them everything. And then they'd kill us.

"Is Kali's tattoo the reason she can't be entranced?" Viggo asked next.

"Yes."

"How?"

"There's hawthorn powder mixed with the ink."

"Mm," Zan breathed into my ear. "Clever little human. Too bad he didn't get one, isn't it?"

I bit my tongue, not responding to his taunting. Pax came into my sight, his focus on Viggo and Warner. Viggo went on to ask his next question.

"Do you know a secret way into Project Hope?"

"Yes."

"Are you able to get to it?"

"Yes."

"Are you or Kali part of PARA?"

"No."

Zan shifted behind me. "Ask him how old she is."

The back of my neck prickled when Viggo repeated the question.

"Twenty-four," Warner answered.

"You haven't been tested yet?" Zan asked, keeping his lips near my ear.

The image of the platform in the city center with

Norman and his knife flashed in my head, but I stayed completely still, refusing to answer him.

"Ask him," Zan ordered. Viggo asked Warner the same question.

"No."

Pax glanced at Zan as Viggo asked the next thing.

"When is her birthday month?"

"June."

"Two months," Pax muttered. "She hasn't been tested yet, Zan."

"She's an orphan," Zan added, sounding thoughtful.

"Yes," I spat out. "I guess it doesn't matter, does it? I either die now by you or get killed by the sickness if I do have black blood."

Pax exchanged a look with Zan for a long moment while Viggo asked Warner how old he was and if he'd been tested already. Which he was a couple of years ago.

"Enough for now," Zan gritted out. "He has what we need. Put him back in the cage. We'll get everything later."

Viggo stepped back, releasing Warner's neck, and I watched as he blinked a couple of times and anger flooded back onto his face as Viggo manhandled him back into the cage.

"And her?" Viggo asked, nodding at me. "A human who can't be entranced. Never thought I'd see that."

"There's more of us too," I snapped. "And growing by the day."

Viggo raised an eyebrow, looking amused. "You'll never have the numbers to beat us."

Zan passed me to Pax. "Take her upstairs. She's staying with us."

"Maybe I should do that," Viggo sneered, glaring at his

twin. "For all we know, Pax might let her get away on purpose."

"Fuck off." Pax gripped my arm tightly. "You know I would never put you in danger."

Viggo's mouth fell. "She had a fucking stake to Zan's heart."

"Pax, take her upstairs," Zan said again, turning toward the bar. "We're going to have to let Dad know what we learned."

He and Viggo began speaking in hushed voices while Warner started yelling when Pax dragged me toward the stairs. My fighting did nothing once he just lifted me up.

"If you're going to kill me, just get it over with," I snarled.

"We're not killing you tonight, Kali," Pax said tightly. "The night I met you, I told you we try to save the humans who bleed black. I was telling the truth. You haven't been tested yet. Which means your life is safe until you turn twenty-five."

Chapter 27
Zan

"I didn't know the couch was that comfortable," Viggo mocked as he shoved my legs off the cushions and plopped down.

I shot him a glare as I sat up, running a hand down my face. There was a thud behind me, and I looked into the kitchen to see Pax drinking from a blood bag. Our living quarters were sparse and small. It was open concept with the living room being right next to the kitchen, with a small counter and some mismatched stools separating them. Most of the big furniture, like the leather couch and our beds, had been shipped in from our father, but my brothers and I got everything else in here on our own.

I didn't care that the wooden floors were old and scratched. Or that the walls desperately needed a new coat of paint. The kitchen wasn't usable, but we never cooked, so that wasn't an issue. It was the complete opposite of how we'd lived on our father's property, where we had everything at the snap of our fingers. I loved this even more. Because it was ours. There were no vampires watching us and reporting everything to our father. This house and the city were my freedom. We'd built this city on our own.

I glanced down the hallway, where our three bedrooms were. "How is she?"

Viggo arched an eyebrow. "Do you care?"

"I brought her food an hour ago," Pax spoke up. "She still won't say a word."

"Maybe she'll talk to you," Viggo mused with a chuckle. "Or not. Seeing as you locked her in your room two days ago."

I gritted my teeth, wishing we hadn't soundproofed our rooms so I could hear her. But living so close together, I never would have gotten sleep with Viggo's room right next to me, since he loved to bring women home nearly every day.

Pax had been the one bringing her food and books for the last two days. He was trying to make up for lying to us about her. I wasn't sure what I was pissed about most. The fact that my brother had lied to us for over a week for a human had fury burning my veins. Knowing she'd lied about who she was stung nearly just as much. When I'd thought she was a new vampire, I'd opened up to her. It wasn't much, but it was more open than I'd ever been with anyone besides my brothers.

"We going to tell Dad about her?" Viggo asked. He leaned over the small coffee table to roll his cigarettes.

"Not yet," I answered gruffly.

We were getting word to him about what we learned from Warner about how we had a way into Project Hope. But the messenger wasn't told a word about Kali. If Dad found out about her, the torture he'd inflict on her would make her wish she was dead. A human in our city for a week acting as a vampire? He'd have to make a show of what happened to people who tried playing us.

"What are you doing here, Zan?" Viggo murmured, slipping into his big brother role. "She's human. Lied to us. Found out things that make it impossible to let her leave here alive."

"We're waiting for her birthday month. If she bleeds black, then it won't be an issue—"

"And what if she doesn't?" Viggo cut me off. "What if her blood is bright red and she's a normal human? She can't be entranced. She's a liability. What are you going to do? Turn her or kill her?"

"I'll decide when I need to," I snapped as I jumped to my feet.

"I don't even know if turning her would help at this point," Viggo mumbled. "She hates us—you especially. I don't think that will change, even if she does become one of us."

"Did our scouts get what I wanted?" I asked, changing the subject.

"Yes," Pax answered from the kitchen. "They'll be back tonight."

I nodded before striding down the hall. "I'll meet you downstairs later."

"Wait," Viggo called out, his voice laced with amusement. "Be careful going in there. If you have any wood in your room, she's most likely going to try and stab you. Again."

I ignored him, even though I'd already had the same thoughts. The only wooden thing was the dresser, and it was thick, old wood. I'd notice right away if she tried breaking it. My bedframe was metal, and I'd already had

Pax take my desk out. Pulling the key from my pocket, I unlocked my bedroom door and pushed it open.

Kali was sitting at the edge of the bed, and she scrambled to her feet when I stepped into the room and kicked the door closed. My eyes widened when I took in what she was wearing. My fucking clothes. The black T-shirt was long, brushing her thighs as she stood to her full height while glaring at me. Her legs were bare, and my eyes raked over her skin just like the first night I met her.

Why? Why the hell did she have this hold on me that I couldn't fucking shake? After learning who she really was, I should have killed her. If she were anyone else, I would have. But with her? I couldn't. This was why I'd stayed away from her for the last two days. I tried distancing myself to think clearly about her, but it didn't help. Was I furious with her? Yes. I didn't trust her for anything. Yet here she was—alive and in my room.

And her scent? *Oh my fuck.* It was seared into my brain. When I tasted her, something snapped inside me. And seeing her in my clothes only strengthened this foreign emotion. *Possessiveness.* As much as I wanted to hate her, there was a jagged piece of me that refused to let her go. Which only infuriated me.

Human or vampire, she was fucking mine.

"Come to kill me?" she asked, making my eyes snap back to her face. She crossed her arms, her glare frigid as she stayed in front of my bed. "Death would be better than being trapped here anyway."

I leaned against the door, and her eyes followed my hand when I put the key back in my pocket. "Pax said you haven't spoken a word since we brought you up here."

"Pax and Viggo don't make the decisions about me," she sneered. "You do."

She wasn't wrong. My brothers wouldn't make any choices when it came to her. It was all on me. Meaning that if she continued to be a threat to us, I had to make the decision.

"Why did you decide to grace me with your presence instead of sending your brother?" she asked, her feisty attitude out in full force. She raised her chin, turning her head to expose her throat. My jaw clenched when I saw the two scabbed marks from my bite. "Did you want another taste of something you had no right to take?"

I strode forward, my movement catching her off guard. Immediately, her stance went defensive, and she backed up until her legs hit the bed. Out of the corner of my eye, I noticed one of the dresser drawers was crooked, and my lips lifted in an amused grin. I'd bet my life she had a makeshift stake hidden somewhere in here.

I stopped in front of her, and she narrowed her eyes, not flinching away when I raised my hand, letting my fingers drift over the mark I'd left on her.

"You shouldn't offer something so tempting," I murmured, bringing my lips closer to hers. "Unless you're willing to accept the consequences."

"I didn't offer it last time," she snapped, swatting my hand away. "How long have I been locked in here?"

I glanced at my boarded-up window, realizing she had no way to tell time in here. "A little over two days."

A bit of fight left her eyes as she met my gaze. "Is he still alive?"

"Warner is exactly where you saw him last."

"Locked in a cage," she said bitterly.

"Better than him being dead."

"I'm not sure about that," she countered, shifting her weight from one foot to the other. She didn't want me so close, but she didn't make a move to push me away. I was positive it wasn't fear holding her back. No, she was plotting something.

"Would you like me to kill him?" I questioned, tilting my head. "Because that can be arranged."

"I have a feeling he's useful to you until you've forced every piece of information you can from his head."

"True. We haven't asked him everything yet."

"And why am I useful?" she gritted out. "You can't control me by entrancement. Why are vampires so interested in the Shadows?"

I tsked, shaking my head. "You've learned enough secrets since being here. I'm not supplying you with any more."

"I'm not staying in here for two fucking months," she hissed, her palms slamming against my chest.

I caught her wrists, stopping her attempt to shove me away and bringing her closer instead. She arched her back, trying to put some space between us, but I followed, my hold the only reason she didn't fall onto the bed.

"You *are* staying here," I said in a low voice, watching fury slide into her gaze. "But...if you behave, then you can leave this room."

Rage. Defiance. A touch of fear. They all clouded her features until she decided to plaster a smile on her face. A fake one, but still better than the glare she'd been giving me since I stepped inside.

"I want to leave this room," she stated.

"Where's your bag?" I asked. "Pax said you had one, but it's not in the room you were staying in."

"Somewhere you can't find it."

"Too bad," I said with a sigh. "Because you aren't leaving this room until you can use that lotion again."

"Why?"

"Because I was going to let you work at Impulse again, but not when you smell this delicious. You'll attract all the vampires."

She scowled. "There are other humans down there."

"Who get fed on," I shot back. "Is that what you want?"

I didn't know why I was even giving her an option. She was absolutely not going down there when her scent was so strong. I didn't want any other vampire to taste her.

"I'm not telling you where it is."

"More secrets?" I shrugged when she didn't respond. "Fine. Enjoy the room."

"You can't just keep me locked in here," she seethed, her hands clenching into fists.

"Watch me. Oh, and I'm tired of the couch, so I'll be sleeping in here once morning comes."

There was a sudden banging on the door before it swung open and Viggo rushed in. He didn't have to say anything for me to know something was wrong. He was tense, his usual grin replaced with a deep frown.

"We need to talk," he said, shooting Kali a look. "Not sure if you want her to hear."

"Does it have to do with her?" I asked.

"Maybe. If it's her fault." Distrust lined his features as he stared past me at her. "I have a feeling it is."

Fuck. "What's wrong?"

"A raid," he hissed. "PARA. Some are already in the city."

I whirled around, anger rushing through me as I faced Kali. "You *did* get word out when you went into the woods," I accused.

"Wait," she shrieked when I advanced toward her. "I didn't give PARA anything."

"Liar," Viggo muttered darkly. "It's a coincidence it's happening now?"

"It's happened before," I reminded him. "They never get far into the city."

"It's an entire fucking unit, Zan," he snapped, the worry in his voice putting me on edge. "We're calling everyone out. The only person still at the bar is Gia."

"Shit." I met her gaze. "What did you do, Kali?"

"It wasn't me," she screamed, backing away from me. "Pax told you I was running that night. PARA wants me dead. Why would I tell them where I'm trapped?"

I swiped a hand over my chin, glancing at Viggo. "Get clothes from Gia for her. She's going downstairs. I want eyes on her."

Kali shouted at me when I left the room with Viggo, locking the door behind me. My chest tightened as Viggo started explaining how many humans were trying to enter our city. It was a fucking lot. A planned attack. We'd known they were gearing up for something for a while, but we weren't expecting it so soon. This city was large, and we needed to keep them out of the city center where most of us lived.

"Your girl did this," Viggo said in a low voice. "If we find out that's true, she can't stay. You understand, Zan?"

"I know," I clipped out. "Gia will watch her while we deal with this."

"Why are they coming at night?" Viggo voiced his thoughts out loud. "All the other times, it was during the day."

"I don't know."

I followed him out of our place, heading downstairs. There had been a handful of times humans had come into the city, and we'd pushed them out. They knew we were here but didn't know our numbers. We made it look like just another run-down city where random vampires lived. I had a bad feeling tonight was going to change all of that.

Chapter 28
Kali

Zan gripped my arm, keeping me beside him as we entered Impulse from the stairwell. My stomach was in knots, and it only got worse when we stepped into the empty room. Zan was tense. On edge more than I'd ever seen him.

"I didn't do this," I muttered as he tugged me toward the bar. "I'm running from the government."

"Do not try to leave," he ordered gruffly, acting like I hadn't said a word. "Gia is watching you. I don't want you upstairs when no one can be up there to listen for you."

"Go, Zan," Gia said, appearing from one of the back rooms. "She won't leave my sight."

She gave me a small smile, which confused the hell out of me as Zan dropped his hand from me. I turned my head, catching sight of Warner in the same cage as last time. I jerked when Zan suddenly lowered his head, bringing his lips much too close to my cheek.

"Just because it's only Gia doesn't mean you can try anything," he breathed in my ear. "She is old, which means she's strong. You don't stand a chance against her."

"Kali is smart enough to know that," Gia said with a wave of her hand. "Go help your brothers."

Zan cursed under his breath and spun away. I watched as he slammed open the door before disappearing into the darkness. Turning my attention to Gia, I slowly backed up, going closer to Warner's cage.

"Go talk to him." Gia reached under the bar. "It's not like we have anything else to do right now."

Her voice was cheery as usual, but her smile was cracked, and her eyes kept darting to the door. She was nervous too. My lips parted when she set two guns on the counter. One was a small pistol and the other was a long shotgun.

"Vampires use guns?" I muttered.

"Our teeth and strength usually do a good job," Gia replied. "But they bring big weapons. We need our own too. How do you think the war lasted so long?"

"I'm surprised you're talking to me." I cleared my throat. "Zan and his brothers hate me after finding out I'm not one of you."

"Zan doesn't hate you. If he did, you'd already be dead."

"They're waiting until my birthday."

She sighed. "Kali. I've known Zan since before he became a vampire. Believe me when I say he does not hate you. I have a feeling you'll be around a long time. Which is fine with me. I like you. As long as you aren't a threat to my family. And I consider Zan family."

Her warning wasn't lost on me, and her eyes flashed dangerously before she shook her head and went back to loading bullets into the guns. My gaze trailed to the back room, where my own weapon was hidden.

"Kali," Warner whispered from behind me.

I spun around, grabbing the bars. His hands covered

mine, and relief flooded his face. I opened my mouth before immediately closing it again. There was so much I wanted to say, but Gia was listening to every word, so I had to be careful.

"Hey," I said softly. "Are you okay?"

"Are you?" His gaze slowly trailed down my body. "I thought they were going to hurt you after finding out you were human."

"They just locked me in a room upstairs. I'm fine."

"How the hell did you make them think you were one of them?"

"I had the lotion on the first night. They guessed that, and I just ran with it."

"Smart," he muttered. "I'm glad that you're still...you."

A lump grew in my throat. "I wanted to tell you, but they hear everything."

"Yes, we do," Gia sang out.

Warner shot her a death glare. "PARA is going to destroy this place."

"And us along with it," I mumbled. "They're going to kill us, Warner."

He gave me a small lopsided grin, trying to ease my worry like he'd done when we were kids. "Hey. We survived this long. We'll get out of this too."

I returned a weak smile of my own. I pulled my hands from the bars and glanced over my shoulder at Gia. She was staring at the front door, her head tilted slightly, making a chill run down my spine.

"Can you hear them?" I whispered.

"They're closer than they should be." Her eyes snapped to mine. "I want you to go into a back room, and don't come out until I say."

"No," I protested. "I'm not leaving Warner—"

"Go," she demanded sharply. "Or I'll lock you in a room."

"Let him go with me," I pleaded, staying right next to the cage. "If they get in here, they'll kill him."

"No. This is the last time I'm telling you. Go, or I'll make you."

"Kali, just go," Warner said in a low voice. "I'll figure it out."

I gave him one last look before backing away. I had every intention of getting my gun, and I didn't want Gia to put me in a different room where I didn't have a weapon. I slipped inside, gripping the edge of the door while keeping it halfway open. Warner was pacing, watching Gia as she stayed behind the counter with a shotgun in her hands. My mouth grew dry when flashlights began shining through the dark in the front windows.

"Close the door," Gia hissed, not looking away from the windows. "Now."

"Fuck," I muttered, shutting the door and locking it.

Rushing to the couch, I ripped the cushion off and hurriedly unzipped it. My fingers wrapped around the gun, and I checked to make sure it was loaded with a bullet in the chamber. They might be wooden bullets, but they were still deadly to humans. I fell to the floor when there was an explosion loud enough to shake the entire building. Glass shattered from outside the room, followed by yelling and gunshots.

I scrambled to my feet, flinging myself forward and pressing against the wall right near the door. There was a feminine scream, and my heart thudded painfully. Was that Gia? Worry sat on my chest before I could force it away. She was a vampire—I shouldn't care. I tightened my hold on the gun. She'd been nothing but nice to me since I got here.

I stared at the doorknob, trying to listen hard enough to guess how many soldiers were out there, but it was suddenly silent.

"Holy shit." A man's muffled voice came through the door. "Is that Warner Mackley? We've been looking for you."

"Should we bring him back with us?" another voice rang out.

"He has a bounty on his head. Dead or alive."

My heart sank, and I reached forward and silently cracked open the door. From here, I couldn't see the bar, but I could see the cage Warner was in with three men surrounding him. They were all wearing tactical gear, but two of them had taken off their helmets. Their necks were wrapped with something to make it harder to get bit. Panic slid through me, my steps heavy as I moved out of the room.

"Kill him," one of the men ordered. "We don't need to be dragging him back."

Warner saw me, but he didn't say a word as I lifted the gun. I'd been shooting for three years and had gotten amazing at hitting my target, but a human was completely different from practice. Plus, I was sure they were wearing thick vests, so I had to aim for their heads. I crept closer, giving me a better chance at hitting my mark. Sucking in a slow breath, I aimed for the one who had just spoken.

He was about seven feet in front of me, and I stared at the back of his head, putting it in my sights. I squeezed the trigger right when one of the other men turned and saw me. His shout of warning was too late. My bullet hit the guy in the back of the head, and he dropped to the floor. This was the first time I'd ever taken a human life. I wasn't sure if it was because this was about pure survival or just plain adrenaline, but I didn't feel a flicker of remorse as I backed away.

"Hey," the man snarled, whipping out his own gun. "Put it down."

Warner's hand shot past the bars, and he grabbed the side of the guy's head and smashed it against the cage. I aimed and shot at the man in the helmet who was charging at me. The bullet hit him in the upper chest, and it slowed him down, but it didn't stop him. He lowered his shoulder, as if going to tackle me, and I fell to the floor a second before he reached me. His momentum didn't allow him to stop in time, and he tripped over me, letting out a grunt when he slammed into the floor.

I jumped to my feet, leaping on top of him before he could get back up. I let my gun fall from my grip, knowing I'd need both hands to do this. He was on his back, and I dodged his first hit while reaching for his belt. I felt the handle of the knife and quickly tugged it from its holder.

I rolled off his stomach before turning and stabbing the blade where he was least protected. When the knife slid into his thigh near his knee, he jerked, screaming loud enough for me to hear through the helmet. I went to stab him again, but he kicked his other leg up, hitting me in the ribs. Pain jolted up my side, and I lost my balance. My palms hit the floor for a second before I scrambled back to my feet. By this time, the man had taken off his helmet. His brown eyes were lit up with rage, and his longer blond hair was a mess from being under the helmet.

Had he not learned anything in training? Never take off the armor that protected him. With a scream, I jumped back on top of him, slicing my knife at his hands when he tried reaching for me. He still had an edge on me with all his tactical gear, but I'd been learning to fight for years. I had a better chance against him than the vampires I'd been surrounded by.

"Not a vampire," he spat out. "You're the one on the run with him."

He reached up, his hand tangling in my hair, and I gritted my teeth when he yanked. This was why I always wore my hair up, but Zan's bedroom didn't have anything for me to use to tie it up. I swung my arm, trying to hit his face with the blade, but he yanked me back by the hair before I could hit him. He threw me off him, and my eyes watered from the pain on my scalp as I landed on the wooden floor. I kept a tight hold on the knife as I rolled away even farther before getting back to my feet.

"Fucking bitch," he snarled. He had gotten up too but was limping from the stab wound. "I'm going to enjoy gutting you."

He lunged at me, and I shot my foot out, kicking him in the leg where he was bleeding. He crumpled to the floor with a howl of pain, his hands going to his thigh. In three steps, I was in front of him, and I jammed the blade into the side of his throat. He gurgled out breaths, his leg forgotten as I pulled the knife away.

"Look out," Warner bellowed.

I whipped around to see another man running through the bar from the back area. His helmet was off, and his black hair was buzzed short. He had a gun in his hand. I ducked low, running the other way and scooping my own gun up before diving behind a pool table. I cursed under my breath, knowing this was a horrible spot.

I peeked around the side, and a bullet whizzed past my ear. Falling back, I dropped to my stomach and aimed at the man's leg from under the table.

"Fuck," I hissed when my first shot missed. I squeezed

the trigger again, and this time, I hit him in the leg. When he fell, I took aim at his head until Warner's voice shot ice through my veins.

"Three of them," he screamed. "Behind you."

Their shadows fell across me, and I rolled onto my back, taking another shot at the first person I saw. My bullet hit a man in the shoulder, and he stumbled back, but two others were on me in a second. I didn't even get a chance to look at my attackers before a fist cracked against my jaw. Hot pain filled the side of my face, and I blinked, unable to recover before boots kicked me hard enough to break one of my ribs.

I choked out an agonizing breath, curling into a ball when the gun was wrenched from my hand. I screamed, blindly swinging as someone heaved me up by grabbing me under the arms. More hands grabbed my ankles, picking me up off the floor as I struggled against them.

"Get off," I shrieked, twisting and writhing as I was carried away from the pool table.

My legs were suddenly free, and a second later, I was flung into something hard. The back of my head spasmed with pain as I slumped to the floor. The world was spinning, the pain making me nauseous as I tried getting my bearings.

"Leave her the fuck alone," Warner snarled from behind me, making me realize I'd been thrown against his cage.

Before I could move, someone stepped over me, straddling my legs as he stood above me. I steeled myself, raising my chin to meet his gaze. My head was pounding, my ribs screaming with agony, but I bit my tongue, refusing to show them any of that. It was the man whose leg I'd shot from under the pool table. His wound was bleeding, but I must not have hit a vital spot, seeing as he was still standing. He had a gun in his hand, and he stared down at me with a vile smirk on his face. Three other men who were still wearing their helmets stood behind him.

The guy crouched down, putting his gun to my forehead when I tried moving. His weight fell on my legs as I sat there, and my heart thundered in my chest when I met his gaze. His brown eyes gleamed with cruelness as he studied me.

"Kali, I'm guessing," he murmured. "We've been searching for both of you all over these damn woods this week."

"She didn't do anything," Warner hissed from behind me. "She wasn't there. It was all me and my sister."

"That's not what we were told," the guy replied.

A shot rang out, and Warner let out a grunt of pain, his footsteps stumbling farther away from me.

"No," I cried out, jerking forward, only to freeze when the guy pressed the gun harder against my forehead.

"Don't fucking move," he warned. "I have a choice. Bring you back alive. Or kill you here. What do you think I should do?"

"We should probably hurry. We don't want any vampires running in here," one of the others said nervously.

I swallowed thickly, wanting to look behind me, but the gun on my head made that impossible. I could hear Warner's labored breathing, meaning he was still alive. For now, at least.

"Have you two been in this city the whole time?" The guy cocked his head. "We've been looking in the wrong place. What a waste of our fucking time."

Without warning, he moved the gun, backhanding me across the face with his other hand. I felt my lip split, tasting blood on my tongue as I glared at him, my chest heaving. My body was shaking, and I couldn't stop it, no matter how hard I tried. Everything fucking hurt, and I couldn't even shift slightly without feeling like I was choking for a breath. I had at least one broken rib. But that was the least of my worries when the guy holstered his gun and took out his own knife.

"You stabbed one of my men. It's only fair I do the same to you."

He didn't hesitate, and the scream didn't leave my throat before he plunged it into my stomach.

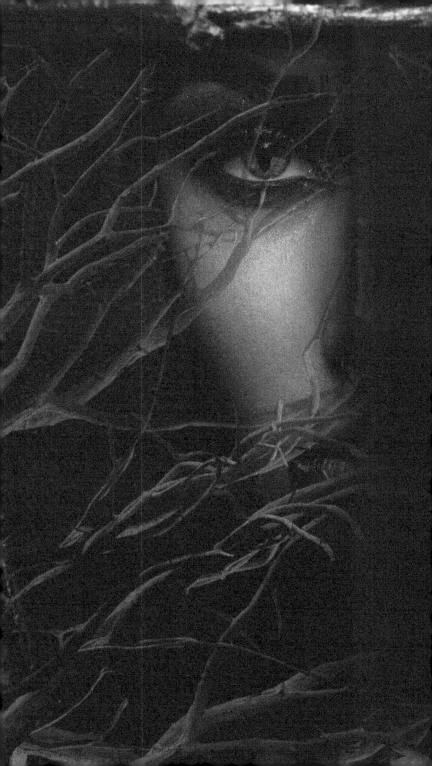

Chapter 29
Kali

Pain like I'd never felt traveled through my body like a wildfire, and I let out a tortured wail when he twisted the blade that was still buried inside me.

"Kali. Fuck. Kali." Warner was shouting, but he sounded so far away. I sagged against the cage, slipping more toward the floor when the guy yanked the blade out of me. My hands went to my wound, the blood already seeping out. I blinked rapidly, trying to stay alert, but the pain—*fuck*—it was so bad. The guy climbed off me, and I fell to the side, my head hitting the floor as I curled into myself.

There was a muffled scream, and I forced my head up slightly to see that one of the men with a helmet on had fallen. The other two were drawing their weapons until one was thrown into a nearby table. Black spots dotted my vision when hands wrapped around the other guy's helmet. There was a sickening crack when the man's head was twisted at an unnatural angle before he fell to the floor.

I couldn't see where the third guy went, but the man who'd stabbed me was up and rushing away until someone stepped in his way. If I wasn't slowly dying, the shock of seeing Zan would have been much more jolting. He looked downright fucking terrifying. His eyes were dark, clouded with fury. Blood soaked nearly every inch of his clothes, and I had a feeling it wasn't his. I choked out shallow breaths, keeping my eyes on Zan as he threw a punch to the man's face before gripping the collar of his jacket and yanking him close.

"If I had more time, I'd fucking tear you limb from limb. I could make it last days," Zan murmured, his icy tone holding only violent promises.

"Because you're all killers," the guy spat out. "Nothing but filthy fucking monsters."

Zan's chuckle was cruel. "I'll gladly live up to that name. But merciful? That word isn't in my vocabulary."

In a quick move, Zan ripped the guy's neck protection off before going for the two stakes that were on the man's belt. He threw the stakes across the room while keeping his other hand wrapped in the guy's jacket to hold him in place when he tried getting away. Zan's fangs slid down, and with a growl, he lowered his head as the man screamed in horror. His fangs ripped into the guy's throat, but he didn't feed. He literally bit down and then ripped his head away, taking part of the guy's throat with him.

The man's mouth was open in a silent scream, and his face was twisted in agony as he fell to the floor. Blood slowly poured out of his neck as Zan reached down, ripping his jacket open and then tearing at his Kevlar vest. The knife stained with my blood was on the floor, and Zan snatched it up, stabbing the guy in the chest. He leaned over him, twisting the blade slowly as the man writhed under him.

"Those two wounds are some of the slowest—and most fucking painful—ways to go." Zan pulled the blade from the guy's chest, tossing it on the floor. "Enjoy your last minutes."

I struggled to keep my eyes open as he turned to me. I couldn't feel the pain anymore. My body was going numb, my head in a hazy fog. His gaze trailed over my battered body as he strode closer before suddenly halting and looking past me.

"Leave her alone," Warner snapped, his voice weak.

A muscle in Zan's jaw flexed as his eyes darted back to me before he stepped past me. Warner let out a shout before there was a loud thud.

"Let me go," Warner's voice was right behind me, and with huge effort, I twisted my neck to see Zan gripping Warner's arm, keeping him right by the bars.

"Look at me," Zan commanded, his voice sharp. He finally caught Warner's gaze, and Warner's face fell flat, his emotions suddenly gone. "You're going to forget the last twenty minutes. You did not see anything that happened in here. Do you understand?"

"Yes," Warner answered, his voice expressionless.

"You did not see Kali get hurt. All you remember is getting knocked out and waking up to see Kali on the floor. Understand?"

"Yes."

"Now, you're going to turn the other way and count in your head. Do not stop until you reach five hundred. Do it now."

Zan released him, and Warner immediately turned around, facing away from us. His body relaxed as he silently counted. I didn't have the capacity to understand what Zan was doing when he focused back on me and dropped to his knees beside me. His eyes cut to the floor that I was sure was covered with my blood. He reached over me, gently pressing his hand over mine that was still covering my stab wound.

"Fuck, Kali," he gritted out. "I shouldn't have left you here."

"Why?" I choked out, the word barely coherent. "Now you don't have to worry about me knowing your secrets."

His eyes darted to mine, indecision swirling in them. Until he lifted his other arm, bringing his wrist to his mouth. His fangs appeared before he bit his own wrist. Fear tore through me, hitting me even through the numbness. I jerked, but his other hand stayed on my stomach as he tore open the skin on the inside of his wrist.

I pressed my lips together, but he shoved his wrist toward me, using his other hand to grip my chin, holding my face still as he pressed his open wound against my lips. The copper taste of his blood coated my tongue, and he tilted my head back, refusing to let me move as more of his blood hit my throat. Terror sliced through my heart, remembering watching the man die from ingesting vampire blood. Their blood was toxic to us. It was a torturous way to die, and I waited for the pain to start. Did Zan really hate me that much?

"I'm going back on my word. Something I never do," he murmured, making sure his blood was still dripping into my mouth. "I told you that I won't give you any more of our secrets. But here I am."

I tried not to swallow, but it was useless. Once his blood hit my throat, it was a losing battle. Tears streamed down my face, and he finally moved his arm away. I glared at him, opening my mouth, but nothing came out when someone in tactical gear suddenly appeared behind Zan.

Zan noticed immediately and he stiffened, his muscles tensing as he looked ready to jump to his feet. But before he could, the masked man pressed a gun to the back of Zan's head.

"Wooden bullets," the man said in warning. "I wouldn't move."

Zan stayed completely still, his lips twisting in a murderous scowl. The bullet wouldn't kill him, but one shot to the head, and he'd be knocked unconscious until the wood worked its way out of his brain. Footsteps alerted me that others were coming, and I lay there, just waiting for Zan's blood to hit my system. Why try to move when I was going to die anyway?

"Kali," a voice gasped before someone fell beside me.

Shock coursed through me when I looked at Jill. Tim was standing behind her, and I glanced around, seeing more members of our group. I whipped my head back around to stare at the man who was holding the gun on Zan.

"Hey, Kali," the guy said softly. This time I recognized his voice, knowing who was under the mask. He was one of our guys, though he'd infiltrated PARA. Collin. The same one who helped me get out of Project Hope.

"Warner." Tim snapped his fingers. "Warner. What the hell is wrong with him?"

Zan was still on his knees, his eyes heated with rage as he looked at every human before focusing back on me. I wondered if he'd be able to move fast enough to get away before Collin got a shot on him. Since the muzzle of the gun was firmly pressed against his head, the chance was slim, which was probably why he hadn't moved.

"Kill him," Jill ordered, loathing in her voice as she glanced at Zan.

My heart thudded, and I shook my head. "Kane."

"What?" Jill asked.

"He's a Kane. Amaros's son," I whispered hoarsely.

Jill exchanged a glance with Tim before muttering something to another Clover member. If I thought Zan was enraged a second ago, it was nothing compared to now. His glare was scathing as I shifted slightly. They wouldn't kill him. As a Kane, he had secrets they wanted.

I sucked in a sharp breath when a wave of pain suddenly crippled my body. The numbness trickled away, and I could suddenly feel every one of my injuries again. I let out a cry, pressing my hands to my stomach. My head thundered hard enough that I squeezed my eyes shut.

"Jesus, that's a lot of blood," Jill muttered. I felt a soft touch on my arm. "Where are you hit?"

"We need to get out of here," Tim said in a rushed voice. "Before any more vampires or soldiers find us."

I forced my eyes open, meeting Jill's worried gaze. "Get Warner out. He can walk. There's a key for the cage...in the drawer behind the bar."

Jill relayed the order to someone else, and I heard hurried footsteps as I trembled, the agony still squeezing every part of my body. Jill ran her hands over me, searching for my wounds before tugging me up until I was sitting. The move stole my breath, and I winced, my ribs screaming in pain.

"Fuck," I hissed. "Just leave me here. Get out while you can."

"Whatever hurts, you can handle it," Jill said sharply. "You have no open injuries. We'll check for internal ones once we get out of here."

My lips parted at her words, and I brought my hands to my stomach, realizing my blood wasn't seeping out anymore. I clawed at my shirt, lifting it up and swiping at the drying blood on my skin. I stared in absolute shock, seeing a small, jagged cut that looked barely skin deep.

Another jolt of pain had me flinching, but I realized it wasn't as bad as the last one. I snapped my head up, meeting Zan's eyes. He didn't give me anything, glaring back with his lips pressed in a line.

Was his blood...healing me?

No, that wasn't fucking possible. I saw with my own eyes what happened to the man who'd drunk vampire blood. My entire city had witnessed it. Before I had time to process anything else, Jill grabbed my arm, hauling me to my feet.

"Shoot him," Tim demanded. "We're taking him with us."

Before the words were out of his mouth, Zan ducked, moving so fast that by the time Collin shot, he was already out of the way. Zan grabbed Collin's ankle, yanking hard, and he crashed to the floor with a grunt. Zan was on his feet, his fangs out as he whirled around to attack the closest human. He got his hands around the guy's neck, letting out a roar when Tim came up behind him, shoving a stake into his lower back. Jill joined in the fight, stabbing Zan in the stomach before he shoved her away.

"You take me, you'll fucking die," Zan threatened, his voice sending chills down my spine. "No one fucks with the Kane family."

He grabbed the closest man, flinging him across the room before spinning toward Jill. Even though my wounds were healing, I was still no help with anything. I could barely fucking move. Tim leaped on Zan's back, jabbing a needle into his neck before Zan was able to flip him off. Tim landed on his back, wheezing out breaths as Zan fell to his knees, reaching up and ripping the needle out.

He tried climbing back to his feet, but the hawthorn that Tim had shot into his bloodstream was already working. He fell forward, landing on his palms as he groaned in pain. Jill came up, stabbing another needle into his neck, pushing even more hawthorn into his system. He slumped to the floor, going unconscious. I bit my tongue, guilt clutching me as two men heaved him up. He'd just saved my life. And now he was about to be tortured for information.

"Kali." Warner appeared beside me, his hands cupping my face as he searched my eyes. "Are you okay?"

"Yeah," I choked out weakly. "I'm fine."

"Let's go," Tim ordered. "We're running out of time."

Warner swept me into his arms, lifting me up. The two guys in front of us were dragging Zan with them, and Warner started walking with Jill at our side.

"How'd you get here?" Warner asked as we kept moving, leaving the club.

"We got Kali's note," Tim answered from my other side. "Collin knew about the raid, and we thought this was the best time to try and get to you."

"You did all this to get us back?" I asked in a whisper.

Jill sighed. "We care for our own. But—"

"Yes," Tim cut her off, giving her a pointed look. "We're family, Kali."

I glanced up to see Warner giving Tim a curious stare, but he didn't say anything as we rushed down the street. We weren't moving as fast with Zan being dragged, but there were no soldiers or vampires around. I could hear shots and screams, but it sounded like they were near the street I'd first come here through, which wasn't very close.

"I know a way out," I said. "The same way I used when I snuck out to put the note in the tree."

Tim nodded. "Let's go. We have a truck waiting in the woods."

"Where are we going?" Warner asked.

"To the Clovers who live outside the city walls. One of their members will drive you there," Jill answered. "It's about six hours from here. You two will stay there."

"And him?" I asked, my eyes going to Zan.

"He's going to give us all the answers to end his race," Tim stated coldly. "I don't care what it takes. He's going to fucking talk."

Cold slid through my veins, even though his answer was exactly what I expected it to be.

"His brothers will come looking for him," I whispered. "We're all dead if they find us."

Jill shot me a small smile. "Don't worry, Kali. They won't find us. This is the break we've been waiting for."

Her words didn't ease the knots growing in my stomach, but I didn't say anything as we got closer to leaving the city. Warner's hold tightened on me as he ran, and I rested my head on his chest, running a hand over my stomach again. Zan had saved me. And I wasn't sure how I felt about that.

Chapter 30
Zan

White hot pain seared through my chest when the stake was stabbed into me only inches from my heart. I clenched my jaw, slamming my teeth together to stay silent. They'd been at this all fucking day. Jabbing stakes into every part of my body and then waiting for me to heal before starting all over again. Hawthorn was still coursing through my system, keeping me weaker than my usual strength. The guy—who I'd learned was named Tim—pulled the stake out, only to ram it into my stomach.

The chains holding me hostage rattled when I jerked, unable to stay still when he pushed it deeper. I swallowed a grunt, refusing to give him the satisfaction of showing my pain.

"I'll keep doing this," Tim threatened, ripping the wood out of me. "And I have other ways to make you talk. Even worse than stabbing you with this."

I forced out a dark chuckle. "By all means, keep doing it. When my family comes, I'll make sure your death is nice and slow."

"No one is coming," Tim snapped. He dropped the stake and then swung his fist into my jaw. It stung but was nothing compared to the stakes they'd been stabbing me with. I caught him shaking out his hand, and I threw him a leering smirk.

"I'm not some weak human you can torture until I break," I taunted. "I can sit here for as long as it takes and I won't say a fucking word."

"Where is your father's property?" he gritted out.

I sat there, keeping my mocking grin even when he shoved the stake back into my gut. He let out an annoyed snarl before straightening up and glaring at me.

"I do have a few things I'll share with you," I said, cocking my head. "But not until I get what I want."

"You're not making the rules," he snapped.

I straightened out my legs, the chain that was wrapped around my ankles dragging along the floor. "Sure, I am. You just don't know it yet."

That remark earned me another stab, this time in my shoulder. Pain flared down my arm, but I forced my body to stay relaxed as Tim backed away.

"I'll be back in a while," he stated. "Maybe some time alone will make you realize you should start talking sooner rather than later."

"If the last fourteen hours are anything to go by, I think I'll be fine."

He sneered at me before pulling open the basement door and slamming it behind him. I heard the dead bolt slide into place. As if that could keep me in here. His footsteps grew quieter as he went up the stairs, and I shifted slightly, letting myself sag back now that I was alone.

I was conscious when they dragged me into this house, but the hawthorn and chains were the reason they'd gotten me into the basement. The walls were made of gray cement blocks, and the floor was a dirty slab of the same color concrete. There were thick poles every ten feet for support, one of which I was chained to. There was a bare bulb that was close to me, dimly lighting the area I was in. I'd rather be in the dark.

It was clear that it wasn't PARA who'd taken me. Most likely the group that we'd entranced Warner to tell us about. The Clovers. A group that hated the government *and* vampires. It was almost worse than soldiers taking me. These kinds of humans did things on their own, and they were reckless. Which could be more dangerous for me.

But that also meant they had limited means. Which was why I was locked in the basement of a run-down house instead of a secure location in a human city. The basement wasn't even soundproofed, making it easy for me to listen to others in the house. Tim was smart, leaving the house if he wanted to talk about something he didn't want me to hear, but I'd still picked up a few things already. There were twenty people in this house, plus they had another house close to here with more people.

I tried stretching my bound arms behind me, more than a little annoyed that I could barely move. I was sitting on the floor with a metal collar wrapped around my neck, and it was fastened to the steel pole behind me. My arms were pulled behind me, my wrists chained tightly together around the same pole.

I'd already tested the strength, and unfortunately for me, the pole was strong enough to hold me, most likely even at my full strength. However, the chains they'd wrapped my wrists in weren't as thick or durable as the chain and collar around my neck. I'd be able to get my arms free at some point. Then I'd just wait for the fucker to get close enough so I could grab him.

But it wasn't time yet. I wasn't worried about being stuck here. My brothers would find me. It wasn't a question of if, but when. And I was fine to stay here for the time being. Because there was one person I wanted to talk to, and she should be waking up any time now.

I'd already heard Warner voicing his worries about her, proving that she was in the house I was trapped in. My blood might have healed her, but her body still needed rest. I expected her to be sleeping through most of the day, but I was getting impatient. Closing my eyes, I rested against the pole, focusing on the voices outside the basement. I heard Tim's first.

"Don't let anyone else down here." I listened to Tim once he got to the upper floor. "I don't want anyone knowing about his blood."

"Got it." The feminine voice was familiar, and I placed it as the woman who'd shot me up with hawthorn. A few others throughout the day called her Jill.

I scowled, my fists clenching behind me. That was one thing I was less than happy about. I'd been worried Kali had seen it the night she'd stabbed me on the beach. But since my shirt was dark and already wet, she'd missed it. I knew Tim had caught it when he'd stabbed me in the club because they made sure I was covered until they brought me to the basement. They didn't want others to know. Probably a good thing he wasn't blabbing it to anyone.

Because before I left here, I'd have to kill every human who knew my secret.

Tim's and Jill's voices faded away as they went outside, and I sucked in a long breath, blocking out every voice I heard until I found his.

"She's awake," Warner was telling someone. "I'm going to check on her."

"We're going to need to talk to her," the guy replied. "Ask her about everything she learned while in their city."

"It can wait," Warner snapped. "She's been dead to the world for the last fifteen hours. Give her some time."

"Fine. But it won't be much."

I listened to Warner's footsteps before they paused again. A door clicked shut, and he moved more quickly before halting abruptly.

"Warner," Kali choked out. "Where are we?"

My heart pounded when I finally heard her voice. And as much as I hated it, relief swept through me. She'd been so close to death by the time I'd gotten to her in the club that I'd been worried I was too late. After my brothers and I had pushed the unit out of the city, I went back to the club while Viggo and Pax helped organize the clean-up. I had no idea some humans had slipped past the vampires or I never would have left Impulse. I didn't even know if Gia was alive.

By giving Kali my blood, I shared a secret with her that I'd sworn to my father I would never reveal. Humans could not know, or they'd be bloodthirsty. We had done so much over the last several decades to keep it hidden. When I saved her, I thought she'd stay in my city. But now she was here. And if she told the Clovers, there was going to be a problem. I could not let that get out. Even when I gave her my blood, I made sure to keep my wrist hidden once I broke skin. Though I was so panicked when I saw her that I'd almost forgotten to hide it.

I banged the back of my head on the pole. Viggo was right. She was a liability. One that I couldn't seem to leave alone.

"We're in Galvin," Warner answered. I forced my thoughts away so I could listen. They were at least two floors above me, and I had to concentrate to hear everything. "Tim and Jill ended up staying. Collin is covering for them at Project Hope."

"Where's Zan?"

Her question had my lips pulling up into a small grin. I was on her mind enough for her to ask about me nearly as soon as she woke up.

"He's locked up. He can't touch you anymore, Kali."

She didn't respond to Warner, and I ground my teeth when I heard something creaking. I had a feeling he'd just climbed onto the bed she was sleeping on.

"What happened?" he asked her softly. "I don't remember anything. All I remember was seeing you on the floor with bodies everywhere."

"PARA," she said stiffly. "They came after me. And then...Zan showed up. He killed them before they got to me."

"You were covered in blood," he said in a low voice.

"I had to fight them off before Zan came."

"There's not a mark on you."

She laughed, and I picked up immediately that it was forced.

"Tim did a good job with training me. Are you okay? You got shot."

"Only in my arm. They already stitched it up. I'm good. How are you feeling?" he asked, worry in his voice.

"I'm fine," she promised. Then footsteps softer than Warner's began pacing the floor. "Is he here?"

"Who?"

She paused. "Zan."

"Why?" Warner growled. "You don't need to see him."

"Because I still have questions for him," she said, growing annoyed. "He wouldn't answer when I was stuck with him. Maybe he will now."

I scoffed in amusement. Apparently her brush with death did nothing to her attitude. She also didn't tell Warner about me saving her with my blood. Thank fuck. I hoped she continued to stay quiet about it.

"Tim will get all the answers you want," Warner said tightly. "Just talk to Tim and Jill about it. Stay away from the vampire, Kali."

"I need food." She changed the subject. "Where's the kitchen?"

"Downstairs. I'll go with you." His footsteps joined hers for a moment before they both stopped. "Wait. I'm sorry. I didn't mean to get snappy with you. I'm just—fuck. It was a long nine days. And having to watch that fucking vampire touch you like he owned you. I don't know what he did to you, but I just want to make sure you're okay."

"He didn't hurt me," she murmured. "I'm fine. Just hungry."

"Don't push me away. I couldn't take it. We've lost Lisa and Helena." His voice cracked before he cleared his throat. "We're all each other has now."

Rage clouded my thoughts, but before I could keep listening, the basement door slammed back open. I flicked my gaze toward Tim as he filled the doorway, irritated that he was interrupting me.

"Ready for some more questions?" Tim asked, holding a stake.

"Not from you," I drawled. "I'll give you a few answers —of my choosing. But I'll only talk to one person."

"You only talk to me," he seethed as he stepped closer.

"That's not going to work. But feel free to keep

tormenting me while I stay silent." I kept his stare. "I could do this for days. And I hear you're on a time crunch. How long can you be away from Project Hope before they figure out you're gone?"

His face turned a shade darker, and he glared at me with murder in his eyes. "Who?"

"I'll only talk to Kali."

Chapter 31
Kali

"**D**on't do this." Warner grabbed my arm, pulling me away from the stairs. "You don't have to."

Tim frowned, his eyes dropping to Warner's hand. "He's chained up. He won't be able to touch her. And we need answers. He agreed to talk to her."

"You couldn't torture the answers out of him?" Warner snapped. "Isn't this what you've been waiting for? You're not prepared?"

"Kali is a Clover," Tim said slowly, trying to keep his composure. "We're a team. She can help get this done faster. Let her go, Warner."

"She's dealt with enough," Warner exploded, not backing down. "She was trapped with him for almost two weeks. She gave you everything you needed in that note. Which was how you got into the city in the first place. She did her part."

Chills raced up my spine as my eyes darted to the basement door. Fucking great. I was positive Zan was listening, and him learning that I was the reason they were able to capture him was not a great way to start the conversation. I doubted he'd give me any answers Tim wanted, and I had a feeling he wanted to talk to me for a whole different reason.

"Warner, I can do this," I told him, pushing his hand off me.

His jaw clenched. "I'll be right out here."

I nodded before opening the basement door and going slowly down the stairs. It had only been a couple of hours since I'd woken up, and after food and a shower, I sat in the room with my thoughts flooding through my head. When Tim approached me about talking to Zan, I jumped at the chance.

My body felt perfect, buzzing with energy I didn't even know I had. I couldn't help but wonder if it was Zan's blood racing through me that was making me feel this way.

Once I got to the bottom of the stairs, I hesitated, staring at the closed door. Zan had saved me, and now I was with the people holding him hostage. I had no idea what to expect when I faced him. His voice suddenly drifted through the door, making me freeze.

"I know you're out there, Kali. Don't make me wait any longer. Get in here."

I frowned, my pulse thudding nervously as I slid the dead bolt and pulled open the door. My eyes widened when I saw him, and I slowly stepped into the room as he stared at me. His neck had a thick collar on it that seemed to be connected to the pole behind him. His arms were bound behind him, and his legs were stretched out in front of him, with his ankles chained together.

It was the first time I'd seen him shirtless, and I tried and failed not to study the black ink sprawled all over his skin. Nearly every inch was covered in beautiful work, and drops of water speckled his skin. I raised my gaze, seeing his dark hair was still soaked and dripping. I knew Tim had been down here hurting him, but there wasn't a mark on him. Vampires healed so fast. About as fast as his blood had healed me.

Before I could stop myself, my eyes darted back to his body when he shifted. I knew he was in shape, but fuck. Before I could inspect him more, he spoke, making my gaze go back to his face.

"Go back upstairs."

"What?"

"I told Tim that I didn't want anyone on the first floor when I talked to you," he murmured. "They either go upstairs or outside. Or I don't talk. I can hear him and Warner at the top of the stairs."

"They're not going to leave," I snapped.

"Then I won't say a fucking word."

With a huff, I spun around and ran back up the steps. Warner pushed off the wall, and Tim cursed under his breath.

"What's wrong?" Warner asked in alarm.

I looked at Tim. "He won't talk until you do what he says."

"Do what?" Warner glanced at Tim.

Tim sighed. "He doesn't want anyone trying to listen. We need to go outside."

"Fuck that," Warner hissed. "What if he gets free and Kali's down there with him? We wouldn't get to her in time—"

"He can't move." Tim cut him off. "I locked him up myself. And he still has hawthorn in his system. He's weak."

"Go," I told them. "I'll be fine. Just let me get this done."

Warner grumbled under his breath, not moving until Tim grabbed his arm and forced him to walk down the hall with him. I sucked in a deep breath and headed back downstairs. Zan was watching me as I stepped back into the basement, his face unreadable.

"Close the door," he said in a low voice.

I did what he said, and then leaned against the door, crossing my arms and attempting not to show my nerves. Just like Tim said, Zan was locked down. But I had a feeling even those chains wouldn't stop him once the hawthorn was out of his system. He oozed confidence and strength even now.

"What—"

"Wait," he cut me off, tilting his head. "They aren't outside yet."

I bit my tongue, wondering how good his hearing really was. Could he hear me on the second floor in the room I was staying in? I stood there, the silence making it seem like every second was dragging on. Finally, Zan straightened, the chains clinking against the pole as he focused on me.

"We're alone now."

His words had a mixture of fear and curiosity washing over me. He might be the one chained, but he was acting like he was still in charge. And seeing as he'd gotten me down here like he wanted, he still was, in a way.

"Tim wants to know where your father's property is," I said tightly.

"Is that what you want to know?"

I stared at him. "Yes."

"Too bad. I'm not talking about that. I'll give you enough to make him happy before you leave. But for now, I'm choosing the topic."

His words weren't a surprise. He wouldn't just blurt out his secrets because he was talking to me. No, he was playing a different game. He gave me a small grin, jerking his head in a nod.

"Come closer. I can't see you."

I scoffed. "You can see perfectly."

"Come here, Kali."

"We're not in your city," I ground out. "You can't boss me around."

"If Tim wants any answers, then yes I can."

My irritation flared, and I bit my tongue as I glared at him. Tim was counting on me, and I didn't want to let him or the Clovers down. I shuffled forward, still keeping at least ten feet between us. His eyes raked over my body, dropping to my feet and then raising again, only to stop on my chest.

"You took off my necklace," he said with a frown.

"You think I would have kept it on?" I bit out.

A muscle in his jaw ticked. "You should have. Even if I'm stuck here, you should never take it off."

"Why?" I asked. Warner had broken the lock on it almost immediately after I woke up. It was up in my room right now.

"Because other vampires will leave you alone. You can't go back to your city, which means you have to be careful. It would protect you."

"That's why?" I asked skeptically. "Not because you'd be able to find me if I had it on?"

"Can't do that if I'm chained up here, now can I?"

I crossed my arms. "I didn't come here to talk about the necklace."

"Then let's talk about that note Warner mentioned."

My heart dipped, my nails digging into my arm as I stared at him. "I was telling the truth about not being the reason PARA raided your city."

"But you told your group."

"Yes."

"What was in the note, Kali?"

"Everything I learned while I was with you."

He cursed under his breath, a dangerous gleam hitting his eye. "About new vampires?"

"Yes."

"You told them about me and my brothers being Kanes?"

"Yes."

Oh, he was pissed. He jerked in the chains, and I took a step back, ready to bolt up the stairs. He had a scowl on his face. The cool and calm look he'd worn when I first came in was long gone.

"So they knew about Impulse?" he asked quietly.

I swallowed thickly, realizing where he was going with this. "Yes. They knew that's where you'd be."

He forced out a cold laugh. "You set me up in my own city."

"I had no idea they'd come like that," I hissed. "I didn't know they'd take you."

"You did," he accused. "That's why you told them I was a Kane. So they didn't kill me."

"You saved my life; I saved yours. We're even now."

He fell still at my words, his intense gaze not leaving me. "That's what you think?"

"Why did you save me?" I asked, anger building inside me. He was a vampire. Someone who kept me for almost two weeks. Yet I cared about whether he died. I shouldn't fucking care.

"Why didn't you tell Warner what I did?" he countered.

"Because I have a feeling whoever knows that secret will find themselves at death's door," I muttered.

"You'd be right."

"Except me?"

"Yes."

"Why?"

"You can know all my secrets, Kali." His lips tipped up in a grin that had the back of my neck prickling.

"Why?" I repeated, not sure I wanted to know the answer.

"Because you're coming with me when I leave here."

My jaw dropped. "The hell I am."

"With or without my necklace, I'll find you. We're not done yet."

"So confident for someone who's chained to a pole," I snapped. "I'm not going anywhere with you. And how did your blood heal me? The humans think your blood kills."

He grinned. "Optics."

"Excuse me?"

"If humans knew the benefits of our blood, they'd want it. We didn't want to be hunted any more than we already were."

"I saw a man die with it in his system. With my own eyes." I froze, realizing I'd moved closer to him without noticing. "How do you explain that?"

He paused, sucking in a deep breath as he studied me. "Your government doesn't want the civilians to know either."

My heart stuttered. "What the hell does that mean?"

"I'm not telling you everything today," he said. "But just know that the higher-ups of PARA already know about our blood. And they're the reason that the humans in your cities *looked* like they'd died from our blood. It was a show."

"You're lying."

There was no way. Was there? PARA was shady and controlling about a lot of things. But this?

"You're part of a group that despises the government."

He arched a brow. "I'm surprised you're questioning it."

"I question everything."

"Good. You should." He shifted again, looking mildly annoyed about not being able to move. "Now for the bit of information you can tell Tim—we have a medical building in a city about three hours from Project Hope. It's in Victor."

I scrunched my face. "Why is that important?"

"There are only human women there. Who are there for one purpose. Why do you think that is?"

Nausea claimed my stomach, and I stared at him in horror. A medical center with only women meant one thing. They were there breeding the women with vampires. It was the entire reason why every Clover woman got a hawthorn tattoo. Vampires wanted to mate with women to make children who would grow up and bleed black. We didn't know why. But clearly, we were missing something. They wanted to keep me until I got tested at twenty-five. Pax had told me they tried to save them. There was a deeper reason that I hadn't figured out yet.

"That is vile," I spat out.

"I agree." His words shocked the hell out of me. "It's under my father's order. I feel that women should have the choice to mate with vampires. They don't have a choice there. Which is why I don't mind telling you about it."

"You want us to save the women," I said slowly. "Why don't you just do it?"

"It's complicated."

"Because you can't go against your father?" I sneered.

"I gave you something to tell Tim," he said, his voice growing serious. "Tell him. And only that. Nothing else we talked about. Understand?"

I gave him a curt nod, the bile rising in my throat from

thinking of those poor women. What else was out there that we didn't know about?

"Warner is coming back inside. He must be worried about you." His eyes drifted to the door behind me. "I'm guessing we're done talking for today."

"And I'm guessing you want me to come back tomorrow?" I grated out.

"Come back whenever you want. As long as no one is listening, then I'll talk to you."

"Kali," Warner yelled from upstairs. "I'm coming down if you don't get up here."

After giving Zan one last look, I turned toward the stairs and reached for the door until he spoke up again.

"One more condition—keep him out of your bed."

I whirled around. "Excuse me?"

"If you want me to keep giving you information, then Warner stays the hell away from you." Danger lurked in his eyes, and he was giving me a smirk that only riled me up more. "He wants you—"

"He's my family," I cut him off.

"That's the deal, Kali. He doesn't kiss you. Or touch you. Nothing. Or I won't say another word. That goes for any man."

"You're fucking ridiculous. And you have a control issue." I glared daggers at him as Warner called my name again.

"I'll be listening."

That statement proved what I'd already guessed. He could hear me in my room upstairs. Or he was lying. But I wasn't sure I could take that chance. Once I told Tim about the medical center, he'd want more. And since I was the easiest avenue to get it, he'd be relying on me. From the way Zan was gloating, he knew that too.

Chapter 32
Kali

I pulled my hair back, tying it up in a ponytail before slipping into the clothes Jill had brought me. The baggy pants were a bit large, and I swam in the T-shirt, but it was better than having nothing. Jill promised she'd grab my clothes when she was in Project Hope. She and Tim had already left to go home, since Collin could only cover for them for so long. Tim wanted me to keep talking to Zan to see what else I could get him to admit. Although Tim was annoyed that I wasn't getting the information the group wanted.

There was a light knock on the door before Warner poked his head in. He didn't wait for me to invite him in, but why would he? I'd been living with him and Helena for years. It was habit. Zan's words rushed back into my head about keeping Warner out of my bed, and I frowned in annoyance, positive that he was listening right now.

Warner stepped into the room, giving me a small smile as he made himself comfortable on the edge of the bed. The room was as old and run-down as the rest of this house, but I was grateful we had walls and a decently safe place to stay.

335

Although I still felt like we were in the open. It was a neighborhood of houses that had been abandoned years ago. Apparently the Clovers had been living here for a long time, and PARA never came this way. Other than a couple of rogue vampires, this place had never been bothered.

"Tim and Jill should be back in a few days," he said. "I've been getting to know a couple of the people here. They seem good. We could make a life here, Kali. Live free outside the city like you've always wanted."

He'd just jumped into the serious talk. I sighed and leaned against the wall. "I've already told this to Tim, but keeping Zan here? They're going to come looking. If they find us—"

"They won't," Warner cut me off. "We're hours away from there."

I wasn't so sure about that. After seeing how their city worked and how organized the vampires were, I felt we were underestimating them. Especially with how calm Zan was about being trapped here. He was expecting his brothers to find him.

"I'm going to talk to him again," I stated, watching Warner's eyes harden. "Can you make sure everyone leaves the house?"

"You just woke up," he grumbled.

"Tim wants me to find out as much as I can."

"Is that the only reason you're rushing to talk to the vampire?"

My gaze met his. "What's that supposed to mean?"

"Fuck," he breathed out, running a hand down his face. "You talk about him like you know him. Not like he's a vampire—a fucking Kane—who held you hostage. Who locked me in a cage. If I didn't know better, I'd think you didn't hate him."

336

I stared at him, choosing my words wisely since I was sure Zan was listening to this entire conversation. "I know what he is. I also know that he's only talking to me right now. What do you want me to do, Warner? Tell Tim to fuck off when he asked me to do something to help the Clovers?"

"Of course not," he muttered, standing from the bed. "I just want to know what's going on in your head. What did he do to you when we were stuck in his city?"

"Not much," I answered. "He thought I was a vampire. They were teaching me."

"Just...be careful with him," he said slowly. "Don't let him get into your head."

"He can't," I replied stiffly. "He can't entrance me."

"That's not what I meant, and you know it."

"I'm doing what the group needs me to do. That's it."

He crossed the room, stopping inches in front of me, his eyes searching mine. "I changed my mind about something."

My stomach flipped. "About what?"

"We promised we'd wait until after you were twenty-five to talk about it. But after everything, I don't want to wait anymore."

Fuck. "Warner—"

"I want to start a life—with you," he said softly. "You're my best friend, Kali. I want you to know you can always rely on me."

"I already know that." My stomach knotted. I didn't want to talk about this when Zan was listening.

"I thought we were going to die in that city," Warner said gruffly. "And I know life won't be fairy tales and rainbows. But I want to go through it with you at my side. As mine."

"And what happens if I bleed black? If I'm a Shadow?"

I whispered. "There's a reason we agreed to wait until after my birthday."

"You won't," he said confidently. "You'll be fine."

My heart panged as I stared at him. It was what we'd always promised each other. I loved Warner. But I loved him like I did Helena and Lisa. He was my comfort. And I used to think that would be enough.

I cleared my throat. "I can't do this right now. My head is all over the place from everything. I just need things to slow down. Then we'll talk."

He frowned. "You don't want it anymore? Us?"

"I love you, Warner," I choked out. "You know that. But I don't know if we're going to survive into next week, let alone past my birthday. I can't think of the future. Not right now."

My words angered him, but he only blew out a breath and backed away. "Fine. I'll get everyone outside so you can talk to the vampire."

He turned around and strode out the door, and I rubbed my temples. I didn't want to upset Warner, but I couldn't give him what he wanted. And not just because of Zan's threat about listening. Although it was still his damn fault.

Because the one kiss I'd shared with him had ruined everything.

It brought emotions that I'd only read about. The spark. The fluttering. The all-consuming fire that heated my veins when my lips touched his. And now I didn't want to go through life without feeling that again. I'd never kissed Warner, but his touch was only comforting. It didn't give me the chills. Or make my heart pound in excitement.

Now that I had experienced that, I wanted it again. I clenched my jaw. *Not* with Zan, though. The fact that he was the one to draw those feelings out didn't mean anything. I could find that with someone else—someone who wasn't a vampire. But I had a feeling it would never be with Warner.

With a sigh, I left the room and made my way to the first floor, seeing that Warner had already kicked everyone out. It was dead silent. My stomach knotted as I reached the basement stairs. I never knew what to expect with Zan. I never did.

I bounded down the stairs, sliding the dead bolt and slipping into the room. I could feel his eyes on me as I closed the door behind me. Spinning around, I found him in the same position as yesterday.

"You just missed your friend," he drawled, his voice weaker than yesterday. "Apparently, he wanted to make sure I wasn't a threat to you."

I crept closer, studying him. His gaze wasn't as sharp as usual, and his body was relaxed, not rigid like he was yesterday.

"Or maybe he shoved hawthorn down my throat because he was pissed that you denied him upstairs," he continued, a ghost of a smirk on his lips. "And he knows it has to do with me."

"It has nothing to do with you," I gritted out.

He cocked his head, his eyes dancing in a way that made me feel like he could see right through me. "You're wasting your supplies on me. I know hawthorn is hard to get."

He was right. Vampires had been trying to destroy plants that could harm them for years. Hawthorn trees took years to grow. And even with PARA planting them, it was difficult for the Clovers to keep up with the need for it.

"I'll stay weak even without it if I don't get blood," he murmured.

My eyes widened at his admission. "How long can you go without feeding?"

"Technically I could go years." He chuckled. "But it wouldn't take long for my heart to stop. I'd go into something that you humans call a coma."

"How long?" I pressed.

He ignored me. "Have you slept with him?"

I scowled. "That's none of your business."

"I'm guessing not from that conversation. Have you slept with anyone else?"

I could feel my cheeks getting hot, but I refused to be the first to break the stare. "Why the hell would you even ask that?"

"First, because you get flustered when I talk about sex, and it's easy to read you," he answered, sounding amused. "Second—I've enjoyed claiming your firsts."

"My firsts?"

"Your first time dancing. And I brought you to the ocean." His stare stayed locked on mine. "Your first kiss with a vampire. I'm curious if that was your first kiss ever."

"It wasn't," I retorted, trying to calm my heart. "And I only kissed you—"

"I know why." He cut me off. "But you can't deny that you liked it."

"I can absolutely deny that."

"Then you're lying."

I didn't bother to argue anymore because it was clear he wouldn't believe me anyway. Instead, I walked closer and crossed my arms, deciding to play into his game. He wanted to get under my skin? I could do the same.

"I've slept with more than one guy. That first was taken years ago," I told him. "And even if it wasn't, you'd never be the one to claim that one. If that kiss is anything to go by, then you would be a disappointment in bed."

Challenge brightened his eyes, and he sat up straighter. "Careful, Kali."

"Or what?" I sneered, letting my eyes trail over him. "Going to threaten me? It looks like the chains you're in are much worse than the one you locked around my neck."

"Come here," he ordered, his gruff voice shooting a jolt down my spine. "I want you to claim one of my firsts."

I didn't answer right away, trying to figure out where he was going with this. I had a feeling I wasn't going to win this little game of words.

"What first?" I said, keeping my voice steady.

"I've never made a woman scream while I've been chained up. And I've been craving another taste of you." He broke the stare-down first, his eyes dropping lower, telling me exactly *what* he wanted to taste. "You want to stand there and lie about what you felt about that kiss? Get your ass over here and I'll make you admit the truth a different way."

"No," I snapped, ignoring the way heat curled in my lower stomach.

He grinned. "Next time, then."

"How about never?"

A frown appeared on his lips as he lifted his eyes toward the ceiling a couple of seconds before I heard footsteps. "His obsession with you is getting tiresome."

I nearly choked in disbelief. "His obsession? He worries about me. You're the one who won't leave me alone."

"Get rid of him," he said, nodding toward the door. "We aren't done talking."

I bristled. "I decide when we're done."

"Really?" He arched an eyebrow. "Tim won't be happy if you don't get any information from me."

"If I don't, then they'll just torture you like they did before I woke up."

"You think they've stopped?" he asked, a hard edge in his voice. "One of Tim's lackeys was in here all night trying to get me to talk. He left an hour ago, after I said fucking nothing. I'll only talk to you, Kali. You want to help your precious Clovers? Then tell Warner to fuck off. I want you in here with me for the rest of the day."

His words were a surprise to me. I had no idea they were still hurting him to get information. I heard the door at the top of the stairs open but didn't look away from Zan.

"If you walk out with him, then I won't say another thing. Nothing that Tim wants to know," he murmured in a low voice. "Maybe even some other secrets that you're curious about."

"What kind of secrets?"

He didn't respond, and a moment later, the door swung open. I glanced over my shoulder, seeing Warner rush inside. He studied me before his eyes turned hard when he looked at Zan.

"I'm making breakfast," Warner said, focusing back on me. "Come eat."

I could feel Zan's stare on my back as I turned and faced Warner. "Thanks, but I need to question him longer."

"Fuck him," Warner drawled. "You can come back later. You need to eat."

"She can eat down here," Zan said from behind me, his voice full of smugness. "Can't you, Kali?"

"You don't speak for her," Warner growled. He moved, and I stepped in front of him, putting my palms on his chest.

"He won't talk to me about anything if I leave," I gritted out. "I'm fine down here."

"He's messing with you," Warner burst out, his glare full of loathing as he looked past me. "Just like he did when you were in his city. He's the one in chains. You don't have to fucking listen to him."

Zan tsked, only making the entire situation worse. "She does if Tim wants any more information."

"I should just kill you now," Warner hissed. "Then we can just go get one of your brothers. Maybe they'll talk."

"I didn't peg you for someone with a death wish." The taunting tone Zan had a second ago was completely gone, and in its place was a violent threat. "You go after my brothers, and I'll kill you myself."

Warner opened his mouth, but I spoke up first. "Warner. Walk away. Let me get this done."

He stared at me for a long moment before he spun around and stormed up the stairs, slamming the door at the top. I rubbed my hands down my face as I turned to look at Zan.

"Are you going to talk now?" I asked irritably. I didn't like when Warner was upset, but at the same time, he knew why I was doing this. It was understandable that he hated Zan after everything, but he wasn't looking at the larger picture. It was for us. For the Clovers. At least that's what I kept telling myself.

Zan grinned. "Let's talk."

Chapter 33
Zan

"How long can you really stay silent?"

The guy stabbed me again, and I swallowed my grunt, keeping my lethal glare on him as he pulled the stake back out. This motherfucker took pleasure in torturing me for hours every time Kali left. His name was Garrett, and he was high on my list of who was going to die when I got out of here.

Garrett stepped back, swiping his black hair off his forehead before glancing at the other man, who was standing watch near the door. They made sure no one else came in when I was bleeding, but at least I had a shower before Kali came, since they didn't want her to know I was a different breed of vampire. My body was fucking aching, every nerve on fire from this round of trying to get me to talk.

And I was fucking weak. Much worse off than I'd been expecting. I'd only been here maybe three days, but with them practically draining me from staking me so much, my body was working overtime to heal, and I hadn't drunk a drop of blood. My mind was hazy and my limbs heavy. I was so damn thirsty.

I tensed when Garrett stepped over my legs and crouched down, getting eye level with me. He smirked, his yellowing teeth flashing as he raised the stake and put the sharp tip under my chin. I gritted my teeth when the wood cut into my jaw, splitting my skin open as he forced my face up.

"Why do you only want to talk to the girl?" he asked, cocking his head to the side. "Wouldn't it be better to just give in to me and stop all of this?"

The room stayed silent when I didn't answer.

"Do you have a hard-on for her?" he questioned, his eyes gleaming with cruelty. "I don't blame you. She's a looker. Maybe when I'm done down here, I'll go find her and see if she'll get on her knees for me."

Rage scorched my veins, and it took everything in me to stay still. Garrett grinned, pushing the stake harder into my jaw. Pain spasmed, and I clenched my teeth, letting loathing filter into my glare.

"Do you like her?" Garrett mocked, attempting to see if Kali was a way to get under my skin. She absolutely was. Not that I was going to show him that.

"He needs to get washed off soon. She wants to come down and talk to him. Tim is getting impatient since the asshole isn't giving us what we want," the guy at the door said, his lip curling in disgust at me. "Hurry up."

"Maybe we're going about this wrong," Garrett murmured. "Maybe we should be focusing on her to get you to talk."

I bit down hard on my tongue, refusing to show a response. I wouldn't put it past him to drag Kali into this. These kinds of groups acted like they were family and cared for each other. The truth was the people in charge would throw the rest under a bus if it helped them toward their end goal.

"How about I fuck her in front of you?" Garrett paused, studying me as I silently seethed. "She wouldn't agree to that. Especially with her friend always at her side. But he doesn't have to know. I could bring her down here and let you watch while I make her choke on my cock."

This fucking slimy bastard wasn't just going to die. He was going to suffer. I wasn't exactly sure how long I'd be stuck down here, but Viggo and Pax would get here eventually. When they did, half the humans in this house wouldn't survive. Garrett would be the first in fucking line.

Garrett let out a harsh laugh, pulling the stake away from my jaw and standing back up. Like he did yesterday, he unwrapped the chains around my ankles and then moved behind me to free my wrists. The chains clanked when he unhooked something I couldn't see even though I knew what it was. The chain connected to the collar was long but stayed tied tightly against the pole to keep me in place.

Except for when they needed to wash me off.

Garrett gave me a shove, and I stumbled a step, letting out a growl and whipping back toward him. My fangs were out, and he nearly crashed into the wall trying to get away from me. Fucking coward. Only talked shit when I couldn't fight back. Although with how bad off my body was right now, I wasn't even sure I'd have the strength to do much.

But as I heard Garrett's heart thrash, I was sure I could subdue him fast enough to get some blood. But they probably wouldn't allow Kali down here if I murdered one of them. It almost killed me to back off as Garrett whipped out a gun that was no doubt filled with wooden bullets.

He jerked the gun to the left. "Ten fucking minutes."

I glared daggers at him as I moved in the direction he wanted. Only because the faster I got this done, the sooner they'd leave. The weight of the metal collar felt heavier today, with my strength waning. The chain connected to it just reached this tiny bathroom that was in the back of the room. All there was in here was a toilet with a cracked seat and stand-up shower with no curtain. A pair of shorts were tossed in the corner, and the only reason they were supplying clothes was because of the bloodstains on the ones I was wearing now.

I twisted the faucet, stepping right under the water since I'd realized the first time they had me do this that there was no hot water. Not that cold bothered me. I let water run down my face as I stood there, hating how weak I felt. I was nearly dizzy from just standing. I had guessed I would have been able to go a week without blood before feeling like this. But with how much Garrett enjoyed seeing me bleed, it was draining me much faster. I needed to feed. Soon.

I took my time washing my body, my anger spiking when my hand hit the chain. I'd already tried testing the strength of the collar and chain connected to it. I wasn't strong enough to even try to free myself from it.

"Let's go," Garrett called out gruffly.

I scoffed, his words only reminding me that I scared them. They could yank on the chain and drag me back out there, but they wouldn't. Not when my hands were free. I rolled my neck, fucking despising that they were going to tie me back to the pole again when I got out of the water.

But then I'd get to see Kali. I'd been waiting all damn night. I'd made her stay with me all day yesterday, and I could tell she was annoyed the entire time. Only giving me clipped answers, and we didn't talk as much as I'd wanted because of it. She was so damn stubborn. I knew she wanted to ask me questions, but she barely initiated conversation because I'd forced her to stay with me instead of going with Warner.

I muttered a curse and turned the water off, giving myself a minute to air dry since there wasn't a towel. I grabbed the shorts and slipped them on, even though I was still wet. My mouth was bone dry, and the scent of Garrett's blood when I stepped out of the bathroom was nearly too tempting for me to ignore.

He stood near the pole with the gun aimed at me. The floor was wet from them washing away any remnants of the torture session. My eyes cut to the man near the door to see he had his own pistol raised. I blew out a breath, striding toward the pole and resting my back against it before sliding down until I was sitting. The only time in the three days that had gone fast was when Kali was in here. Other than that, time seemed to be at a standstill. I wasn't sure how much longer I could go without trying to escape.

I'd been patient, trying to plan. Because I had every intention of taking Kali with me. She knew too much about me and the vampires. Plus, these people were going to get her killed. Not that she'd ever believe that if it came out of my mouth. My patience was nearing a breaking point, though, and if Garrett ran his mouth one more time, I was going to snap. Especially if he threatened Kali again.

Garrett grabbed my arms, bringing them behind the pole and wrapping the chain around them. Then he wrapped the other chain that was connected to the collar, making sure I couldn't move. Before he could go for my ankles, I heard her footsteps coming down the stairs. Then she knocked on the door. The guy waited for Garrett's approval before he moved and unlocked the door.

"Kali," Garrett greeted her as she stepped inside.

She glanced at me first before raising her eyes to him. "Hey, Garrett."

He sauntered over to her, completely forgetting about chaining my ankles as he focused on her. "Once you're done here, come find me. We need to talk."

Rage coiled through me, and I glared at Garrett's back while Kali frowned in confusion. If this fucking bastard touched her, he was going to be begging me to kill him by the time I finished.

"Sure," she said uncertainly. "But right now you all need to leave so he'll talk."

"Tim wants something bigger," Garrett said. "He's giving small stuff. It's not enough."

Kali's eyes darted to me as she nodded. Garrett and the other guy left, shutting the door behind them. Kali moved toward the door, locking it from the inside, and I watched her curiously as I bent my knees; glad they'd forgotten to chain my ankles. That was the first time she'd locked it so others couldn't come while she was in here.

"Were they in here with you all night?" Kali asked, her gaze sweeping my body.

I waited a little longer until I was sure no one was upstairs and within earshot. Although it was getting hard to throw my hearing farther. My head was pounding, and I sucked in a breath, realizing a second later that it was a mistake. Kali's scent filled the room. Oh, it was so fucking good. Her blood was so unique to me that I would recognize it anywhere.

I forced out a small grin. "Why? Worried about me?"

"No," she snapped, stepping toward me. The longer she was in here with me, the more she ventured closer when we spoke. The first time she came in here, she'd hovered near the door. This time, she was already close enough she could reach out and touch my foot if she wanted. It was progress.

I opened my mouth to tell her to stay away from Garrett, but before I could, she came even closer, and I caught a wicked gleam in her eye. I tilted my head, watching with interest as she stopped right near me. My jaw muscle flexed from having to stare up at her. Even with my legs free, I couldn't stand up with this collar on my fucking neck.

"What are you doing, Kali?" I murmured.

She stepped over my legs just like Garrett had earlier, but this time my heart was thudding for a whole different reason. She lowered herself down, a flash of uncertainty hitting her eyes when she sat down on my legs.

"I've been thinking," she said, her voice much sweeter than usual.

Sweet and scheming.

The same exact way she'd spoken before she kissed me that night in the park. She was definitely up to something. Not that I was complaining. Having her body on mine was pushing away the blood thirst that had been consuming my head all damn night.

"Thinking about what?" I asked, playing into whatever she was doing.

"Claiming one of your firsts."

Shock coursed through my veins when she scooted up farther until her face was inches from mine. She licked her lips, and my eyes dropped to her mouth when she suddenly let her palms fall on my bare chest.

"And what first would that be?" I asked, my voice gruff.

She only smirked deviously, dragging her nails down my chest that immediately had my dick stirring. Her fingertips brushed the waistband of my shorts, and my gaze cut to hers.

"Do I look flustered now?" she asked, her eyes widening with false innocence. "Can you read me better? Do you know what I'm going to do next?"

"I have a guess," I forced out, my focus solely on her hands touching my body.

"And what guess would that be?"

I grinned. "I think I'll keep those thoughts to myself for now."

Our conversation from yesterday had gotten under her skin. The control I had even when stuck down here was driving her crazy. And now she'd decided to take a different approach. I wondered how far she'd take this.

"Have you ever been touched while chained up?" she purred, her eyes staying on mine.

"I've never been chained up before this, so no."

My breath caught when she stroked my cock over my shorts, and she giggled at my reaction. She ran her hand over me again as my dick hardened, and though I could sense some slight hesitation, she didn't stop. My body tensed, and even though the pain was still there, her touch was overpowering all of it.

"If you give me the answers I want, then maybe I'll keep going."

And there was her motivation. I chuckled before stopping abruptly when she suddenly full-on wrapped her fingers around me through the shorts. *Holy fuck.* It felt good. She moved her hand up and down a few times before pausing and shifting her weight on my legs.

"What answers do you want?" I questioned, raising an eyebrow.

"You know what I want, Zan. I've been asking the same questions for the last three days."

Everything about my father. His property. My city. I knew what she wanted. I wouldn't give it to her. Although I had a feeling this kind of torture was going to be even worse than what had already been inflicted on me if she kept going. Not that I wanted her to stop.

"You'll have to try a lot harder than that to get those kinds of answers," I told her, letting challenge flood my voice.

My attention went to her throat when she swallowed thickly. Having her this close was fucking with me in more than one way. I could smell her blood, and it was affecting me just as much as her touch was. I needed to feed, but I fought back the urge. She wouldn't freely let me drink from her, and I wasn't ready for her game to end. I wanted her hands to stay on me as long as fucking possible.

"How about I keep my mouth busy while you talk?"

She didn't even give me a chance to respond before she tugged the waistband of the shorts and dipped her hand inside. I bit my tongue when her soft hand wrapped around my cock before she freed it from the shorts. I didn't miss the way her eyes widened when she looked down. She squeezed my cock as she took in my large size, and I was enjoying her shock.

"Fuck," she choked out before clearing her throat.

I grinned smugly. "Keep your mouth busy, Kali. Maybe you'll even be able to drag some answers from me."

Her eyes flashed with defiance for a split second before she glanced at the door. I had a feeling she hadn't told anyone her plan to try to get me to talk. Especially Warner. He would have probably locked her upstairs if he even had an inkling she'd do this. That fucking human was going to be an issue when I took her away from here. But that was a problem for another day.

She slid farther down my legs, lowering her head until I could feel her warm breath on the tip of my cock. Before I had time to process anything else, she flicked her tongue, and a hiss left me when she did it again. She grew more confident, taking me farther into her mouth as I threw my head back. It slammed against the pole, but I barely noticed as pleasure tore through my lower stomach. Something I hadn't felt since the last time she kissed me.

Her tongue flattened, and she sucked, going deeper. I wrenched against the chains, beyond frustrated that I couldn't touch her. She couldn't take all of me into her mouth, but she wrapped her hand around the base of my cock, shooting more pleasure through my body. Her head bobbed as she moved faster, and I couldn't stop the groan that slipped past my lips.

Until she halted, lifting her mouth off me. I'd been expecting that, but that didn't stop my annoyance from flaring when she raised her eyes to mine. She was smiling wickedly, keeping her hand around me and stroking slowly.

"Kali," I warned. "I'm letting you know one thing—I will be getting out of here at some point. And when I do, I'm going to turn all this teasing back onto you. So be very careful about choosing what you do next."

Only heat built in her gaze, and she went down on me again without another word. I jerked when her teeth grazed me, pleasure burning every inch of me. She sucked and licked until I could feel my balls tighten as I got closer to my release.

And then she stopped and scooted farther back on my legs. I tried following her, a snarl burning my throat when the chained collar kept me from moving. The way she was playing with my body was draining the little energy I had left, but I shook my head, forcing the starving pains away when she dropped her head and started her teasing all over again.

"Shit," I hissed. She licked from the base of my cock all the way to the tip before dragging her tongue down the other side. Her moves were slow and driving me fucking insane.

This torture was much fucking worse than all the pain I'd endured. And I had a feeling she was just getting started. I could admit I'd underestimated her. I hadn't thought she'd ever turn sex against me, but clearly, she was full of surprises.

"Tell me something, Zan," she murmured after she slid her mouth off me for the fourth fucking time.

"What do you want to know?" I gritted out, my hands clenched into fists behind me.

"Where does your father live?"

"You want to know so badly? I'll show you once we leave here."

She scowled. "I'm not going anywhere with you."

"I fucking love your mouth," I murmured. "I could do this all night just for you to keep going."

Her face scrunched in anger, and her calculating gaze swept down my bare chest as the tension built during the silence. Her next move had me frowning when she tucked my dick back into my shorts before standing up.

"Giving up already?" I taunted, trying not to reveal how much I wanted her touching me again.

She played with the hem of her baggy shirt before she suddenly lifted it and pulled it over her head.

Chapter 34
Zan

I couldn't have hidden my reaction even if I tried. My lips parted, my eyes instantly falling to her bare skin. She wasn't wearing anything underneath, and my eyes stayed glued to her hands when she ran them along her breasts.

She was fucking stunning. Her smooth skin was marred with a few old scars on her stomach, and I stared at them, wondering how she'd gotten them. Who I'd fucking kill if I found out someone was the reason for those.

"Do you find me attractive?" she asked, her voice quiet.

My eyes raised to meet hers. "I find you a lot more than just attractive. You are fucking gorgeous, Kali."

She didn't break the stare as she prowled closer before falling back on my legs again. Her hands returned to her breasts, and I tracked her movements, letting out a growl when she stopped.

"Keep touching yourself," I ordered, desperately trying to twist my arms out of the chains. But until I got some blood in my system, I wasn't strong enough to slip out. Fuck, my head was still in a fog while my body just ached. But having Kali on top of me was helping me deal with the pain.

"I will—when you tell me what I want to know."

"Are you wet right now?"

She reared back, not expecting my question. I smirked, letting my heated gaze trail slowly down her body. Indecision sparked in her eyes as she stayed sitting on my ankles.

"I bet your pussy is throbbing, just begging to be touched," I murmured in a low voice.

"Something you can't do since your arms are bound," she shot back, her voice a notch higher.

"You could unchain me."

"No."

"Then take your own pleasure from me," I replied, my cock twitching just from that thought. "Climb back up on my lap, Kali. Come prove just how much of a *disappointment* I'd be after our kiss."

She stared at me, listening to the words she had thrown at me yesterday. For once, her face wasn't unreadable. Her cheeks flushed pink, and I stayed quiet, not pushing her anymore. I didn't want her to keep doing this to force answers out of me. I wanted her to give in to the desire for me that I knew she fucking had.

"I won't have sex with you," she stated firmly. "It's not enjoyable anyway."

"Sex isn't enjoyable?" I sputtered out, genuinely shocked by her words.

"No," she snapped. "Every time just reminded me that I could go the rest of my life without it."

"Oh, Kali," I murmured, wishing I could convince her to free my hands. "The things I could do to you to change your mind. I would have you writhing with pleasure. You just haven't experienced the good kind of sex yet. Please, let me be the one to teach you."

She bit her lip, her resolve slipping for a moment before something stopped her from giving in to it. She raised her chin before crawling back over me and sitting down with her thin sweatpants and my shorts being the only barriers between her pussy and my cock. My head was still pounding, and pangs of starvation jolted through my body, but I only focused on Kali as her hands landed on my shoulders.

"Use me," I demanded, losing my self-control. "If you come while on top of me, then I'll give you something to tell Tim."

Her jaw flexed at my order, because I was once again taking the control back. I didn't give a fuck. I wanted to see her come apart, and I was willing to play dirty to get it.

"I won't have sex," she repeated stiffly.

"Then don't. Grind against me. Rock your hips. Find the spot that shoots pleasure all over that beautiful body of yours. Then don't stop until you fall over the edge."

"And you'll tell me what I want to know?"

"Are we really going to pretend that you're sitting on top of me half-naked because you want answers for your group?" I tsked. "Fine, I'll play along for now. But once I'm out of these chains, we'll be having a conversation."

She bristled but still didn't make a move to get off me. I jutted my hips, making her nails dig into my skin to keep her balance.

"Move," I told her, keeping her stare. "Back and forth, Kali. I promise you'll fucking love it."

To my surprise, she did what I said, and I sucked in a breath when she rubbed herself over my cock. Fuck me. I wished her pants were off so I could see all of her, but I smartly kept my mouth shut as she moved faster. This was pushing her to her limit. I could see the tension lining her face. She was torn about this because of who I was. What I was. But she still didn't stop.

She was sliding back and forth against me, and I shook my head. "Don't move so much. Grind. Quick, small movements. And make sure it's hitting right where you need it."

She shot me a glare as I spoke, but she still switched up the way she moved. Soon, the rigidness she was carrying fell away, and her heart began pounding faster. She'd found the sweet spot. I didn't even blink as I watched her lose control. All her defenses came down as she chased her own release, and I loved every damn second of it.

The way she was grinding on my cock had spasms of pleasure mixing with the pain my body was still in. As good as it felt, I wasn't even sure I could get my own orgasm. Not when I was so starved. Although, that really wasn't on my mind at the moment. I'd be perfectly fucking happy watching her come again and again while sitting on me.

Her breaths came out faster, and she squeezed her eyes shut as she kept moving. My cock was rock hard underneath her, and she used that, rubbing her pussy against me. I blinked, wishing I could enjoy this fully instead of my body fighting between pain and pleasure.

"Oh my God," she breathed out, still keeping her eyes closed.

"Just wait," I ground out, listening to her heart beat out of control and knowing she was getting close. "Next time, when my hands are free, it'll be even better."

"There won't be a next time," she said, her voice lacking any kind of vigor. "One-time thing."

I didn't respond, not bothering to argue with her. There was no way this would be the only time this happened. But I wouldn't push it for now.

She raised her hand, clamping it over her mouth, muffling a scream as she came hard. Her hips didn't stop rocking as she drew out the orgasm as long as she could. She finally slumped forward, her head resting on my shoulder as she caught her breath.

I went utterly still. Her throat was so close that I could turn my head and easily feed on her if I wanted. Her scent smothered me, and I sucked in shallow breaths through my mouth, trying to think about anything that wasn't her blood. I could feed on her. But I wouldn't. Not now. She'd never venture this close to me again if I did that.

After about a minute, her body went stiff, and she scrambled off me as her senses won out. Her cheeks were bright pink while she grabbed her shirt and rushed to slip it back on.

"Give me something to tell Tim," she grated out, acting like she hadn't just been on top of me.

I crossed my ankles, watching as her walls came back up. She was going to bolt as soon as I told her what she wanted. I needed to tell her something else first.

"Don't talk to Garrett," I warned her in a low voice.

She rolled her eyes. "This whole controlling thing really doesn't have the impact it did when I was stuck in your city."

I decided not to bring up how she'd just come all over my lap when I demanded it.

"Kali," I said stiffly. "Don't go anywhere alone with him. You can't trust him."

"But I can trust you?"

"Oh my fuck," I muttered, my head spinning so much I could barely concentrate. Having her so close where I could smell her but couldn't drink was almost too much. My entire body was begging to feed, and it wouldn't be too much longer until I couldn't function until I had blood. "Garrett is not a friend to you. If you have to speak to him, then at least have Warner with you."

Shock flashed in her eyes. "What did Garrett tell you?"

"Doesn't matter."

"It does if it concerns me."

My jaw muscle flexed. "They want me to talk. And they'll do whatever they need to get it. They'll hurt you if they think I care about you."

"They would never hurt me," she said fiercely. "I've been a Clover for years."

"Believe me, they would. With the exception of Warner."

"I trust them," she muttered. "They saved me. Gave me a family."

"They need soldiers. That's all you are to them."

Her mouth twisted into a scowl. "You have no idea what you're talking about."

I chuckled and closed my eyes, resting the back of my head against the pole. "I've met a few groups like this over the years."

She stayed silent, and I kept my eyes closed, listening to her heartbeat. It was a bit faster than usual, but it still calmed me enough to think through the haze in my head. I wasn't sure how long we sat there in silence before she spoke up again.

"Do you care if they hurt me? Are you trying to use me for a way out of here? Because I won't help you. I can't."

I snapped my eyes open to see her sitting on the floor and watching me. "I wouldn't have saved you with my blood if I didn't care."

"But why do you care?" she asked, a desperate edge in her voice.

"I don't know," I answered bluntly. "I have no fucking idea why I care. But I do. As for helping me leave—no need. I can handle this myself. But mark my words, Kali. I'm taking you with me when I do leave here. You stay here, and you won't survive."

Her anger came back full force. "You are delusional. This is my home."

"Project Hope was your home. That's gone for you now. Don't put your entire life into this Clover group."

She took that about as well as I expected. I should have just kept my mouth shut. But my thoughts were muddled with how badly my head was pounding. Every time I swallowed, it felt like I was eating glass. I even had fucking chills. Almost like the worst flu in the world, but the only cure was blood. Or it was only going to get worse.

"Don't tell me how to live my life," she snapped. "You don't know me."

I sighed. "I know that you don't belong here."

She let the room lapse into silence, and I closed my eyes again, almost dozing off. I could survive on little sleep, but between Kali's visits and Garrett's, I hadn't slept at all since being here.

"What do you want to tell me to give to Tim?" she asked quietly.

I twisted my chained wrists, jerking my arms slightly in annoyance. "There's an entire warehouse of hawthorn. Government building. We have plans to get rid of it. But if you can get to it before us, then go for it. I'll give you the coordinates tomorrow."

"You're dragging it out," she mumbled. "Tim won't like that."

"I really don't give a shit right now. He's lucky he's getting this."

I didn't open my eyes, waiting for the sounds of her getting up and leaving. Time passed, but she stayed on the floor near me with her heart rate fluctuating. I didn't even have the energy to fight with her anymore today. Which pissed me off because I loved riling her up.

"Why are you still here?" I grunted. "I gave you what you wanted."

"Does Garrett come in here every time I leave?"

Her question surprised me, and I cracked an eye open to look at her. "Why do you care?"

She played with the end of her ponytail. "I don't know."

Her answer was the same as mine, and we stared at each other for a moment before her eyes roamed over my face.

"You look sick," she murmured.

"I am."

"You need blood."

"Mm," I hummed out in agreement.

"Is it painful?"

I frowned, not liking showing my weakness. But she could easily see something was wrong with me. Not that I'd be acting like this if Garrett was in here. "Yes."

She nodded, stretching her legs and leaning back on her hands. She didn't say anything, looking content to just sit there. My eyelids fluttered closed again, and I heaved out a pained breath. Fuck. This was getting worse much faster than I expected.

"Here."

I snapped my eyes open to see her standing right next to me. She crouched down and shoved her wrist into my face.

"What are you doing?" I asked slowly.

"You need blood," she answered, her voice uneven.

If I thought I was shocked when she went down on me

earlier, it was nothing compared to right now. I gaped at her, unsure of what to even say.

"You want me to feed from you?" I asked roughly.

"You won't even be conscious in a couple of hours if you don't," she said stiffly. "How can I ask you more questions if you can't even talk?"

I chuckled. "Right. You're not offering because you care."

"Definitely not."

"I can't feed from your wrist," I said, keeping my eyes on hers. "Not unless I can hold it. The vein is small, and I'd need to maneuver your arm where I need it."

"You can't bite my neck," she retorted. "Everyone will see."

"Mm," I mused. "I'd love that. I want them all to see my marks on you."

She scowled. "Watch it, Zan. Or I won't freely offer this again."

"Your thigh, then. You can cover that."

She froze, not expecting that. After some hesitation, she straightened up, and then pushed her sweatpants down. Her shirt hung to her thighs, but my eyes raked over her bare legs as she stepped toward me.

"The inside of my thigh?" she questioned nervously. "Where do you need me to stand?"

I swiped my tongue over my bottom lip. "I can think of a place where I want you to sit right now."

Fuck, the thought of tasting her pussy had my dick hardening all over again. But when I raised my gaze to her face, I could tell that now wasn't the time. She was already more on edge about letting me feed from her. And I fucking needed it.

"Come closer. Put one foot on either side of me," I told her. "Just press your thigh to my face."

She did what I said, her posture like a steel rod. This decision was tearing her apart. Now that I knew who she was with, it made sense. They had been trained to hate us. Even more than regular civilians. The fact that she was doing this was still shocking the hell out of me.

"Thank you," I murmured in a low voice.

She didn't answer, turning her leg until the inside of her thigh was close to my face. I slid down my fangs, my heart pounding out of my chest as I leaned forward slightly, letting them graze her skin. A shiver ripped through her, and I heard her breath catch when I lightly kissed her. If I thought she could handle it, I'd drag this out just so I could kiss her more. But she wasn't ready.

My nostrils flared when I caught another scent that wasn't her blood. She wasn't wearing any panties. J*esus fuck.* My face was inches from her pussy, but I forced myself to focus on feeding. I carefully bit down, trying to be gentle—something I'd only ever done one other time. And that was the first time I fed on her. Usually, I didn't care how rough I was. But I did with her.

I sucked softly, relishing in the taste of her blood. It was just as sweet as it smelled, and I groaned, swallowing a large amount before sucking some more. My body was already buzzing, my strength quickly returning, even from this small amount. I wouldn't be at my full strength, but it would be enough to last me a few more days.

It took everything to pull myself away after I drank some more. I didn't drink near enough to affect her, but I didn't want to chance it. She stepped away from me, tugging her pants up quickly, her face flushed as she glanced at me.

"You have..." She trailed off and kneeled beside me before brushing her thumb over my lips to wipe off her blood. "You can't tell anyone I did that, Zan. They wouldn't like it."

I grinned. "Are we trading secrets now?"

Footsteps began coming down the stairs, and my lips turned down in a frown when there was a banging on the door. I wasn't fucking ready for her to go yet.

"Kali." Warner's voice came through the door. "Why is this locked? Are you okay?"

"I'm fine," she called out. "I'll be out in a second."

"Stay away from Garrett," I warned her again. "I'm serious, Kali."

She didn't respond, almost looking like *she* didn't want to leave. But after a moment, she stood back up and muttered a goodbye before unlocking the door. Warner shot me a glare before the door shut again, and they both went upstairs.

I rested my head against the pole, listening to them talk as they moved into another room upstairs. Her blood had worked, and I felt a hundred times better. If I wanted, I'd be able to get out of this the next time they undid my chains to make me shower. I could kill Garrett and the other guy who usually came down with him before they knew what was happening.

But I could be patient for a while longer. Maybe I could convince Kali to go with me willingly before I decided to leave.

Chapter 35
Kali

"Whats going on?" I asked Tim. "Why can't I go down there?"

Tim crossed his arms. "They're talking to him."

"I thought he wasn't saying anything," I said, glancing at the basement door.

"He's not," Tim gritted out. "But he's giving you small things. Nothing about his father or brothers. Important locations. We need all of that."

"I'll get it," I promised.

His face softened, and he patted me on the shoulder. "I'm not blaming you, Kali. Of course we know you're trying. And it must be so hard to face him after being with him for two weeks. We appreciate your work for us."

The back of my neck flushed as I thought about what I'd done with Zan yesterday. Getting off against his dick was not benefiting the Clovers. Neither was letting him feed from me. What the hell was I thinking?

"You okay?" Tim asked with concern.

I forced out a smile. "I'm fine. When do you go back to Project Hope?"

"In a few hours. Did Jill give you your clothes?"

I nodded. "Yeah. Thanks."

The basement door swung open, and Garrett strode out. He gave me a smile that instantly made me uneasy. Even before Zan's warning, I wasn't a fan of Garrett. He lived here, and I had only met him when we arrived. He was in charge of this faction of the Clovers, like Tim was with ours, and I could tell in the short time that he loved the power.

"You're not talking to him today," Garrett said, locking the basement door and pocketing the key. "Go enjoy your free day."

I frowned. "Why not?"

"He's too weak to get a word out," Garrett answered with a shrug, glancing at Tim. "I think he needs blood. We need to discuss what to do."

I stood there, unmoving, carefully keeping my face blank. He was weak? Was the blood I gave him yesterday not enough? He had looked better right after he fed on me. Garrett turned his attention to me, his calculating stare giving me the creeps.

"Go, Kali," Tim said with a smile. "We'll let you know when you're needed."

"Yeah," I muttered. "I'm going to find Warner."

"He mentioned something about going down to the pond earlier," Garrett said. "I can take you."

"Thanks, but I'm fine."

I nodded a goodbye to Tim before walking toward the back door. My thoughts were muddled, and I pushed open the screen, stepping into the muggy air. It was so hot today that I was wearing a tank top and a pair of shorts that were just long enough to cover Zan's bite mark. I had planned on wearing pants, but the heat was too stifling. So now I'd been tugging on the hem of the shorts all morning to make sure they stayed in place.

I walked through the tall grass, thinking about Zan. Why was disappointment weighing me down? I'd gotten used to talking to him every day, and it felt odd not being in the basement with him. I groaned, wiping sweat off the back of my neck. I should not let him into my head like this. Yesterday had been a mistake. What I did with him...my face flushed. It had started as a way to question him but had turned into so much more.

The pond came into view, and I paused near the edge of it, scanning the area for Warner. The pond was large, and it was kept stocked with fish for food. I was sick of fish since it was pretty much all we'd eaten since arriving. But at least we weren't starving. Warner was nowhere in sight, and I sighed, deciding to go back to the house. The sun was too damn hot to be walking around.

"Did you find him?"

I whipped around, my heart skipping when I saw Garrett standing a few feet behind me. How had I not heard him following me?

"Uh, no," I answered. "I'm going back to the house. I'm sure I'll find him later."

He stepped in my way when I moved to go around him, and I raised my chin, silently giving him a warning. He grinned, moving with me again.

"I just wanted to talk for a moment," Garrett said. "Having new people in my house is something I'm not used to. If you and Warner plan to stay, I want to get to know you."

"I appreciate you giving us a room," I said slowly.

"Are you and Warner together?" he asked, cocking his head. "You two seem close, but he didn't give me a straight answer."

I paused, choosing my words carefully. "We've never been without each other."

"Except when you're downstairs with the vampire."

"Not really my choice," I said, my eyes growing cold. "Tim wanted me to question him, so that's what I was doing."

"Of course." Garrett advanced toward me. "And you've done great getting information out of him."

"Thanks," I muttered. "I'm going to get some food."

This time, he grabbed my arm when I attempted to go past him. My eyes snapped to his, and I frowned when his fingers tightened on my upper arm. I had a small pocketknife in my bra, but I stayed still. Garrett was the boss here. If I attacked him, things could go very badly for me.

"What are you doing?" I asked, keeping my voice steady.

"I want to know why the vampire only talks to you." Garrett's voice bled with authority, and I bit back my retort. He was important here, and making waves with him was not smart.

Instead, I forced a smile. "I'm honestly not sure why. But we can talk about it if you want. In the house. It's too hot out here."

"No," he said curtly. "I don't want the vampire listening in."

Nerves skittered through me when I realized there was no one around us. And I couldn't see the house from here at all. Zan's warning about Garrett rushed through my mind again, and dread climbed down my limbs when I wondered what exactly Garrett had said to Zan.

"The only reason he talks to me is because it's a way for him to keep control," I ground out. "Because I was trapped with him."

"I think he has something for you."

"Something like what?"

"I'm not sure," Garrett murmured, a cruel glint in his eye. "But I think we could use it."

"I have been. By talking to him."

"I like you, Kali." He tugged me closer, and I stumbled a step, clenching my jaw from his nails digging into my arm. "You're a breath of fresh air here. Living with the same twenty people can get boring."

Fear slithered through my chest, the dark undertone of his words putting me more on edge. He might be the boss, but I had to show him I wasn't one to be messed with.

"Let me go," I snapped, narrowing my eyes. "You have no right to put your hands on me."

"I don't think so," he tsked. "You're in my house. I can do whatever the hell I want."

"You answer to the Clovers," I shot back. "Respect is an important rule. I might be new here, but I've been a Clover for years. Watch yourself."

His other hand came up too fast for me to dodge, and pain exploded across my face when he backhanded me. It hurt, but the shock of him attacking me outweighed that. He kicked my feet out from under me, and I let out a cry when I crashed to the ground. I rolled in the tall grass, my heart stuttering when he grabbed my ankle, yanking me toward him.

"You need to show me some respect," Garrett growled, grabbing my other ankle when I kicked at him. "You're here, taking up my space. Eating my food. You need to pull your weight around here."

"Get the fuck off me," I snarled, reaching into my shirt to get my knife.

Then he froze, his hold staying on my ankles. I flicked the knife open, but when I noticed what Garrett was staring at, panic smothered me. My shorts had ridden up, and Zan's bite mark was plain as day. I had planned to bandage it, but all the medical supplies were under lock and key, and I didn't want to explain why I needed it.

"He fed on you?" Garrett accused. "You let him?"

I opened my mouth, but I couldn't think of one thing to say. There was no defending it. I had no way to free Zan from the chains, which meant Garrett knew that I'd allowed myself to get close enough for him to bite me. And the fact that the mark was on the inside of my thigh made it so much worse because I was hiding it.

Garrett's laugh sent a shudder through me. "Oh, this is good. Don't worry, Kali. I can keep your secret. You let a vampire feed on you. How would the Clovers feel about that?"

Cold terror lined my veins, and the humid air suddenly felt suffocating. If Tim found out, I had no idea what he would do. Kick me out? Kill me? The Clovers were all I had. And the one thing instilled in us was how vampires were the enemy. They wouldn't tolerate someone who was soft for them.

Garrett released my legs and leaned back on his knees. I scrambled away from him, keeping a tight hold on my knife. He ran a hand through his black hair, his smug grin making me want to stab him. He was going to use this in a way that wouldn't bode well for me.

"You and I are going to talk," he drawled. "And you're going to do what I say. Or I tell Tim what I just found out."

I glared at him, my chest heaving as I slowly climbed to

my feet. Before either of us said anything, voices drifted closer, and I peered over the grass to see a small group heading this way. Garrett noticed the same, and he frowned before getting up and brushing off his shorts.

"I'll see you later," he said, warning filling his voice. "This isn't over."

He stalked off, and I stood there with my heart pounding in my ears.

I was so fucked.

"Kali. There you are."

I spun around to see Warner coming toward me, and I rushed to pull the hem of my shorts down. He got closer, his eyes darting to my cheekbone near my ear, which was no doubt red. I was sure it would bruise with how hard Garrett had hit me.

"What the hell happened?" he asked with a scowl as he inspected the rest of my face, and then my body. I was glad my T-shirt sleeves covered where Garrett had grabbed me.

"Nothing," I muttered, pushing his hand away when he reached for my face. "I was training with someone and they got a hit on me."

"Training?" he repeated skeptically. "You haven't trained since we got here."

"I know," I answered with a forced laugh. "That's why I needed to do it. I can't let myself go."

He was still studying me, and I turned away to head back to the house. Warner could read me better than anyone, and he probably knew I was lying, but I couldn't admit anything to him. Like everyone else here, Warner hated vampires. After what Zan had done to him, he had a special loathing for him. He would never understand why I let Zan feed. I still didn't fucking understand it. But Warner would see it as a betrayal, and I couldn't even blame him for that.

"They're planning a mission in the next couple of days," Warner informed me. "I know you've been busy with the vampire, but I was thinking we could volunteer to go."

I thought for a moment. "Yeah. I want to go."

It would give me a chance to get to know the area. If things went south because of what Garrett had found out, I'd need to find a way to leave. Although once the bite mark healed, I wouldn't be as worried. He'd have no proof of anything, and Tim trusted me. I just needed to play along for a while until I could find a way to fix it.

"I'll let Tim know," Warner replied as he opened the back door for me. "Do you like it here?"

I grabbed a plastic cup and poured some water from the huge jug on the kitchen counter before facing Warner.

"It doesn't feel like home," I admitted. "And I'm not a fan of some of the people here."

"Garrett," Warner stated. "I don't like him either."

My eyes darted around, making sure we were alone. Talking about someone high up in the Clovers like this wasn't the smartest.

"We can talk to Tim," Warner said in a low voice. "There are other places around here we can stay. I know another small faction that's about three hours from here."

Zan's face was the first thing to enter my mind at Warner's words, and I scrubbed my hands down my face. If I left here, then I wouldn't see him. That shouldn't have any bearing on my decisions. Yet here I was.

"Come on," Warner grabbed my hand, pulling me back toward the door. "I found an amazing spot in the woods that you'll love. It doesn't have a river like back home, but there's a small creek."

I glanced over my shoulder toward the basement door. If they wouldn't let me talk to Zan today, then spending the day outside the house was the smartest thing. At least I wouldn't have to deal with Garrett.

I followed Warner back into the heat, pushing all my worries out of my head.

Chapter 36
Kali

I had always been a light sleeper, but the threat from Garrett had me even more on edge. Which was why I was instantly awake when the floorboard creaked. My eyes snapped open, and I was met with nothing but darkness. It was still the middle of the night, and I didn't move a muscle, waiting to hear another sound. Maybe it was Warner. But he would have alerted me instead of sneaking into my room.

"I know you're awake, Kali. Your heartbeat gave you away."

Zan's voice knocked shock into me, and I rushed to sit up, only for the bed to dip, and a second later, a hand clamped over my mouth. He pushed me back down until my spine pressed into the mattress before his hand left my mouth just long enough for him to trap both of my arms above my head. Keeping one hand around my wrists, he brought his other back over my mouth, smothering my yell. He was straddling me, with most of his weight on my stomach.

I writhed under him, my screams muffled as I tried

bucking him off. He chuckled, and I raised my glare upward, where I guessed his face was. I couldn't see anything, but I was sure he could see me. Everyone knew vampires had great eyesight in the dark, but I didn't know how good.

"I'm going to move my hand," he murmured quietly. "But if you scream, it's going back over your mouth. I'm not ready for anyone to interrupt us yet. Understand?"

I jerked a curt nod, anger and panic clinging to me. How did he get out of the basement? The house was still silent. Did they even know he'd escaped? My stomach dropped. Had he killed everyone?

He slowly pulled his hand away, making sure to keep a tight hold on my wrists.

"How the hell did you—"

My whispered question was cut off when his fingers suddenly grazed the side of my face where Garrett had hit me. When I flinched, he snarled a curse under his breath. Apparently his sight in the dark was much better than I guessed.

"Who did this?" he growled, returning his fingers to my face and gently touching the bruise again. "Give me a fucking name, Kali. Right now."

I really didn't give a shit about my injury. The fact that he was here instead of in the basement was still making my head spin.

"How did you get out?" I hissed.

"A name," he countered sharply. "I already have a list of humans who are dying in this house. If you don't tell me, then I'll kill every last one of them instead of just the ones who wronged me."

"Garrett," I bit out.

Zan stayed silent, and I could feel the waves of rage

rolling off him. I squirmed, but he only scooted down so that he was straddling my hips instead of my stomach.

"Get off me," I demanded.

He sucked in a deep breath, as if trying to calm himself before he responded. "Not yet. I don't trust that you won't try to escape me."

"How did you get free?" I tossed back. "Did you kill them all?"

He scoffed. "The one human I killed was gullible. They usually have two people with me, but since they thought I was weak, only one came down this time. It wasn't hard to get a hold of him and grab the key once my arms were free."

"*Thought* you were weak," I breathed out. "But you weren't, were you? Not since I let you feed."

"Kali." Warning filled his voice. "Don't."

"You used me," I tried keeping my voice hard, but it trembled slightly as anger tore through me. "You—"

"I didn't use you," he cut me off. "I had no plans to leave when you offered me your blood. But things changed."

"What things?"

"I can hear *everything* that's talked about in this house," he murmured. "And I overheard a conversation that made me re-evaluate when I wanted to leave."

"Wanted to leave?" I forced out a small laugh. "How long have you known you could just escape when you wanted?"

"Since they stopped giving me hawthorn."

"That was days ago."

"I know."

"Then why have you stayed?"

He didn't reply, and even if I couldn't see him, I could feel his stare on me.

"What do you want?" I gritted out, breaking the silence.

"I'm leaving." He paused. "You're coming with me, Kali."

"No the fuck I'm not."

"Yes, you are." His voice left no room for arguments. "You know too many secrets about me and vampires. I can't let you stay here when you know about all that. And...I don't particularly care for the feeling I get when you're not near me."

"You can't just force me to come with you," I snapped, ignoring his last sentence.

"I can," he stated. "But I want you to come by choice."

"No."

"So stubborn," he grumbled. "You can't stay here."

"I'm not going with you." My voice began to rise as panic set in.

Did I want to stay here? Not really with Garrett or other people I didn't know. But I sure as hell wasn't going with him either. I didn't belong with vampires. And even after everything, I couldn't forget what he was. Or what I'd done to him. I'd given up his secrets—most of them anyway. I was the reason he'd been held hostage and tortured.

"Shh," he said in a hushed voice. "They don't realize I'm up here yet. I'd rather they not know until I'm out of this fucking house."

"You have to sneak out," I said, the realization dawning on me. "That's why you're trying to convince me to go. Because you can't drag me out of here without raising suspicion."

His tense silence had me guessing I was right. I struggled against him again, but he only pressed more of his weight on my hips, and I clenched my teeth at the reminder of when I was on top of him in the basement. Something I did not need to be thinking about right now. Or ever again.

"What if I let you bring him?" he forced out gruffly.

"Who?"

"Warner." He spat out the name with disdain.

I couldn't hold back the sarcastic laugh. "So you can lock him in a cage again? Or threaten him to keep me in line?"

"No," he answered slowly. "Because I know he's the only reason you want to stay here."

"I want to stay here because it's where I belong," I retorted. "I sure as hell don't belong with vampires when I'm *human*. Or did you forget?"

"Believe me, it's impossible to forget that."

"You're wasting your time. I'm not going with you."

"Fuck, Kali," he growled. "You're infuriating."

"So you've told me before."

He lapsed into silence again, and I wasn't sure if he was listening for noises or thinking. But either way, he stayed on top of me the entire time.

"Even if you stay here tonight, I'm coming back for you," he warned, his voice low. "And next time, you won't have a choice."

"You won't find me after tonight," I snarled furiously. "Once you're gone, we'll move. We won't stay where vampires can find us. And I don't have your little necklace on anymore."

"Necklace or not, I'll find you."

"Good luck."

"I've never had anyone push me like you do," he murmured. "And as much as it drives me crazy, it also excites me. In more than one way. I don't want to let that go. Let you go."

The way my stomach fluttered seriously terrified me. He was sitting on top of me, threatening to kidnap me for a second damn time. His words or actions shouldn't affect me in any way. But clearly, that wasn't the case. The way my body reacted to him. How I was content to sit in that fucking basement and talk to him. If I let him in, he'd consume me. I knew it. And I also knew it would end up with me dead. Which was why there was no way I was leaving this house with him. After tonight, we'd move, and I'd never see him again.

"I'll start screaming if you don't get off me," I threatened, desperate to put some space between us.

His dark chuckle growing louder was the only warning I had before his lips suddenly brushed my cheek. Goose bumps covered my skin at the contact, and I sucked in a quick breath when he nipped at my earlobe.

"I'd love to hear you scream," he whispered roughly. "But we can't do that tonight."

"Zan," I choked out, trying to keep my voice steady. "What the hell are you doing?"

"You won't leave with me tonight?"

"No," I answered firmly. "I won't."

"You're right. I've already checked outside, and there are more humans than I was expecting." His lips were still touching my skin between every word, and he was slowly drifting down to my neck. "I can't sneak away from all of them when I have you over my shoulder and screaming. And I can't go back to the basement. So it looks like you get your way—you're staying. For tonight anyway."

"Then go."

"You really think I won't find you?"

"I can promise you won't."

"Then let me give you a goodbye present," he murmured. He suddenly kissed the side of my throat, and then he sucked hard enough that I knew it was going to make a mark.

"Fuck," I breathed out. "A hickey as a present? I guess it's better than you biting me."

"If I had more time, I would bite you," he said, barely lifting his lips from me. "I could mark your entire body, and you'd still be begging for more."

"If you stay any longer, you're going to get caught," I gritted out.

"I can hear everyone in this house," he told me. "I have plenty of time."

I swallowed, my heart pounding faster. "Time for what?"

"Let me teach you." He kissed the other side of my throat as he repeated the words from the other day. "You enjoyed sitting on my lap. Let me show you how much you can enjoy being underneath me."

Chapter 37
Kali

I really should have started screaming. If I did, he'd be gone in a flash. But I couldn't push out a word even if I tried. Because his lips were now skimming my collarbone, and I couldn't form a complete thought. What was one night? One time, and he'd leave. And I'd be gone as soon as the sun came up.

"Fuck it," I muttered.

"I need to hear you say it, Kali," he demanded.

"Say what?"

"Tell me yes. That you want me."

"Yes," I whispered. "But only for tonight."

That was apparently all he needed because a second later, his lips crashed down on mine. He kept my wrists trapped above me, and his other hand went to my hip. He pushed his tongue into my mouth, taking control. And I let him. Because it felt too good to think rationally right now. I shouldn't be doing this. Knowing this was about as forbidden as I could get had my heart racing. If someone walked in right now, I was done for. The Clovers would disown me.

I was relying on Zan to make sure we weren't interrupted. I stilled when that realization hit me. I was
putting trust in him. Something I really shouldn't be
doing.

"Stop," he said gruffly, pulling his lips off mine just
enough to speak. "Don't think about it."

I scowled. "Don't act like you know what I'm thinking."

"But I *do* know," he murmured. "You're letting outside
problems in right now. I don't want you thinking about that.
Or anything else. Only me."

I sucked in a breath when he wedged his knee between
my legs, spreading them farther apart. His head dropped
back down, and he kissed my neck again, no doubt feeling
my thudding pulse. This time, he sucked hard enough to
leave another mark. What was I doing? If he wanted to feed
or bite me, he had every opportunity right now, and I was
helpless under him.

My worries fled from my mind when his hand drifted
from my hip to the inside of my thigh. His fingers traced a
trail upward until they brushed my clit over my leggings.
Heat flushed through my veins at his slight touch, my body
already begging him to keep going. It had been over a year
since anyone had touched me there. And I was already
enjoying Zan's hand much more than any other man I'd
been with.

He finally released my wrists, and the next thing I
knew, he was slipping my shirt over my head. Since I wasn't
wearing a bra, my top half was exposed to him. He
muttered a curse, dragging his lips across my collarbone.

"Why are you so goddamn addicting?" he breathed out.
"I can't get you out of my fucking head."

"I thought I was infuriating," I snarked, my breath
catching when his tongue flicked over my nipple.

He chuckled. "That too. But I think you'll be a little too distracted tonight to try and get under my skin."

His mouth covered my nipple, and I let out a small yelp when he teased it with his tongue. Jolts of pleasure traveled through me when he switched to my other breast, giving it the same attention. His fingers were still rubbing my clit through the leggings, and he didn't stop, even as I was practically writhing underneath him.

Nothing was in my head except the pleasure he was overwhelming me with. I'd never had a man have me so close to the edge so fast, and Zan hadn't even taken off my pants yet. My past experiences were nothing like this. Every guy I'd been with just jumped into sex without a care about getting me off.

My muscles tensed, and I could feel myself getting close until Zan suddenly stopped. He pulled his hand away from my pussy but kept teasing my nipples with his mouth. I arched my back, silently demanding more, but he only grabbed my hip and pressed me back into the mattress.

"You're lucky we're on a time crunch," he muttered, scooting down and grabbing the waistband of my leggings.

"Why?" I breathed out, lifting my ass as he pulled them off me.

"You think I forgot what you did to me in the basement?" he questioned roughly. "I told you I would turn all that teasing back on you. But it'll have to wait until next time, when you don't have to stay quiet. And I want to taste you while you're making a delicious mess all over my tongue."

My cheeks flushed, and I tried finding my words to remind him that this was *never* happening again. But before I could, he lifted my legs until my thighs were on his shoulders, and he wrapped his arms around them, pulling me exactly where he wanted. The next thing I felt was his tongue sliding across my pussy, and I slammed my mouth shut to keep from crying out.

He flicked and nipped at my clit, making me buck in his hold. His arms tightened around my thighs, preventing me from escaping the overwhelming pleasure. He wasn't gentle or slow, but his movements were exactly what I needed to climb to the edge all over again. Heat flushed through me, and I slapped my hand over my mouth, barely remembering that I had to be quiet.

My body trembled, and I rocked my hips, whimpers escaping me as he coaxed my climax to the edge. Every nerve exploded as I came, and I screamed, my hand swallowing the noise as he kept licking and sucking. I squeezed my thighs around his head, unable to handle the sensations anymore. He finally pulled away, and I heard him moving around.

When he fell back on top of me, my heart stuttered, feeling his naked body on me. He'd taken off his shorts, and he pressed his body onto mine, his hard cock pressing against my pussy.

A coherent thought shoved its way through my muddled mind, and I raised my arms, finding his chest and pressing my palms against him.

"I can't get pregnant." I spoke slowly. "I will never bring a child into this world. Especially with a vampire. Having black blood is a fate I will never put on a child."

He was silent for a moment, and I wished there was a light on so I could see his face.

"Do you trust me, Kali?" he asked, his voice low.

My chest tightened. "I honestly don't know how to answer that question right now."

He shifted his weight over me, and after a small click,

the room was bathed in dim light. He'd turned on the lantern that was on the table next to the bed. I blinked, my eyes adjusting to being able to see again. Zan only gave me a second before he grasped my chin, making sure I was looking into his eyes.

"I will *not* get you pregnant," he swore. "Like you, I have no plans of bringing a child into this life."

I swallowed thickly, unsure of how to answer. I was now regretting being able to see him. In the dark, I could keep my emotions hidden. Facing him made it all too real. I shouldn't want this. Want *him*. He was everything I'd been taught to hate. But why was the little voice in my head begging for this night to never end?

"Do you trust me about this?" he asked, his eyes searching mine.

"Yes," I whispered hoarsely. I wasn't ready for him to leave yet.

He lowered his head, kissing me deeply. My heart pounded when I felt his cock nudge my entrance before he slowly inched inside me.

"Holy fuck," he groaned once he filled me completely. "You feel so damn good."

He pulled out and thrust again, his mouth smothering my cries as he picked up his pace. Every time he plunged back into me, the waves of pleasure built, and I eagerly met his thrusts, wrapping my arms around his neck. His tongue clashed with mine, and he kissed me like he was starved.

My hips rocked, and I could feel myself getting close, but the pleasure waned each time he moved when my clit wasn't grazing his body. Letting out a frustrated noise, I moved my hand down my body until it was awkwardly between my legs, but Zan slowed when he realized what I was doing.

He pulled out of me, ignoring my protests, and then stood up before pulling me until my ass was nearly hanging over the edge of the bed. He lifted my legs, putting my ankles on his shoulders before he plunged back into me.

"Fuck," I choked out, my body flailing under him as he gripped my hips. This hit a whole new angle.

Zan shot me a smoldering grin. "Now I want you to touch yourself."

I did what he said, realizing this position made it much easier to rub my clit. Pleasure racked my body as I touched myself. Zan's strokes were deep and fast, and I squeezed my eyes shut, losing myself to the sensations.

"Eyes on me," Zan demanded in a low voice. "I want to watch you come apart this time."

There was no more struggle or guilt about this. He was working my body up in a way that I couldn't form a thought about anything other than what he was doing to me. The pleasure was overtaking everything else, and when I opened my eyes, my gaze locked on his.

"Feel it, Kali?" he asked, thrusting again.

I shook my head, trying to understand what he meant. "What?"

"How right this is."

Shock tore through me. "No, it's not."

His eyes flashed dangerously, and he suddenly moved both of my legs to one of his shoulders without changing the pace he was fucking me. With one arm gripping my legs to keep them in place, he pushed my hand away from my clit, replacing it with his own. He circled it slowly before pinching it, making me choke out a breath when a whole new gripping sensation of pleasure ripped through me.

Fuck me, that felt good.

"It doesn't matter what I am. Or who you are," he

gritted out. "This...is something that can't happen only once. It's not fucking enough."

I was practically a writhing mess under him, but his heated stare was burning through me. He was expecting an answer, even with me on the brink of an orgasm.

"It matters," I forced out. "You kidnapped me. Kept me in your city."

"I protected you."

"You kill humans."

He slammed back into me, his eyes never leaving mine. "*You* kill vampires."

"You locked me in your room for two days."

"You've stabbed me—twice."

"You deserved it," I breathed out, my hands fisting the blanket as my pussy clenched around him. "You're a controlling asshole."

"Only with you," he muttered, almost too low for me to hear.

I threw my hands over my mouth right when my orgasm slammed into me. Even with my mouth covered, I wasn't quiet. But Zan didn't seem worried that someone had heard, so I rode out the waves, my body going tight as the pleasure swallowed me whole. I moaned when he thrust again, drawing the orgasm out even longer.

His fingers left my clit, and he suddenly pulled out of me while keeping a hold on my legs. He fisted his cock, pumping it twice before his hot release shot out, covering my lower stomach. He groaned, his arm tightening around my legs as he sagged against the bed.

I lay there, catching my breath as reality slowly sank back in. Zan's face was unreadable as he slowly let go of my legs before he turned around and grabbed a towel from the pile of clothes I had on the dresser. He dropped the towel onto my stomach, gently cleaning me up.

"You think I'd hurt you if you came back with me?" he asked quietly, his head tilting up to look at me.

My heart squeezed. "I don't know."

"I wouldn't."

"What if I decided to spill your secrets?" I asked bluntly.

A muscle in his jaw ticked. "You wouldn't."

"You don't know that. And if I did, then what?" I asked, keeping his stare. "You kill me? Turn me?"

"It wouldn't happen," he gritted out. "You'd be with me all the time."

I blew out a laugh. "I'm not going back to be watched all the time. I had enough of that the last time I was in your city."

He tossed the towel onto the floor and then grabbed my legs, spreading them before falling back on top of me. His lips landed on my throat where he sucked hard, and my protest did nothing as he gave me another hickey.

"Zan," I hissed. "What are you doing?"

"We could do this all the time if you came with me," he murmured, propping himself up until he was looking down at me. "You wouldn't be a prisoner. You'd be *mine*."

My body flushed. Just the thought of doing this again was getting me worked up again. That was a damn problem.

"No," I said stiffly. "Being yours would be the same as being trapped there. I'm human, Zan. I will never belong there."

He frowned, irritation etched on his face. I had no doubt that if it was possible to drag me out of here, he'd do it in a heartbeat. He shook his head and climbed off me. I watched him in silence as he looked for his clothes. I didn't know if he was telling the truth.

He and his brothers had made it clear they wanted me until my birthday. Was he doing all of this just to take me until they could test my blood? Or did he really want *me*? My emotions were so fucking torn. I didn't know what to think. It was ingrained in me that vampires could not be trusted. They were all the same. Vicious. Deadly. Cruel. Zan was all of those things.

But he was also more. No matter how much I fought it, I couldn't look at him like I did all other vampires.

He spoke again, pulling me out of my head.

"Last chance," he said, pulling his shorts back on. "Come with me."

I sat up, pulling the sheet to my chest. "That was a one-time thing. I won't see you again."

He scoffed. "Keep telling yourself that."

I leaned against the wall, staying on the bed as he stood up and quickly crossed the room. My stomach dipped when he pulled open the drawer of the dresser and stuck his hand in. After a couple of moments, he pulled out his necklace.

"How'd you know it was in there—"

"I'll hold on to this. Until I see you again," he cut me off as he slid the chain over his head.

I rolled my eyes. "You'll be holding on to it for a long time."

He glanced at the door before his gaze darted to the window. In three quick strides, he was standing next to the bed, and he reached down, wrapping his hand around the back of my neck. He slowly slid his hand up until his fingers tangled in my hair, and he tightened his hold before tilting my head back.

He lowered his head, and his lips crashed onto mine.

He nipped at my bottom lip immediately and pushed his tongue in the second I relented. His taste overwhelmed everything else as I kissed him back. Until I heard the click of my door. My eyes snapped open, and I tried jerking back. But Zan wasn't done. He kissed me for a second longer before pulling away.

I whipped my head to the door, my blood turning to ice when I spotted Warner standing in the doorway. He wasn't moving a muscle, looking utterly shocked. Until his gaze cut to Zan, and murder filled his eyes.

"Even if I'm not here, I want him to know." Zan untangled his fingers from my hair. "That you're mine."

Warner let out a loud yell as he charged across the room. Zan ducked away from Warner's fist before swinging his own into Warner's ribs and sweeping his leg out, knocking him to the floor. Zan had the window open and was halfway out before Warner got back to his feet.

Zan glanced at me one last time. "Bye, Kali."

Then he was gone. There was shouting throughout the house, showing that others had woken up. My hands were clenching the sheet as I stared at Warner. Oh my fuck, this was bad. Warner cursed under his breath and stuck his head out the window before turning his attention to me. His eyes traveled down to my throat, horror filling them when he saw the marks that Zan had left.

"What the fuck happened, Kali?"

Chapter 38
Kali

I stared at Warner, unable to say a damn word. He stomped across the room, shutting my door and then turning back to look at me. His eyes were hard and unreadable, and I swallowed thickly, the knots in my stomach threatening to tear me apart.

"Did he attack you?" Warner hissed, his gaze going back to the hickeys on my neck. "That kiss didn't look forced."

Before I could answer, there were heavy footsteps in the hall, heading straight to my room. Warner mumbled a curse as he quickly reached for the light with one hand while pulling off his shirt with the other. I frowned, not understanding what he was doing. The room fell into darkness again once the light was off and a couple of seconds later, Warner slipped into the bed with me. His arm went around me, and he pulled me with him until we were both lying down.

"Warner—"

I snapped my mouth shut when my door suddenly burst open. I fought against Warner to sit back up, keeping a tight grip on the sheet. The light flicked back on, revealing

Garrett and another man standing in the doorway. Warner put his arm around my waist, keeping me close while Garret stared at us, his eyes going to my neck.

"What the fuck, Garrett?" Warner snapped. "You can't just come barging into our room."

"You two have been in here all night?" Garrett asked slowly.

"Not that it's any of your business, but yes," Warner answered curtly. "What do you want?"

I stayed silent, feeling much too exposed since I was naked under the blanket. My heart was pounding against my ribs, and I leaned against Warner, only to feel him stiffen. He was protecting me. But it was clear he was pissed.

"The vampire escaped," Garrett spat out. "Get dressed and meet us in the basement. Now."

With that, he spun around and strode away with the other man following. Warner climbed out of bed and grabbed his shirt off the floor.

"Get dressed," he told me, keeping his back toward me. "We'll talk about this later."

He stepped out into the hall, closing the door behind him. I bit my lip, not moving a muscle. Warner would never understand what I'd just done. But I didn't have time to dwell on it now. With a sigh, I rolled out of bed and quickly threw on a bra and a T-shirt before slipping on a pair of leggings. After tying my boots, I glanced in the mirror, attempting to rearrange my hair to hide the hickeys.

"Shit," I mumbled, giving up. There were two that were in plain view, and I didn't have any clothes that would cover them.

There was a knock at my door, and I hurried across the

room, pulling the door open. Warner was waiting, and he wouldn't even meet my eyes.

"They want us downstairs right now," he said gruffly. "Well, they want you downstairs. Since you're the one who has been with the vampire every day, they want to talk to you."

He headed down the hall, and I trailed after him, the silence tense and suffocating. He was my best friend, and he wouldn't even fucking look at me. Once we got to the first floor, it grew chaotic. There were people running around, packing their things and making plans. I wasn't kidding when I'd told Zan that we'd leave. Staying here when he knew the location wasn't happening.

We didn't stop to talk to anyone, making our way past the kitchen. The basement door was already open, and we bounded down the steps, hearing arguing coming from the room where Zan had been held. Warner entered the room first, and he sucked in a quick breath. I peered around him, my eyes widening in shock.

The floor was wet and stained red. A mangled body was in the middle, and it was impossible to recognize who it was. His limbs were bent at odd angles, and his throat was completely torn apart. My stomach rolled with nausea. Zan had done this. There wasn't a question about it. He was a ruthless monster. A creature I'd been taught to hate. Taught that the world would be better with vampires extinct. And I'd had him in my bed.

"Kali. What did you talk to the vampire about the last time you were down here?" Garrett asked in a dangerous voice.

Memories of sitting on Zan's lap filled my head, but I kept my face blank. "Exactly what I told you. The warehouse with hawthorn."

"You were down here for hours," Garrett snapped. "That's all he fucking said?"

"He's not very forthcoming," I retorted. "He only gave me what he wanted to share."

"Did you know he was going to escape?" Garrett asked.

"I had no idea." I crossed my arms, keeping my eyes off the body on the floor.

A cruel gleam lit Garrett's eyes when he glanced at my leg where Zan's bite mark was. "Did you help him escape?"

"No," I snarled, my pulse thudding. "I would never help him."

"Don't pawn off your mistake on her," Warner spoke up, glaring daggers at Garrett. "She didn't have the key to his chains. She wasn't on watch. There's only one body. I thought there was always supposed to be two men down here. Where was the second?"

"We had business to deal with, and I needed more men outside," Garrett gritted out, clearly unhappy with Warner's accusations.

"That's on you," Warner stated, standing at my side. "Kali was with me all night. Don't try and blame her again, or I'll tell Tim that you're using your role as leader here to throw others under the bus for your mistakes."

Garrett's face turned a shade darker, and the two other men in the room shifted uncomfortably. Garrett was the boss here, and everyone followed his orders. Warner and I were new and clearly rocking the boat.

"We can't stay here," Garrett finally bit out, breaking the tense silence. "We're all leaving in small groups and staying in safe houses until we can set up somewhere new. I want you two to go with Matt and Paul to a cabin a few hours from here. I'll meet you there in a few days."

It wasn't lost on me that those two men were Garrett's

trusted friends. He wanted eyes on me. Warner nodded, his fingers interlocking with mine.

"Go pack," Garrett ordered, running a hand down his face before glancing back at the body. "What a fucking shit night."

Warner didn't release my hand as he turned around, pulling me with him back up the stairs. We didn't say a word as we went back to my room. People were still running around, and by sunrise, we'd all be gone from this house. Once I stepped into the room, I tugged out of Warner's hold and grabbed the duffel bag that was in the corner. I heard the door close, and nerves skated through me.

"What are you doing, Kali?" Warner asked, his voice barely controlled. "Why the hell was he in here? Did you free him?"

"No, I didn't." I turned to face him. "I had no idea he'd gotten out until he showed up in my room."

"Did you sleep with him?"

"Yes," I whispered in a strangled voice. I couldn't lie to him. No matter how badly I wanted to. Even if I did, he'd know. He could read me better than anyone.

"Fucking Christ," Warner muttered, looking at me like he didn't even know who I was. "He can't entrance you. You willingly let him fuck you. A vampire. Did you see what he did to Rick? He's a monster, Kali."

"I know," I cried, crossing the room until I was standing in front of him. "I don't know how it happened. He acts differently with me. Sometimes it's hard to remember what he is—"

"He's a fucking Kane," Warner snarled. "Who kept you on a leash and me in a cage for two weeks. How can you forget that?"

"I don't know," I mumbled, guilt squeezing my heart. "It was a mistake."

Even as I spoke those words, my brain was refuting them. It didn't feel like a mistake when Zan was in my bed. It felt *right*. My heart dipped. I couldn't think like that. I'd never see Zan again, and whatever the hell my tangled emotions were, I needed to shove them deep down and forget. Warner was my family. This group was my life. Vampires were the reason we were living like this. They had started the war that lasted nearly two decades. I needed to remember that. And after overhearing Amaros, it sounded like they were still plotting against humans. Zan was a part of that.

Zan was the enemy. He always would be.

There was a knock at the door, and Warner stepped away from me, pulling it open. Matt stood there, his reddish blond hair sticking up everywhere. He must have been sleeping when everything went down. His hazel eyes darted around the room nervously before he looked at Warner.

"Paul is waiting for you two at the truck," he informed us. "I have to do something, and I'll meet you at the cabin in a day or two."

"Have to do what?" I asked, wondering why Garrett hadn't mentioned anything.

"Get word to Tim and Jill about what happened."

"You're going alone?" Warner asked doubtfully. "We can come with you—"

"I've done this trip alone tons of times," Matt interrupted. "I'll be fine. I'm taking a bike."

Without waiting for an answer, Matt turned around and disappeared down the hall. Warner took a deep breath, still facing the door.

"I have to grab a bag," he said quietly. "I'll meet you at the truck."

He left my room, and I stared at the empty doorway. I wasn't sure he'd ever look at me the same way. Or forgive me. I doubted he trusted me like he had before. I needed to make it right. I couldn't lose him after all of this. With a sigh, I went back to the duffel bag and grabbed the few articles of clothing I had. I wasn't sure how things were going to change after tonight. But my mind wasn't on the Clovers.

It was stuck on Zan.

Chapter 39
Zan

"**I**s that everything?"

I glanced at my dad when he asked the question. "Yes. I told them about the hawthorn warehouse and that was it."

Amaros nodded while leaning back in his chair. "I'll have the building burned by the time they get to it."

I felt a slice of guilt for not telling my father the complete truth. If he knew I'd provided the location of the medical center, that would be his first priority. But what I'd told Kali about that place were my honest thoughts. I didn't share my dad's feelings when it came to human women mating with vampires when they didn't have the choice. I hoped they actually succeeded in tearing that fucking place down.

Heavy footsteps filled the air, and I turned my head to see Viggo and Pax appearing from the darkness as they walked toward us. My dad and I were sitting outside on the patio behind his house. Being back on this property wasn't something I enjoyed, but I had to fill Amaros in on everything that had happened. Well, not everything, but enough to satisfy him. He was furious that I was taken in the first place.

"The scouts went to the house," Viggo said as he sat in the chair next to me. "The humans were already gone."

"I told you they would be," I muttered. "They wouldn't stay there when I knew the location."

It had been two days since I'd left there. I'd come straight to my father's property, knowing he'd be able to get word to Pax and Viggo that I was fine. Two fucking days since I walked away from Kali. And the unease smothering my chest hadn't left. I should have dragged her ass out of there with me. I'd stayed outside her window long enough to make sure Warner covered for her like I figured he would. But then I had to leave, since they had started searching for me.

"None of this changes our plan for Project Hope." Amaros lifted his whiskey glass, finishing the rest in one swig. "The few who know about you will be dealt with."

"We're already working on it," Pax added as he took the seat next to Amaros. "Two of the humans who know are hiding in Project Hope."

Tim and Jill. They were aware that I was different from the average vampire, and out of the rest, they'd be the most difficult to get to since they lived in a human city. Hard but not impossible. Thanks to Warner, we now knew another way into Project Hope. We just needed to sneak in.

Viggo pulled out his pack of rolled cigarettes, and I snatched it away, pulling one out for myself. Pax raised an eyebrow as Viggo handed me the lighter. I smoked, but not as often as Viggo. After the week I'd had, I needed to let go of some stress. Though it wasn't the torture that had been inflicted on me that was plaguing my mind. It was the fact that Kali wasn't near me. I didn't fucking like it. I'd gotten used to having her close. Hearing her heart. Becoming accustomed to her human scent. She made it perfectly clear that she didn't want to come with me. That night, she had a choice. Next time, she wouldn't. She wasn't staying with that damn group.

She was right—I was obsessed. And I didn't care. Sleeping with her had only enhanced it. I didn't want to let her go.

"Is your city back in order?" Amaros asked, pulling me out of my thoughts.

Viggo nodded. "The soldiers who got past the perimeter were killed. They still have no idea how many of us there are. Only the Clovers know."

"They won't get in again," Pax stated with a frown. "The only reason they were able to was because they hid behind PARA to do it. They don't have the numbers on their own."

"I'm still not pleased they know," Amaros murmured, setting his glass on the table. "We need to speed up the plan. And I want that entire group handled."

"We will," I said gruffly before inhaling a drag of the cigarette. "We're leaving now to go home. We'll start making plans right away."

"Now?" Amaros repeated. "I thought you'd want to stay a bit longer."

"Too much to do, Dad," Viggo said with a grin. "Humans to kill and all."

My mind was focused on getting Kali, but I hadn't said a word to Amaros about it. He didn't need to know anything about her. If he knew I was thinking like this about a human, he'd be curious, and I wanted to keep her far away from my father.

"Keep me updated. I'll see you in a couple of weeks."

Amaros nodded in farewell before standing and striding back toward the house. He was never one for emotional goodbyes. Or emotional anything. But he loved us. I just wasn't sure if it was because we were his sons or because we were the ones carrying on his legacy.

"Let's go," Pax muttered, rushing to his feet. He hated being here more than either me or Viggo.

I followed my brothers back to the front of the property and climbed into the truck. It was going to be a long seven-hour drive back to our city. I took the passenger seat while Viggo stuck the key into the ignition. Pax didn't say a word from the back seat as Viggo pulled onto the dirt road. Pax had been quiet ever since I'd gotten back, besides apologizing to me multiple times.

He blamed himself for me being taken in the first place. Technically, it was his fault. If he'd been honest about Kali in the beginning, I doubted any of this would have happened. But I wasn't angry, just like I told him. If I'd known Kali was human when I first met her, my decisions might have been different. Maybe I never would have let myself get close to her like I did when I thought she was a vampire. Everything happened for a reason.

"We haven't found her yet," Viggo informed me, keeping his eyes on the road.

"It doesn't matter," I answered.

I wasn't worried about finding Kali. If I didn't have a way to locate her, I never would have left her.

Viggo glanced at me out of the corner of his eye. "She isn't wearing your necklace anymore."

"The Clovers used up their hawthorn," I said, remembering the conversation I'd heard at the house. "Most of it was used in our city against the vampires. The rest was used on me to keep me weak. Most of the men wear it on them like Warner did since they don't have enough to ingest every day. That made it easy."

"Interesting," Viggo muttered. "Let me guess, you entranced one of them before you got away?"

I smirked. "Two of them. One of them close to one of the bosses in the Clovers. Any information he hears, he'll relay back to me. Including where Kali went."

"She's going to be on edge," Pax piped up from the back seat. "And she probably won't be alone. We need to go in prepared."

"I hope she's not alone," I said in a low voice. "I have a list of names to cross off. Garrett is at the top."

"Gia will keep watch on the city while we deal with all that." Viggo sighed. "I still think it's a bad idea. Kali is human. What are you going to do? Keep her locked up until you grow bored of her?"

I gritted my teeth, not responding. I didn't know what I was going to do yet. But she wasn't staying away from me any longer than necessary.

"You'll have to turn her," Viggo continued. "Or kill her. But I have a feeling you don't want to do that. You're even worse than Pax now. She hates vampires. Doesn't want to be with you. It's going to be a fucking problem."

I scrubbed my hand down my face. "I'll figure it out."

Viggo let it go, focusing on driving while I leaned the back of my head against the seat. I wanted everything ready once I found out where she was. Because I wasn't leaving her behind a second time.

Chapter 40
Kali

I shifted on the thin cushion of the couch, staring at the same page I'd been trying to read for the last hour. We'd been at this cabin for four days, and I was bored out of my damn mind. And jumpy. Zan warned he'd come after me, and I had a feeling that it wasn't an empty threat. There was no way he'd be able to find me at this isolated cabin, but I still couldn't get his words out of my head.

With a sigh, I tossed the book onto the couch next to me and glanced at Warner, who was sitting at the small wooden table, snacking on some berries we'd picked earlier. Paul was sitting in a chair near the front door, using his knife to make more stakes. He lifted his head and smirked when he saw me looking at him. I let my gaze turn cold as I kept his stare. He was as bad as Garrett, leering at me like he knew my secret. I had a feeling Garrett had told him about the bite mark from Zan. But he'd left me alone—mostly because Warner had made it clear early on that I was with him when Paul made a comment about the hickeys the first night we got here.

This cabin was tiny. The living room and kitchen were

in the main space, with one bedroom in the back and a small bathroom. The entire structure was made of logs, and there was no electricity. We used gas lamps and candles, although we usually tried to keep lights to a minimum at night.

Luckily, we had running water, unlike some of the other safe houses. We were deep in the forest, with no cities around for miles. A fireplace was on the wall across from me and was the only source of heat for when it was cold. The furniture was all old and falling apart. Since we only used this place for short durations, we didn't see the need to update anything.

"I'm going for a walk," I announced, getting to my feet.

My eyes widened in surprise when Warner stood up and crossed the room until he was in front of me. He'd barely spoken to me since we'd arrived, and I understood why he was mad. I really did. In his eyes, I'd let myself fall into bed with someone we were trained to kill. And Zan was even worse, since Warner had been locked in a cage because of him. I knew he needed time to process and hadn't tried talking to him. But I missed my best friend.

He pulled me into a hug, burying his face in the crook of my neck. I sagged against him, hoping this meant he was getting over what I did.

"I'm not going to lie and say I'm not still mad," he said in a low voice to keep Paul from overhearing. "But I want you to know I'm here for you, Kali. I'm not going to just abandon you because of what happened. The last three weeks have been fucking crazy. I don't know everything that happened to you when we were in that city. But I do know you. And I trust you. You just need to remember what side you're on."

It took everything in me to stay still. Heated anger rushed through my veins as he squeezed me tighter. *What side I was on?* He'd known me nearly my entire life. I would never betray him or the Clovers. I could see why he was questioning my choices, but it didn't make it hurt any less.

"I made one mistake," I whispered. "It's not fucking happening again."

"I know." He pulled away from me. "I'll go walk with you. This damn cabin is driving me crazy."

I nodded in agreement, following him toward the door. Paul was watching us, and he stood from the chair, letting the half-made stake fall to the floor. Warner's shoulders tensed when Paul got in the way of the door.

"Maybe we should stay inside," Paul said, running a hand over his curly black hair. "The whole point in staying here is to be safe."

"It's noon," Warner retorted curtly. "Nowhere near sunset. We're miles from any city. Which means we don't have to worry about PARA or vampires. Get out of my way."

"Matt never made it back," Paul argued, crossing his arms. "It's not smart to split up. And Garrett should be here soon. He's going to want to talk to you both when he arrives."

"He won't be here for a while," I said. "We'll be back by then."

Paul looked like he wanted to argue, but Warner shoved him to the side, ignoring Paul's curses when he stumbled back.

"Watch it," Paul hissed. "You're both guests here—"

"No," Warner cut him off. "We're Clovers just like you. It doesn't matter that we used to live in Project Hope, not outside the walls like you. We are all on the same side. So stop acting like a fucking prick."

Without another word, Warner unlocked and opened

the front door, only to freeze. My stomach knotted as I peeked around him.

"Did the messenger leave this?" Warner asked skeptically. "I don't remember seeing him carrying anything."

Someone had come yesterday to inform us when Garrett would be here and to let us know that Matt never made it to Project Hope. He'd brought supplies but had unpacked everything before he left again.

My eyes dropped to where Warner was staring, and my heart seized. Sitting right in front of the door was a small basket nearly overflowing with apples. If the messenger had brought them, he would have carried them inside. I stared at the bright red fruit, my panic rising fast enough to steal my breath.

"Warner," I choked out.

He must have heard my frantic tone because he quickly pulled me outside, making sure to step beside the fruit basket before slamming the door to keep Paul from following. He grabbed my upper arms, peering at me in concern.

"What's wrong?" he asked in a hushed voice.

"Those apples..." I took a deep breath. "They're the same ones that were stocked at Impulse. I ate them every night."

"They're just apples, Kali. The messenger probably brought them—"

"The basket is the same," I nearly screeched, tugging out of his hold. "It's the one that Gia kept under the bar for the human girls who worked there to eat from. It's from their city, Warner."

I could picture Dee refilling the basket every night. And I was always grabbing apples from it when I needed a snack. There wasn't a doubt in my mind about who had put these here.

"Zan," I breathed out. "He knows where we are."

I turned my eyes, scanning the thick forest around us. Other than birds chirping, there were no other noises. Warner grasped my chin, pulling my focus back to him.

"You don't know that it's him," he said, his eyes narrowing.

"I do," I argued. "We need to leave."

"We have time before it gets dark." Warner dropped his hand from my jaw when I backed away. "We'll wait for Garrett to get here and see if there are any other safe houses around here."

My heart was beating painfully as I nodded. We needed to leave. But why was there a tiny part of me that wanted to see Zan again? I bit my tongue, forcing that away. Zan had already told me that he wanted the people from the house dead. If he found us, people were going to get killed. I didn't think he wanted me dead, but what about Warner? And the other Clovers? I couldn't chance it. We had to get the hell out of here before night fell.

"If Garrett isn't here in a couple of hours, then we leave on our own," I said.

"Fine. We need to tell Paul," Warner grumbled. "As much as I want to, we can't just leave him here alone."

As if knowing we were talking about him, the door swung back open. I spun around to face Paul as he stood in the open doorway.

"What's going on?" he asked, his eyes going between me and Warner.

"We might have to leave sooner," Warner said, grabbing my hand and leading me back into the stuffy cabin.

Once we were all back inside, I pulled my hand from Warner's and moved toward the kitchen area to get some water. My mind was racing, and I wondered how the hell

Zan had found out where I was. And why he left the apples instead of just storming in here. It didn't make any sense.

"Why would we have to leave?" Paul questioned with a suspicious frown.

"The vampires might have found us," Warner said tightly. "Once Garrett gets here, we should go."

Paul looked between us, a scowl on his face. "Ever since we saved you two, there's been nothing but trouble."

"It wasn't our choice to kidnap a Kane vampire," I shot back.

"You feel bad for the vampire?" Paul asked quietly.

"No," I snapped. "I'm just saying that's where the trouble started. Not from rescuing me and Warner."

"We aren't going anywhere until Garrett gets here." Paul patted his pants pocket. "I have the keys to the car."

Warner rolled his eyes. "We aren't going to leave without you. Or without talking to Garrett."

"Good." Paul leveled me with a glare before turning toward the bedroom. "I was the one on watch all night. I'm going to sleep for a while. Wake me when Garrett gets here."

He disappeared into the bedroom, slamming the door behind him. Warner grabbed my arm and pulled me toward the couch, not letting go until we were both sitting.

"Is there anything I should know?" he asked, keeping his voice low so Paul couldn't hear.

"What do you mean?"

"About the vampires. Or when you were in their city." He hesitated. "There's something different, Kali."

"With me?" I asked with a frown. "No, there's not—"

"With us," he clarified. "You used to tell me everything. But you're keeping secrets from me."

"Only because I don't want to hurt you," I whispered, my chest tightening.

"You slept with him," Warner murmured, trying to hide his disgust. "Was it just sex? Or do you actually care for him?"

"He saved my life," I admitted. "He didn't have to do that."

"He's using you for something. He's a vampire. They want to control everything. That's why we became Clovers. To protect humans *from* them."

"I know." I covered my face with my hands. "I...don't know. It was a stupid thing to do."

Hands circled my wrists before he pulled my hands from my face. "I don't hate you. I don't blame you. He fucked with your head."

I had to bite my tongue to keep from responding defensively. It didn't seem like Zan was using me or messing with me. But...what if I was wrong? My group had kidnapped him. His father was making plans against Project Hope. I was human. What if he was purposefully getting close to me? Ice crawled through my veins at that thought, and I tugged my wrists out of Warner's hold.

"It doesn't matter," I muttered. "He's gone. We won't see him again."

"Thank fuck," Warner mumbled before clearing his throat. "I just feel like this whole thing has changed us too."

"Us?" I repeated.

"We never finished the conversation from last week," Warner said, his eyes meeting mine. "I still want you, Kali. If that's what you want. If not...I'll always be here as your best friend. But I need to know."

I didn't say anything, unsure of how to answer. I loved him, and he knew that. But was I in love with him? My heart panged when the truth slammed into me. I wasn't. If I'd never met Zan, if I'd never felt the rush that he'd given me, I could have happily been with Warner. But not anymore. Not when I knew those feelings existed.

If I found love in this life, I wanted it to be all fulfilling. I wanted the excitement. The butterflies. The heat. I didn't have that with Warner.

Warner sighed, taking my silence as an answer. "Friends it is."

"Warner—"

"It's fine," he said, giving me a small smile. "I always knew a life with me wasn't what you wanted, Kali. I want a quiet life with someone by my side who is content living away from everything. You want to leave here. See whatever you can. I've always known that you wouldn't be happy with just the short adventures out of Project Hope. You crave freedom. I just want to find a small niche for myself and live. But that's not what you want, is it?"

I shook my head. "No. I want to see everything I can while I'm alive."

"I know." He gave me a quick kiss on the forehead. "And I hope you get everything you want. You know I'm always here for you."

Before I could answer, he abruptly stood up and headed to the kitchen area. He was hurt, even though he was acting like he wasn't. Deciding to give him some time, I got up and took the chair by the front door. I picked up the knife and stake that Paul had been carving and continued sharpening the edge of the wood.

The silence was strained, and time dragged on as Warner ate a snack while pretending to read the book I'd thrown down earlier. My body was heavy with guilt, even though I wouldn't change my mind. He was my best friend.

My family. I just hoped he felt the same and wasn't *in* love with me so that our relationship wouldn't change.

There was a knock on the door, and I stiffened while Warner gave me a look.

"It's daylight, Kali," he said softly. "It's not them."

"Hey," a voice called from outside. "It's Matt. Let me in."

My eyes widened as I set the stake and knife down. I recognized Matt's voice, but he should have returned two days ago. Where the hell had he been? When Matt knocked again, I stood up, seeing Paul exit the bedroom.

"Unlock the door. I've had a long damn trip," Matt complained through the door. "I'm tired as hell."

"Open the door," Paul demanded, glaring at me.

Warner stayed near the couch, purposely keeping himself between Paul and me as I turned around to unlock the two dead bolts. My hand fell on the doorknob, and I slowly twisted it before pulling it open. There was a body in the doorway, and I raised my head, meeting the eyes of the person in front of me.

I expected Matt. But it wasn't him.

He wasn't a human at all.

Chapter 41
Kali

Shock held me hostage, and I stood there completely frozen as Zan gave me a wicked smirk. He was leaning against the doorframe, holding an apple. Viggo and Pax were standing behind him, and Matt was off to the side, staring blankly at me. The blood drained from my face. I couldn't believe what I was seeing.

"Did you miss me, Kali?" Zan asked, tossing the apple into the air and catching it.

Not fucking possible. The sun was high in the sky, yet Zan was standing right in front of me. Never had I heard of a vampire being able to walk in the sun. I opened my mouth, but not a sound came out as we stared at each other. Amusement danced in Zan's eyes, and he raised an eyebrow, as if waiting for me to say something.

"Kali," Warner yelled. "Get back."

His voice knocked me out of the shock, and I tensed. But before I could move a step, Zan dropped the apple, his hand lashing out and snatching my wrist. I screamed in protest when he hauled me against his chest while striding into the cabin. He quickly turned me around until my back was to him, keeping his arm around my waist, trapping both of mine at my sides. My heart thrashed when his free hand went around my throat. His hold was firm, but he didn't cut off my air, even when I struggled against him.

His lips brushed my hair. "I told you I'd find you. Ready to come home?"

"I'm not going with you," I hissed, panic clutching every part of me.

Zan ignored me. "Viggo."

Warner was darting across the room, going for one of the guns we had in a kitchen drawer, but Viggo raced past us, getting to Warner right when he pulled the gun out. Paul was already disappearing into the bedroom, and he slammed the door shut.

"Stop," I screamed when Viggo threw his fist into Warner's jaw.

Warner tried raising the gun to shoot, until Viggo wrapped his fingers around Warner's wrist, pushing his arm upward. Zan's hold tightened around my waist, keeping me in place.

"Pax, get the asshole who went and hid," Zan said quietly.

Pax strode across the small room, sliding past Viggo and Warner. He rammed his shoulder into the bedroom door hard enough for it to splinter. He did it one more time, making the door crash open. Pax disappeared into the room, and the next sound was Paul shouting. Viggo and Warner were fighting for the gun, and even though Warner was holding his own, his strength was nothing compared to Viggo's.

"If you want her to stay alive, you better do what my brother wants," Zan warned loudly.

Warner fell still when he saw me in Zan's hold, his eyes

darkening when his gaze dropped to my neck. Viggo ripped the gun from Warner's hand before quickly emptying it of the wooden bullets and tossing the weapon onto the counter.

Keep me alive? I might not trust Zan, but I was confident he didn't want me dead. Not after everything he'd done. Something I planned to voice until Zan's grip on my throat tightened in warning. His head dropped next to mine again.

"Not a word, Kali," he ordered under his breath. "Not if you want him to walk out of here."

Rage filtered through my panic, and I twisted my neck as far as I could to glare at him. He met my eyes for a split second, his face unreadable before he focused back on Warner.

"Let her go," Warner gritted out.

A mocking grin tipped up Viggo's lips as he slung an arm around Warner, forcing him across the room.

"Look at you," Viggo taunted. "Freedom suits you. But if you try anything, I'm throwing you back into a cage."

"Fuck you," Warner snarled, trying to wrestle out of Viggo's hold.

"Sit," Viggo ordered sharply, pushing Warner toward a chair at the table.

Warner rigidly sank into the seat, glaring daggers at Viggo, who stayed standing beside him. My attention went to the other side of the cabin when Pax appeared in the bedroom doorway, holding Paul by the back collar of his shirt. Paul was yelling curses, fighting against Pax's hold.

"I know you," Zan drawled. "One of Garrett's guys. I warned you of what would happen before you started using that stake on me. Should have fucking listened."

"Does he know about you?" Pax asked, throwing Paul to the floor in front of the table where Warner was sitting.

"Yes."

"How?" Paul spat out, climbing back to his feet. "Vampires can't walk in the sun."

"Most vampires can't," Viggo corrected him. "We're a bit different. Although, you already know that from torturing Zan, don't you?"

I frowned in confusion but couldn't look at Zan like I wanted because of the grip he had on my throat. Warner stayed quiet, his murderous gaze darting between Zan and Viggo. Pax grabbed Paul by the hair, forcing him to his knees. Ice rushed through my veins as the atmosphere shifted, the tension rising as Viggo stepped forward, ready to help Pax if needed.

"You helped hurt my brother?" Pax asked, his voice low.

"He deserves worse," Paul snapped. "You all do."

Pax's laugh was cruel, something I hadn't heard from him before. "Probably. But that's not going to change what happens next."

Paul craned his neck to glare at me. "You bitch. You told them where we were."

"Watch it," Zan growled. "You're in no position to talk to her like that."

"Garrett told me," Paul shouted, grimacing when Pax tightened his grip in his hair, yanking his head up, making it impossible for him to look at me. "That she let him feed. Fucking traitor. She'll get what's coming to her."

My heart sank when Warner's eyes filled with shock. He stared at me, hurt sprawled across his face. A lump grew in my throat, regret smothering me as I looked at my best friend. Paul tried swinging at Pax while getting to his feet, and Pax kneed him in the ribs, sending him back to the floor.

"Don't look so sad, Kali. He'll forgive you, even for that," Zan breathed in my ear.

"He won't," I ground out, my voice cracking.

"After that conversation I heard, he'll forgive you for anything." His quiet words had me freezing. My heart thudded, realizing he'd been listening to us all day. "But I heard you too. He's a good *friend*."

"What I said has nothing to do with you," I whispered furiously, my cheeks flushing.

He chuckled. "Sure it doesn't."

"Do we need him anymore?" Pax questioned, hauling Paul back up by the hair.

"No. Don't make a mess," Zan answered.

"Wait—"

My shriek did nothing as Pax grabbed both sides of Paul's head. He twisted hard, and I cringed when the bones in Paul's neck snapped. Pax released him, and Paul's body hit the floor with a thud. Guilt invaded me as I stared at his lifeless body. This was my fault. Zan was here because I'd refused to go with him that night.

"He was going to do worse to you," Zan told me gruffly. "And he knew too much about me. He needed to die."

"I know too much about you," I hissed, writhing in his hold. "Are you going to kill me too?"

Instead of responding to me, he spoke to Pax. "Take him out back where they won't see."

They. Zan was waiting for Garrett to get here. Nerves swarmed me, my chest tightening painfully. Zan finally let go of my throat but kept his other arm firmly around my waist. I raised my eyes to see Warner staring at Paul's body, panic etched on his face. Viggo stayed near him while Pax heaved Paul's body over his shoulder and headed out the front door.

"Into the bedroom, Kali," Zan ordered, walking us forward. "I don't want Garrett to see me yet, and he'll be here in a few minutes."

Warner jumped to his feet, only for Viggo to drop a hand to his shoulder to stop him. Zan let go of me but grasped his hand around mine, keeping me close. He glanced over his shoulder at the open front door.

"Matt," he called. "You can come in now."

Matt strolled inside, his face blank of any emotion as he stopped right inside the doorway. Warner met my gaze for a moment before he looked back at Matt. There was no point in trying to talk to Matt since it was clear he was entranced.

"Matt," Zan drawled, pointing at Viggo. "Who is he?"

"He's someone who came with me from Project Hope," Matt answered. "A Clover who knows Warner and Kali."

"That better be what you say too," Viggo said, his voice laced with threat as he shot a look at Warner. "Got it?"

"Get fucked," Warner ground out. "I won't play along with whatever you're planning."

"Fine," Zan replied.

I cried out when he suddenly spun me around and began tugging me toward the door. Warner started shouting, and Zan stopped, turning around to face him. I did the same, seeing Warner on his knees with Viggo's hand on his shoulder to hold him down.

"If you don't do what we want, then I'll leave my brothers here to deal with you, and I'll take Kali away right now," Zan said in a dangerously soft voice. "And you won't see her again."

My heart stuttered. "Zan—"

"Play along, and I'll just take her into the bedroom like

I'd planned and wait for Garrett to get here," Zan continued. "Your choice."

Warner's face grew a shade darker, his chest heaving as he met my eyes. "I'll do it. Just don't take her."

He was going to take me anyway. I didn't voice that thought, though, because I wanted Warner to survive this. If he knew Zan wanted me, he'd fight. And he'd lose. I didn't struggle against Zan as he led me toward the bedroom. Before we stepped inside the room, Zan stopped and looked at Warner one last time.

"Behave," he warned. "Or she'll be the one who pays for it."

Warner cursed at him, but Zan kept a firm grip on me while going inside the room. Then he pushed the busted door closed behind him before I could say a word. His grip on me loosened, and I tore away from him, scrambling to the other side of the room. Other than an old bed with a thin blanket on it and a broken dresser, this room was empty. There was a window I could try to escape out of, but I wasn't leaving this cabin without Warner.

I slowly turned around to see Zan leaning against the door with his arms crossed. He seemed content to just stare at me, and I lifted my chin, glaring at him.

"It'll be me that pays for it?" I sneered, repeating the words he said to Warner.

Zan shrugged. "You know I won't hurt you. Warner doesn't. It works in my favor."

"I don't know that," I snapped. "What are you planning on doing with me, Zan? You seem to want to kill everyone who knows your secrets."

His eyes didn't leave mine. "Not you."

"Not yet," I muttered.

"Once you hear what Garrett has to say, you'll want to come back with me," he murmured. "Trust me, Kali."

I let out a cold laugh. "Trust you? You're killing Clovers. I will never trust you."

A muscle in his jaw ticked. "You'll change your mind."

I didn't argue with him, knowing he wouldn't listen to anything I said. Instead, I glanced toward the top of the dresser, where my bag was. Where my weapons were.

"Don't," Zan warned. "You wouldn't get it before I get to you."

I flexed my fingers, resisting the urge to try anyway. But with Viggo out there next to Warner, I didn't want to chance anything.

"Why are we hiding?" I gritted out.

"Because I want you to hear what Garrett has to say," Zan replied. "I'm going to crack this door so you can listen. But you need to stay silent. Got it?"

"Yes."

"I'm serious, Kali," he said with a frown. "I'm doing it this way for you. I could have dragged you out of here last night. But I didn't. Because I want you to understand why you can't stay with this fucking group."

His reference to last night had me straightening my spine as I stared at him. "How can you walk in the sun?"

His lips lifted in an amused grin. "You're more on guard at night. Daylight was best to surprise you."

"You didn't answer my question."

"I will." He tilted his head. "But not now. Garrett is about to walk in. Come over here."

I hesitated, not moving from my spot as he cracked the door open. When he saw I hadn't moved, he scowled. In five steps, he had crossed the room, and he snatched my hand, pulling me back toward the door with him.

"Stop—"

"Shh," he hissed, pressing my chest to the wall, right near the door. "He's walking in."

His chest was at my back, and when I pushed against him, he only pressed me to the wall even more. I bit my tongue, staying still when Garrett's voice filtered in from the other room.

"Who is he?" Garrett asked, already sounding suspicious.

Matt told him the same answer as earlier. "He's someone who came with me from Project Hope. He knows Warner and Kali."

"Tim never mentioned him," Garrett said. "This is a safe house for a fucking reason."

"He needed to get out," Warner said, his voice tight. "He got caught sneaking food out of the pantries. The food that was coming here."

"Fine, whatever," Garrett snapped. "Where's Kali?"

"Out for a walk," Warner answered. "She should be back soon. Why?"

There was a long pause before Garrett spoke again. "We need her. The vampire liked her. We can use that."

The hair on the back of my neck prickled. Whatever Garrett had planned involved me, and I had a feeling he wasn't going to give me a choice.

"Use that how?" Warner questioned sharply.

"You swore your life to the Clovers," a new voice spoke, and I stilled, wondering how many people had come with Garrett. "Would you choose to protect her over doing what we need?"

"Protect her from what?" Warner shot back. "From you? The Clovers? She didn't do anything."

Garrett chuckled darkly. "That's where you're wrong.

She let the vamp feed from her. And kept it a secret. She's not on our side anymore. She'll be used as a way to draw the vampire out. That's it."

If I wasn't pressed between Zan and the wall, I would have fallen to my knees. Panic swelled inside me, my breaths coming out fast as I comprehended Garrett's words. They wouldn't turn on me. Would they? I'd done everything for them. I'd risked my life to get them that note when I was stuck in Zan's city.

"She would never turn against us," Warner practically shouted. "What the fuck are you thinking, Garrett? I want to talk to Tim."

"Tim signed off on this. Every single one of us lives and dies for the Clovers. I'm not risking my life for a girl who is soft for vampires. She's done."

Tears slid down my cheeks, and I didn't move a muscle when Zan's hand landed on my hip. *He knew.* This was why he wanted me to listen. I didn't have my city anymore. And now I didn't have the Clovers.

"I told you this was a bad idea," the guy grumbled. "Look at him. He won't go along with this."

"I can see that now," Garrett agreed. "I thought we could give him a chance."

"You're wrong," Warner snarled. "About Kali."

"It doesn't really matter," Garrett replied casually. "You and your friend won't be leaving this cabin. Tim wanted you to choose us, but clearly, he didn't know how lovesick you are for that girl."

"She's my family."

"You'll be dead before she gets back."

Chapter 42
Kali

Fear washed through me, and I pushed back against Zan, ready to do whatever I needed to get to Warner. But Zan was already moving, ripping open the door and striding out. I quickly rushed after him, my eyes widening at the unfolding chaos.

Pax was racing in from the front door, going after the two guys Garrett had come with. Warner was still sitting at the table, looking unsure, and when he spotted me, he jerked his head to the door, silently telling me to run. I shook my head. I wasn't fucking leaving him here. Viggo was fighting with Garrett, and I stumbled to a halt when Viggo ripped the hawthorn bracelet off Garrett's wrist.

"Shit," Garrett hissed in panic.

He spun around, sprinting for the door, only to slam into Zan. His hand went to Garrett's throat, and he squeezed until Garrett was choking out small breaths.

"Wearing hawthorn is so dangerous," Viggo mocked, tossing the bracelet onto the table. "I guess you shouldn't have used your supply on my brother."

"Calm down," Zan said in a low voice, staring at

435

Garrett. "You're going to stand here and answer my questions. Understand?"

Garrett's eyes stayed trained on Zan's as he fell under entrancement. "Yes."

I tore my eyes from Zan to see Pax wrestling a stake away from one of the men. He didn't hesitate. He spun the wood in his hand before stabbing the guy in the stomach. Viggo was already on the other man, slamming him into the wall before sinking his fangs into the guy's throat. Screaming filled the cabin, and Warner flew to his feet, getting to me while Viggo was still ripping the guy's throat out.

"Out the window," Warner breathed out, grabbing my arm to pull me toward the bedroom. "Come on."

I wasn't sure how he expected us to outrun three vampires who could walk in the sun, but I let him push me back toward the bedroom until fingers wrapped around my other arm, yanking me back.

"Get the hell away from her," Warner snarled, darting in front of me, pushing Zan's hand off me.

"Warner, no," I screamed when he punched Zan in the jaw.

Zan stayed completely still until Warner swung at him again. He caught Warner's wrist, squeezing hard enough that Warner let out a pained grunt while trying to free himself. But Warner's other arm shot out, stopping me when I tried getting between them.

Zan cocked his head. "Trying to protect her from me?"

"Whatever hold you have on her is going to get her killed," Warner gritted out.

"No," Zan corrected, letting go of Warner's arm. "It's your fucking group that will do that. Which is why I'm fixing it."

Warner stepped back, taking me with him, keeping himself between Zan and me. I didn't move, my heart racing as I caught Viggo's eye from across the room. Blood dripped from his chin, and he smirked while wiping a hand over his jaw, smearing it even more. The man he'd bitten was slumped on the floor, unmoving. Pax was leaning against the wall, the stake still in his hand as he looked at Zan.

"I don't know why you're hiding her behind you," Zan murmured, pulling my eyes back to him. "She's the reason you're still alive. If anything, she's protecting you."

Warner scoffed. "Please. You wouldn't hesitate to kill me."

"Believe me, I've thought about it." Zan chuckled. "But I won't. Not unless I need to."

My stomach knotted, and I tried to slip past Warner, but he banded his arm around me, keeping me beside him. Zan watched with interest but didn't make a move to grab me again.

"Garrett," Zan said, turning to look at Garrett, who was standing off to the side. "What did you plan to do when you walked into this cabin?"

"Take Kali," Garrett answered in a monotone voice. "Use her to find you."

"Then what were you going to do to her?" Zan asked.

"Kill her once she wasn't useful anymore."

"Was that your decision or the Clovers'?"

"Clovers'."

Garrett's answer had my heart squeezing painfully. The people I considered family would just turn on me like that? Warner's arm tightened around me in silent comfort.

"And Warner?" Zan pressed. "What were you going to do to him?"

"Kill him if he chose to side with her."

Viggo let out a low whistle. "Sounds like a great group of people to be with."

I glared at him, my body shaking as I fully grasped what Garrett was saying. I couldn't go back with them. I was now considered an enemy. Just like the vampires.

"How many people know about me?" Zan asked in a low voice.

"Six," Garrett replied.

"Only three left alive out of those six," Pax piped up.

Zan nodded. "The two in Project Hope will have to wait. But Garrett can be dealt with now."

He was talking about Tim and Jill. He planned to kill them. What the hell kind of secret had they found out about, and why did Zan want to keep quiet?

Zan turned to fully face Garrett as he took a small folded knife out of his jeans pocket. "Now, you can say whatever you want. Let your true feelings out. But while you're talking, you're going to do exactly as I say. How many times did you hit Kali?"

Warner stiffened, his head whipping to the side to look at me. "He what?"

"Once," Garrett answered, his eyes darkening with anger. "She fucking deserved it."

Why Zan told Garrett to spill his true thoughts, I wasn't sure, but his words shot anger through me. The asshole had hit me before he even saw the bite mark.

"Where did you hit her?" Rage saturated Zan's voice.

"Her face."

"Where?"

Garrett paused for a moment. "I don't remember."

Zan studied him for a moment, the dangerous glint in his eye making my stomach churn. He flicked open the pocketknife and held it out toward Garrett. Warner pulled me back a step, making Zan glance at him in warning.

"If you try to take her out of here again, I'll entrance you too," Zan threatened. "You can't outrun us, even if you did make it out of the cabin. So stop fucking trying."

The fact that he was aware that none of them had hawthorn in their systems made me wonder what else they knew. Having Matt under their control could wreck the Clovers.

"You're going to do worse to me if we stay in this cabin," Warner snapped.

"That's entirely up to you," Zan replied, his eyes meeting mine. "But before we talk about that, I want Garrett to take this."

He turned to look at Garrett again while handing the knife to him. Garrett's eyes didn't leave Zan's as he clutched the knife, standing completely still.

"I want you to cut yourself," Zan ordered softly. "In the exact spot you hit Kali."

Garrett stared at him without a speck of emotion. "But I don't remember where I hit her."

Zan shrugged. "Shame for you. Why don't you start on your left cheek?"

Garrett raised the blade to his face, flinching when the sharp edge grazed his skin. Warner sucked in a quick breath, his arm staying tight around me.

"Harder," Zan commanded, his voice colder than I'd ever heard. "You left marks on her. I want scars on you."

A thin line of blood appeared on Garrett's cheek when he dug the blade deeper, slicing himself down to his jawbone. Pain was etched on his face, but he didn't stop, dragging the knife back up toward his ear.

"You're fucking sick," Warner hissed in disgust. "You like watching humans suffer?"

"Only the ones who deserve it," Zan murmured, not breaking eye contact with Garrett. "Tell us why you hit Kali."

"Because I could," Garrett answered, his voice thick with pain. "She's nothing. A girl who owed me for taking her in."

"Taking her in?" Zan repeated, as if pretending to be interested in his words. "I thought she was a Clover."

"We lost three people trying to save her from your city," Garrett grunted, still moving the blade along his jawline. "She's lucky all I wanted was sex."

Zan's hands clenched into fists. "And if she didn't want to have sex with you?"

"I would have taken it anyway."

I blanched at his words, wondering what could have happened if I'd stayed at that house. Warner froze, his glare focused on Garrett. Viggo and Pax stayed quiet, both staying on the other side of the cabin. Zan's eyes didn't leave Garrett's as blood continued dripping onto the floor. The entire left side of Garrett's face was a mangled mess, and his hand was shaking as he dragged the blade across his skin again.

My stomach roiled with nausea from watching. Yet I couldn't make myself feel sorry for him. I should be screaming at Zan to stop. But after knowing what he wanted to do to me, I really didn't care if he lived or died. My heart thudded, wondering if I was as bad as Zan. I wanted Garrett to suffer.

"I want you to do the same to the other side of your face," Zan said, his voice mockingly cruel. "You're free to think whatever you'd like, but I don't want to hear another word out of your mouth. Don't stop cutting yourself until I say."

Garrett gasped in pain when he switched the knife to his other cheek. Tears were mixing with the blood as he slowly sliced through his skin. Hatred was deep in his eyes as he glared at Zan, but his lips stayed pressed together.

When Zan turned to face me, Warner pulled me behind him again, and I didn't miss the flash of annoyance in Zan's eyes before he masked it.

"Now, to deal with you," Zan murmured, his gaze going to me. "I told you that night that I'd let him come too. That still stands—as long as I know he won't try to go against me."

"Let who come?" Warner snapped. "What are you talking about?"

Before I could answer, Zan spoke again. "I'm taking Kali back with me. She has a connection with you. As long as you can promise me that you'll listen, then I'll allow you to come too."

Panic washed through me as Warner fell absolutely still, processing Zan's words. My gaze cut to Viggo, who was watching me with a frown on his face. He didn't want me coming back to their city, but clearly, it was Zan's decision, since neither twin was arguing.

"Taking her back for what?" Warner forced out. "She's human. You need another living blood bag? Your club seemed to have an abundance of women who freely let you feed. Why do you want her?"

"That's none of your concern," Zan responded. "I just need one answer. That if you come, you'll obey me. And my brothers."

I licked my lips, my nerves nearly overwhelming. Warner would never agree to that. Especially after they kept him locked up last time. Even if he answered yes, he'd be lying. Warner would never bow to vampires. Not even for me. And I wouldn't want him to.

"Yes," Warner hissed. "I'll listen."

Zan stared at him thoughtfully before stepping closer. "Look me in the eyes and answer again."

"Fuck you." Warner was purposefully not looking at him in the face to prevent Zan from entrancing him. "I gave you my answer."

Zan's arm lashed out, and he gripped Warner's jaw. Warner spewed out curses, trying to fight his hold, and I darted forward, grabbing Zan's arm.

"Don't," I cried out.

"I just need his honest answer, Kali," Zan replied, forcing Warner's face up. "Tell me, Warner. If you come back to my city, would you try to kill me?"

The anger that had been covering Warner's features faded, his expression going slack. "Yes."

"Would you ever be able to live with vampires?"

"No."

"Why?"

"I want you all dead."

"Will anything ever change your mind about that?"

"No."

My heart sank as Zan dropped his hand from Warner's face, breaking his mind control. Warner shook his head, scrambling away from Zan.

"Just let him leave," I pleaded, not letting go of Zan's arm.

"Can't do that," Zan said quietly. "He knows too much."

"Then entrance him," I screamed. "Make him forget about it all."

"Kali." Warner looked at me in disbelief. "What are you doing?"

442

I tore my eyes from my best friend to look back at Zan, taking a long breath to make sure my next words were clear. "Make him forget. About it all. Everything he learned in your city. That you can walk in the sun. Everything."

Zan searched my eyes. "He'll come looking for you."

"Then make him hate me," I whispered, my voice trembling. "Tell him that I sided with the vampires, and I'm the reason all these men died. Let him go back to the Clovers."

"No," Warner shouted, grabbing my arm and pulling me in front of him. "Don't do this, Kali. Please. You'll die there—"

"I'll die if a Clover sees me again. And he can't entrance me." I cut him off. "This way we both have a chance at survival."

"That's what you want?" Zan asked me, his face unreadable.

"Yes," I said firmly, ignoring the ache carving itself through my chest. "Do it."

"Don't," Warner snarled when Zan reached for him again. "You fucking piece of shit. Look what you did to her."

Zan ignored him, grabbing Warner's jaw again in a tight hold. Warner swung his fists and struggled, but only for a moment until Zan caught his eye. The fight quickly left him as Zan entranced him.

"All you remember from the time at Impulse was that you were trapped in a cage. Kali was there too, but she didn't say a word to you the entire time. You know nothing about vampires that you haven't already told the Clovers about." Zan spoke slowly, as if choosing each word carefully. "When you were both rescued, Kali seemed different. More sympathetic to vampires."

My gut twisted, but I stayed silent, wiping the tears away as Zan continued.

"Kali helped me escape. She planned it so we could find this cabin. She's the reason your men are dead. She's *mine*. She chose me over everything."

Warner didn't move a muscle as he listened. Viggo was moving across the cabin toward Matt. Garrett was still cutting his face, and he could barely hold the knife now. His face was nearly unrecognizable, and I wasn't sure how long he'd be able to keep doing it before passing out. But I didn't bother to worry about him. Not when my best friend was now being fed fake memories that would make him hate me.

"Matt will back up your story," Zan said. "You two barely escaped this cabin with your lives after we tried killing you both with Kali beside us. She doesn't care about you anymore. Or about the Clovers. Do you understand?"

"Yes," Warner answered, not looking away.

"The cabin caught fire, and you and Matt ran into the woods. And after this conversation, you will not see her as family again. I want you to walk out the front door and start running with Matt. Do not look back. You'll only remember seeing the cabin up in flames. This is all you'll remember. Until I say otherwise."

I choked back a sob, my heart breaking as Zan stepped away from Warner. This was it. I wouldn't see Warner again. I had no one to save me this time. The Clovers would kill me if they saw me again. Warner would kill me. I had no one.

Viggo was talking in a low voice to Matt, making me guess he was telling the same story that Zan had just told Warner. Pax stayed leaning against the wall, and when he met my gaze, pity filled his eyes. He felt bad but wouldn't go against Zan on this. I doubted he'd ever help me again after what happened when he lied for me before.

"Go."

Zan's one-word command had Warner bolting to the front door with Matt on his heels. I couldn't help myself. I ran to the door, watching the two of them disappear into the trees.

"We need to go before they find others and come to check out the cabin," Viggo said.

I stayed in the doorway, debating whether I should run too. Zan wanted me alive right now. But what if that changed? What if I went back to their city, only to be used as a human to feed on like Warner said? They wanted to wait until my birthday because, for some reason, they wanted humans who bled black. What if I was an ordinary human? Would I lose my value to them? Fear invaded my bones as my thoughts raced, and I tensed.

I'd rather try to survive on my own than live in terror until they killed me. Zan might have saved me with his blood, but then he'd used me. I let him feed, and he escaped. I slept with him, and fuck me for feeling something because of it. Because I couldn't trust him. I couldn't allow myself to. Not when they were hiding so many things.

"Don't run, Kali," Zan murmured, like he knew exactly what I was thinking. "You wouldn't get far."

"Why do you want me so badly?" I gritted out without turning around.

"For one," Viggo drawled. "You can't be entranced, and you now know we can walk in the sun. Can't let you run away with that information."

"Because I want you with me," Zan answered, sounding annoyed by his brother's answer. "We're not going to hurt you."

I finally spun around to look at him. Pax was standing in front of Garrett, speaking so low I couldn't hear him, but I kept my eyes on Zan.

"For how long?" I asked, my voice getting high. "Until my twenty-fifth birthday? Until I disobey you? Then what? You kill me? Or turn me? Those are the only options that keep me from being a liability."

"We're not talking about this now," Zan said gruffly. "We need to go."

Without thinking about it, I crouched down and snatched up the stake I'd been making earlier. Zan watched, raising an eyebrow as I held the stake in front of me.

"I told you this was a mistake," Viggo muttered. "She's going to try to run the second she can."

"She won't get the chance." Zan slowly prowled closer to me. "Put it down, Kali. I entranced Warner and let him go like you wanted. I promise I'm not going to hurt you."

"Can you promise you won't turn me?" I shrieked, my grip on the wood turning almost painful as I held it tighter.

"I can't promise that," he said carefully. "But I don't want to turn you."

"I'd rather take my chances alone in the world than become a vampire," I hissed, backing up until I was nearly outside.

"That's not an option." Zan suddenly lunged at me, and I swung the stake at him, even though I knew there was no chance I'd hit his heart. I sliced his arm with the sharp edge of the stake before he grabbed my wrist, forcing the weapon out of my hold with his other hand before quickly putting his arm behind him.

But it was too late. I saw what he was trying to hide.

"Was that...?" I trailed off, staring at the arm he was hiding. With my free hand, I grabbed his, and he didn't fight me as I tugged his injured arm back into view.

The wound was already closing, healing as fast as I'd

cut him. But the blood trail was still there. And it wasn't red.

His blood was black.

"What is this?" I breathed out, trying to understand what this meant. "Are you a half vampire? A Shadow? Or is your blood black for a different reason?"

Viggo cursed, glaring at Zan. "Do you plan on telling her literally all of our damn secrets?"

Zan's eyes were hard, but he didn't answer me or his brother as he pulled me into his arms. He turned me until he was behind me, keeping his arms around me.

"We'll talk about it later," he said, sounding torn about something. "Finish it, Pax."

Pax handed Garrett a full bottle of whiskey, and I stared in shock when Garrett began pouring it onto himself. His face was cut so badly there wasn't a spot that wasn't covered in blood. But he stayed completely silent while emptying the bottle over his body.

"Once we walk out the door, light this." Pax handed him a pack of matches. "Then drop it."

I swallowed thickly, unable to say a thing before Zan dragged me backward out of the cabin. Pax and Viggo strode out after us, and a second later, agonized screams filled the air. Zan pulled me with him, and I looked over my shoulder to see smoke billowing from the open doorway. Garrett was still screaming, but as we got farther away, the yells grew weaker until he was silent.

"Let's go," Zan said, upping his pace.

"I don't want to go back with you," I gritted out, pulling against his hold. "I don't want to become a vampire."

"You won't," Zan snapped, losing his patience.

He dragged me through the trees with Pax and Viggo behind us until we got to a small clearing where a truck was waiting. My heart was pounding out of control, and my screams and struggles did nothing as Zan hauled me into the back seat before coming in after me. I clamored to the other side, away from him as he closed the door.

"It's locked," Zan murmured. "No point in trying."

I reached for the handle anyway as Pax and Viggo got into the front seats. The door didn't budge, and I hit the window with a frustrated scream. Viggo began driving, tearing down the small path as I curled up in the seat, refusing to look at any of them.

"Don't fight it, Kali. I told you this was going to happen." Zan's voice was soft. Something I rarely heard from him. "You don't belong with them."

"I don't belong with vampires either," I retorted.

"You belong with me."

I whipped my head toward him at those words. "No, I don't."

Zan sighed. "You do now. Everyone you know thinks you're with us. Might as well make it true."

I didn't answer him, turning away to look out the window. The life I knew was over. There was no going back. What would happen now? I'd stay with them until my birthday? And then what? They'd turn me?

I sagged in defeat. There was nothing I could do right now. But I sure as hell wasn't going to sit back and allow them to turn me into one of them. The second they let their guard down, I'd try to leave.

I just needed to be patient and wait until I got the chance.

* * *

Are you ready for the next adventure with Kali and Zan? Get it HERE.

* * *

Experience fast cars and heists in RUNNER. A why-choose gang romance that will leave you on the edge of your seat begging for more.

Note from Author

Thank you so much for reading! I hope you enjoyed Bite of Sin. I loved writing this story so much and can't wait to continue into book two! Writing paranormal was so different than my other books, but after having this story in my head for a couple years, it feels amazing to see it on paper.

Until next time,
Kay Riley

Also By Kay Riley

SUNCREST BAY SERIES:

FATEFUL SECRETS

TREACHEROUS TRUTHS

RUTHLESS ENEMIES

HEIRS OF BRAIDWOOD

BURIED BETRAYAL

DEVIOUS DESIRES

RECKLESS REDEMPTION

STAND-ALONE:

RUBY REVENGE

SAPPHIRE DUET

RUNNER

ENDGAME

LITTLE HAVEN SERIES

TAINTED DECEPTION

TAINTED DESIRE

SHADOWS OF WAR SERIES

BITE OF SIN

Made in the USA
Las Vegas, NV
29 August 2024

94305269R00254